TWO BROTHERS

www.transworldbooks.co.uk

Also by Ben Elton

Stark
Gridlock
This Other Eden
Popcorn
Blast from the Past
Inconceivable
Dead Famous
High Society
Past Mortem
The First Casualty
Chart Throb
Blind Faith
Meltdown

TWO BROTHERS

Ben Elton

BANTAM PRESS

LONDON • TORONTO • SYDNEY • AUCKLAND • JOHANNESBURG

TRANSWORLD PUBLISHERS
61–63 Uxbridge Road, London W5 5SA
A Random House Group Company
www.rbooks.co.uk

First published in Great Britain
in 2012 by Bantam Press
an imprint of Transworld Publishers

A CIP catalogue record for this book
is available from the British Library.

ISBNs 9780593062050 (hb)
9780593062067 (tpb)

Addresses for Random House Group Ltd companies outside the UK
can be found at: www.randomhouse.co.uk
The Random House Group Ltd Reg. No. 954009

The Random House Group Limited supports the Forest Stewardship Council (FSC®),
the leading international forest-certification organization. Our books carrying the
FSC label are printed on FSC®-certified paper. FSC is the only forest-certification
scheme endorsed by the leading environmental organizations, including Greenpeace.
Our paper procurement policy can be found at
www.randomhouse.co.uk/environment.

Typeset in 11/14.5 Sabon by
Falcon Oast Graphic Art Ltd.
Printed and bound in Great Britain by
Clays Ltd, Bungay, Suffolk

2 4 6 8 10 9 7 5 3 1

Two Brothers is dedicated to two cousins, my uncles:

Heinz Ehrenberg, who served in the Wehrmacht
1939 to 1945,
and
Geoffrey Elton, who served in the British army
1943 to 1946.

The Girl on the Cart

Berlin, 1920

Frieda Stengel woke from a dream filled with tiny kicks to find her nightdress and her bedding soaking wet.

It was past dawn but the coming of day had done little to relieve the darkness and gloom of the long freezing night that had preceded it. Her breath hung heavily in the dull light as she shook her husband awake.

'Wolfgang,' she whispered. 'My waters have broken.'

He sat up in bed with a jolt.

'Right!' he said, staring about wildly, struggling to surface. 'Good! Everything's fine. We have a plan.'

'I'm not in labour yet,' Frieda said soothingly. 'No pain. No cramps. But they're on their way, that's for sure.'

'Keep calm,' Wolfgang said, tumbling out of bed and tripping over the boots he'd left close at hand for just such an awakening. 'We absolutely have a plan.'

Frieda was expecting twins and so had been guaranteed a place in a hospital for the delivery. The Berlin Buch medical school was several kilometres across the city from Friedrichshain, where they lived. As she struggled into her clothes Frieda could only hope that the babies were in no hurry.

Wolfgang took his wife's arm and they groped their way down the five flights of stairs from their apartment to the street below. There was a lift but it was ancient and rickety and they had decided that the tiny iron cage was not to be trusted for such a crucial journey.

'Imagine if we got stuck and you had the babies between

floors,' Wolfgang joked. 'It's only licensed for three people! That bitch of a concierge would probably report us to the housing collective.'

The sky that lowered over the young couple as they stepped out on to the icy pavement was so dark and so grey that it might have been forged from iron in the furnaces of the famous Krupps foundry in Essen and then bolted above Berlin with rivets of steel. Berlin seemed always to be huddling beneath such gunmetal skies. The war winters and those that followed had been cruel indeed and as the wet and frozen early morning workers hurried past the young couple, bent low in the teeth of biting eastern winds, it was hard for Frieda and Wolfgang to remember that there had ever been any other season in Berlin but winter. That there had once been a time when every tree on Unter Den Linden had dazzled in garish bloom and up and down the Tiergarten old gentlemen had removed their jackets and girls had gone without stockings.

But spring and summer were a distant memory in that February of 1920, a dream of better times before the catastrophe of the Great War exploded over Germany. Now the skies seemed always to have been beaten out of cannons and to thunder as if just beyond the horizon in the fields of Belgium and France and across the endless Russian steppes real cannons still roared.

There were of course no taxis to be found even if they could have afforded one, and inevitably the trams were on one of their regular strikes. The Stengels had therefore arranged to borrow a hand cart from the local greengrocer.

Herr Sommer was waiting for them when they arrived outside his shop, with the cart and a bouquet of carrots tied up with ribbons.

'Pink and blue,' Sommer said, 'because Wolf assures me you're going to have a boy and girl. An instant family, all the bother done with in one go.'

'They'll both be boys,' Frieda replied firmly. 'So watch out for trouble, they'll be pinching your apples in a few years!'

'If I have any apples,' the grocer replied ruefully as Wolfgang began to push the cart away, slipping and clanking across the icy stones and cobbles.

Just then there was a burst of automatic gunfire somewhere in a nearby street, but they ignored it, as they also ignored the shouts and the screams that followed the clattering boots and the sound of breaking glass.

Gunfire, boots and breaking glass were just the sounds of the city to Wolfgang and Frieda, they didn't really notice them any more. As commonplace in Berlin as the cry of the newspaper vendor, the bird song in the parks and the rattle of the trains on the elevated railway. Everybody ignored them, keeping their heads down, hurrying along, hoping not to be delayed in getting to whatever queue it was they were planning to join.

'Fucking idiots,' a one-legged veteran muttered as he scuttled past on his crutches.

'You got that right,' Wolfgang replied to the back of the man's shaven head and little army cap.

The newspapers called these ongoing disturbances a 'revolution' but if it was a revolution it was of a peculiar German kind. Civic authority continued to function and business was still done. Kids still played on the pavements. Secretaries were at their typing machines by eight thirty. The police still checked the licence discs on parked cars, even while their owners were in a nearby cellar kicking somebody to death or being kicked to death themselves.

Berlin simply carried on with its own affairs while Communist gangs and right-wing *Freikorps* militia killed each other during their lunch breaks.

Frieda and Wolfgang carried on too, or at least Wolfgang did, sweating over the cart handles, despite the cold, as he pushed his wife through the rubble-strewn streets, swearing and cursing his way around the occasional barricade until finally arriving before the splendid steps of the famous five-thousand-bed teaching hospital on Lindenberger Weg, the largest in all Europe.

Wolfgang pulled up his cart, drawing deep, painful breaths of freezing air, and took down Frieda's bag.

'Heavy enough, isn't it?' he gasped. 'Do you really need all these books?'

'I might be in for a while,' Frieda replied, sliding herself heavily over the tailboard and down on to the pavement, wincing as her swollen ankles took the weight. 'I need to get some work done.'

'Well, I'm with you on that, Fred,' Wolfgang agreed, treating himself to a smoke. 'You married a musician. A musician who at some point hopes to find himself living in the style to which he would like to become accustomed.'

'You're a *composer*, Wolf.' Frieda smiled. 'Not just a musician. I told my parents I was marrying the next Mendelssohn.'

'God help us, I hope not. Too many damn tunes. *Kaffee und Kuchen* music ain't for me, Freddy, you know that.'

'People like tunes. They *pay* for tunes.'

'Which is why I grabbed myself a nice clever girl when I had the chance. Every jazz man needs a besotted lady doctor to look after him.'

Wolfgang took Frieda around her huge waist and kissed her.

Frieda laughed, disengaging herself. 'I'm not besotted, I'm barely tolerating. And I'm not a doctor either. Not yet, there's the little matter of my final exams. And be careful with my books. They're all borrowed and they fine you if there's even a tiny crease in a page.'

Frieda was studying medicine at the University of Berlin. She even had a grant of sorts, a fact her deeply conservative parents still had difficulty believing.

'You mean they *pay* for your education? Even *women*?' her father had enquired incredulously.

'They have to, Pa. Most of the boys are dead.'

'But all the same. Women doctors?' her father replied, confusion reigning behind the solid, timeless certainty of his close-cropped Prussian moustache. 'Who would trust them?'

'Who will have a choice?' Frieda countered. 'It's called the twentieth century, Pa, you really ought to join some time, it's been going two decades already.'

'You're wrong,' her father said with sombre gravity, 'it began only recently, when his Imperial Highness abdicated. God only knows where or when it will end.'

Frieda's father was a policeman and her mother a proud housewife. He brought in the salary, she ran the home and raised the children. Their attitudes had been formed under the Kaiser, and the political and cultural earthquake of the post-war Weimar Republic had left them reeling. Neither of them understood a government which while unable to stop gunfights on the high streets concerned itself with sexual equality.

Or a son-in-law who was happy to begin a family despite not being able to afford to pay for a taxi to take his wife to the hospital.

'I think if Papa saw you pushing his pregnant daughter to her confinement in a grocer's cart, he'd take out his gun and shoot you,' Frieda remarked as they laboured up the hospital steps together.

'He nearly shot me for *getting* you pregnant,' Wolfgang replied, searching in the pockets of his jacket for the hospital admission papers.

'If you hadn't married me he would have done.'

'Right, this is it. We're here.'

All around them sick, cold people crowded, bustling in and out of the great doors of the hospital.

'I'll come back this evening,' Wolfgang said. 'Make sure there's three of you by then.'

Frieda gripped his hand.

'My God, Wolf,' she whispered, 'when you put it like that . . . Today there's just you and me, tomorrow there'll be you, me . . . and our children.'

A gust of wind caused her to shiver. The harsh, rain-speckled chill penetrating her threadbare clothing. Once more Wolfgang folded her in his arms, no longer playfully but this time passionately, almost desperately. Two, small, cold people huddled together beneath the unforgiving granite columns of the enormous civic building.

Two young hearts beating together.

Two more, younger still, warm in Frieda's belly.

Four hearts, joined by love in the harsh squalls of another, greater heart. One made of stone and iron. Berlin, heart of Germany.

'That's right,' Wolfgang replied. 'You, me and our children. The best and most beautiful thing that there ever was.'

And for once he spoke without smiling or trying to make a joke.

'Yes, that ever was,' said Frieda quietly.

'Well then. Let's get to it, Fred. It's too bloody cold to be standing around being soppy.'

There was no question of Wolfgang waiting at the hospital. Very few expectant fathers in post-war Berlin had the leisure to hang about outside maternity wards waiting to hand out cigars in the traditional manner. Herr Sommer needed his cart back and Wolfgang, like everybody else in the city that terrible winter, needed to begin queuing.

'There's meat at Horst's,' he said, as he began to descend the steps to where he had left the cart. 'Lamb and pork. I'm going to get some for you if I have to pawn my piano. You'll need the iron if you're going to feed our little son and daughter.'

'Our little *sons*,' Frieda replied. 'It'll be boys. I'm telling you, a woman knows. Paulus and Otto. Boys. Lucky, lucky boys.'

'Why lucky?' Wolfgang called back. 'I mean, apart from having the most beautiful mum in the world?'

'Because they're *twins*. They've got each other, Wolf. This is a tough town in a tough world. But no matter how tough it gets – our boys will always have each other.'

Tea and Biscuits

London, 1956

Stone stared at the hessian-covered table in front of him. At the teacups and the biscuits and the block of yellow notepaper with the fountain pen on top. He focused on the black Bakelite telephone with its sharp angular edges and its frayed, double-twisted, brown fabric cord. It must have dated from the early 1930s.

What had he been doing when that cord was new?

Fighting, no doubt. Or running in terror along some Berlin pavement looking for an alley to dodge down. He and his brother chasing each other's heels, two teenage boys in mortal fear for their lives.

Stone's eye followed the cord down off the table, across the slightly warped, ruby-coloured linoleum and into a largish black box screwed to the skirting board. He fancied he could hear the box humming but it might have been the distant traffic on the Cromwell Road.

He shifted nervously in his seat. He had never quite got used to being interviewed in bare rooms by government officials. Even now he could not quite persuade himself that he was safe. Even now some part of him expected violence.

Except of course that this was England, they didn't do that sort of thing here. Some of Stone's more left-leaning acquaintances sneered when he said that. But then they had never had the misfortune to live in a country where sudden and absolute violence was the norm and not the exception.

Stone looked once more at his interrogators. A classic pair. One short and rather plump, balding, with an officious little soup stain of a moustache, his beady eyes flicking constantly at the biscuits. The other not much taller but thinner, standing in the corner of the bare windowless room, watching through slightly hooded eyes. It felt to Stone like he was in a scene from a movie. That he was being questioned by Peter Lorre while Humphrey Bogart looked on inscrutably, keeping his own counsel.

'You are travelling to Berlin in the hope of meeting up with your brother's widow.'

This was the second time the shorter man, Peter Lorre, had asked this question.

Or was it a statement? It was certainly true. But how did they know?

They had read Dagmar's letter. Obviously.

'*Presumed* widow,' Stone replied, evading the question. A lifetime's experience had taught him that it was usually wise to withhold any information from the authorities until forced to divulge it.

'You don't think your brother's dead?'

'There has never been any actual proof of it.'

'You mean a corpse?'

'I suppose so.'

'Your brother is certainly *presumed* dead,' Lorre replied, finally capitulating to the biscuit plate and choosing a shortbread finger. 'Killed by the Russians during the battle for Moscow in 1941.'

'That is what I was told,' Stone said, 'after the war, by the East German authorities.'

'Have you any reason to doubt it?'

'No. None at all. I've always hoped, that's all. My brother generally had a plan. He would have been a hard man to kill.'

'The Waffen SS tended to be made up of hard men to kill. At least until they started recruiting boys. Your brother joined in 1940, didn't he?'

Was there a hint of a sneer? Stone felt his anger rising. What right did this smug little man, munching on his shortbread finger, have to judge? He hadn't been where his brother had been. Where his mother and father had been. And Dagmar.

Again the guilt.

Survivor guilt, the shrinks called it.

'My brother wasn't a Nazi,' Stone stated firmly.

'Of course he wasn't,' Peter Lorre replied, and now the sneer was unmistakable. 'None of them were Nazis, were they? Or so they all claim *now*. And the Waffen SS wasn't really *proper* SS anyway, was it? They never ran the camps. You can't blame *them*.'

'My brother was married to a Jew,' Stone said.

'Yes, we know. Dagmar Stengel, née Fischer. You are travelling to Berlin to meet her. Is that not the case?'

Stone stared at the cups and saucers once more. He didn't like telling them his business, but it was clearly a rhetorical question and he didn't want to be caught in a lie.

'Yes. Dagmar Fischer,' he admitted.

'Dagmar Stengel.'

'I knew her as Dagmar Fischer. She married my brother after I left Germany.'

'When did you last see Mrs Stengel?'

Stone drew deeply on his cigarette and closed his eyes. How often had he relived that moment? The whistling and shunting of the trains. The smell of her hair. The martial music on the loud-speakers that made it so hard to whisper the things he needed to say.

'In 1939,' he answered.

'In Berlin?'

'Yes. In Berlin.'

'And after the war? Did you try to find her?'

'Of course. I tried to find all my family.'

'You were in Germany?'

'Yes. With the army. I worked in the Displaced Persons camps, with the UN Relief and Rehabilitation Administration. You know all this, it's in my records.'

'So,' Peter Lorre observed through a mouth filled with biscuit, 'well placed to look for an elusive Jewess?'

Elusive Jewess. Such a phrase. The little man clearly had no idea of the casual contempt and innate suspicion contained within it. 'An *elusive Jewess*?' Stone repeated. 'What the hell do you mean by that?'

'I mean Frau Stengel of course.'

'Then bloody well say so.'

There was a moment's silence.

'Frau Stengel then?' Lorre resumed. 'You didn't find her?'

'No.'

'What happened to her?'

'I never found out.'

'One more anonymous victim of the Holocaust?'

'I presumed so.'

'But you now think she survived?'

Stone paused for a moment, considering his reply.

'I have recently allowed myself to *hope* that she did.'

'And why would that be?'

Stone was trying very hard not to become angry. Getting angry never helped. Not with the sort of people who sat behind green hessian-covered tables with cups of tea and empty yellow notepads.

'What is this about?' Stone asked. 'I don't understand why you want to know, or why I should tell you for that matter.'

'It's very simple,' the plump man replied, breaking a second biscuit in two and taking the larger half. 'If you cooperate with us you'll soon be on your way. If you don't, then there's any amount of red tape we can tie you up with pretty much indefinitely. You might not get to Berlin until the year 2000, by which time you will be a very old man and Berlin will long since have been reduced to a pile of smouldering radioactive rubble. So just be a sensible chap and answer our questions. Why do you now hope that Dagmar Stengel is alive?'

Stone shrugged. The supercilious little swine knew anyway.

'Because she contacted me.'

'Out of the blue?'

'Yes. Out of the blue.'

'After seventeen years?'

'That's right.'

'And you're sure it *was* Frau Stengel?'

That was the rub. He *was* sure. He was absolutely sure. The writing, the tone, and the memories the note contained. And yet . . .

'She said she'd survived most of the war in Berlin as what they called a "submarine",' Stone replied, avoiding Lorre's question. 'But the Gestapo picked her up in June '44 and shipped her to Birkenau. It seems she escaped.'

'A rare feat indeed.'

'Such things happened, rarely, but they happened. She says she got out during the *Sonderkommando* revolt at Crematorium IV and saw out the war fighting with Polish Partisans. After that, the Soviets put her back in a camp along with the rest of the surviving Polish resistance.'

'Quite a story.'

But not impossible. Dagmar had been tough and resourceful for all her refined manners.

'I can see you found it hard to credit,' the plump man said, looking steadily at Stone. 'Not surprising, after so long. However, I am here to tell you that the story is true. Or at least its conclusion is. Dagmar Stengel is alive and well and living in East Berlin.'

The surge of joy he felt was like the sudden, heady rush that sometimes overtook him in his dreams. When it was he and not his brother on the beach at Wannsee entwined in Dagmar Fischer's rain-dappled arms.

'How do you know?' Stone asked, trying to keep his voice from shaking.

'We know lots of things.'

Stone banged the table with his fist. The cups rattled. The ancient telephone receiver jumped in its cradle. This was his business, not theirs. His family. His life. How dare they act as if it was some game!

'How do you know!' he demanded. 'Tell me!'

'Sources,' the plump man replied, ignoring Stone's passion and idly succumbing to the other half of his second biscuit, '*confidential* sources.'

'Are you MI6?'

'MI6 does not exist, Mr Stengel.'

'Stone! My name is Stone. It's been Stone for fifteen bloody years!'

'Yes, you changed it, didn't you?'

Again a tiny sneer. This time not for the German who claimed not to have been a Nazi but for the sneaky Jew who had changed his name to hide his Jewey-ness. That was the Brits, they liked it both ways. Just because they'd saved the world for decency and fair play didn't mean the bloody Yids could start getting above themselves.

'I changed my name,' Stone snapped, 'because the army advised me to. The *British* army. If I'd been taken in action and they'd found out I was Jewish, I'd have been gassed.'

'All right. Keep your shirt on,' the little man said with a patronizing smirk. 'We knew that.'

'You know a bloody lot.'

'We try to.'

'Because you're MI6,' Stone said. 'The Secret Service.'

'Can't tell you that, can we, Mr Stone? Then it wouldn't be secret.'

Peter Lorre smiled and wiped his mouth, clearly pleased with his little joke.

Stone should have guessed it from the start. Just the layout of the room was proof enough. Bare, save for a table, tea, biscuits, paper and a phone. Not a book, not a pamphlet, not a memo. No chart on the wall, no wastepaper bin under the table, not even a paperclip. What normal office was ever like that? Even the police had posters on their walls.

And then there was the double act. The chatty one, the silent one. Classic, of course. Such a cliché. He really should have guessed. They were spooks all right.

And they said Dagmar was definitely alive.

Once more the surge of joy.

She'd survived. Berlin. The camps. The gulags. She'd survived them all.

And through all that dreadful darkness she had remembered him. He who had loved her.

He who still loved her.

Who would always love her.

Twins
Berlin, 1920

It turned out that Frieda was right, she was carrying two boys, but the labour was long and difficult and only one of them survived it, the other choked on a twisted cord.

'I'm sorry, Frau Stengel,' the doctor said. 'The second child is stillborn.'

Then they left her alone.

Not out of any sense of delicacy but simply because the hospital was so busy. Four years of war, followed by the spitting, spluttering dud of a 'revolution', had left nobody with much time for niceties, particularly the medical profession. Frieda, who had not herself suffered any complications during the birth, was aware that they would be wanting her little bare yellow-painted room back. She did not have much time.

'Hello, little one,' Frieda whispered, struggling to find it in her heart to welcome one baby while bidding farewell to the other. 'And goodbye, little one.'

She did not want her joy in the living, breathing creature that lay in one arm to be drowned for ever in her tears for the lifeless little bundle that lay in the other, but at that moment Frieda did not see how it could be any other way. She knew that she would forever mourn her child who never was.

'*Auf Wiedersehen*, my darling,' she breathed.

The mean light from the single forty-watt bulb that hung unshaded above her bed fell on the bundle's tiny grey face, pinched and wrinkled like an ancient Chinaman. The other bundle began to cry, a tiny bleating sound at first, which grew in volume as the little creature discovered the power of his lungs. Frieda turned her gaze from the miniature Chinese death mask to the crying baby and then back again. One pale and dull in death, the other shining and growing redder and redder in the dawning of life.

'*Auf Wiedersehen und guten Tag. Guten Tag und auf Wiedersehen.*'

Then the doctor returned with an old nurse who took the dead baby from Frieda's arms. 'Smile for this one most of all, Frau Stengel,' the nurse said, making the sign of the cross over it. 'He's spared the misery of this world and instead begins at once to savour the joy of the next.'

But Frieda could not smile. She didn't believe in a next world and so knew only the misery of the present one.

Then the doctor spoke.

'Frau Stengel, I hesitate to speak with you being so recently bereaved but I feel I must. There's a young woman in a nearby ward. Or rather there was. She died an hour ago. You survived and lost a child, this woman died while a child lived . . . a boy.'

Frieda only half heard him. She was watching as the old nurse took a part of her away. Not to the better place she promised but to the cellar of the hospital and the incinerator. There would be no flowers, no prayers. Germany's ongoing agony dictated that the disposal of corpses, no matter how innocent and tiny, was an efficient and mechanical affair. The bundle had been in her body for nine months; it would be ashes in not many more seconds.

'I'm sorry, doctor,' Frieda said, 'what was it you were saying? A mother and child?'

'Just a child, Frau Stengel. The mother died delivering him and his father is dead too. A Communist. Shot at Lichtenburg.'

Frieda knew about the massacre in the suburb of Lichtenburg. A *thousand* workers arbitrarily rounded up by *Freikorps* and shot in the street with the full connivance of the Minister of National Defence. It was scarcely even mentioned in the papers at the time, murder being so common in Berlin, even mass murder. But Frieda was the sort of person who took trouble to remain informed.

'The dead girl was estranged from her parents,' the doctor continued. 'They didn't want the child of a Red in the family and now that their daughter is dead they want it even less. They're tired and poor and not interested in any bastard orphan grandchild.'

It was as if the dull bulb above her bed burned a little brighter as Frieda began to understand.

The bundle was gone but it could live again. All the preparations she and Wolfgang had made, all the love that had grown in their hearts for two babies, would not go to waste. That love was needed, desperately. A little soul was waiting to be claimed. She would have twins after all. Paulus would have his Otto and Otto would have his Paulus.

'Frau Stengel,' the doctor was saying, 'I know that you are distressed but would you possibly consider—'

'Bring me this baby please,' Frieda replied before the doctor could even finish his sentence. 'Bring me my son. He needs me.'

'But your husband,' the doctor began, 'surely you must ask—'

'My husband is a good man, doctor. He will feel as I do. Bring me our second son.'

Moments later there was a new bundle on Frieda's arm where the ancient grey Chinaman had lain so briefly. This one red-faced, bespittled and howling like its new twin. Two healthy babies, one in each arm. It was as if time had stood still for the previous hour and only now was Frieda's labour complete.

'*Guten Tag, und guten Tag*,' Frieda whispered.

The adoption was a simple matter to arrange, the wheels of the process being extremely well oiled. Germany might have been short of young men in 1920, but after the war and the influenza pandemic that followed it, it certainly had plenty of orphans, and the hospital was anxious to be done with this one. Wolfgang was summoned from his place in the butcher's queue and the necessary papers were produced even before Frieda's milk had begun to flow. The child's maternal grandparents appeared briefly at Frieda's bedside and signed away the child with scarcely a glance at it. They wished Frieda and Wolfgang a gruff good luck and disappeared from Frieda and Wolfgang's lives for ever. Gone before the ink was even dry.

And so it was the four of them just as had been planned and as Frieda had predicted. Frieda and Wolfgang and their two boys, Paulus and Otto. Otto and Paulus. Two sons, two brothers, equally wanted, equally loved. Equal in every way.

Just the same.

Except not quite the same.

There was one difference between the two boys. A difference that went almost without comment at the time. A difference that was entirely irrelevant to Frieda and Wolfgang. But a difference that would in the fullness of time become a matter of life and death. One child was Jewish, the other was not.

Another Baby

Munich, 1920

On the same day that the two Stengel brothers were born, 24 February 1920, some few hundred miles from Berlin, at the Hofbräuhaus Bierkeller in Munich, another baby came into the world. Like many babies (not least Paulus and Otto themselves), this one was noisy and wild. When it found its voice it was only to shout and to scream, and when it found its fists it was only to beat the air in fury because the world was not as it wished it to be.

Most babies grow up. They develop reason and a conscience, they become socialized. This baby never did. It was the National Socialist German Workers Party, named that day out of the ashes of a previous, failed incarnation. The voice that screamed and the fists that pounded were those of its emerging leader, a thirty-one-year-old corporal in the political unit of the Bavarian *Reichswehr*. His name was Adolf Hitler.

That fateful night, along with giving the party its new name, Hitler outlined twenty-five points that were to be the 'inalienable' and 'unalterable' basis of the party programme. Most of these points were quickly forgotten by both Hitler and his rapidly growing party, sops as they were to the quasi-socialist principles of its roots. Other points, however, were very much Hitler's own and he never wavered in his commitment to them until the moment he drew his last breath. A union of all German-speaking peoples. A complete repudiation of the Treaty of Versailles. And, above all, a 'settlement' with the Jews. This was the most crucial point of all and on that cold winter evening the penniless, unknown soldier, voice almost gone after three hours of oration, fists clenched, arms flailing in the air, spit floating in the smoky beams of light, gave notice that the Jews were the source of all Germany's ills and that he, Adolf Hitler, would be their nemesis. He would deprive every one of them of their Reich citizenship. No Jew would be allowed to hold any official office. No Jew would be allowed to write for a newspaper. And any Jew who had arrived in Germany after 1914 would be instantly deported.

It was heady stuff and the crowd roared their approval. Here at last was a man who knew why Germany had lost the war. Why instead of being victors living fat in Paris and London, decent Germans were paupers eking out their beer and tobacco in Munich.

It was the Jews. Despite being only 0.75 per cent of the population, the Jews, in their fiendish cunning, had done it all and this man would cut the bastards down to size.

No one, not even Hitler himself, imagined that night in 1920 just how much more he would do to them than that.

An Operation is Cancelled

Berlin, 1920

Frieda and Wolfgang took the decision not to have Paulus and Otto circumcised for the strangest and most incongruous of reasons. It happened as a result of a failed attempt by reactionary fanatics to seize control of the German state.

'It was pure Dada really,' Wolfgang liked to joke when he told the story in later years (the boys glowing red in the corner at having their penises discussed at their parents' parties). 'The ultimate Surrealist non-sequitur. Some idiot tries to do a Mussolini in Berlin and my lads get to hang on to their foreskins – figuratively speaking, I mean, of course. How's that for a random and chaotic juxtaposition? Life imitating art!'

They had certainly *intended* to have their boys circumcised.

'We have to do it,' Frieda said, when they brought the babies home from the hospital, 'it means so much to my parents.'

'My mum and dad wouldn't care either way, but I suppose being dead their opinions don't count against the mighty Tauber family,' Wolfgang commented.

Wolfgang's parents had both died the year before. Like so many millions of other Europeans, they had survived the war only to be struck down by flu.

'Please don't turn this into another rant about my dad,' Frieda insisted. 'I say we just get on with it. It never did you any harm.'

'You don't know, do you?' Wolfgang growled with mock lasciviousness. 'Who knows what powers of passion I'd deploy if I had a hooded helmet?'

Frieda silenced him with one of her looks. Having given birth only days before she wasn't in much of a mood for dirty jokes. 'Just book the rabbi,' she said.

But as fate would have it, Wolfgang's misgivings were irrelevant because there was to be no circumcision anyway. On the date when tradition required the deed to be done, all the water dried up in Frieda and Wolfgang's apartment.

They were standing by the kitchen sink into which they had just placed two shitty-bottomed babies in dire need of a bath and all they got when they turned on the taps was a distant clanking sound.

'We've got no water,' Frieda said.

'Shit,' Wolfgang replied, glancing ruefully at his soiled babies before adding, 'and lots of it.'

At which point the twins, who although as yet unable to speak could still sense a crisis in the air, knew it was their job to compound it and began to scream blue murder.

'Why us!' Frieda shouted above the din, but in fact it was not just them, the water had dried up all over Berlin. The electricity had gone too. Also the gas and the trams, the post and the police. The whole municipal infrastructure which had continued to function throughout the war and then somewhat more sporadically through two years of famine and street fighting had suddenly ground to a complete halt.

The reason the great city had been left without a single modern convenience was that there had been an insurrection. A local political nonentity named Kapp had marched through the Brandenburg Gate at the head of a notoriously brutal brigade of *Freikorps*, occupied the President's Palace on the Wilhelmstrasse and announced that he was Germany's new leader and that everybody had to do what he said. In reply the unions had called a general strike, cutting off all services and bringing Berlin to a filthy, stinking standstill. Wolfgang and Frieda had no water for their babies and the hapless Kapp had no paper on which to print a proclamation informing Germany that due to his firm leadership their nation was strong once more.

It was of course the water that the parents of the two puking, pooping new babies missed most. There was enough to drink from local standpipes but they couldn't clean the kids.

Therefore when Frieda's father brought Rabbi Jakobovitz round on the appointed day with his little bag of ancient-looking tools and powders, Frieda refused to let him near the boys.

'It's an operation, for God's sake, Papa,' she said in reply to her father's embarrassed protests. 'It's a medical procedure which requires proper hygiene!'

'Oh don't be ridiculous,' her father replied. 'It's just a little nick, there's hardly even any blood.'

In vain did the old rabbi protest that he'd scarcely lost a boy in years, that his shield, knife and spice box were all regularly polished and he always rubbed his sharpened thumbnail with alcohol before he did the deed. Frieda was adamant.

'You're not doing it. Certainly not until the taps are back on. What's wrong with foreskins anyway?'

'Please, Frieda!' Herr Tauber spluttered. 'The rabbi!'

'Yes, the rabbi,' Wolfgang commented laconically from the corner of the room where despite the early hour he was pouring himself a glass of schnapps, it not being possible to make any coffee. 'Perhaps he can answer the question. What *is* wrong with foreskins?'

Herr Tauber began to stammer his apologies but the rabbi insisted sagely that he was perfectly happy to engage in theological debate.

'Azariah said,' the rabbi intoned sombrely while laying out his ancient collection of implements on an equally venerable stained and dusty old cloth, 'that the foreskin is loathsome, since it is a term of opprobrium for the wicked, as it is written.'

'Ah yes, it's all so much clearer now.' Wolfgang smiled.

'The foreskin is loathsome?' Frieda asked.

'So it is written,' Rabbi Jakobovitz replied gravely.

'By Azariah,' Wolfgang added. 'That well-known penis expert.'

'It is the Babylonian Talmud,' the old man said with equal gravity, oblivious to Wolfgang's sarcasm.

'Damn! I've been meaning to read it.'

Herr Tauber tried once more to intervene.

'Nothing's wrong with foreskins in their place, Frieda, my love,' he said, attempting a conciliatory tone, while throwing furious glances at Wolfgang.

'In their *place*, Papa! They *are* in their place. What better place could there be for a foreskin than the end of a penis?'

'*Temporarily*, dear,' her father continued. 'That is their place temporarily. For God put them in that place in order that they may be removed from it.'

'That's just completely ridiculous, Papa,' Frieda said. 'I mean, pardon me, rabbi, no disrespect and all that but really, when you come to think about it, what is the point of the whole business?'

'Just because there is no obvious reason for doing something does not necessarily mean that one shouldn't do it,' the rabbi replied, having happily accepted the schnapps Wolfgang pressed upon him.

'Exactly! There you are, you see!' Herr Tauber said triumphantly, seizing on the remark as if the rabbi had imparted some great and transparent wisdom. 'There is such a thing as tradition, Frieda, and we reject it at our peril. If you knock out every brick in the foundations of a house, that house will surely fall down.'

Wolfgang picked up his babies in a bear hug and set them down on either knee.

'You hear that, boys?' he said. 'Your dicks are holding up a house.'

'Shut *up*, Wolf,' Frieda hissed, but she couldn't help but smile too.

'I mean, come on, Pop,' Wolfgang went on. 'Really, why do you care? You're not religious. When did you last even go to a synagogue?'

'We do things because we do them,' Herr Tauber said angrily, while the rabbi continued to nod sagely at every remark while accepting a refill of his schnapps from Wolfgang. 'Just like the Orthodox Greek fellow with his smoking incense or the Catholic with his wafer, which he knows very well isn't a piece of Christ's flesh. These things are done. That's reason enough. It binds a person to his own past. It honours our elders and keeps us steady. Tradition is what has made Germany great.'

Wolfgang snorted once more.

'Germany isn't great, Konstantin,' Wolfgang said, knowing full well that his father-in-law hated him to address him by his first name, preferring either 'Herr Tauber' or 'Papa'. 'Germany is a basket case. Germany is crippled, bankrupt, starving and insane. If Germany was a dog, you'd put a bullet in its head.'

Konstantin Tauber flinched. Despite having been well over forty in 1914, he had served with distinction in the Great War, winning an Iron Cross which he wore always on his uniform and in civilian clothes on the slightest excuse.

'Germany *was* great,' he said angrily, 'and it will be great again despite the best efforts of you and your leftist friends.'

'Wolfgang's not a leftist, Papa,' Frieda said, 'he just likes jazz.'

'It's the same thing,' Tauber replied, 'and only a leftist would deny his sons their cultural birthright.'

'What? To have their pricks interfered with?' Wolfgang enquired. 'Some birthright!'

'Can you please moderate your language in front of my daughter and the rabbi!' Herr Tauber thundered back.

'This is my home and I'll say what I like, mate!'

'Look!' Frieda snapped. 'I have just given birth to twins. There isn't any water. There isn't any heat. There isn't any light and there isn't any food. Can we please leave the question of the boys' foreskins to another day?'

The rabbi shook his head sadly.

'Another day is not possible, Frau Stengel,' he said, 'for this is the eighth day and circumcision must be proffered on no day but this unless the child's health is at risk, as it is written.'

'Their health *is* at risk,' Frieda protested. 'There's no water in the taps.'

'For three thousand years we did without taps,' Rabbi Jakobovitz replied, 'just as we did without heat and electric light. I'm afraid that it's now or not at all, my dear.'

'Then it's not at all,' Frieda said firmly, 'because we're not doing it until they turn the water on.'

'In that case,' Jakobovitz said, seeming to perk up somewhat, 'since a steady hand is no longer required, perhaps, Herr Stengel, I might trouble you for another schnapps?'

Wolfgang looked ruefully at his half-empty bottle, but hospitality was one tradition he did subscribe to.

Eventually the rabbi and Herr Tauber took their leave and, as the sound of their stumbling progress down the stairs faded away, Frieda and Wolfgang looked at each other. They were smiling but also serious; they both knew what the other was thinking.

'Perhaps now was the time,' Frieda said, 'perhaps we should have said.'

'I wanted to tell the old bastard, I really did,' Wolfgang replied, 'when he was banging on about tradition and birthright I was itching to tell him that one of his grandsons' traditions and birthright were Catholic and Communist.'

'Actually, I'm glad you didn't,' Frieda said.

'I couldn't find the moment.'

'I know. It's difficult. I think we've already left it too late.'

Wolfgang and Frieda had never meant the adoption to be a secret. They had fully intended to tell everybody immediately, both friends and relations. They were not ashamed, they were proud, proud of what they had done and proud of their son. Of both their sons.

But somehow they had missed the moment.

'Why should anybody be bothered about it anyway?' Frieda said. 'It isn't an issue for us, we don't even think about it.'

'No, I thought I would,' Wolfgang agreed, 'but I don't.'

'The funny thing is it feels to me as if it never really happened anyway. That the little bundle they took away was just a part of the process, just the boys messing about a bit, that's all. There were two of them, then one disappeared for a moment and then he came back. Three little souls just became two.'

Together they looked at the sleeping boys, swaddled tight, side by side in a single cot.

'I don't want there ever to be any distance between them,' Frieda continued, 'or between them and us. We're a family and by going into how we became a family it feels as though we're saying it's important when it isn't. Why should anyone ever know? Why would anyone ever be interested?'

'Well, it's in the records at the hospital,' Wolfgang said.

'And as far as I'm concerned it can stay there,' said Frieda. 'It has absolutely nothing to do with anybody but us.'

A Whimper and a Scream

Berlin, 1920

The Kapp Putsch, as it came to be known, lasted less than a week. While Berlin shivered in the cold and stood in line at standpipes for a trickle of icy water, Kapp, the would-be dictator, spent a lonely five days shuffling about the President's Palace, staring forlornly out over the Wilhelmplatz, wondering how to bend the nation to his unalterable will. Eventually he decided that he couldn't and instead took a taxi to Tempelhof airport and got on a plane to Sweden, never to be a head of state again.

Berlin was jubilant and hundreds of thousands gathered on Unter Den Linden to watch as Kapp's *Freikorps* troops marched out under the Brandenburg Gate through which they had strutted in triumph less than a week earlier.

Frieda and Wolfgang decided to join the celebration.

'This is a big day for Berlin,' Frieda said excitedly as they worked their way into the crowd, pushing the pram before them. 'It's not often that a bit of union solidarity gets the better of an army. Solidarity, that's all you need.'

'All I need,' Wolfgang replied, seeing a stall selling beer and fried potatoes, 'is a drink. This is a party after all.'

There was indeed a carnival atmosphere in the crowd. Hawkers were out in force and there were numerous street musicians busking for pfennigs. But as the retreating army could be heard approaching, the mood of the crowd began to change, turning sullen and angry as Charlottenburger Chaussee and Unter Den Linden rang to the harsh crash of thousands of hobnail boots smashing in deadly unison on the stone flags.

'Shit,' Wolfgang whispered nervously, 'this has got to be the first time German soldiers have paraded through the Brandenburg Gate to complete silence.'

'These aren't soldiers,' Frieda replied, 'these are just crazy thugs.'

'Well, I don't like it,' Wolfgang muttered nervously. 'It's weird.'

'Too late now,' Frieda observed.

So they stood with their pram as the hated columns marched past them and on through the great stone columns of Friedrich Wilhelm's famous gate. Ragged-looking men with bitter angry faces. Soldiers still, despite what Frieda said, in old army uniforms and coal-scuttle steel helmets.

'What's that funny crooked cross,' Wolfgang hissed, 'painted on some of their helmets?'

'I don't know,' Frieda said. 'Actually, I think it's Indian.'

'*Indian?*' Despite the strange solemnity of the occasion, Wolfgang almost laughed.

'Yes, Buddhist or Hindu. I'm not sure which. I think it's called a swastika.'

'*Buddhist?*' Wolfgang observed incredulously. 'That is just fucking weird.'

The silence seemed to deepen now. As loud almost in its way as the marching boots.

Frieda was to remark later that it was beautiful. That the silent contempt of a great city spoke more loudly than any amount of shouts and noise. Wolfgang disagreed. He thought it was terrifying from the start. That people had remained silent only out of fear. Fear of what those marching men were capable of. Of what might happen.

Of what did happen.

The column was almost past when it began. The vanguard of the troops were already nearly at the bridge over the river Spree and still the sullen mass of people kept their silence and the strutting troops their order. The two sides remained apart. The strange truce held.

And then, close to where Wolfgang and Frieda stood, their pram in front of them, a boy called out.

His high, half-broken voice clear despite the ringing, echoing noise of synchronized boots. Perhaps if the boy hadn't been so young and his voice so shrill it wouldn't have been heard, lost instead amongst the rhythmic crashes.

But the boy was no more than twelve or thirteen.

'Piss off, you bone-headed bastards,' he shouted. 'Vlad Lenin for German Chancellor!'

Instantly two of the troopers broke ranks and pulled him from the crowd. A woman screamed and onlookers stood momentarily in shock as the *Freikorps* men clubbed the boy to the ground with their rifle butts, knocking his teeth from his mouth with the first blow. Then men and women from the crowd ran forward trying to save the dying boy, surrounding the two troopers and grabbing at their flailing rifles.

'Oh God!' Wolfgang shouted. 'Get the babies out of the pram, get them high, quick, above your head. Quick!'

In that instant the silent crowd around them became a furious mob. People from behind surged forward while some in front stepped back. Immediately the little buggy went over, twisted and trampled underfoot in the very moment that Frieda and Wolfgang had snatched their babies from it.

'Back! Back!' Wolfgang barked. 'For God's sake don't lose your footing.'

Terrified, each holding an infant above their heads, they struggled to move away from the trouble, pushing against the mob, staring into the contorted faces of outraged citizens who were trying to force their way towards it.

'Let us through! We have babies,' Frieda cried.

Some, immediately in front of her, tried to give way but those behind them kept pushing, imagining in that frantic moment that in their numbers they could be a match for well-drilled soldiers. The terrible minutes that ensued were to teach them their mistake.

A harsh voice called out. An order given and a bugle sounded. Instantly and as one man the troops brought their boots down to a crashing halt and then with another crash they executed a fault-less quarter-turn to face the seething crowd. Then another shout, another bugle blast, and with a slap and a rattle the field-grey lines brought their rifles to the shoulder.

At this point the nightmare could have ended. Already the crowd had paused. Faced with so many gun barrels raised as one and hearing the sinister double snap of massed rifle bolts cocked in perfect unison, the unarmed civilians checked themselves mid-stride and began to fall back. Here now could have been an end to it. The boy who had dared to insult the mighty *Freikorps* was already dead and his would-be avengers had been properly subdued.

But this was Germany. This was Berlin in 1920, and the genie of violence *never* returned to its bottle once released, no matter how briefly the stopper had been off.

'Fire!' the voice shouted.

No bugle was needed this time, a volley of shots followed on the voice instantly, sending a fuselage of bullets thudding into the chests and faces of the stunned citizens.

As people fell dying to the pavement the rifle bolts double-clicked again but this time their perfectly drilled rhythm went unheard beneath the screams.

'Fire!' the voice shouted again and a second round of bullets tore into the people, into their backs now as the crowd was already in full retreat.

There was no third round. The anonymous voice spared the defenceless people that, but hundreds were already dead and more were dying in the blind panic of flight.

The Stengel family were just a few steps ahead of that panic, just emerging from the crowd as the first shots were fired. Wolfgang's quick thinking had certainly saved Paulus and Otto's lives, and possibly his and Frieda's too, but they did not stop running for almost two kilometres and never once paused to look back.

At the Brandenburg Gate the troops were left alone with their victims. The voice cried out once more, then the *Freikorps* reformed their column and marched out of the city.

The following morning the briefly deposed government returned to office and the water was turned back on.

A Proposal
London, 1956

Stone swallowed twice before he replied.

He had only just begun adjusting to the certainty that Dagmar was alive after so many years of wondering. And now this.

'A spy? My sister-in-law is a spy? I find that –' he struggled for the right word and failed – 'very strange.'

'Well, not necessarily a spy,' the plump little man whom Stone had begun to think of as Peter Lorre conceded. 'Shall we try and drum up some fresh tea?'

'I don't care about bloody tea!' Stone snapped, the swear word sounding rather strange and forced in his half 'foreign' accent. 'What do you mean, not necessarily a spy? Is she or isn't she?'

'Let's put it this way, she definitely works for the East German secret police,' Lorre replied, 'that much we do know. Your sister-in-law is a Stasi girl.'

The Stasi. The very word made every hair on his body stand on end. All German police organizations made Stone's skin crawl and would do until the day he died. Even the innocent, smiling young pastel-green and khaki-clad West Germans with their untidy hair and deliberately non-militaristic insignia were hard for him to stomach. But the Stasi were a new Gestapo. Working in the Foreign Office Stone knew enough about their activities to feel physically sick at the mere mention of their name.

This was his old enemy reborn.

Stasi. Even the word sounded like Nazi.

'You're wrong,' Stone replied. 'You must be. I simply can't believe the woman I knew is a member of . . . that organization.'

'Oh, she's one of theirs all right. We can be very clear on that.' It was the other man who answered, speaking for the first time since the interview had begun. The one Stone had cast in his mind as Humphrey Bogart. Except that Humphrey Bogart had never spoken with a Yorkshire accent.

'Dagmar Stengel née Fischer works for the Stasi,' Bogart went on, 'which is why we're interested in the fact that she made contact with you. Why *do* you think she wanted to make contact with you, Mr Stone?'

It was such a soft accent with its friendly vowels and timeless Englishness, like J.B. Priestley on the radio in the war. But it seemed to Stone that there was nothing soft or friendly about the intent of what the man was saying.

'She's my sister-in-law,' he said.

Bogart merely smiled, leaving Peter Lorre to reply.

'Yes. Your sister-in-law,' he said, brushing shortbread crumbs from his tie, 'and such was her filial affection that it took her seventeen years to get in touch. And then on the strength of this one contact, a contact that you could not even be sure was genuine, you began immediately to plan a trip to East Berlin, a trip which in your position you must have known would raise eyebrows within certain departments.'

'My position?'

'Oh come on, Stone!' Lorre snapped. 'You work in the Foreign Office. The *German* Department of the Foreign Office.'

Stone said nothing. He could see their point, of course.

'It just seems to us,' the Yorkshire voice said, calm and low, 'that it is a little injudicious for a mid-ranking official of the British Foreign Office to be so eager to make contact with a Stasi officer, sister-in-law or not.'

'Except I didn't know she was a Stasi officer! And I have to say I'm astonished that you think Dagmar is – she was never remotely political as a girl.'

'If you live in East Germany you're either a Communist or you're pretending to be a Communist,' Peter Lorre said. 'I don't think the authorities care which. Besides, the Red Army liberated her. A girl would be grateful, I imagine.'

'From what I know of what the Red Army did on their way west in 1945, very few German women would have had reason to be grateful to them.'

'But your sister-in-law was Jewish.'

'And the Soviets have always loved a Jew, haven't they?' Stone replied with bitter sarcasm. 'You know as well as I do what the NKVD attitude was to Jews. Those Kremlin wolves weren't much better than the Nazis.'

'Which brings us to the point,' Bogart said with a smile.

'There's a point? I mean apart from virtually accusing me of planning treason?'

'Yes. There's a point. Your sister-in-law is not an obvious fit for the Stasi, not least because of its endemic anti-Semitism.'

'Which is why—' Stone began to protest.

'And yet Dagmar Stengel is definitely one of their officers,' Peter Lorre interrupted, anticipating Stone's objection, 'there can be no doubt about that. No doubt at all. We looked into her the moment she wrote to you.'

It was a horrible thought but it *was* possible. The teenager Stone had known might not have been political but she had been intelligent and tough and self-motivated. Dagmar was a survivor, and who could imagine what horrors she had been through in the years since they had last met. What compromises she had made. How much she had changed.

'A Jew working for the Stasi suggests to us a person who would work for anyone,' the Bogart figure remarked, resuming his calmer, almost disinterested tone, 'and we wondered, since you're going that way, if you might like to try and persuade her to work for us.'

The man smiled as he said it. As if he had been asking Stone to deliver a small gift or return a book.

Brand New Model
Berlin, 1921

'You mean you'll have to take your clothes off?' Wolfgang demanded. 'In front of the bastard?'

'If Herr Karlsruhen requires it, which I imagine he will,' Frieda replied with a coquettish toss of her thick, dark, recently bobbed hair. 'I don't imagine nymphs wear an awful lot of clothes, do you?'

Wolfgang was changing Paulus's nappy on the kitchen table, holding the baby's feet in the air in order to wipe him, and for a moment it almost looked as if he might wave the baby about in protest.

'Well, I don't want you to do it,' he said. 'In fact, I . . . I *forbid* you to do it.'

Loud though Frieda's hearty laugh was at this doomed attempt at exerting husbandly authority, it was drowned out by Paulus who at the same moment gave a piercing yell, having clearly decided that his arse had been wiped long enough and it was time for Wolfgang to put his legs down.

Inevitably Paulus's cries set Otto off, the two babies having long since learnt that they could create more chaos if they worked as a team.

'Now look what you've done,' Frieda chided.

'What *I've* done?' Wolfgang exclaimed. 'He's probably crying because his mother wants to be a stripper!'

'*Model*, Wolf!'

'*Nude* model, Frieda.'

Wolfgang finished Paulus's nappy and pretty much dumped him back down beside Otto where the screaming ramped up another notch or two and Frieda was forced to spend ten minutes rocking the boys and singing '*Hoppe Hoppe Reiter*' to them. This always cheered them up, it was their favourite song, particularly the verse about the poor fallen rider getting eaten by the ravens, which the boys seemed to understand was a good bit, despite not yet being able to talk.

'Look, nude modelling is easy work, Wolf,' Frieda said, when finally the babies had calmed down, 'and we could certainly do with the money.'

'We don't need it that much!'

'Oh don't we?' In answer to her own question Frieda marched across their tiny kitchen and flung open the doors of the little wall-mounted cupboard that they called their pantry. In it, apart from a few assorted spices and condiments, was a small piece of cheese, a few centimetres of sausage, a handful of carrots, five decent-sized potatoes and half a loaf of black bread. Besides that, there was a bottle of milk sitting in a bowl of water on the window sill and above the sink a jar of ground coffee and some sugar.

'That's it, Wolf,' Frieda said angrily. 'The lot, our entire supplies until you find another band to play in or we go begging to my parents *again*. I am a student, you are essentially unemployed and we have babies to feed! We need money and if this silly man wants to give me some for getting goosebumps for a couple of hours, I'm going to grab it with both hands.'

'He'd like to grab *you* with both hands if you ask me.'

'He's an *artist*, Wolf. And a rich one too. He pays way above the odds.'

'We don't need his money. We get by.' Wolfgang sulked. 'We don't starve.'

'*Just*, Wolf. We don't starve *just*. And what sort of ambition is that, by the way? *We don't starve*. Nice to know you've set your sights so high. Personally I'd like to do a bit better than not *actually* starving. I'd like to have some nice cakes at the weekend and extra milk for the children, and if taking my clothes off three evenings a week can get me that then every sculptor in Berlin can immortalize my bum in marble as far as I'm concerned.'

Wolfgang scowled but didn't answer.

A rat ran across the lino. He hurled a shoe at it in fury.

This futile gesture did nothing to harm the rat but the bang startled Otto who began crying again. This caused Paulus to throw out an arm in irritation, scratching Otto's face with fingernails which Frieda had been absolutely meaning to get to that evening. Otto screamed blue murder at this which, of course, according to the brothers' unspoken rules, required Paulus to start screaming blue murder as well.

Peace was finally restored but only after Frieda had been forced to put the boys on her breasts, which she absolutely hated herself for doing. She was trying seriously to wean them in an effort to bring some order into her increasingly chaotic life, a district nurse having told her that breast on demand after the first nine months was the road to anarchy and source of all evil.

When Wolfgang broke the angry silence that followed, to Frieda's amazement, instead of being contrite, he was *still* complaining about her new job.

'I didn't mind so much when it was at the Art School,' he said. 'That was legitimate.'

'Oh. So it's fine for *fifty* people to see me naked but not for one? Is that it? Ow! Bugger!'

Frieda yelped in pain. The babies' new teeth were another reason for her wanting to get them off the breast as soon as possible.

'Yes, that is it exactly!' Wolfgang exclaimed. 'You'll be *alone* with this horny old bastard, in his bloody studio.'

'Earning five times what the college pay.'

'And *for what*? What does he expect to get from it? That's what I want to know.'

'He expects tits and ass, Wolf!' Frieda hissed, trying both to shout and to keep her voice down at the same time. 'Which I happen to have in abundance since the twins put ten kilos on me and which, despite the fact that I eat only *one crumb of bread a day*, I don't seem to be able to lose!'

'But why *your* tits and ass? That's what I'd like to know,' Wolfgang asked, still not prepared to give in. 'What's he see in you?'

'Well, thanks very much!'

'I think he fancies you.'

'I've just said, Wolf, he's an *artist*, he needs models to inspire him, and he says that with no meat and no butter in the city all his usual girls have lost their bloom. I, on the other hand, have apparently hung on to mine.'

'Bloom? Is that what he calls it? *Bloom?* Dirty little swine.'

But Wolfgang could not help but admit to himself that the sculptor was right.

Frieda had always turned heads, with her girlishly open face with wide-set eyes, small upturned nose and deep shining auburn hair. She had a trim, athletic-looking 'modern' shape but with a generous bust, and while she had certainly acquired an extra curve or two at the hips during her pregnancy, she was no less a beauty for that.

'Well, quite apart from anything else,' Wolfgang said, changing tack, 'the man's a terrible, *terrible* artist.'

'He's a Victorian Realist.'

'I *think* that's what I said. I mean, honestly. What is the *point* of realism? The camera has been invented. Take a bloody photograph! It does the job *better* and at shutter speeds of a hundredth of a second.'

'Lots of people like realism.'

'Lots of people are idiots.'

Frieda put the babies down and banged a pan on the hob to boil some water. 'I'm not going to continue with this ridiculous conversation.'

'And I'll tell you another thing—' Wolfgang said.

'Not listening.'

'Karlsruhen's a complete reactionary. I read an interview with him. He supports the *Stahlhelm* for God's sake!'

'What? So it would be all right for him to see my tits if he was a Communist?'

'Well, no, maybe not,' Wolfgang conceded. 'But it certainly would if he was an Expressionist or a Surrealist!'

'You're being an absolute idiot, Wolf.'

'Oh, I'm the one being an idiot, am I? Well, tell me this. Will your precious Karlsruhen be making you hold a spear and wear a winged helmet?'

Frieda paused. He had her there. She couldn't help but smile, it *did* seem slightly absurd, a little Jewish girl pretending to be the spirit of *völkisches Deutschland* while hoping that her nipples wouldn't start to drip.

'Well . . . yes,' she conceded, 'he did mention spears and helmets. I admit that.'

'A *winged helmet*.'

'Sometimes apparently. If we're doing a Rhinemaiden.'

Now a shadow of a smile appeared at the corners of Wolfgang's mouth also.

'You are going to stand there, completely naked except for a *winged helmet*?'

'I think I just told you that.'

'Aren't Rhinemaidens supposed to be nymphs?'

'In this case, nymphs in helmets.'

'Which isn't very nymphy.'

'It is to Herr Karlsruhen. Look, Wolf, be realistic,' Frieda said, trying to make peace, 'if he thinks I look like the spirit of German womanhood, then bully for us. I've told you, he pays top hourly rates and all I have to do is stand still and listen to Wagner.'

'He *should* pay you top rates to listen to that crap.'

'I don't mind a bit of Wagner.'

'He was a raving anti-Semite.'

'What's that got to do with his music?'

'I'm just saying that he was as shitty a man as he was a composer.'

'We can't all be cool jazz guys, Wolf. Somebody has to write a tune occasionally. You're being really stupid.'

'And I refer you to my previous point that I'm not the one who is planning on standing about naked in a helmet! Think about that. Naked. But in a helmet. It defies logic, or do people only get hit on the head in Asgard?'

'Now who's interested in realism?'

Frieda turned her attention to a load of nappies that were soaking in a bucket.

'This man lives in the hottest, craziest city in Europe. Every studio's got some wild genius in it breaking all the rules of form – and this prick wants to set the Ring Cycle in stone.'

Frieda fished a dripping terry towel out of the bucket and began running it through the mangle.

'You're being pathetic and self-righteous and actually totally reactionary in a reverse kind of way,' she said, 'which is frankly not attractive.'

'Keep mangling,' Wolfgang replied. 'Karlsruhen's going to love those muscles. If you're lucky he might even promote you to Brünnhilde.'

'There can be more than one style of art you know,' Frieda said through gritted teeth as she worked the heavy handle. 'Not everybody wants to look at pictures of babies on bayonets and limbless soldiers like the stuff you like. We can't all be George Grosz or Otto Dix.'

'Bloody geniuses, both of them. Jazz on canvas. People like Karlsruhen and his moronic *Stahlhelm* go on about making Germany great again. It's *already* great. Stuff is going on here in Berlin, within a few hundred metres of where we're sitting, that they haven't even started *dreaming* about in Paris or New York.'

'Just listen to yourself, why don't you?' Frieda said as the water from the nappies cascaded into the mangle tray. 'You're actually more chauvinist than the Steel Helmets with your "we've got better art in Germany than those bloody foreigners" – even the avant garde are nationalists. It's pathetic.'

Wolfgang's tone showed that despite himself he could see her point. 'I'm just saying that for once we have something going on here that we can be proud of.'

'So you'd feel better about it if I was posing for someone who gave me square tits and three buttocks. That would be all right, would it?'

'It would be a lot better.'

Frieda said nothing. But she gave the mangle an extra vicious turn.

Rhinemaiden
Berlin, 1922

Despite Wolfgang's protestations, Frieda took the modelling job and posed for Herr Karlsruhen throughout 1921 and into the following year. It was while she was on her way to the sculptor's studio in the summer of 1922 that she heard the horrible news that Germany's Foreign Minister had been shot, murdered while on his way to work by a teenage gang put up to it by reactionary anti-Semites. A newspaper boy was calling out a special edition of the *Berliner Tageblatt*. 'Walther Rathenau dead!' the boy shouted. 'Shot in his car.'

Frieda felt sick to her stomach. Just when things had been looking up a little, the republic's foremost statesman was dead. That old German madness had reared its crazed, iron-clad head again.

She got off the tram on the busy Müllerstrasse and turned into a side street which had once contained small businesses and store houses but which was now principally residential. The street was on the edge of the working-class district of Wedding, which was much favoured by artists for its earthy credibility and somewhat Bohemian air. Karlsruhen rented a studio just close enough to the centre of things to gain a little cachet from the borough's reputation, but not so close as to be fully immersed in a dangerously left-wing area that was known throughout the city as Red Wedding.

The concierge of Karlsruhen's building gave Frieda the usual dubious glance as she let her in, clearly under the impression that nude models must be whores. Frieda returned the woman's look with proud disdain before making her way up the stairs to the attic studio in which Karlsruhen worked. The door was half open and she could hear him singing along to a gramophone recording of *Götterdämmerung*. He always had music on while he worked but he did not normally sing. Frieda wondered if he might be a little drunk. Karlsruhen loved his beer and schnapps.

She knocked firmly, causing the door to swing fully open under the force of her fist. She knew that Karlsruhen would shake his head at this. He had once rebuked her for 'banging on the door like a stevedore', admonishing her to be more 'gentle and reserved' and a credit to her sex. This of course made Frieda knock all the louder the next time, and from then on she was always sure to give his door a knuckle-rattling bang whenever she visited. Such displays of spirit, however, seemed only to increase Karlsruhen's attraction to her. He would giggle with silly indulgence as if she were a naughty girl and he her long-suffering father.

All this made Frieda pretty uncomfortable, but she had final exams to prepare for and standing about naked had to be the easiest way to make money in Berlin. She knew plenty of girls who would kill for her luck.

Recently, it was true, Karlsruhen's behaviour has begun to get a little bolder. He had taken to calling her his 'cheeky pet' and his 'little bud', which made her squirm. Wolfgang had said she should demand a pay rise. Instead she had taken strength from reminding herself that once she qualified as a doctor she would never have to see the silly old fool again.

'Enter,' came the familiar, self-important voice from within. 'Advance, sweet child, and be recognized.'

Karlsruhen had never served in the army but he loved to affect a slightly military air.

He was alone, of course, as Frieda had been certain he would be. Before, there had always been one or two young men busying themselves with plaster and tools in distant corners of the studio, Karlsruhen's 'pupils', as he called them. He made much of the fact that he had 'pupils' (although to Frieda's eye they seemed more like paid assistants), clearly fancying himself in the Michelangelo mode. Recently, however, Karlsruhen had taken to ensuring that these pupils were away purchasing supplies or on some other errand when the time came for Frieda's sittings.

Frieda entered the huge space, which spanned the entire length and width of the building. In the daytime the studio was flooded with beautiful natural light, which shone through the skylights even on cloudy days. But night was falling and Karlsruhen had turned on the meagre forty-watt bulbs that hung from the ceiling eaves and cast eerie shadows across the silent plaster figures standing about the room.

At the far end of the studio a desk lamp stood on an empty plinth, its shaded bulb pointing to the place where Frieda would be posing, like a theatrical spotlight.

The great man was standing at his usual place, wearing his habitual white smock and beret, although Frieda did not think he had been doing much work as there was a schnapps bottle in his hand.

Karlsruhen worked mostly in clay, producing mildly erotic figures from which a mould was cast and numerous plaster replicas made to be sold at markets. But he also had pretentions to greater things and sometimes worked in bronze and occasionally even marble, although such materials were of course not readily available.

The white-clad figure watched in silence as Frieda walked the length of the room, her shoes clicking on the dusty bare floorboards. Past half-finished heroic figures and shy nymphs, round stepladders and sacks of plaster powder, over brushes and palettes, past trestle tables laden with knives, chisels, pencils and paper. Perhaps twenty metres in all with Karlsruhen's eyes on her every step of the way before finally she arrived at the little screen in the corner, which Karlsruhen referred to as her dressing room.

It made Frieda laugh inwardly that he insisted on this ludicrous 'courtesy'. After all, there was no 'dressing' to be done, only undressing, which she did as quickly as possible because her hours only began once she stood naked and in position. It would have been simpler to strip off beside her podium. Frieda had pointed this out but Karlsruhen insisted that there was a proper way to do things and she must disrobe in 'private', as feminine modesty demanded. Recently Frieda had noticed that her screen had moved further and further away from her podium. Clearly Karlsruhen enjoyed watching her walk naked across the studio –

more fun, no doubt, than leering at her in frozen immobility.

'Good evening, Fräulein,' Karlsruhen said. 'What joy it is to see you, the sun has set but its light still shines in your smile.'

'I'm not smiling today, Herr Karlsruhen. Have you heard? They shot Walther Rathenau.' She had not really meant to bring it up, she always tried to avoid exchanging views with Karlsruhen on any subject, but it was better than engaging with the leaden and saccharine horror of his unwanted compliments.

'Yes, I heard,' Karlsruhen remarked dismissively. 'But don't think of it so much as losing a Foreign Minister as getting rid of a Jew!'

And he laughed as if he had made an excellent joke.

Frieda didn't reply. She was used to casual anti-Semitism. It was generally assumed that she herself was not a Jew and so she heard it all the time. It was as common in Berlin as remarks about the weather. Nothing much was meant by it, and if she had spent her days confronting it she would have had no time for anything else.

'I can't claim credit for that line,' Karlsruhen went on, 'a friend phoned me with it. He heard it on the Tiergarten within moments of the assassination. People are so clever, aren't they?'

'Perhaps we should start,' Frieda said.

'Yes! At once, little one. Let us not dwell on Germany's terrible present, but instead journey together to her mythical past! Although I fear that my poor talent cannot hope to match the beauty with which you grace my studio, and no cold clay nor bronze nor even marble could ever aspire to capture the warm and subtle tones of your exquisite soft, pale skin.'

On another evening Frieda might have tried to force a smile at the man's creepy compliments, if only to cover her nauseous embarrassment at them, but this time she remained stony-faced as she disappeared behind the disrobing curtain. There was something a little different in the atmosphere. Karlsruhen was more confident than usual, more full of himself. Clearly the schnapps had emboldened him. Frieda hoped he wouldn't drink any more.

She threw off her clothes as quickly as possible and emerged naked, feeling unaccustomedly embarrassed. She was used to

Karlsruhen's hungry gaze and normally almost indifferent to it, but this time as she felt his eyes explore her she felt suddenly revolted. She took her place on the little podium and assumed the pose on which they had been working over the previous session, perched delicately on a stool that Karlsruhen assured her would later be transformed into the rock on which a bewitching Rhinemaiden would disport herself within the foaming fury of the great river.

Karlsruhen turned on the reading lamp and Frieda blinked as she felt herself bathed in its glare.

'My dear, is it a little cold for you?' she heard the shadowy figure behind the lamp enquire. 'I see that the points of your breasts are proud. A lovely detail for me as an artist, particularly since my mythical creation is to be depicted in freezing mountain water, but I fear you might catch a chill.'

Frieda could feel herself reddening beneath her mask of stillness. Karlsruhen had begun to speak like this more and more. Offering extravagant compliments and making personal observations about the detail of her body. Becoming less and less careful to conceal his obvious desire beneath the pretence at professionalism.

Thank goodness she would be leaving soon. And in the meantime, just block it out. After all, weren't all artists secretly somewhat in love with their models?

'Your hair is a mystery, my dear,' Karlsruhen was saying, not even bothering for the moment to work away at his clay but instead simply standing and staring. 'Is it auburn? Is it brunette? I swear sometimes when the light from my lamp catches it just so, it almost glows a fiery crimson.'

Frieda sensed that it was not her hair that Karlsruhen was looking at, but she could not be sure as he had positioned himself just out of her eye line and she was not allowed to move her head.

'How I wish you would let it grow and be your true crowning glory, instead of these ridiculous pageboy monstrosities with which you and your modern sisters vandalize yourselves. You know that when I come to begin upon my Rhinemaiden's head I must make you wear a wig of golden plaits, for a true German daughter of the soil lets her hair flow all the way down to her . . . to her . . . *derrière*.'

There was a catch in his voice. He was circling her. She could feel him pause behind her and she knew what he was looking at.

Frieda set her mind to blocking out his uncomfortable chatter and the thought of his big sweaty face leering behind her. At least she was not required to respond, that was the one redeeming feature of the job really. She was absolutely not required to speak. He paid her to remain still, expressionless and mute.

That was how he liked it too. She knew that. He enjoyed her silence, her compliance. Her *obedience*. Wasn't that the biggest part of the whole *Kinder*, *Küche*, *Kirche* thing that these old *völkische* dinosaurs obsessed about? Children, Kitchen, Church. Those were the duties of a good German woman. And above all obedience to her man. Well, it was 1922 and all that was changing, thank God. Her medical degree would be proof of that. Frieda set her mind to considering her studies. That was always how she tried to pass the long weary hours of posing, by reviewing in her mind the reading she had done the day before. Her current subject was circulation of the blood so she set herself to leafing through the pages of her mental textbook, exploring the anatomy of the heart.

She was just trying to sort out the arteries from the veins when she felt it. Karlsruhen's hand on her breast.

She jumped as if she had been electrocuted, stumbled off the small podium on which she had been perched and ended up in a bruised and naked heap on the floor.

'Please. Please,' Karlsruhen said stepping forward. 'Let me help you up.'

'Get away from me!' Frieda scrabbled to her feet. 'What do you mean by touching me! I'm a married woman. I want to get my clothes.'

But Karlsruhen was in her way, standing between her and the curtained changing area, his expression a mixture of fear and lust.

'You stumbled,' he protested. 'Your leg must have gone to sleep.'

'That's a lie! You touched me!' Frieda exclaimed in fury. 'You felt my breast. Let me past.'

'I adjusted your hair. An inadvertent movement. My hand slipped. What are you suggesting, Frau Stengel? It is I who am wronged. You offend me.'

Frieda stared at him hard. She knew what had happened but he was denying it and there was an end to it. In a way she felt relieved. Money or no money, their relationship was over. She'd never have to see him again.

'Get out of my way, Herr Karlsruhen. I'm afraid I will no longer be able to model for you.'

'No! Don't say that, please.'

'Yes. I must. Please get the money you owe me while I dress.'

She walked past him, thinking the incident was over, but to her horror he grabbed her from behind. Suddenly his arms were around her and his face was buried in her hair.

'Please,' he mumbled. 'I love you, little one. You are everything. Everything to me!'

Frieda struggled in his grasp, shouting once more that she had a husband, and also that he had a wife.

'That heifer!' Karlsruhen blurted, spinning Frieda around, his hot breath on her face. 'She doesn't understand me. You do! You are everything a woman should be, you are my muse. My love.'

He gripped her closer now, clamping her naked body against his chest. She could smell the schnapps on his breath. He was not a young man but he was strong and booze and lust had given him power. Frieda struggled but she could not free herself. Now she could feel his hand behind her, clawing between her buttocks as he ground his erection against her stomach.

'My little Rhinemaiden,' he was gasping, '*meine kleine Woglinde, Wellgunde und Floßhilde!*'

Then Frieda realized how to stop the madness.

Naked, much smaller than her assailant and caught unawares, she could not hope to fight him off, but she didn't need to. She had seen his weakness. He wasn't pawing her, he was pawing a fantasy, a warped romantic obsession.

One word would still his ardour.

'Herr Karlsruhen!' she shouted, forcing her face into his. 'I am not your little Rhinemaiden, you arsehole! I am a grown-up woman! I am soon to be a doctor and, above all, I am a JEW!'

There was a pause of perhaps a second or so before his grip loosened and he stepped backwards, astonished.

Frieda seized the opportunity to rush behind the curtain for her clothes.

'You're . . . a Jewess?' he said. 'You never said.'

'I ought to call the police!' Frieda shouted in fury, pulling on her underwear and buttoning up her dress.

'You . . . you don't look like a Jew,' she heard him mumble.

'What does a Jew look like, you fatuous bastard?' Frieda shouted as she emerged from behind the curtain, pulling on her shoes. 'Do you think I should have a nose like a boat hook, you stupid old prick!'

'Please . . . such language. It is not fitting for—'

'*Language!* You were trying to rape me!'

'No!' he protested, 'just an embrace, a kiss, I thought you wouldn't mind. I'm sorry. You must go.'

'Give me my money first!' Frieda said, grabbing at a large palette knife and pointing it in Karlsruhen's face.

Karlsruhen reached into the pocket of his smock and pushed a bundle of notes into her hand.

'Go. Please go,' he said.

Frieda threw down the knife and ran to the door.

'And let me tell you, Herr Karlsruhen. The only reason I won't be telling my husband what you did today is that he'd kill you. Do you understand? He'd kill you!'

District and Circle Line

London, 1956

It was mid-morning when Stone emerged from the house on Queensgate in which he had been interrogated. A troop of cavalry from Chelsea Barracks were rattling their way up the road towards Hyde Park. They were in khaki, not dress uniform, but nonetheless made an impressive sight. An echo of imperial greatness. Stone found himself offering a wry salute. Force of habit, perhaps. You can take the man out of the army, as they say. But Stone actually liked the army, not the spit and polish bullshit, but the courage and the comradeship. Briefly the British army had given him a home.

He headed down towards South Kensington tube station. Lorre and Bogart had told him to go home, call in sick at work and keep himself available. They promised to square things with Stone's head of department, assuring him that he would lose neither wages nor credit.

Stone didn't care about wages. He had thoughts only for the shocking revelation that Dagmar was an officer of the Stasi.

And yet was it so shocking? The war had changed them all so much. Were he to go back in time and look at his own carefree, soccer-mad, rebellious pre-war self, he would surely not have predicted the journey that boy would take. That at the end of it he would find himself fading to grey behind a desk in Whitehall, doing his long weary penance for surviving.

Dagmar would scarcely recognize the man he had become. Would he recognize her?

Stone made his way through the fine red-tiled entrance of the nineteenth-century tube station, declining the offer to buy a first edition *Standard*. The news was the same as the day before anyway. The aftermath of the Suez debacle still dominated the front pages with its ongoing humiliation of Britain at the hands of Eisenhower and the US State Department, not to mention Nasser himself. The UK was finished, Egypt was in the ascendant and all over the Middle East Arabs were flexing their muscles.

There was Lonnie Donegan music playing through the open window of one of the flats that sat above the station entrance. Usually Stone quite liked Lonnie Donegan, except for the stupid one about chewing gum and bedposts. He liked skiffle in general because it was scruffy and disrespectful of authority. Now, however, he found it irritating. He found the chatter of girls in front of him on the stairs irritating. And the platform announcements too.

He was trying to think.

Dagmar had said in her letter that she'd been in a Soviet gulag. That made grim sense. The Russians had imprisoned hundreds of thousands of recently liberated innocents after the war, however much the craven apologists of the London Left might try to deny or excuse it.

Dagmar was, after all, a bourgeois Jew. Two strikes against her in Stalin's book.

But that had been ten years ago. She could not possibly have spent all of the intervening period in a Soviet camp and yet now be a Stasi official. At some point during those years she must have been released and 'rehabilitated'. And yet only now had she got in contact. Why had she taken so long to try and find him?

And why had she done so now?

The train arrived. Stone found a seat and lit up a Lucky Strike. His father had always loved American cigarettes.

The answer to the first question was obvious. Dagmar had not *wanted* to resume contact. Association with people from the West would do her no good at all. Particularly a person like himself, an ex-German, living in Britain and working at the Foreign Office. In her position Dagmar would certainly know of these things about him and would understand that association with him was bound to bring suspicion down on her. The fact that MI6 wanted him to contact her on their behalf was chilling enough evidence of that.

So why had she approached him?

The answer to that was so exciting that Stone had scarcely dared acknowledge it, even in his deepest, most private thoughts.

She needed him.

Stone held the cigarette between his teeth and took the letter from his wallet. Written in that still familiar hand, if shakier now, sadder somehow, less optimistic.

> *When last I saw you, dear friend, at the café at the Lehrter Bahnhof, you held my hand and whispered so that no one, not even your brother, could hear. You whispered that you loved me and that you always would. You promised me that day I would see you again. Will you keep your promise? We are strangers now, of course. But will you come? Perhaps we can find a smile together, over half-remembered happiness from another world and time. Everyone is looking for Moses.*

That last line. *Everyone is looking for Moses.*

It was his mother who used to say it. In the first year of the nightmare. In 1933. People used to come to her and ask for a way out. She was a doctor after all, doctors had the answer to everything. Perhaps even how to get an exit visa. But for all her cleverness and her compassion, Dr Stengel did not know that. She could only smile and whisper gently, *Everyone is looking for Moses. Hoping he'll lead them out of Egypt.* She said it so often that first year but less so later and then not at all.

Well, Dagmar had a new Egypt now.

And this time Moses wouldn't fail her.

Money Gone Mad

Berlin, 1923

Paulus and Otto were playing together on the thick blue English rug which had come from Wolfgang's parents, while Frieda sat at her little desk bureau looking over the family finances. She had been staring at a particular banknote for a few moments when quite suddenly she began dabbing at her eyes with a handkerchief.

The little boys stopped playing and stared at her for a moment, caught up in the unfamiliar spectacle of their mother's tears, having imagined up until that point in their lives that crying was their prerogative alone.

'Don't cry, Mum,' Otto pleaded.

'I'm not, darling. Just an eyelash in my eye, that's all.'

Frieda blew her nose on a handkerchief and then more urgent issues claimed the boys' attention as Paulus took the opportunity to steal the parapet from Otto's fort and add it to his own. Paulus, thoughtful behind deep-set, dark eyes, was already the superior strategist of the two boys, while Otto, although by no means stupid, was wild and impulsive. His impulse now was immediate and violent. He slammed his fat little fist into the side of Paulus's head and the fight that ensued was only ended when Wolfgang stormed in from the bedroom (where he had been sleeping after a late show) and sprayed the flailing knot of arms and legs and fists and feet with water from a toy pistol. This was a trick he'd picked up in the park from a man who bred dogs.

'When they brawl, I throw water over them,' the man had said. 'They soon learn.'

Wolfgang decided that the same cause-and-effect training might work on his endlessly battling three-year-olds.

'They're just a couple of little wild animals, aren't they?' Wolfgang argued when Frieda objected to her children being trained like dogs. 'And you have to admit it works.'

'It doesn't work. They just think it's funny.'

'I prefer the laughing to screaming.'

Once the twins had been subdued, Wolfgang noticed Frieda's red eyes.

'What's wrong, Freddy?' he asked. 'You've been crying.'

He sat beside her at her desk, sliding himself on to the piano stool she was using as a chair. 'Come on, girl, I know times are pretty tough but we're getting by, aren't we?'

Frieda didn't reply. Instead she handed him the banknote, a ten-million-mark one she had the previous day received in part change for a litre of milk.

Scrawled on the note in a naïve, girlish hand were the desperate words: *For this very bill I sold my virtue.*

Wolfgang frowned and then shrugged.

'Must have been at least a month ago,' he said. 'Even a country girl would want a hundred million for her virginity now.'

'I hadn't believed Germany could get any more crazy,' Frieda said, sniffing back the tears.

'I suppose when you lose a world war things don't get back to normal overnight.'

'It's been *five years*, Wolf. I don't think anybody in Germany has the faintest idea what normal is any more.'

Outside their apartment the clanking of the lift announced its ponderous arrival at their floor.

'Edeltraud,' Frieda said with a long-suffering smile.

'About bloody time.'

'We need to get her a watch.'

'We need to give her a kick up the arse.'

Edeltraud was the Stengels' maid and babysitter. A seventeen-year-old street waif who had wandered into the Community Health Centre where Frieda worked, with her two-year-old daughter on her hip, and simply collapsed on the floor from hunger and exposure. Frieda had fed her, clothed her, managed to find her a place in a hostel and also, for the sake of the giggling little girl at her feet, promised Edeltraud a job.

This surprised and also exasperated Frieda's colleagues at the Health Centre, who were on the whole stern-faced Communists and did not approve of bourgeois sentimentality.

'If you're going to give a job to every basket case that walks through our doors,' a young colleague called Meyer grumbled, 'pretty soon you're going to be employing the entire population of Friedrichshain. You need to channel your social guilt into organized political action, not pointless and reactionary acts of counterproductive Liberal charity.'

'And you need to shut your face and mind your own business,' Frieda replied, surprising herself.

Wolfgang hadn't been too happy about the arrangement either, although his reservations were practical, not dialectical. He just didn't fancy the idea of having a scatter-brained, unskilled and uneducated teenager lolling about the house pinching his food. After a month or two, however, he was prepared to admit it was working out quite well. It was true that Edeltraud had never once been on time and she was certainly not the most hard-working girl in the world and she had an *unbelievably* annoying habit of rearranging his shelves. But she was pleasant and meant well and the twins loved her, which Wolfgang put down to them all having a similar age of maturity.

Edeltraud was only six years younger than Frieda but Frieda sometimes felt that she had a teenage daughter in the apartment, and a young and naïve one at that.

It was in fact the thought of Edeltraud that had made Frieda cry over the pathetic inscription on the banknote.

'It could easily have been her who wrote this,' she said.

'Darling, when Edeltraud gets any money, she doesn't waste her time writing poignant little notes on it, no matter how she earned it. She spends it on chocolate and film mags. Furthermore, Edeltraud can't write.'

'Actually she can a bit now, I've started to teach her.'

'Don't tell that arsehole Dr Meyer – he'll say you can't liberate the underclass by private initiatives, you need coordinated mass action.'

'I don't want to liberate the underclass, I just want Edeltraud to be able to read my shopping lists.'

A key scratched in the latch and Edeltraud bustled into the

room with the bread delivery under one arm and her little daughter Silke under the other. Silke was the result of an extremely brief relationship the fourteen-year-old Edeltraud had had with a sailor, about which she was disarmingly frank.

'He took me to this lodging-house bedroom,' the young girl had explained to Frieda, still seeming to be getting over the surprise of it, 'and when he finished doing what he wanted to do, which I can't say as how I'd enjoyed very much, he said he was going to the toilet down the hall. Well, for about an hour I just thought he was constipated. I only realized he'd buggered off when the landlady starts banging on the door for her money, which of course I didn't have. A nice way to lose my cherry, I must say.'

Silke was now two and a half years old and already a cheerful charmer with a mass of curls so blonde they were almost white. Curls which were of course an object of fascination and terrible temptation to Paulus and Otto, who tugged them at every opportunity.

'Good day, Frau Stengel, Herr Stengel,' Edeltraud said from the door. 'I brought Silke; I hope you don't mind.'

'You know we don't mind, Edeltraud,' Frieda replied, 'we love to have her. Just watch those boys and if they pull her beautiful hair whack them with the wooden spoon.'

'Right,' said Wolfgang, 'I'm going to try and grab another forty winks. Don't use the vacuum machine for a bit, will you, Edeltraud, there's a love, and try to resist the temptation to rearrange the sheet music on the piano.'

'Of course, Herr Stengel,' Edeltraud replied, unconsciously swapping the positions of a framed photograph and an ashtray on the mantelpiece above the gas fire.

Wolfgang returned to the bedroom and Edeltraud, who was more than happy to be told not to work, started in with the latest news from the neighbourhood.

'Did you hear?' she said, breathless to tell.

'What?'

'The Peunerts gassed themselves!'

'No!' Frieda gasped in horror. 'My God. Why?'

Even as she said it Frieda knew it was a stupid question, it was obvious why.

'He was on a fixed pension from the post office,' Edeltraud went on. 'They left a note saying they'd rather die by their own hand than starve. They sold every stick of furniture they had to get the gas turned back on and then lay down together on the bare floor by the tap in the skirting board, with their heads under a blanket!'

'Oh my God,' Frieda whispered.

'I think it's really really romantic,' said Edeltraud.

Edeltraud was not yet eighteen and told her gruesome story with all the unconscious callousness of youth.

Frieda did not think it was romantic. Living together into old age was romantic, committing suicide together was simply appalling and terribly sad. She had known the Peunerts by sight, had nodded to them often in the street, and yet she had been oblivious to the despair that had enveloped them.

'I should have talked to them. Asked if they were getting on all right, if they needed help.'

'Wouldn't have done any good, would it?' Edeltraud said. 'You can't make their life savings worth anything, can you? There was a woman at the ciggy kiosk this morning. Said she'd saved all her life and now the whole lot wouldn't buy her a pack of smokes and a newspaper. If you ask me, the answer is, don't save it. Get it, spend it.'

Edeltraud put Silke down on the floor and began rearranging the breakfast dishes that were piled up in the sink. 'They put on their best clothes to do it, you know, her in a long granny frock from before the war and him in city coat and tie. Imagine that! The two of them, dressed up for Sunday in the Tiergarten, stretched out on the bare boards with a blanket on their heads. It's almost funny really when you think about it.'

Little Silke waddled across the floor of the apartment to where the twins were playing. She stood in front of them for a moment, apparently deep in thought, strong, bare little legs planted firmly apart on the carpet, arms folded purposefully. Then, having clearly come to a decision, she sat down heavily on Otto's fort, collapsing every single brick. Otto of course howled in fury and Paulus rolled about on the rug and laughed and laughed. Then Silke hauled herself to her feet, took a step towards Paulus and sat down on his fort, chuckling happily amongst the collapsed wooden blocks of two great military installations. Now it was Paulus's turn to howl while Otto laughed. Then they fought, ignoring Silke, the cause of their distress, and flying at each other with tiny fists, rolling on the rug yelling and whacking as hard as they could. Silke, clearly pleased with the way the situation was developing, jumped on top of them both and joined in, laughing with delight.

Despite Frieda and Edeltraud's efforts to quieten them it wasn't long before Wolfgang came charging out of the bedroom with his water pistol blazing. This did eventually stop the fight but only after all three children were soaked, which meant they all had to be stripped and the clothes set out on the tiny balcony to dry. After which they happily began their favourite game of all. The boys piled all the cushions in the apartment on top of Silke and then jumped on them while she screamed with pure joy.

'No point trying to get back to sleep now,' Wolfgang said ruefully, putting a pan on the stove and contemplating the snake pit of limbs writhing amongst the cushions. 'Got a lunchtime gig in Nikolassee.'

'Can I make the coffee for you, Herr Stengel?' Edeltraud asked brightly.

'No, Edeltraud, you can't. And when I say that, I mean it literally. You can't. You *could* make the strange brown gritty solution you *call* coffee, which somehow manages to be both too strong and without flavour at the same time, but what you *can't* do is make *actual* coffee so if it's all right by you I'll make it myself.'

'Well, whatever suits,' Edeltraud shrugged, 'but personally I don't think it matters as long as it's warm and wet.'

'And there, Edeltraud, in a brief and horrifying sentence you have the entire problem.'

'You're *funny*, Herr Stengel.'

Wolfgang contemplated his reflection in the polished wood of the beautiful old upright Blüthner piano, polished at least above toddler-finger level. 'Better shave. I'm supposed to look presentable.'

'I haven't sponged the sweat stains out of your dinner jacket yet,' Frieda said, 'and it'll need pressing too because you just left it in a crumpled heap on the bathroom floor when you got in, even though I've asked you a million times to at least hang it over a chair.'

Wolfgang took the jacket from where Frieda had hung it and began making pointless little smoothing gestures at the concertinaed creases.

'Why we're supposed to play music dressed up as head waiters is beyond me, anyway,' he said. 'The audience is supposed to listen to us, not look at us.'

'You have to look smart, Wolf, you know that. I think the only solution is to get a second dinner suit. You have so many jobs now that there's just no time to clean it between them.'

'Everybody's dancing,' Wolfgang said, pouring out the coffee and handing Frieda a cup. 'It's *so* weird. I mean it, everybody. Grannies. Cripples. Cops, fascists, commies, priests. I see them all. The madder the money gets, the more frantically everybody seems to want to throw themselves around the room. I'm telling you. Berlin is now officially the world capital of crazy. I'm playing with guys from New York who say the same thing. They have nothing on us.'

'They dance on top of taxis in America,' Edeltraud said, 'and on aeroplane wings. I saw it on a news reel.'

'And that's the point,' Wolfgang said. 'They're doing it for fun, we're doing it for therapy. It's like the last party before the world ends.'

'Oh don't say that, Wolf,' Frieda said. 'I've only just graduated.'

'It's brilliant for us musicians, of course. We love the inflation. We love war reparations and the bloody French for occupying the

Ruhr. We're glad the mark has gone down a rabbit hole and ended up in Wonderland. Because the more screwed up the country becomes, the more work we get. I have five shows today, did you know that, *five*? Lunchtime waltzes for the old ladies and gents. An afternoon tea dance for the horny spinsters.'

'Wolf! Please!'

'You're *funny*, Herr Stengel.'

'I'm telling you, the whole country's dancing.'

To the delight of Edeltraud and the children, Wolfgang performed a little tap routine. A skill he had perfected at the end of the war to augment his income as a busker.

'*Yes! We have no bananas!*' he sang, beating out the rhythm with dexterous toe and heel. '*We have no bananas today!*'

Frieda smiled too but she couldn't help thinking of those who weren't dancing. Of those who were lying cold on the floorboards of their empty homes. The old, the young, the sick, dying in their hundreds as once more starvation and despair returned to the capital after only the very briefest of absences.

If the people of her beloved Berlin were dancing, for many it was a dance of death.

Young Entrepreneurs

Berlin, 1923

The kid who approached Wolfgang at the bar was eighteen years old and looked younger. In one hand he held a bottle of Dom Pérignon, and in the other a solid gold cigarette case with a large diamond at its centre. The arm that held the bottle was clamped around the pencil-thin waist of a fashionably bored-looking girl with quite the severest 'bobbed' haircut Wolfgang had ever seen. A shining black helmet with a high straight fringe cut at an angle across her forehead, and a crimped wave at the sides that reached barely beyond her ears. An extremely striking 'look', both forbidding and alluring at the same time. Which was more than could be said for the young man, who at first glance struck Wolfgang as a complete pain in the ass.

'You there! Jazz man, Mr Trumpet!' the youth brayed. 'I'd like a word.'

Wolfgang glanced at him but said nothing.

There were so many of them in Berlin that fruitcake summer. Kids, stupidly young and completely ridiculous, with their money, their self-consciously loud chatter and their drunken arrogance.

Downy-cheeked boys in faultless evening dress, hair brilliantined straight back into a hard shell. Sometimes a hint of rouge on their lips, it being suddenly fashionable to look a bit queer.

And the girls, so sophisticated and world weary at all of eighteen. With their *Bubikopf* and *Herrenschnitt* hairdos, smokily made-up eyes and the newly fashionable, sheath-like, waistless dresses hanging from their bony, boyish frames.

Germany's new kindergarten entrepreneurs, crazy alcohol- and drug-fuelled chancers. The *Raffke* and the *Schieber* – spiffs, gamblers, profiteers and thieves. Teenage wideboys in coffee bars dealing in shares, setting up private banks amongst the cakes and coffee cups. Buying up the treasured possessions of war widows for a few loaves of bread, then selling them to French soldiers in the Ruhr for foreign currency.

The youth who was approaching Wolfgang at the bar was young even by the topsy-turvy standards of the great inflation. He looked as if he had borrowed his father's tuxedo for a school dance and got his mother to tie his tie.

'Hello, Daddy,' the young man said with a broad smile. 'I'm Kurt and this divine creature is Katharina. Hey! Kurt and Katharina. Sounds like a song! *Kurt and Katharina, flew in from Sardinia!* Not bad. You can have that if you like. Just needs a tune. Say hello to Mr Trumpet, baby.'

The girl gave Wolfgang a cool nod, which may or may not have included the tiniest hint of a smile. Or perhaps it was a sneer. It was difficult to tell with a girl so clearly intent on remaining sultry and enigmatic.

Wolfgang wondered whether she practised such studied mystery in her dressing-room mirror when she was applying all that dark shadow to her large grey eyes and teasing the lashes to twice the length nature intended them to be. She looked a little older than Kurt, perhaps as ancient as nineteen or even twenty. At all of twenty-five, Wolfgang felt ancient.

'Hello, Katharina,' he said. 'Pleased to meet you.'

'Look but don't touch, Mr Trumpet!' Kurt admonished, wagging a heavily bejewelled finger. 'This hotsy-totsy baby already found her daddy.'

Wolfgang smiled at the boy's absurd posturing but he was secretly annoyed that his appreciation of the girl had been so obvious. Katharina herself gave Kurt a look of such endless and absolute contempt that Wolfgang could only wonder how the youth did not shrivel up into a heap of ashes inside his suit.

'We often breeze into this particular gin mill,' he went on, 'me and my crowd. It's our favourite dive. Do you want to know why?'

Wolfgang was about to remark that frankly he could live without that information. He had only stopped at the bar on his way out for a quick cigarette and a shot of whisky against the night chill, and was in no particular mood for drunken intimacies from complete strangers. Particularly teenage ones.

But there was something undeniably compelling about this young peacock, if only his immense self-satisfaction. Also, if Wolfgang was honest, he had no objection to spending a few moments longer under the cool appraisal of Katharina's smoky gaze.

'I imagine you're going to tell me anyway. So put me out of my misery. Why *do* you come to this particular gin mill, Kurt?'

'Well—'

'I'm dry,' Katharina interrupted in a lazy drawl, tapping a long, black-painted fingernail on the rim of her empty glass. Kurt, whose gushing *joie de vivre* was as unaffected by being ignored as it was by being derided, happily poured out the last of his champagne into Katharina's glass and then called for another bottle.

'Make sure it's French, mind!' he shouted, putting real American dollars on the bar, 'and another malt scotch for my friend.'

As Katharina raised her glass to her lips, the wispy silk of her dress rippled against her breasts. It was as if a naked girl had walked through a cobweb.

Once more Wolfgang tried not to stare.

'Light me,' she said, helping herself to one of Wolfgang's American cigarettes that were lying beside his drink. 'I like a Lucky. They're toasted, you know.'

Wolfgang struck a match on the sole of his shoe and held it up for her. She touched his hands as she leant forward to place the tip of her cigarette into the flame. The light flared, highlighting her fine cheekbones and casting shadows across her temples.

'We come here,' Kurt said finally, '*if* I might be allowed to get a word in edgeways, because of the music. And more to the point, Mr Trumpet, because of you.'

'Thanks a lot,' Wolfgang said, draining the double shot he'd been given in one gulp. 'Well, I'm here each night, and all paying customers are welcome.'

'You are very hot,' Katharina said slowly, and for a moment she fixed her heavily lidded eyes upon his, gazing unblinkingly into them through the smoke that curled up from her purple-painted lips. 'I like trumpet players. They know how to coordinate their mouths and fingers.'

Wolfgang actually blushed at this and Kurt roared with laughter.

'Stop flirting, you goofy Dora!' he shouted, slapping Katharina's bottom. 'I'm doing business here.'

'Really?' Katharina replied. 'OK, well here's some business for you, sonny: give me fifty American dollars now or try and find another girl as beautiful as me to make you look like a man instead of the damned little schoolboy that you are. And don't *ever* slap my ass again.'

Kurt giggled foolishly. 'Isn't she a scream? Too too cruel. It's what I love. I must be a masochist.'

Then to Wolfgang's astonishment, Kurt took out a gold money clip and counted out five US ten-dollar bills, which Katharina took without a smile or even a nod of acknowledgement. Then raising her slim coltish leg on to the foot of a bar stool, she briskly pulled the hem of her dress along her thigh and slipped the money into her garter.

Her eyes flipped up and caught Wolfgang staring.

'I'm afraid my dress doesn't have any pockets,' she said.

Wolfgang gulped. He needed to get home.

'Business?' he said quickly, trying to pretend it had been the hard currency and not Katharina's leg he'd been looking at. 'What business are you doing and what's it got to do with me?'

'You're the fixer in this juice joint, am I right?' Kurt enquired. 'You book the band, do the sheets and work out the set list?'

'Yes, they're all my arrangements. I do it all.'

'Well, I *like* what you do, Daddy. I'm starting up my own club and I want you to fix for me.'

Wolfgang tried not to laugh.

'You? Starting up a club? Forgive me, Kurt, but how old are you?'

'I'm eighteen.'

'He's seventeen,' said Katharina.

'I'm using the Russian calendar,' Kurt shot back, 'out of solidarity with the murdered Romanovs.'

Wolfgang laughed. The kid certainly had charm.

'They shouldn't even let you *in* a club, let alone buy one,' he said.

'They let in anyone with dollars,' Kurt pointed out. 'I have a *lot* of dollars. And francs and gold sovereigns. Anything you want. Come and join me at my table. Meet my friends, we can discuss it.'

Wolfgang looked across the crowded room towards where Kurt

was nodding. Kurt's friends looked almost as young as he was.

'Shouldn't you all be studying for college or something?'

'There is nothing old people can teach us. Absolutely nothing,' Kurt said with a weary shrug, 'except how to crawl. How to starve. How to sit about wishing that it was still 1913 until you curl up and die. We know more already than those stupid old bastards ever knew, which is why we're drinking French champagne and listening to hot jazz while they queue for soup or march about the streets in tin helmets looking for Jews to shoot. Come on, I want you to meet my friends.'

Perhaps it was Kurt's money that made Wolfgang linger. Perhaps it was his girlfriend. Either way he allowed himself to be led over to the table where Kurt's 'crowd' was seated and where he was greeted with enthusiastic applause.

'This is Hans,' Kurt said, referring to an athletic-looking young man with a thin Douglas Fairbanks moustache, which Wolfgang suspected had been beefed up with mascara. 'One year ago he failed his final Latin exam, now he deals in automobiles.'

'Anything from a Flivver to a Roller,' Hans boasted, slurring his words somewhat. 'You want it, I'll get it. Take my card. Discount for a man who plays like you.'

Wolfgang explained that he was happy with his bicycle but took the card anyway, noticing that Hans's pupils were mere pin-pricks. There was also a girl slumped on his shoulder, dead to the world.

'This is Dorf,' Kurt went on, ignoring the unconscious girl and indicating a bookish-looking man with horn-rimmed spectacles sitting on the other side of her. 'He's in currency, his father thinks he should be studying law.'

'He wants me to be an articled clerk when I'm twenty-one,' Dorf said primly, 'which is rather funny actually because, without me, my old man would starve! Mother doesn't tell him of course.'

Kurt and Hans both laughed at this, causing the girl between them to begin to slide slowly under the table. Hans put an arm across her to arrest her progress.

'And here's Helmut,' Kurt said, referring to a beautiful blond youth with piercing blue eyes that matched his cobalt blue earrings. 'He's what you might call—'

'A queer pimp,' Katharina interrupted.

'Actually I was going to say a social consultant,' Kurt said.

'I prefer queer pimp,' Helmut remarked archly, at which there was more laughter, and once more Hans's girl had to be set up straight.

'So now you know my friends, Mr Trumpet. They're all big fans of yours.'

Again there was applause.

'You haven't said what you do?' Wolfgang asked. 'What's your game, Kurt?'

'Well, as I mentioned before, amongst other things I am a club owner,' Kurt replied.

'Oh? Which club do you own?'

'I haven't decided yet. Maybe this one, or one of the others. Perhaps all of them, we shall see.'

'So you don't own them yet?'

'Details. Details. I'll get them if I want them.'

'How will you get them, Kurt?' Wolfgang asked, wishing he could think of a smart way to cut this cocksure youth down to size, but uncomfortably aware that Kurt would not even notice if he did.

'Improvise, of course! Like the good little jazz kid that I am . . . In fact,' Kurt went on, clearly delighted with this image, 'that's what I do! I'm a *jazz economist*. I improvise. You borrow notes. And so do I! *Banknotes!* Isn't that a scream?'

'But where do you borrow them from?'

'The same place you get yours! Thin air! I borrow what I need on the security of the thing I'm buying and pay off the loan next week when it's worth a thousand times less. Anyone could do it.'

'Why don't they, then?'

'Why don't you?'

Wolfgang knew Kurt was right. He *could* do it. He could buy anything he wanted. Anything at all. He just had to have the guts. The sheer chutzpah to borrow enough to do it. It didn't really even take guts, because with money depreciating so quickly debt was just an illusion.

Anyone *could* do it.

But it was only people like Kurt who actually *did*.

And the big boys of course. The industrialists who were manipulating the same situation as Kurt, except they were buying whole industries while Kurt bought only champagne and drugs.

And in the meantime everybody else was trying to work out where their next meal was coming from.

Which reminded Wolfgang he needed to get home so Frieda could go to the markets. The wages in his pocket were depreciating at the same speed as Kurt's debt. By simply standing right there, he was getting poorer while Kurt got richer.

'I'll tell you what,' Wolfgang said, draining his glass and putting it on the table, 'you buy your club and make me an offer. If it's a good one, then I'll be your fixer. Meantime I really do think I should be getting home.'

Katharina was standing beside him at the table and he had felt her hand brush against his more than once. He was pretty sure that she knew it too. Hands didn't brush against each other more than once by accident.

Which was rather exciting.

And also why he needed to get home.

Wolfgang had never been short of female admirers, girls made eyes at him all the time. He was good-looking and, more importantly, he was a jazz man and the jazz babies loved nothing better, particularly trumpet players.

Usually Wolfgang was entirely resistant. Immune to the coquettish glances of over-excited flappers on the dance floor. He was happy to look at their shaking, shimmying bottoms and swinging breasts bouncing in front of his little stage in their next-to-nothing dresses, but he was not tempted to touch. Katharina, however, was different. She had truly caught his eye, and that was dangerous, because he seemed to have caught hers.

'I'll be playing here tomorrow night,' Wolfgang said to Kurt matter-of-factly, 'you can speak to me then.'

'If you're playing here tomorrow night,' Kurt said, 'then I'll already be your boss. So I certainly will speak to you.'

This splendid piece of bravado elicited further cheers and much table thumping from Kurt's friends, the vibrations of which caused the unconscious girl to finally slide fully under the table.

Wolfgang shook Kurt's hand and nodded briefly at Katharina. Her face remained as cool and impassive as ever as she nodded back, a brief, dismissive farewell.

And then, as if on impulse, she leant forward and kissed him on the mouth. For one brief moment her lips were alive against his, he felt the waxy quality of her lipstick and smelt the perfume in her hair. Then, just as abruptly, she stepped back, her face a mask once more.

'You see!' Kurt shouted. 'Told you she was flirting. You're honoured – she never kisses *me* goodbye.'

'You don't play trumpet,' Katharina said, smiling properly for the first time.

'Yes, well,' Wolfgang said, trying to regain his composure. 'Like I say, got to go. Wife and kids at home and all that.'

He said this last sentence for Katharina's benefit. He didn't normally talk about his domestic status at work. Too humdrum. Not very jazz.

Which was why he said it now. He wanted to make Katharina aware at once, because she had disturbed him, and in his experience nothing dampened a jazz baby's libido quicker than mention of the wife and kids.

'Give Frau Trumpet our love,' Kurt said.

'Yes, yes I will.'

He needed to get home.

Funny Money

Berlin, 1923

The crucial thing was to move fast. When a kilo of carrots could leap in price fifty-thousand-fold in the space of a day, a young couple with children to feed were wise not to leave their shopping until the afternoon.

Wolfgang was fortunate in that being a musician he finished work only an hour or two before the commercial day began. He would grab his pay from the manager, in bundles of freshly printed notes, some still damp having been produced only hours earlier on one of the twelve printing presses that the Reichsbank kept running twenty-four hours a day. Then he'd rush out of the back door of whatever club he had been playing at, lash his trumpet and his violin to the rack of his bicycle and pedal off in a fever of anxiety lest the inflation render his wages worthless before he had the chance to spend them.

In February he had two or three hundred thousand marks stuffed into his pockets in five- and ten-thousand-mark notes. By the summer he had begun carrying his instruments on his back and his wages strapped to his bicycle rack in a bulging suitcase.

Knowing that the drinks he had had with Kurt and Katharina had made him late, Wolfgang laboured mightily at the pedals of his bicycle. His teeth rattled as he forced the ungeared old bone-shaker across the cobbles and uneven flagstones of Berlin's nineteenth-century back streets, his mouth clamped firmly shut for fear that he would bite his tongue as he bounced along.

He chained his bike up by the communal bins in the internal well of their apartment block, rushed in through the front entrance and summoned the lift. For some reason, wherever Wolfgang was in the building, be it at the top or the bottom, the lift was always at the opposite end of the shaft. Usually he stood cursing quietly at this purest example of sod's law, but on this occasion he had cause to be thankful, for as he waited on the ground floor, listening to the lift's laborious, clanking descent, his mind returned to his recent encounter and in particular of course to Katharina and her goodbye kiss.

He remembered her hand drawing his face towards hers. The lazy eyes behind the cigarette smoke. Her mouth momentarily alive.

And then he remembered her lipstick. Thick, glossy and purple.

If there was one thing that Wolfgang knew it was that a woman could detect another woman's cosmetics at fifty paces and from behind closed doors. He grabbed at his handkerchief and wiped vigorously at his mouth.

Looking down at the little linen cloth he saw that he'd had a lucky escape, there were hints of dark purple on the cloth. Of course he had no reason to feel guilty, he hadn't invited the kiss. But Wolfgang knew that when it came to other women's lipstick, innocence was no defence.

Frieda was waiting for him in their apartment, her hat and coat already on, her bag ready at her feet and Otto in her arms.

'You're late,' she said in a loud whisper, nodding towards the children's bedroom door to remind him that one child was still asleep.

'Sorry. Got talking. A fella said he wanted to offer me a job. Could be interesting.'

'Take Otto, he's been up an hour,' Frieda said, shoving the toddler into Wolfgang's arms and grabbing her bag. 'Had a nightmare I think. Got to rush. I'm meeting Ma and Pa before surgery starts. It's Dad's day.'

As a police officer Frieda's father was on a monthly salary, an arrangement that only a few months before was a mark of success and stability. A middle-class achievement which meant that if a person was sacked they had a whole month's notice with which to cushion the blow. But in Germany in 1923, a monthly pay cheque was a curse. The recipient was forced to buy everything they needed for the month to come in the first hour of getting their money, because by the following day when the new dollar exchange rates were announced it wouldn't buy a pod of peas.

'I still think it's stupid that you have to go with them,' Wolfgang grumbled.

'They're no good at all on their own, you know that,' Frieda replied from the doorway. 'They still think it's 1913 and spend so long squeezing each orange and sniffing the cheese that by the time they've decided to buy something they can't afford it any more. I'm going straight to the clinic from the market so you've got the boys until Edeltraud comes at ten. I'll try and get back before you go out tonight. See you!'

'Don't I get a kiss at least?' Wolfgang asked.

Frieda turned around, her face softening in an instant. She dropped her shopping bag and ran back to him.

'Of course you do, my darling.' She put her hands to his face and pulled him towards hers.

Then she stepped back.

'Whose perfume is that?' she asked.

'What?' was the best Wolfgang could do in reply.

'You smell of perfume, whose is it?'

'Well, I . . . my aftershave, I suppose. My cologne.'

'I know your cologne, Wolf. I'm talking about perfume. Women's perfume. I can smell it. Even over the sweat and the booze and the gaspers, so it's been rather close to you I'd say. Did you kiss someone at the end of the evening, Wolfgang? Just asking.'

Wolfgang could scarcely believe it. In *seconds* she'd recreated the entire crime scene.

'Frieda, for goodness' sake,' he stammered.

'Is that why you were late, Wolf?' Frieda's voice was now a steely combination of disingenuous innocence and flint.

'No! I've told you, I was talking to this fella about a job. His girl gave me a peck . . .'

Frieda put a hand back up to his face and wiped a thumb across his mouth. 'There's grease on your lips, Wolf. They're still waxy. On the lips is not a peck. You *peck* cheeks. You *kiss* lips.'

Wolfgang was stunned. He'd always known his wife had a smart, analytical mind, she was a doctor after all, but this bordered on witchcraft.

He pulled himself together. Time to get on to the front foot.

'I didn't kiss anybody, Frieda,' he said firmly. 'Somebody kissed me, which is a very different thing.'

The best defence was the truth.

'Who?' Frieda asked, still narrow-eyed.

'I have no idea.'

Or at least as much of it as you could afford to tell.

'Some stupid flapper,' Wolfgang went on. 'She was with the man I was telling you about, the one who wants to offer me a job. She just flung her arms round me and kissed me. Said she was a jazz fan.'

'Hmmm.'

'I can't help it if I'm irresistible.'

'Was she pretty?'

'God, Frieda, I don't know! I doubt it or I'd have noticed. I was trying to get away and she kissed me. Like I said, I didn't kiss her, she kissed me, and if you want to know, I'm a bit unhappy at what I think you may be implying.'

Frieda's narrow look softened a little.

'We-ell,' she said, 'you can see why I wondered.'

'Only if I first presume that you don't trust me.'

That got her.

'I work in nightclubs,' Wolfgang continued, pressing his advantage. 'They're full of silly young girls. What do you want me to do? Have six bodyguards like Rudolph Valentino? I refuse to let my sexual magnetism make me a prisoner.'

She was laughing now. He could always do that to her.

'You're right. I'm an idiot. Sorry, Wolf.'

'Well *really*. As *if* I look at other girls.'

'I know. I'm sorry. I'm tired . . . But if you see that little flapper again just you tell her to keep off, all right?'

'If I do, I will. But I doubt I'll ever lay eyes on her again, babe. And by the way, I thought you were supposed to be in a hurry.'

'God, I am!'

Once more she reached up and took his face in her hands and pulled him towards her.

'And by the way, whoever she was *didn't* kiss you. *This* is a kiss.'

Frieda pushed her mouth against his and for a few moments kissed him with hungry passion while Otto gurgled happily in between them.

'Let me put the kid down,' Wolfgang gasped, his free hand grabbing at her.

'No! Can't. Sorry, Wolf,' Frieda said, breaking away. 'Got to run. Dad'll be livid if he can't afford any herring.'

And for the final time she picked up her bag and ran for the door.

'We need to make more time for each other,' Wolfgang said, following her into the corridor.

'I know, darling,' she replied. 'But I work days, you work nights, and we have two toddlers. We'll make time for each other, I promise, but it might have to be when the boys are grown up.'

The lift arrived, in its shuddering and laborious manner. Frieda pulled open the concertinaed metal doors and stepped inside.

'Maybe around 1940,' she said, 'when they're at university. Book a restaurant.'

Wolfgang was not smiling. 'I'm serious,' he said.

'I know, I know, just kidding,' Frieda said through the diamond gaps in her cage. 'We *will* make time, we really will. We'll make the effort.'

Then there was a clunk and a shudder and she disappeared down the shaft. Ankles, waist, chest. A final smile and she was gone.

Wolf was left with Otto in his arms, who having happily watched his mother disappear now found it hard to come to terms with the fact that she had actually gone and began to wail. Wearily Wolfgang turned back towards the apartment.

He thought about Frieda. How much he loved her. How much he wanted her. How very very frustrated he felt.

Involuntarily Katharina intruded on his thoughts.

She was probably still out there enjoying the night. Still drinking, still dancing. Still living the jazz, baby.

Wolfgang went back inside the flat and into the kitchen in search of a rusk.

Not very jazz, baby.

Fuck Frieda's dad.

'Why can't your Gramps do his own fucking shopping?' Wolfgang said to Otto.

'Fucking,' said Otto. 'Fucking shopping. Fucking. Fucking. Fucking.'

Renewed Acquaintance

Berlin, 1923

Outside in the street Frieda ran for a tram and nearly got herself run over in the process. City traffic was getting out of control.

Wolfgang said it was just 'mechanized Dada'. It was his joke. He said that Surrealism had become so ubiquitous that even Berlin drivers were challenging structure and form.

However, as the mother of two wilful toddlers, Frieda did not find the situation funny at all. She had in fact spent several chilly Saturday mornings standing outside the *U-Bahn* station collecting signatures for a petition of complaint to the local council, but had so far heard nothing back. The newspapers said that there were plans to install Berlin's first traffic lights in Potsdamer Platz along the lines of what had been developed in New York. But Frieda reckoned that no such refinement was likely to reach the less glamorous streets of Friedrichshain in the near or even distant future.

Two tram changes later she was in her old childhood district of Moabit where her parents still lived and where she was to meet them on the steps of the Arminius Markthalle on Jonasstrasse.

Frieda was always happy to visit the Arminius with its great arched red and yellow brick entrance. It had been built in 1891, nine years before she was born, and had always been a part of her life. An enormous, noisy, frantic, bustling Aladdin's cave of a building in which it always seemed to Frieda that every magical and wonderful thing on earth could be found.

She had wandered its great steel arched aisles through all the weekends of her growing up. First, pushed in a pram, and then holding on to her mother's hand. After that, giggling and gossiping with school friends, and finally shyly with boys. It had been at the Arminius that Frieda had first met Wolfgang. He had been busking for pfennigs during the starvation winter of 1918 and she had given him a bite of a piece of dried beef jerky her mother had managed to find for her lunch.

And now she was back, as if she'd come full circle, except that this time it was her parents who were holding *her* hand.

It was towards the end of the shopping trip that Frieda quite unexpectedly bumped into Karlsruhen. It was the first time she had laid eyes on her ex-employer since her final day as his model when he had assaulted her in his studio, and Frieda was startled to see the depths to which he had sunk. For Karlsruhen was not at the market to shop but to sell. He and his wife had set up a little stall in amongst the junk dealers at the back of the great hall from which they were trying to unload his previously valuable works.

It was a chastening sight. Both Karlsruhen and his wife looked thin and haggard. The skin of the sculptor's previously fat jowls hung in creases from his face. Neither of them had overcoats and they were clearly feeling the cold. Despite it being summer the hall was draughty.

Karlsruhen and Frieda caught each other's eye but did not acknowledge it. Frieda certainly had no wish to renew their acquaintance and he clearly felt the same way.

Unfortunately Herr Tauber had also spotted the stall and was pushing his loaded shopping cart straight for it.

'Look at this, Mother,' he called to his wife. 'This stuff's very good, proper art, not like this modern nonsense. Come along, Frieda! Bring the purse, I think I might buy something.'

Frieda had no choice but to hurry after her father, who was already introducing himself to a somewhat alarmed-looking Karlsruhen.

'Tauber. Police Captain Konstantin Tauber at your service. I think your work is very fine, sir. Very fine indeed.'

Now Karlsruhen looked genuinely worried, clearly wondering whether Frieda had decided finally to make a complaint about what had happened. It made her angry because she had always felt that she *should* have reported him, and had only not done so because it would have simply been one word against another and could have done no good. Now, however, she found herself in the position of having to set her attacker's mind at rest for fear that he would blurt out some lie and an awful scene would ensue.

'Hello, Herr Karlsruhen,' she said, 'it's been a while, hasn't it? This is my father and mother. Don't be alarmed,' she added, as if making a joke, 'he's not on duty.'

Frieda forced herself to smile pleasantly. There was nothing to be gained from confronting him now, a year later, and she had nothing but sympathy for the man's wife.

'Goodness gracious, Frieda,' Herr Tauber said. 'Do you two know each other?'

Karlsruhen clearly wished they'd all go away but had no option but to introduce himself.

'Your daughter used to model for me,' he explained.

Frau Tauber had been inspecting one of the figurines and nearly dropped it.

'Goodness!' she exclaimed. 'Modelled? For these?'

Every single statuette displayed on the table was of a naked girl. Frau Tauber's expression hovered somewhere between astonishment and horror.

'Yes,' Frieda said brightly, 'didn't I ever tell you?'

'You told us that you were *modelling*,' her mother replied, 'but not . . . '

'This is me,' Frieda said, picking up one of the figures. 'It's a good likeness, don't you think?'

Herr Tauber took it from her and then immediately handed it on to his wife, clearly feeling that even holding the thing was somehow inappropriate.

'You mean, you *posed* for it?' he said. 'Completely naked?'

'Yes, Dad. Don't you like it? You did before.'

'It is a Rhinemaiden,' Karlsruhen said grumpily, taking it back from Frau Tauber. 'Of course they're naked.'

'Yes, a *Jewish* Rhinemaiden,' Frieda said, giving Karlsruhen a hard stare, suddenly fed up with tiptoeing around the man. 'Think of that? What *would* Herr Wagner have said?'

'Nonsense, Frieda!' her father exclaimed. 'A German's a German. I have two French bullet wounds in my thigh that say my daughter has as much right to cavort in the damned Rhine as anyone. Isn't that right, Herr Karlsruhen? She makes a splendid nymph!'

Karlsruhen admitted that she did and since the Taubers did not seem to be moving on he was forced to introduce his wife. Frieda shook the woman's hand feeling most uncomfortable, not merely because of the unpleasant secret she shared with the woman's husband, but also because of the reduced circumstances to which Frau Karlsruhen had fallen. She couldn't help but suspect that the person who would suffer most from Karlsruhen's wounded pride was his wife.

Herr Tauber, having got over the initial shock of encountering a naked depiction of his daughter, had decided that in fact he was rather proud that Frieda had inspired such fine German art. He thoroughly approved of Karlsruhen's style and subject matter.

'Had you been posing for one of these idiot pornographers our imbecile arts establishment insists on lionizing, then I should have been concerned, but this is the art of a patriot and gentleman. Herr Karlsruhen, I salute you.'

Herr Tauber shook Karlsruhen vigorously by the hand, utterly oblivious to the horrible irony of his description of the man, and the crackling undercurrents flowing between the artist and his daughter.

'In fact, my dear,' Herr Tauber said, turning to his wife, 'I really do think we must have this! After all, it's not every girl who gets to be a Rhinemaiden. And I'm happy to go without my bottle of schnapps this month to get it too.'

Karlsruhen scowled at this graphic illustration of the current value of his work.

'It's bronze and the plinth is marble,' he said sulkily, but his wife had already taken Tauber's money.

'For you, my dear,' Tauber said, making a flourishing gesture and handing it over to Frieda. 'I'm sure Herr Karlsruhen will admit that it is not quite as beautiful as its model but it's a fine piece of work nonetheless and I am proud to make you a present of it.'

Frieda suspected that Karlsruhen would admit no such thing, but the sculptor merely continued to scowl and said nothing.

A New Job
Berlin, 1923

'That was *The Sheik of Araby*, ladies and gentlemen,' Wolfgang said, emptying the saliva valve of his trumpet into the cigarette-filled spittoon at his feet, 'fresh out of the USA! And my many thanks to our genial host Kurt Furst for bringing such a scorching new tune to my attention. *Smokin'!* We'll be back after a break.'

The boisterous crowd of young men and women, their elegant evening dress in disarray, shouted for more as the sweating combo retired to the little band room at the rear of the stage behind a shimmering beaded curtain.

Wolfgang had begun working for Kurt the very day after they first met, when, true to his word, Kurt had bought the club in which Wolfgang was working.

'Say hello to your new boss, Mr Trumpet!' the exuberant teenager had shouted, having waylaid Wolfgang in the alleyway at the back of the venue as Wolfgang was chaining up his bicycle. 'I told you I'd buy this joint. So welcome to the Joplin Club, the hottest hell-hole in town.'

Katharina was there too, standing in the shadows of the little stage doorway, trying to keep her coat from touching the filthy, urine-soaked walls, the tiniest smile creeping across her usual mask of bored indifference.

Wolfgang smiled also.

But nervously.

In the early hours of that very morning he'd been wiping this woman's lipstick from his mouth and lying to Frieda that he could not recall if she was pretty or not. He had in fact recalled very well how pretty she was, and had continued to recall it any number of times that day as he mangled nappies and created amusing faces out of apples and cheese for his children.

But what could he do? Jazz musicians couldn't turn down work because there were pretty girls attached. They'd never work at all.

'Congratulations, Kurt,' he said, 'looks like I'm your new band fixer then.'

'You betcha, Daddy!' Kurt replied. 'We'll make this joint jump!'

And from the moment the three of them walked together down into the darkened cellar, breathing in the stench of the previous night's booze and tobacco and following the morning's toilet bleach, they did exactly that. They made the joint jump.

It was, without doubt, the best job Wolfgang had ever had.

And not just because Kurt was a ridiculously generous employer who paid at least twice what Wolfgang could have got elsewhere. The main cause for Wolfgang to celebrate was that Kurt was a genuine fan. He loved his jazz in a way that only the young love their music. Like a first love. *Their* discovery, defining them and their generation. To Kurt jazz was a religion, a way of living. He knew every record just in from the States and the names of half the side men in New Orleans. But he didn't use this knowledge to impose his vision on his club. He respected Wolfgang absolutely and gave him a completely free hand.

'Just make sure it's out there, Daddy,' he said. 'Blow it hot hot hot!'

Wolfgang could scarcely believe his luck.

'All the other assholes I've worked for don't give a damn about the music,' he told Frieda on the morning after his first night at the Joplin. 'Those cloth-eared pricks only play jazz because it brings in the gangsters and the flappers; they'd play nursery rhymes or bloody Wagner if they thought it would pay. Even the ones who pretend to understand the music would be happy if we played *Alexander's Ragtime Band* and *The Yankee Doodle Boy* back to back all night. But Kurt's different, he's got *soul*. He only bought the club so he can listen to the band. It's like his own great big grown-up toy.'

'That's nice,' Frieda observed dryly between sips of coffee and bites of black bread. She was working away at some statistical papers and did not look up. 'I dealt with three cases of rickets yesterday.'

'Oh?' said Wolfgang rather surprised. 'That can't have been much fun.'

'It was heart-breaking actually. Lack of nutrients, pure and simple. They don't need a doctor, they need a meal. The city Oberbürgermeister says that a quarter of all school kids in Berlin are under normal height and weight due to malnutrition. Imagine that. In the twentieth century.'

Wolfgang was of course somewhat deflated at Frieda's reaction to what he'd imagined was wonderful news.

'What's rickets and malnutrition got to do with my new job?' he asked.

'Nothing really. Except that with the city slowly starving to death it's nice that one big kid got his own club to play with, that's all.'

'And you're saying that it's Kurt's fault the country's completely fucked, are you?'

'Don't swear. The boys might be awake. They're picking things up you know.' Frieda continued to tick and cross boxes on the forms she was working on.

'Well, there speaks the great radical! Swearing is the language of the proletariat, isn't it? I thought you were supposed to be all for the working bloody class?'

'I want a fairer world, not a coarser one, Wolf.'

'You sound like your mother.'

'And that's a criticism, is it?'

'You decide.'

'Wolf, I'm just asking you to watch your language a bit. Edeltraud told me that a couple of days ago in the Volkspark an old gentleman patted Otto on the head and Ottster told him to fuck off.'

'Good for him. You don't mess around with a man's hair, that's well known. They'd kill you for it in the south side of Chicago.'

'Edeltraud thought it was funny, which is of course half the problem.'

Wolfgang lit up another Lucky, his fourth of the morning, but with the money he would now be earning he could afford to smoke as many as he liked.

'Look, I don't want to talk about Edeltraud, or old gits in the park. I want to know why you seem to feel that my new job's got something to do with you treating kids for rickets.'

'Come on, Wolf,' Frieda said, putting away her papers and taking her cup and plate to the sink where she managed to crush a cockroach with a serving spoon. 'You know very well that all these people getting rich quick is making a terrible situation worse. If your Kurt can afford to buy his own nightclub he must have got the money from somewhere.'

'What? From starving children?'

'Indirectly.'

'He got it from *nowhere*, Frieda!' Wolfgang replied angrily. 'He borrows money and he buys things, then he waits for the mark to go down and pays back the debt. Simple jazz economics. Wish I had the guts to do it. He didn't get rich flogging old ladies' jewellery in Belgium, he's just smart, that's all.'

Frieda sat down again and tried to smile.

'Look, I'm sorry, Wolf. I'm being unfair, I know that. It's just very hard at work. I never thought my first job as a doctor would be watching children die. You know TB's up 300 per cent on pre-war levels?'

'No, I didn't know, as it happens. I haven't had time to study the city's medical statistics. I've been busy working all night making sure my own kids don't starve. *And* my wife for that matter.'

Frieda took his hand across the table and squeezed it.

'Yes. I know. And of course I'm glad about your new boss. It's terrific that he likes your music.'

'You know how much I hated trotting out tea dance music in Wannsee and Nikolassee for the old ladies,' Wolfgang said, 'but I did it because we need to eat and because you want to work in a public-funded medical centre where they pay you bugger all.'

'I know. I know,' Frieda conceded.

'And now I've actually got a gig I *enjoy*, I thought you'd be pleased.'

'I am. I am pleased, Wolf, and I mean it, I'm sorry. Sometimes my work gets to me, that's all. And I *am* grateful for how hard you work for us, you know that.' She leant across the table and kissed him. 'It's not quite how your marriage plan was supposed to work out, is it? I seem to recall I was going to support you.'

'Yes, you were.'

'A jazz man supporting a doctor.' Frieda smiled. 'Only in Germany! Only in Berlin.'

Hot Hot Hot!

Berlin, 1923

Everybody came to the Joplin.

High life. Low life. Good guys. Bad guys.

Plenty of beauties, plenty of beasts.

From day one the place simply throbbed with easy money, booze, sex, drugs and jazz.

The sex and the drugs were supplied principally by Kurt's friend Helmut the 'queer pimp', whom Wolfgang now discovered dealt in narcotics as well as prostitutes.

He regularly offered Wolfgang both.

'Take your pick,' Helmut loved to say expansively, pointing out various exquisite young girls (and boys) who were club regulars and whom Wolfgang had no idea were prostitutes. 'Take two and make yourself a sandwich. Don't worry, they're all clean as whistles. Six months ago they were at finishing schools; now, I'm afraid, Daddy's poor and growing girls and boys must eat.'

Wolfgang politely declined the offer of sex but he was happy to accept the occasional chemical stimulant. They were long nights and the trumpet is a demanding task master.

He didn't tell Frieda of course. But Frieda wasn't there and he didn't have to play by her rules. Not at the club.

He was after all a jazz man. Jazz men didn't play by anybody's rules. That was the point. A little cocaine with your champagne? A puff of something dreamy to chase along the single malt? Why not? How could a man say no?

And if, as the nights went by, he found himself chatting more and more to Katharina between sets, so what? Was it a crime? He liked her. And it wasn't just because she was beautiful, although that didn't hurt. Or that she was intriguing and enigmatic.

Fascinating even.

Wolfgang had met lots of fascinating girls.

Lots of girls who did the same impression of a cold-eyed sultry vamp, so popular in the movies.

The point was he really did *like* her.

She was interested in the same things he was, equally inspired and excited by them. Not just jazz either, but all kinds of art. When Katharina talked about art, her face became animated and her eyes started to sparkle. All that carefully posed haughtiness evaporated and it became clear that her world-weary indifference was just a youthful pretension and she was still a gauche teenager at heart.

She wanted to be an actress of course. German film studios were Hollywood's only real rivals and what beautiful young Berlin girl didn't want to be part of the action? But unlike most of those girls, she didn't just dream of stardom. She loved theatre as much as the movies and Wolfgang was delighted to discover that she had been at many of the same performances that he and Frieda had seen on their occasional, precious evenings out.

'You like Piscator?' Wolfgang asked during one of their first serious chats.

'Yes, and I've *met* him too. I waited for him at the *Volksbühne* stage door after he did *The Lower Depths*.'

'You like Gorky too?'

'Of course I do! Why wouldn't I like him? Nobody writes like the Russians. He's a genius, particularly when Piscator does him.'

In fact, to Wolfgang's embarrassment, he soon discovered that Katharina was far better read and versed in the new Expressionist theatre than he was. She had travelled all the way to Munich to see *Drums In The Night*, the first play from a new writer called Brecht whom Wolfgang had not even heard of.

Katharina always knew what exciting Berlin personalities were in the house each night.

'Guess what,' she'd say with excitement, squeezing herself into the tiny band room behind the stage, oblivious to the fact that the boys were stripped to their vests and shorts trying to cool down between brackets. 'Herwarth Walden's in!'

'Herbert who?' was the general reaction from the assembled musicians. It usually was, when Katharina announced that she had spotted some celebrated figure of the avant garde.

But Wolfgang always knew exactly who she meant.

'My God,' he said, peering out through the beaded curtain, 'he's talking to Dorf.'

'Probably selling him a painting.'

'The publisher of *Der Sturm* is listening to *my* band,' Wolfgang exclaimed. 'That is amazing.'

'Hey, Wolf baby,' a deep, heavily tinged American voice interjected, 'be cool. Whoever the gentleman is, he eats and he shits just like everybody else do. And this ain't *your* band by the way. We're a collective and don't you forget it.'

Thomas 'Uncle Tom' Taylor was one of the numerous American *schwarz* musicians who had found life easier, and work more plentiful, in the fevered melting pot of post-war Berlin than they had in the segregated theatres and bars of their own cities. Like most of them he spoke good German with a Mississippi twang.

'We may be *your* collective,' Tom went on, 'I admit that, but I ain't *nobody's* nigger. Who is this Waldorf cat anyway?'

'Wal*den*, Tom,' Wolfgang corrected. 'He's not a salad, he's the *Godfather* of Berlin Expressionism, Futurism, Dadaism, Magic Realism . . .'

'Damn! That cat loves an ism!'

'That *cat's* been painted by *Oskar Kokoschka*.'

'Well, *excuse* my ignorance, sir!' Tom laughed. 'And by the way, if Oskar Kokoschka's a real name I'd like to shake the guy's parents' hand.'

Just then Kurt appeared standing halfway through the beaded curtain, a string of it across his face, swaying noticeably. Katharina stared at him, an expression of irritation, even contempt, crossing her features, which she made no effort to disguise.

'This band is *hot*!' Kurt shouted. '*Hot hot hot!*'

Kurt was getting drunker earlier and using more drugs. Katharina had confided to Wolfgang that he had taken to injecting his cocaine rather than snorting it.

'It's disgusting,' she said. 'Last night he did it in his balls. Can you imagine? *In front* of me. Says it gives an exceptional high. Personally I don't think any thrill is worth that much loss of dignity.'

Kurt was in an exultant mood.

'Great opening set, you guys!' he slurred. 'I loved it, I *more* than loved it, I adored it, I lived it, it spoke to my soul.'

Katharina slipped away while Kurt continued to witter on.

'You were out there, boys. Solid gone. Let me tell you, I know jazz and that was *jazz*, baby.'

Kurt was by nature a talkative man and cocaine made him insanely verbose. He *spewed* words. They tumbled out on top of each other in a vomit of extravagant praise. It was as if he was saying words side by side as well as end to end. It made Wolfgang sad to hear him. The best boss he ever had was becoming a jerk.

He began to usher Kurt out of the room. Had he not done so, Kurt probably would have gone on all night, oblivious to time.

'Got to get ourselves together, Kurt,' he said. 'Have to play the next bracket, that's why you pay us.'

'Yeah! . . . That's right! Get ready! For the next bracket!' Kurt shouted as if continuing with the evening's performance was some brilliant and incisively original idea. 'That's what I like to hear. And make it hot hot hot!'

As the ridiculously youthful figure stumbled away, Wenke the clarinet player snorted in contempt. Wenke was a brilliant instrumentalist but a dark and brooding man, permanently damaged by four years in the trenches. 'Little bourgeois prick,' he snarled. 'We'll have him hanging from a lamp-post one of these days, when the revolution comes. The whole pack of them make me sick. Boys in lipstick, girls with their breasts showing through their dresses. Berlin's turning into a cesspit.'

'Don't you run Berlin down in front of me, Wenke,' Tom Taylor said with a deep friendly laugh, while chugging at a quarter of Bourbon that he kept in the breast pocket of his dinner jacket. 'I *love* Berlin, 'cos ya know what? Right here in this town *Wolfgang*'s the nigger, not me! Ain't that the strangest thing? Back in the States I was a nigger every day of my life but not here!

I finally found a city where they hate someone worse than they hate a black man and I say hallelujah to the Jews.'

'You just let a gang of *Stahlhelm* find you fucking a German girl, Tom,' Wolfgang observed, 'and you'll soon find out who's the nigger.'

'Well, they ain't *going* to find me, Wolf, are they?' Tom laughed, 'because I ain't about to invite no audience in to watch. Not that they wouldn't get one hell of a lesson in humping!' he added, taking another slug of his whisky, '*American* style, slow and easy, like la-a-azy blues.'

Wilhelm the sax player interjected, a man whose face was caked in make-up and who wore a green carnation on his lapel.

'Well, speaking as one of Wenke's boys in lipstick, if you ever tire of working your way through our city's charming show girls, Tom, don't hesitate to call me, I'd love to try a bit of *schwarz* myself.'

'I surely will remember that, *Fräulein*.' Tom laughed. 'You can expect that call just as soon as hell freezes over.'

'You're a bunch of decadent cunts,' Wenke grumbled.

'Of course we are!' Wolfgang shouted. 'We're jazz men! Being decadent cunts is our job description. Now come on, as the boss says, time to go ape, Daddy!'

Halfway through the second bracket Wolfgang saw Katharina slip away. Looking out from behind the dome of his trumpet he watched as she headed for the doorway with a man. A big producer from the UFA film studios whom Katharina had introduced Wolfgang to briefly the night before. A great, swaggering, sweating, arrogant middle-aged movie guy.

It was her business of course.

Certainly none of his.

No need to feel jealous.

She was just a friend.

But as Katharina and her film producer disappeared together, the man's plump, bejewelled hand placed proprietorially upon Katharina's slim, naked back, Wolfgang was shocked to realize just how jealous he was.

St John's Wood

London, 1956

Stone's flat overlooked Regent's Park. He could not have afforded it on his Foreign Office salary but had bought it with the proceeds of the sale of his parents' apartment in Berlin. The home in which he had grown up, which the Nazis stole in 1942 and which had miraculously survived the Allied bombing.

A final gift from his beloved mum and dad.

As he approached the building from St John's Wood tube, Stone wondered if Billie would still be there. She only stayed at weekends and always left on Monday morning but never at any particular time. Billie was not the sort of person to pay much attention to regular timetables.

Waiting for the lift Stone was concerned to discover that he was rather hoping she *would* be there. It would be nice to see her and share a cup of coffee. They might put a record on and continue her jazz education.

Stone tried to dismiss these thoughts from his mind.

He didn't like attachments. He had avoided them since 1939. Always walking away whenever he sensed himself getting too close to a person. Especially a woman. The very fact that he liked Billie and enjoyed her company made him think that he should stop seeing her.

After all, what right had he to such simple pleasures?

He had survived.

And, anyway, he loved Dagmar. He would always love her. He'd promised her that at the Lehrter Bahnhof.

Billie was a West Indian girl Stone had met during the previous summer at a basement party in Ladbroke Grove. Stone liked to spend time in Notting Hill. He had been an outsider of one sort or another since the age of thirteen and felt great empathy with the immigrants who had recently come to live in West London.

'Hey, we're the Jews now,' Billie had once joked. To which Stone had replied that she'd better hope not.

Stone also liked the music and the easy-going attitude that he found amongst Billie's crowd. The disrespect for convention and authority. He liked the laughter, though he never laughed, and the dancing, though he never danced. He had also found that smoking marijuana was a pleasant alternative to blotting out the world with scotch as he had done on most evenings since the war.

After long days spent in the stilted dryness of Whitehall, it was a relief to while away his evenings sitting half stoned in a noisy, sweating, crowded room, listening to unfamiliar music and watching couples dancing so close that they might almost have been single creatures. It reminded him of the places his father used to talk about. The tiny late-night clubs pounding with rhythm and sweating with sex where Wolfgang Stengel had worked in the days before the whip came down. When, according to his father, Berlin had been beautiful, wild, irreverent and life-affirming.

Sitting in those little basement clubs the West Indians had established so quickly and with so little regard for the licensing laws, Stone could imagine himself close to his father. Luxuriating in the thought that apart from the colour of the dancers' skin the scene he saw through his half-closed eyes was not so very different from that which Wolfgang had smiled out at from behind his trumpet on crazy carefree nights long ago and in another world.

Sometimes of course with one puff of smoke too many, or one extra drink, the vision changed, and Stone could not prevent paranoid nightmare fantasies dropping into his addled mind, in which the door burst open and brown-shirted imbeciles with red and black armbands flooded in, flailing about themselves with their truncheons and smashing all the delicate, beautiful young dancers to the ground in a mess of blood, teeth and splintered bone.

Billie said that if he found himself having those thoughts too often he should definitely try putting a higher percentage of tobacco into his reefers.

'When it makes you paranoid it's time to slow down,' she advised.

Billie was still at home.

Across the hallway, the bedroom door was half open and an elegant brown limb was visible, stretched out from under the sheet. The toenails perfectly manicured and painted in rich, deep shining red.

'Still here, Billie?' he said. 'Nice to be a student, eh?'

'Don't worry, I got screen printin' in an hour, baby,' the cheerful, heavily accented voice replied from the bedroom. 'No classes dis mornin' though so I been doin' some readin' here in me bed but I'll be right out of your hair in a jiffy, man.'

Such a wild accent to Stone's ears. Even when she was talking about studying it sounded like she'd been having a party of sorts. Stone wondered if any variant of his native German could ever sound so carefree and organically cool.

'Take your time,' he called out filling a kettle. 'Really, there's no rush. Stay in bed if you feel like it.'

He spooned coffee beans into a little electric grinder and whizzed them up. He had to go all the way to a shop in Soho to get those beans. The coffeeless culture was one aspect of his adopted homeland that he never got used to.

'Hey, baby. I've got t'ings to do meself, you know,' Billie replied from behind the open door where Stone could hear her getting up to get dressed. 'I wasn't just sittin' here waiting t'get laid.'

Stone reddened. 'I didn't mean . . . I mean, I wasn't saying, stay for . . . well . . . what I *did* mean was, have some breakfast.'

He could hear her laughing at his confusion.

'No time, baby. No time for breakfast. *Or* any other mornin' delights for that matter. Haha! I'll have some o' dat coffee though, baby. Fresh ground beans is one smell I never get tired of.'

It was a good relationship. By far the best Stone had ever had. Friendship plus sex. Billie wasn't looking for anything more serious than Stone was, although for the exactly opposite reason. Her whole life was ahead of her, while Stone's was behind him.

She was young, free-spirited and ambitious. She could not afford to be wasting her time falling in love. Particularly with a man like Stone who had made the decision that he did not deserve to be happy.

'You got about a million demons locked up inside you, man,' she had observed on one of the first nights they had spent together. 'Do me a favour, don't let 'em out when I'm around, heh? I got plenty shit of my own.'

'I never let them out,' Stone had replied. And he never did.

After a few minutes Billie emerged from the bedroom, hopping into her shoes as she went. He never understood how she could make herself look so immaculate so quickly.

'Coffee's coming,' he said. 'Two minutes.'

'Plenty time. I can be at college in fifteen. You know I only like you because of your address anyway,' she teased, sitting at his little breakfast bench and taking out a tube of lipstick.

Billie was in her third year doing textiles at the polytechnic in Kentish Town. When she spent the night with Stone she was already halfway there.

'Of course I do. Happy to be useful,' Stone said. 'I wouldn't want you to like me for any other reason. How about you put that stuff on after you have your coffee? It's hell to get off the rim of the cup.'

'Too late,' she replied, pressing a tissue to her scarlet lips and then pushing the tissue into the breast pocket of Stone's jacket, which was hanging over the back of the high-backed stool on which she was perched. 'Something to remember me by in the week, eh? Haha!'

Stone would not have blamed her if truly she did only like him for the convenience of his apartment. He certainly did not consider himself much of a catch, fourteen years older than her and in love with a memory. He was aware that women sometimes found him attractive although never understood why, but Billie could do so much better. She was clever and wonderfully stylish, positively lighting up his drab little kitchen in her smart pink woollen two-piece suit with its pencil-line skirt and matching beret perched atop a stiff, jet-black Marilyn Monroe perm. And such a wonderful smile. A huge smile, it seemed almost to sparkle simply with a love of life.

He poured the coffee. Watching her as she busied herself

packing her student bag. Pencils, paper, books of photography borrowed from the library and a swatch of fabrics which, even as she put it in her bag, she couldn't resist caressing, her slim fingers slipping sensually across the fabric, appreciating its qualities.

'Opposites attract,' she said suddenly, as if reading his thoughts. 'I like quiet boys. Means I got no competition bein' centre of attention.'

Then she drained her coffee, slung her bag over her shoulder and made for the door, the piece of toast with Cooper's Oxford marmalade Stone had just made for himself clamped firmly between her teeth.

'So see you next weekend,' she said through the toast. 'Maybe come to mine. Mum's doin' pork, stir-fried up wi' ginger an' spice. You're welcome if you want.'

'I don't really eat pork. Don't know why. We did when I was a kid.'

'You'll eat it when me Ma cooks it.'

'Yeah. I'll bet I would. But I'll be gone at the weekend, I'm afraid. Remember? I told you, I'm going to Berlin.'

'Oh yeah, dat's right. The long-lost girlfrien' eh? Haha! Good luck!'

'She was my brother's girlfriend.'

'Yeah, an', man, didn' *dat* hurt!'

Stone had never told Billie anything about his feelings for Dagmar but he supposed it was pretty obvious. Women tended to know these things.

'I'll bring you back some sweet pretzels,' he said.

'No t'anks. On a diet. But if you pass a bookshop see if you can find somet'ing on Bauhaus for me. Don't matter if it's in German, it's the photos I love. Give me a call when you get back. That's unless you're all tied up wit' your *brudder's* girlfriend.'

'I'm free tonight,' Stone said without thinking. 'We could have dinner.'

'Can't. I'm modellin' for the art students. They love me, let me tell you. They t'ink I'm exotic. I say to 'em, jus' wait till there's a few million more of me brothers an' sisters gettin' off de boat.

We won' be so damned exotic then. Haha. Dat made 'em t'ink.'

And with a click-clack of stiletto heels, Billie was gone.

Funny how she did life modelling.

Just a coincidence. But it was a nice one. A connection to his mother, like the club in which he had met her was a connection to his father.

Stone took his coffee into the little sitting room of his apartment. The statuette stood on the mantelpiece above the gas fire. He took it up and held it in his hand.

Running his fingers along its smooth, satisfying lines. Was there something slightly wrong about him fondling a likeness of his naked mother? he wondered. Perhaps Freud would have had something to say about it.

A part of Stone hated that figure. He hated it because of who had created it. But he loved it more. Because it was his mother. Frieda, sculpted in the first year of Stone's life, just before he had become fully conscious of her. Twenty-two years old, naked in the full bloom of youth. His grandfather had bought the piece and it had stood in their apartment all through his childhood and youth. It had still been standing there in 1946 when his German agent had collected up what family possessions were left prior to the sale of the apartment and sent them on to Stone in London.

He wondered how many good Nazis had fondled that statue in the years when some unknown family had squatted like murderous cuckoos in his parents' home. How shocked those thieves would have been to understand that they were caressing the likeness of a Jew. There had no doubt been a Nuremberg Law against that sort of thing – *no pure German will caress the likeness of a Jew as defined by the model having had one or more Jewish grandparents.*

His father had hated that statuette.

Stone smiled as he recalled Wolfgang Stengel's intense, semi-comical exasperation when anyone admired it.

It defied every artistic principle Wolfgang Stengel had possessed. Boring realism, nothing but boring realism, he'd protest. Which was why of course Stone and his brother had loved it then and why Stone loved it still. Precisely because it *was* boring realism, and skilfully executed too. A passable impression of his beloved mother. Not as beautiful as she had been but beautiful nonetheless.

For a moment Stone held the statue by the head.

Held it as he had held it on that awful night.

Knuckles gripped white round it.

The marble base crimson with blood.

He saw again the water running over it, washing the red away. The blood gurgling down into the sink as he and his brother began frantically to cover up the evidence of what they had done.

Too Much Jazz

Berlin, 1923

The joint, as Tom Taylor happily remarked, was jumping.

'This band is on fire,' he shouted from behind his kit. 'They don't got no better in New York City.'

Wolfgang was trying out a new piano player, a Russian émigré called Olga, an ex-duchess or princess of some sort, or so she claimed. But then all the Russian refugee girls thought they were Grand Duchess Anastasia, so she might just as easily be the daughter of some semi-literate farmer who owned one too many cows and so got a bullet in exchange for his field. Not unnaturally, Olga loathed Wenke, the Communist clarinettist, and the feeling was fully reciprocated.

Wolfgang enjoyed the tension.

'We can't all be friends. It's bland. A bit of conflict's good for the minor keys,' he said. 'It really puts some bite into Wenke's atonal riffing.'

'I would like to see a crazed dog put some bite into Wenke's atonal arsehole,' Olga spat through her cigar smoke.

'Just keep playing, princess,' Wenke snarled into his clarinet, 'you can't run for ever. The revolution'll catch up with you in the end, then there's a lamp-post waiting for you just outside in the street, you damned kulak.'

'You bloody sauerkraut Reds!' Olga sneered from her piano stool. 'You'll never have a revolution. You won't fart unless Moscow sends you written permission. Here's to Lenin's fourth stroke! They say he can't talk any more. Give me a call when the bastard can't fucking breathe either, I'll buy drinks all round!'

Olga spat on the floor and raised a glass of vodka mixed with pepper provocatively in Wenke's direction. Wolfgang decided to kick into the next number before the two musicians came to blows.

'This one's brand new and straight off the boat,' he called out over the general din. 'I think you're going to love it as much as we do, it's by the great American Negro composer Jimmy Johnson of New Jersey and it's called the *Charleston*.'

Tom Taylor gave an introductory spin around his tom toms and the band struck up the number which, since Wolfgang had put it into the repertoire the previous week, had proved a guaranteed floor filler.

As he played, Wolfgang stared happily out over the brass cone of his trumpet. The club was packed, as it was every night, and through the smoke and the lights was everything he wanted to see. Writhing bodies. Crazy faces. Booze, girls, good times. He loved it. It had already been three months but it felt like hardly a week. The Joplin had become his second home.

Kurt's people had become Wolfgang's people.

Even the unconscious girl who had ended up under the table on their first acquaintance turned out not to be the poor stupid drunken whore he had originally presumed her to be. Her name was Helene and despite being only twenty she was already a fashion buyer at the great Fischer department store on the Kurfürstendamm.

'Sorry about the other night,' she had giggled when they met for the second time. 'Apparently I was awful, not that I remember. Just got the mix of drugs a teeny bit wrong. Easy thing to do.'

Helene was infectiously positive in her outlook, thinking that pretty much everyone and everything was interesting and fun in its own way.

'I see dull people as *projects*,' she told Wolfgang, 'to be reformed. After all, *everyone's* interesting deep down, aren't they? I mean *breathing* is interesting, isn't it? I mean, when you *really* come to think about it. Don't you think? I mean, honestly?'

Helene would laugh and chatter and charm until the very moment when the booze and pills shut her down. She scarcely gave the slightest indication that she was 'fried to the hat' as she put it until her eyes rolled back in her head and she slid under the table. After which Helmut would make sure she got put in a car and taken home to her doting parents. Helene was as gorgeous, spoilt, wild and vivacious as any jazz baby could ever hope to be, and in any other club Wolfgang had ever played in he would certainly have allowed himself the indulgence of seeking her out between band breaks and enjoying her sparkling company.

But not in a club with Katharina in it.

Band breaks were just too precious to spend time chatting with any other girls, no matter how charming they were.

Wolfgang knew he was getting too close. That he shouldn't be looking forward to seeing her the way he was. Looking out from the stage to find her. Searching for her between brackets. Sitting with her at the bar whenever he could. Eagerly exchanging views on the latest play or exhibition.

But surely there was no danger. She was with Kurt. And he was happily married.

Yes, she'd kissed him on the first night they had met but she had never done so again. When he lit her cigarette she didn't touch his hand as she had done that first time either. Or fix him with her stare as the smoke drifted up from those same purple lips.

So when Wolfgang left the stage on the night in November

when the *Charleston* was a week old, he didn't hesitate in searching her out at the bar.

They agreed the new tune was a sensation.

They laughed about the angry Bolshevik clarinettist and his nemesis the foul-mouthed Russian pianist princess.

They discussed the latest Georg Kaiser play, *Nebeneinander*, which was about to open at the People's Theatre with designs by Georg Grosz, whom they both agreed was their favourite artist.

And then he asked her why she had kissed him on the night they'd met.

It just came out of the blue. Or perhaps more accurately, out of a bottle. He had certainly drunk more than usual.

'I wasn't expecting you to ask me that,' she said.

'I wasn't expecting to ask it.'

Katharina sipped her champagne.

'Perhaps I was a little drunk,' she said. 'And I liked you. You remember I told you? That you were hot? I meant it. Aren't I fresh? But you see I didn't know until *after* I had kissed you that you were married. I don't know, when I watched you on stage you just didn't *look* married.'

For once her stare was not bold. Instead she looked down at the ashtray on the bar between them. Avoiding Wolfgang's eye.

'And of course you're also with Kurt?' Wolfgang added.

'That junkie? I was then, I'm certainly not now.'

'So you're single?' Wolfgang said, realizing he had said it rather too quickly. Too eagerly.

'Yes. Fancy-free. That's me,' Katharina said with brittle gaiety. 'Aren't I the lucky one?'

'And if . . . and if . . .' Wolfgang took a swig of his fresh scotch, recklessly aware that he'd already had much more than was usual for him.

'And if what?' Katharina asked.

'And if I had been single?' he asked. 'After you kissed me that night? If I had never mentioned any wife and kids?'

'Then I would have kissed you again the next night, Mr

Trumpet. And every night after that until neither you nor I were single any more.'

Wolfgang felt a thrill run through every fibre of his body.

Katharina's eyes were a little misty.

'But you *did* mention them. And I'm an old-fashioned kind of modern girl, you see, and it makes rather a difference. It would have been nice of course,' she said dreamily, 'if you'd met me first. Instead of your dedicated doctor. I wouldn't have minded a theatre-mad jazz man for a boyfriend.'

The booze was coursing through Wolfgang's veins now. Delivering its reckless courage to his head.

He crept his hand along the bar to where Katharina's hand lay, a cigarette between the fingers. Nails jet black and shining.

'We've met now,' Wolfgang said quietly.

Their fingers touched.

Katharina looked down and for a moment she seemed lost in thought.

Then she took her hand away, putting the cigarette to her lips and drawing on it hard.

'I told you. I'm an old-fashioned modern girl. Let's keep things as they are, OK? We're friends. We talk. You're married.'

Wolfgang felt foolish. And angry. The whisky made him graceless.

'Old-fashioned? What about that producer from UFA?'

'Excuse me?'

Even drunk, Wolfgang knew he had no right to mention it. 'Nothing.'

'I want to know what you mean,' Katharina asked.

Wolfgang shrugged. 'The one you disappeared with that night.' He mumbled, looking down at the floor to avoid her eye. 'I don't think he wanted to discuss film technique.'

Katharina stared at him hard. Her eyes were no longer misty but cold.

'Oh. So you noticed, did you?'

'Of course I did. I . . . I was jealous.'

'You're married to Mrs Trumpet, Wolfgang. What right have you to be jealous?'

'None, I suppose, but I was.'

Katharina's momentary burst of anger subsided. Instead she looked sad. She drew heavily once more on her cigarette, sucking the glowing end right down to the filter. She lit another from it and shrugged.

'That was business. Stupid and completely naïve. But business none the less. The casting couch, I think they call it. He made promises and I fell for it. Or at least I fell for it enough to take a calculated risk and lost. He got what he wanted and I didn't. I turned up at the studio the following morning and he refused to see me. More fool me. It's the first time I've ever made that mistake and it'll be the last.'

Wolfgang was calm again. And ashamed.

'I'm really sorry, Katharina. I shouldn't have brought it up. What a bastard, I'd like to punch his—'

'It doesn't matter. It was over in a second and it's done with. But while I might be prepared to fuck someone I *don't* like for the right reasons, I'm not happy to fuck someone I *do* like for the wrong ones, which is that we are both drunk and tired and full of all that jazz. You more than me, I think, so you go and play me some music and then go home to Doctor Stengel before you ruin my good opinion of you.'

Wolfgang got up from his bar stool.

'Yeah. Maybe you're right, Katharina,' he said. 'Sorry for being an arsehole. And thanks for . . . well, thanks.'

'Just get on stage. And make it hot hot hot, eh?'

Wolfgang made his way back towards the band room, passing Helmut who was heading for the men's toilet leading a shaven-headed military type and a beautiful young man.

'The party never stops, eh, Wolfgang?' he said.

Wolfgang smiled. 'I imagine it will have to stop in the end.'

Two weeks later, on 15 November, the new president of the Reichsbank abolished the worthless Deutschmark and introduced a new emergency currency with draconian restrictions on lending and speculation. The Rentenmark, as it was called, held its value, and almost overnight another German madness was over.

A Screaming Three-year-old
Munich, 1923

That same month far away in Bavaria another, infinitely more terrible madness was growing stronger. The Nazi Party, that screaming, ranting, violent baby, born on the same day as the Stengel twins, threw a tantrum just before its third birthday. Adolf Hitler, the infant's voice and psyche, attempted to overthrow the state by force. Kidnapping three local politicians and marching at the head of two thousand armed thugs from a beer hall to the Bavarian Defence Ministry, where he intended to demand dictatorial control not just over Bavaria but over the entire Reich.

Hitler and his gang never reached the ministry. They were instead met by one hundred police officers who blocked their path. Shots were exchanged and four policemen and sixteen Nazis were killed. Hitler fled but another Nazi leader, Hermann Goering, was seriously wounded. He was helped into a nearby bank where first aid was administered. By a Jew.

Modern Jazz
London, 1956

In the evening Stone could not stand the inside of his flat any longer and decided he must go out. They wouldn't call now anyway. The Secret Service was like the Foreign Office: it kept office hours whenever possible. Overtime claims were severely frowned on.

So having made himself a solitary meal of eggs and baked beans and drunk a bottle of Guinness, Stone decided to head up to Finsbury Park to drop in at the New Downbeat, a Monday-night jazz club he'd spent quite a bit of time in over the years. He didn't visit so much any more, not now that he had discovered the scene in Notting Hill. The illegal West Indian clubs were much wilder and hipper than the well-established London jazz circuit, which tended to be frequented by earnest middle-class students. But Stone still loved the music. Tubby Hayes had a regular gig at the New Downbeat and you didn't hear much better tenor sax than from Tubby Hayes. Stone's father had always loved the sax but had rarely played it professionally because he usually felt there were better exponents than him in the band. He had played it at home, though, and at jams in local bars. Stone always thought of the tenor sax as a sort of 'family' instrument. Dad's hobby, not his job.

He took a taxi. The New Downbeat Club was held at the Manor House pub, which was right opposite Manor House tube station, but he didn't like the underground at the end of the day. Even though he was a heavy smoker himself, he found the stale tobacco stench mixed with a day's accumulation of body odour just too depressing. Settling back in his seat Stone lit up a Lucky Strike and watched the bars of light passing across the interior of the cab as the taxi drove past the streetlamps.

For a moment he had a recollection of watching similar rhythmic flashes. On the Berlin to Rotterdam sleeper. Lying in his little cabin, thundering through the clanking, rattling, shuddering darkness past the lights of some station or other.

Seeing the seconds tick by on his wristwatch.

Stone held up his arm for a moment, letting the light flash once more on that very same watch. Berlin, Rotterdam – London. In a funny way he was still on the same journey.

Stone closed his eyes. Willing himself far away. To somewhere near the start of the journey. Another time. Another place. Where he was happy.

Far away from Camden and Holloway and the Seven Sisters Road. Back in the People's Park. Laughing and shouting in the Märchenbrunnen, with its fountains and one hundred and six sculptures of characters from fairy tales. He and his brother running in separate directions around the great circular path. Trapping Dagmar between Rapunzel and Little Red Riding Hood. Each holding a soft slim golden arm and begging for a kiss, while Silke sulked nearby and called them both pathetic.

In the taxi Stone smoked his cigarette and found himself wondering if Dagmar ever walked amongst those one hundred and six stone statues and remembered. By some miracle the Märchenbrunnen had survived the Allied bombing and it was now in the Eastern sector. Did Dagmar visit? Did she remember kiss-chase under the watchful gaze of Rapunzel and Little Red Riding Hood, and Snow White and Sleeping Beauty and all the population of Fairy Land?

On her way to work?

At the Stasi?

The taxi driver's voice intruded on his thoughts. 'We're here, mate. The Manor House pub.'

Stone hadn't even noticed them pulling up.

He was early and there was still plenty of space but he knew from experience the gig would fill up so he staked his claim immediately. Taking his pint and whisky chaser he found a table down at the front, right where he knew the horn section would be standing. Since he was going to have to share a table, he wanted to be sure that it was somewhere where there was as little chance of idle conversation as possible. He'd had too many experiences of being lost in a faraway melody only to have his concentration shattered by some jazz train-spotter feeling the need to demonstrate his encyclopaedic knowledge of the technical side of beauty.

'Good augmented seventh, don't you think? And how about that melodic minor? Cool.'

Stone was a loner by *choice*. He didn't want to chat, ever. But because he had frequented a lot of jazz clubs over the years, he had learnt to beware of guys plonking their pints and pipes down beside his pack of Luckies on the excuse that they'd seen him at the Florida, the Flamingo or Studio 51, and imagined somehow that this meant they were jazz buddies.

Stone lit a cigarette and took up a newspaper he'd bought at the tube station opposite. Still Suez and Hungary, of course. He didn't want to read it but a paper wall was a useful blocking device to keep out whoever sat down until the music started.

The room began to fill up. The classic jazz crowd, arty, intense. Duffle coats and corduroy shoes. Like a Labour Party meeting in Hampstead, Stone thought. Except rather fuller. There was a sense of reverence in the room, people spoke in quiet voices, with one or two vainer souls laughing too loudly to show what loose guys they were. How had music that at one time had woken up the whole world become so rarefied? In his father's day jazz had been loud and drunken, it was party music, you danced, you didn't sit about and listen. Maybe it was a class thing. Rags and Dixie had once belonged to the poor and to the decadent elite. Now it had settled down firmly between the two and was as middle class as the BBC and Ban the Bomb.

'Is this seat taken, man?'

Stone looked up. A good result. Student types. They wouldn't want to talk to a square-looking daddy like him. Four of them. Two cats, two chicks.

Classic beats. The chicks with their short fringes cut straight and high. Stripy jumpers, tight pedal-pusher slacks. Bare calves. Flatties. The cats in polo-necked sweaters. Wispy goatee beards. Black jeans. Desert boots. One wore a beret and had sunglasses in the breast pocket of his corduroy jacket.

Two cats. Two chicks. Two chairs.

'No. They're free,' Stone said.

The cats sat on the chairs and the chicks sat on the cats. One of the couples had a set of bongo drums and a battered school notebook. Stone suspected that they were hoping later to luck in to the dregs of the audience and offer up a bit of rhythmic poetry. He would not be sticking around for that.

The band began to assemble to polite applause and much worthy nodding of heads. The cats at Stone's table clearly wanted to clap and nod but it was difficult with chicks on their knees. They had to reach all the way around the girls' woolly-covered waists to get their hands together, which of course made nodding almost impossible as their faces were in the back of their girls' jumpers. Pretty soon the chicks gave it up and went to stand at the back. Stone doubted whether they had been much into the music anyway. Jazz seemed to have become mainly a boys' thing. That was another strange development. It had never been that way in his father's time. Back then the girls had loved their jazz. They were the jazz babies after all, they defined the 1920s. According to his father the clubs had been completely packed with them, shaking and shimmying, flashing their big round Betty Boop eyes and pouting bee-stung lips.

Every one a heartbreaker, or so his dad used to say.

His mother always raised her eyes at that.

Stone had been too young to see for himself of course. By the time he and his brother were old enough to think about going to clubs, the Nazis had long since banned 'nigger' music, as they called it, and they wouldn't have been allowed in anyway. Wolfgang would not have been allowed to play. Jewish musicians were allowed only to perform to Jews. And all the audiences at the Jewish *Kulturbund* seemed to want to hear was Mendelssohn. Perhaps because it reminded them that they had once been German.

The trumpet guys had appeared on stage. Unusually tonight there were two of them. Sipping their beer, exchanging a word or two. Warming up their instruments, running rags through the tubes, diddling the keys. Blowing on their fingers. Stone half closed his eyes and tried to see his father. He must have looked much as these guys did, polishing, diddling. Blowing on his fingers.

That was why Stone came, really. He liked the music well enough, but what he really came to do was half close his eyes and try to see his father. And once he had got a fix on that, put his brother in the picture too. Just as they had always planned.

All through their childhood together, on the countless mornings they had woken up to the sound of Dad coming home, they had whispered and plotted, dreaming that one night the two of them would sneak in and see him play. They would stand together at the back of one of those magical places their parents called clubs and share in their father's secret world.

They never did, of course.

But when Stone sat alone in those little London pubs watching a vision of his father through tobacco smoke, whisky haze and his half-closed eyes, he always had his brother there beside him, just like they had planned it when they whispered together, lying in their cosy beds, in their little room, in the apartment in Berlin.

Tubby, the leader, walked on stage and introduced the band.

'We're going to warm up with some trad,' Tubby announced, 'just to keep the chill out.'

They did *The Sheik of Araby*. That one had been new when his father was starting out. Fresh in from the USA.

Stone smoked his Luckies, sat beside his brother and watched his father play.

A Very Proper Little Girl

Berlin, 1926

Wolfgang put down his coffee cup, took up his pen and forced himself to begin.

Music Tutor seeks Pupils. Piano and all other instruments a speciality.

There. The first sentence. Done. He put down his pen.

'Shall I make some more toast?' he said, turning to Frieda.

'Wolf! You've hardly even started!'

'All right! All right!'

He stared at the paper for a moment or two and then showed her his single line.

'What do you think so far?'

'I don't think you can say all instruments are a speciality,' Frieda replied. 'I mean, *everything* can't be a speciality, can it? No matter how good you are.'

'You *see*! I told you this wouldn't work.'

'Wolf! You haven't tried at all.'

'Because my heart isn't in it. Why don't you write it?'

'Because I'm darning.'

They were still in bed. It was a Sunday morning. What should have been the best day of the week. So peaceful. Coffee, toast. Frieda stitching socks, Paulus on the rug reading. Otto biting the heads off his toy soldiers. And he had to write this stupid advert.

He chewed his pen in moody silence.

Specializing in all instruments?

All instruments equally special?

You name it, I can play it?

'Maybe I should just stick to piano,' he said. 'That's all anyone ever wants their little buggers to learn anyway.'

'Whatever you think. Just get on with it.'

He *hated* the idea of having to teach music.

And he *particularly* hated the idea of teaching music to children. But he knew from friends who had been forced into the same grim career compromise that that was where the work was.

'Of course it'll be kids,' he said grumpily. 'Adults are mature enough to *know* they're shit at music. You have to *teach* children to understand that they can't play.'

'*Please* try not to be so negative, Wolf,' Frieda said.

'Well, that's really what teaching music is about, isn't it? I mean, ninety-nine per cent of the time? The long torturous process of revealing to the student that they are complete crap and will never be able to play anything more than O *Tannenbaum*. Teacher and student just waiting it out week after week after week until finally the penny drops and the student gives up, never to think about music again until they force it on their own equally talentless kids.'

'Wolf! Shut up! Either write the advert or don't.'

'I'm just being honest, that's all.'

He had enough trouble trying to get his own kids to pick up an instrument, let alone anyone else's. He could scarcely get Paulus and Otto to even *listen* to anything decent. He strongly suspected he was the father of a couple of Philistines. The only jazz they seemed to like was ragtime, and at very nearly seven they really ought to have got a bit beyond that.

'Are you sure they weren't *both* adopted?' he whispered occasionally to Frieda.

Which she did not find funny at all.

Wolf was a professional musician. Not some glorified nanny.

It was the government's fault, of course. Stresemann and that whole dull Social Democratic crowd with their boring stability and prudence. What was becoming of the country? It was a disgrace! Even in Berlin, in the heart of the youngest, wildest, most hedonistic and avant garde metropolis on the planet, things had calmed down to an alarming degree. There was still club work at weekends but the weekdays were dead.

'People have stopped dancing,' Wolfgang moaned. 'Three years ago I had my pick of twenty gigs a day. Now I'm fighting *top* side men for pfennigs. Guys who have really *got it* are playing piano in fleapits to the Keystone Cops! It's a criminal waste of talent. God, I miss the good old days.'

'What?' Frieda said, focusing on threading a needle. 'You mean revolution and inflation?'

'Yes! Exactly, Fred! That's *exactly* what I mean. Cataclysmic national disaster! That's what a city needs to make it swing. Three years ago when the country was completely knackered, bank clerks and shop girls were dancing crotch to crotch into the small hours! Drinking themselves insane, snorting cocaine and slipping off to screw in the toilets! Jazzing it up like there was no tomorrow because they didn't think that there *was* going to be a tomorrow. Suddenly they've turned into their parents. It's a disgrace.'

'People can't have fun *all* the time, Wolf.'

'Why not?'

'Because they have responsibilities. They need to *save*. They need to start planning for the future.'

'Future! *Future*. As if any German under thirty-five even knows what the word *means*! There never *was* a future up until now! Being *alive* in the morning, *that* was the future. The future was your next meal. Now people are planning for *old age*. Investing in pensions, putting a little aside for their summer holidays. Have we learned nothing? Don't they realize that the next drink and the next dance are the *only* investments worth making?'

'Well it's up to you, darling,' Frieda said. 'Do it or don't do it but you know as well as I do that we could do with the money.' She paused for a moment before adding, 'You know, just until you sell a song.'

Wolfgang smiled. She meant it too. She still believed.

'The next Mendelssohn, eh?'

'No!' Frieda protested. 'The next Scott Joplin.'

Wolfgang kissed her.

'Yuk!' said Otto from amidst his dead soldiers.

'Don't be immature, Otts,' said Paulus from his book, adding 'Poo face' under his breath.

'Frieda, I'm not Joplin,' Wolfgang said with a smile. 'I'm just happy to live in a world where somebody is.'

Frieda smiled. 'So what now?'

'Well. I suppose I try and finish this advert.'

'Oh give it here!'

And exactly a week later, on the very next Sunday morning, instead of lying in bed till noon, Wolfgang found himself dressed in his best suit pouring coffee for a prosperous-looking gentleman who sat gingerly on the edge of the Stengels' cluttered couch next to his exquisitely turned-out six-year-old daughter.

'And the little girl?' Wolfgang enquired. 'Fräulein Fischer?'

'Dagmar,' the gentleman said. 'Please, you must call her Dagmar.'

'Uhm . . . Will you take some refreshment, Dagmar?'

There were suppressed giggles from somewhere in the vicinity of the doorway to the kitchen. Clearly other members of the Stengel household were finding their father's efforts at polite formality amusing. Little Silke was with them too, as mischievous as either of the boys.

Wolfgang glanced furiously over his shoulder but none of the three culprits were to be seen.

'I should like a glass of lemonade, please, Herr Professor,' the little girl on the couch replied in the most refined of voices, 'with quite a lot of sugar.'

This produced a positive explosion of suppressed merriment from the kitchen followed by the sound of little boys' laughter and then, worse, a little girl's voice indulging in a whispered effort at mimicry.

'*I should like a glass of lemonade please, Herr Professor. With quite a lot of sugar.*'

The elegant, refined little girl sitting stiff and straight-backed beside her father could hardly help but hear the ridicule being directed at her and so put her nose in the air, her effortlessly superior expression making it clear that she was used to ignoring boys and other riff-raff.

'I'm sorry,' Wolfgang apologized. 'My sons. I'd chuck them out and let them beg but I'm obliged by law to look after them. Damned Weimar Government, too soft by half, eh?'

Herr Fischer smiled.

'Boys,' he said indulgently. 'I seem to recall having once been one myself.'

'There's a girl too,' Dagmar said firmly. 'I heard her most clearly. A very *very* horrid girl in my opinion.'

Wolfgang smiled apologetically.

'Our maid's daughter. But she's all right, just high-spirited, that's all.'

'My mummy says that there is never *any* excuse to be rude or unkind. Certainly not high spirits.'

This pious observation brought forth further suppressed giggles and Wolfgang decided he'd better move things along.

'I'm afraid we don't have any lemonade, Dagmar. Sorry, just water actually. And I'm not a professor either.'

'If you are to teach me then you *are* a professor, Herr Professor,' the beautifully dressed little girl replied firmly, her huge, dark eyes turning unblinkingly upon him. '*All* of my tutors are professors. It is how things are done.'

Her father, Herr Fischer, smiled indulgently, no doubt under the impression that Wolfgang must be finding his lovely, porcelain doll of a daughter as charming and clever as he did himself. In fact Wolfgang was struggling to conceal his desire to give little Dagmar a slap and get her and her father out of his apartment as quickly as possible so that he could have a cigarette and get back to his piano.

But he had to go through the motions. He had promised Frieda and they really could do with the money. Although Wolfgang was quite certain that he would be turned down. These people were not his people. Wolfgang knew who the man was, everybody did. He was Fischer of Fischer's department store on Kurfürstendamm. And people like Herr Fischer did not entrust their daughters to people like Wolfgang who didn't even have any lemonade in the house and wasn't even a professor.

'May I ask, Herr Fischer,' Wolfgang said, 'why you've come to me? I'm not exactly a society tutor and I'm new to teaching. I can't claim much experience with children either. Particularly one as young as your daughter.'

Particularly snooty-looking little creatures like Dagmar, Wolfgang thought. A Ku'damm princess whom Daddy wanted to acquire a 'refined' and 'dainty' skill to make her more marriageable to the right sort of minor ex-royal or son of an industrial magnate.

'Little experience with children?' Herr Fischer laughed. 'What were those two young maniacs who ran out of the room when we arrived, then? Hobgoblins? They sound naughty enough to be.'

The boys had in fact begun to edge their way back into the room, and were lurking in the doorway just out of Fischer's vision, their faces contorted with exaggerated expressions of hostility and contempt. Paulus and Otto were prepared to tolerate the existence of girls at their school but in their own home they drew the line (Silke being an honorary boy). Particularly girls with perfectly placed pink ribbons in their hair, snow-white trimmed black velvet dresses and clouds of delicate lace at their necks and wrists.

'Boys are rather different,' Wolfgang replied. 'Besides, I only have to *live* with those two, I don't have to teach them music.'

'You mean you don't teach them music?' Mr Fischer enquired. 'I would find that very surprising.'

'Well, yes, of course I *do*,' Wolfgang said, slightly confused, 'as a father, yes, of course. But professionally I have only ever taught adults and quite frankly I'm not even much good at that. I'm really not at all sure that I'm the sort of person you—'

'My husband will be thrilled should you decide to place your lovely Dagmar with us as a pupil,' Frieda said, bringing in a tray of biscuits from the kitchen.

There was a loud raspberry from behind her at this but again, when Frieda glanced round angrily, no culprit could be seen.

'I'm Frau Stengel, Herr Fischer,' Frieda said, offering her hand. '*Frau Doktor* Stengel.'

'Thanks, darling,' Wolfgang said firmly, 'but I think I can arrange my own clients and I really don't think this would work out for either of us.'

'Really?' Fischer enquired. 'Your advert said you were taking on pupils. Is there anything wrong with my daughter?'

'Of course not, no!' Wolfgang said quickly. 'But look, Herr Fischer, I know who you are. Fischer's is a Berlin institution. You're a rich man, you could afford to hire the chief conductor of the Berlin Philharmonic to teach your little girl. You don't want me.'

'Why not?'

Wolfgang gestured at the crowded untidy apartment. The trombone leaning in the corner. The accordion on the table amongst the newspapers and musical manuscripts. Cushions and books on the floor. Coffee cups balanced on the bookshelves. The theatre and film posters on the wall, Piscator and Chaplin side by side.

The framed prints, grotesque cartoons of fat greedy capitalists and homicidal Prussian officers, their hands filled with money and dripping with blood while all around them the poor and the sick looked on in sullen anger.

'George Grosz,' Fischer said, 'from the First Berlin Dada Fair.'

'You know it?' Wolfgang looked surprised.

'You think a shopkeeper can't appreciate art?'

'Well . . . I admit I'm surprised that you . . . Do you like Grosz then?'

'I *admire* him,' Fischer replied warily, 'I can't say I'd hang him in my drawing room.'

There was a moment's silence. Frieda offered Dagmar a biscuit at which the little girl nibbled tentatively, like a bored mouse who can expect better later.

'Look, Herr Stengel,' Fischer said, 'I don't know much about music and I don't know anything about teaching. What I know is selling. Now when I employ a person to work in one of the departments in my store, I try and find someone who's interested in the thing they'll be selling so they can make the customers interested in it too. It said in your advert that you are a composer, arranger and orchestrator as well as being a working professional musician. I like that idea. I can't imagine anyone being more interested in music than a composer, can you? Unless of course it's a piano salesman.'

'You want me to "sell" music to your kid?' Wolfgang asked, unable to disguise his disdain.

'Well, it's like anything, isn't it? If you're going to spend a lot of money on a hat you've got to be really convinced that you love that hat. To put in all the effort it must take to learn an instrument I imagine you'd really have to believe in music, wouldn't you? So, yes, I want you to "sell" music to Dagmar that she might be inspired to learn.'

Wolfgang could not deny the sense in what Fischer was saying or the honesty with which he said it.

'And you have children yourself. I don't think there's any more impenetrable psyche than that of a small child. I personally can't make head nor tail of them, which is why my wife and I employ two nannies. You have children and clearly you're raising them yourself. It all looks like a good fit to me.'

Wolfgang was about to reply but a look from Frieda silenced him and Fischer continued.

'Dagmar's mother and I think that she's shown a bit of talent . . . No, don't worry,' he went on in answer to the flicker of amusement that crossed Wolfgang's features. 'I'm not one of those ridiculous parents who think their child is a genius prodigy. It's just that we've noticed that she'd rather mess around at our piano than with her dolls so we thought we'd give her lessons. I took a look at a couple of expensive chaps in the city but their "studios" as they called them looked like a cross between a prison and a cemetery to me. I want Dagmar to have a bit of fun. I've seen you play a couple of times too.'

'You have?' Wolfgang said, perking up immediately. 'Really? Where?'

Frieda smiled at Wolfgang's puppy-like eagerness.

'Not recently, bit busy for late nights these days, now the economy's expanding again. But during the inflation, we were all a little looser that year, weren't we? I saw you at the Joplin Club.'

'Best gig I ever had.'

'Yes, it was fun. Quite crazy really. I remember the owner, he came up to my table and actually offered to *buy* my department store. There and then. Absolutely extraordinary, he couldn't have been more than eighteen or nineteen.'

'Eighteen, just,' Wolfgang replied.

'Really. A young man destined to go far, I think.'

'Sadly not. He died.'

'Oh dear. Of what, may I ask?'

'Tastes he'd developed during the inflation that he couldn't afford to sustain when it was over.'

'I see.'

'There were a lot of casualties that year. He was one of them.'

'Well, I'm very sorry to hear that.'

'Yes, so was I. He couldn't play a note but he was as jazz as any man I ever met. Whenever a great new disc comes off the boat from the States I still think of him. Of how much he would have loved it. The silly fool. Anyway, Herr Fischer, you've convinced me. I'll take the gig. I'll sell music to your daughter.'

'Wolf!' Frieda admonished. '*You're* supposed to convince him.'

'Oh. Yes, of course. Sorry.'

'Quite all right.' Herr Fischer laughed. 'It works either way.'

There was another raspberry from somewhere just beyond the living-room door, followed by chuckling and the scuffling of feet.

'And I promise you Dagmar will have fun,' Frieda said brightly.

And in that moment the course of the four young lives was set.

The Saturday Club

Berlin, 1926–28

The boys' initial reservations about their father's new music student evaporated at the very first lesson when Dagmar Fischer arrived for her tuition bearing a large chocolate cake.

Paulus and Otto had certainly *seen* such a cake before. On rare holiday visits to Fischer's famous food hall with dirty fingers and noses pressed against the glass of the *Konditorei* counter. But never had they imagined that one would ever be sitting on the table in their apartment. A *slice* of one perhaps, carefully chosen after much debate, cut with great ceremony by the shop lady, wrapped in greaseproof paper and put in a stripy box to be carried home and put away till after supper. Then to be divided up, a process in which Paulus insisted on using scales, a set square and a ruler for absolute fairness.

But never a whole cake.

Shamelessly the boys, who had been dreading the arrival of the posh kid and seriously considering a cup of water balanced over the door, simply melted with gratitude.

Mixed with not a little awe.

After all, a girl who had access to a cake like that must be at least a princess if not a queen in her own right.

'Can we have a bit?' they asked tentatively.

'We can have all of it,' Dagmar said. 'Papa said that in his experience most nasty little thugs could be won over with cake.'

'Your father sounds like an astute man,' Wolfgang said, getting plates and a knife, 'and fearlessly honest.'

Silke (who had never been close to even a slice of so much cream and chocolate) was made of sterner stuff and refused to be impressed. She folded her arms, put her chin out and declined even to taste it.

For possibly as long as fifteen or twenty seconds.

After which the four of them plus Wolfgang demolished the

entire gateau, apart from a rather small portion which they forced themselves to leave for Frieda.

'Just because we ate your cake,' Silke whispered angrily to Dagmar when bidden to show the new guest to the toilet, 'doesn't mean you're in our gang.'

'Just because I let you eat my cake doesn't mean you're in mine,' Dagmar replied with haughty indifference.

Wolfgang had decided to include the boys and Silke on Dagmar's lessons because he felt that getting through ninety minutes with a group of children would probably be easier than doing so with just one. He also thought it would be more fun. He was right on both counts and the lessons were a great success from the very start. Despite or perhaps because of the endless squabbling and fighting that the four young students indulged in.

Secret notes were exchanged. Solemn pacts made and broken. Alliances formed and betrayed.

And in the midst of it all some music was actually taught. Dagmar's father had been right, his elegant little girl did show some talent at the piano. And because of that, the twins, spurred on by jealousy and the desire not to be beaten by a girl, started applying themselves to various instruments. After all, their dad was a composer, Dagmar's just ran a shop. Otto showed more instinctive flair but Paulus was more diligent and by sheer force of concentration made himself the better player.

Only Silke was completely without any ability to play but she could keep a decent enough rhythm so Wolfgang kept her on tambourine and maracas. Then one day he overheard her regaling the other three children with dirty songs she'd been taught by her mother's boyfriend and Wolfgang realized that in Silke he had a vocalist.

By the end of the first year the children were able to mount a small concert for Dagmar's parents, which even had a printed programme, created using a 'John Bull' printing set which Frieda had brought back from a conference she had attended in England.

Edeltraud, Silke's mother, was also invited to the performance and came accompanied by her new boyfriend Jürgen. A pleasant young man, who held his hat in his hand, twisting it nervously and thanking Frau Stengel for allowing him into her home. He was clearly totally in awe of the celebrated Herr Fischer and his wife, and stood up when either of them entered or left the room.

As the months went by Dagmar began to spend more and more of her Saturday afternoons at the Stengels'. The lessons lasted for an hour and a half but she successfully lobbied her parents not to be picked up by her nanny for as long again after that. The Fischers were happy that their daughter was gaining some experience of children from a different class to her own. This was the twentieth century after all and Germany was a proud social democracy. Besides, the music teacher's wife was a doctor and the children's grandfather was a police inspector so clearly this was a good solid household. And if the little blonde daughter of the housemaid was rather rough and ready with her grazed knees, scuffed sandals and a Berlin accent that could have cut glass, then it would do Dagmar no harm at all to gain some experience of such a very different sort of girl. After all, one day she would no doubt be employing them as part of her household.

The Fischers perhaps imagined that the children spent their time in improving pursuits, reading and listening to records. Or playing board games, Snakes and Ladders perhaps, or the newly arrived and hugely popular Monopoly that Herr Fischer thought wonderful and most educational. What the kids were actually doing was wandering the streets of Friedrichshain getting up to whatever mischief they felt inclined to, which was plenty. Frieda worked on Saturdays, and Wolfgang, who could not put up with the noise of four children going wild in a small apartment, simply turfed them out, allowing them to spend glorious free and easy hours ducking in and out of tenement courtyards, playing hopscotch, throwing stones, pinching fruit from stalls and occasionally inspecting each other's private parts.

In this last activity Dagmar was a spectator only. She never ever showed, not even her knickers, although the boys got round that one by simply lifting up her skirt. Silke, on the other hand, was happy to give the boys a look any time they wanted. She couldn't see what all the fuss was about.

Thus, as the months went by, a strong bond formed between the four youngsters, a bond separate to their school friends and their individual lives. They were the Saturday Club, a secret society of which only the four of them were aware and which none other could join. Many solemn oaths and secret vows were taken, binding each of them always to be loyal to the club and to each other. It is true that the bit about loyalty to each other was often broken by internal feuding, particularly by the girls, who made a habit of crossing their fingers behind their backs when swearing, whispering 'except Dagmar' or 'not including Silke' under their breath. But nonetheless the friendship in the Saturday Club was real. Paulus, Otto, Dagmar and Silke were a true gang of four.

Of course the boys saw far more of Silke than they did of Dagmar, and in her innocence Silke fondly imagined that this made her the insider of the two girls, that there was an elite gang within a gang. The opposite was the case. Dagmar's absence lent her mystery, which in combination with her effortless superiority simply made her all the more fascinating. Silke could never quite understand how the meaner and more snooty and more indifferent Dagmar behaved towards the boys, the more they seemed to like her. Whereas her own eagerness to please just led to her being taken for granted or, worse still, ignored.

It was to be two years before the three Friedrichshain members of the Saturday Club bumped into their elegant Kurfürstendamm comrade on anything other than their name day. It happened at Lake Wannsee during an inter-school swimming gala. These were the Weimar years of increasing egalitarianism, and expensive private schools like Dagmar's occasionally found themselves competing in sporting competitions with their state-supported rivals.

Paulus and Otto were sitting about on the beautiful banks of the swimming lake when they spotted Dagmar laughing with her friends quite close by. They decided not to make themselves known, partly out of shyness, there being so many other posh girls with her, but also from the sheer unfamiliarity of seeing her outside their usual haunts. Instead they were content to watch, fascinated to see their long-legged friend in her bathing costume, and in some strange, half-understood way enjoying the spectacle.

That was until they saw her approaching the victory podium.

'What's she doing?' Paulus said. 'Bloody hell! She's not going to mess around with the cups, is she?'

Dagmar was certainly making her way towards the table where the trophies were displayed.

Tea had been announced a few minutes earlier, and with the various teachers and judges all intent on claiming their share of the refreshments, Dagmar had accepted a dare. Paulus and Otto watched in wonder as she sidled up to the table, took up the grand trophy and stepped up on to the little jetty which led to the diving platforms to pose for a photograph.

Unfortunately the jetty was wet and she slipped, dropping the splendid trophy and breaking its base. Stunned at what she'd done, she simply stood, quaking in terror as a whistle was blown to mark the end of tea and the resumption of the gala. It was then that Paulus and Otto charged up and grabbed the broken trophy from her.

'Get out of it, Dag!' Paulus blurted. 'Get back to your friends!'

Moments later the judges returned to find two contrite little boys in bathing trunks holding the broken trophy.

'What is the explanation of this?' the master thundered through his snow-white whiskers. Every inch the old professor with his stiff collar and frock coat and his cane.

'Some rough boys were playing with it!' Paulus said.

'We were playing with it. It was us!' Otto declared simultaneously.

'We chased them into those woods and got the cup back,' Paulus went on.

'We broke it. It was us, we did it!' Otto said.

The two boys turned to each other.

'You idiot,' Paulus said.

The upshot was that the Stengel boys were given a public beating, which Dagmar watched, astonished at their kindness and thrilled at their bravery. And, if she were honest with herself, rather pleased: it's not every girl who gets publicly defended in front of all her friends by two strange tousle-headed boys who don't even cry when they get ten on the backside. Plus four extra for Paulus for trying to make up a story.

They might perhaps have given way to tears if they had received their beatings alone, but neither was prepared to be the first to break in front of the other.

And particularly not in front of Dagmar.

Silke was also present at the gala with her school and, although she hadn't seen the incident, she quickly heard all about it, as word of what had happened spread like wildfire amongst the children. Later when the competition resumed (minus the disgraced Stengel twins), Silke pushed her way through the various school groups to confront Dagmar. Facing each other, the two little girls made quite a contrast. Dagmar, tall for eight, her beautifully fitted school swimsuit of the latest two-way stretch elastic. Silke, small and tough, in a baggy suit of knitted wool (holed in a number of places), her legs bruised and scratched as they always were from some fight or other.

'You got our boys a beating!' Silke snarled.

'Don't be stupid,' Dagmar replied loftily. 'I didn't ask them to take the blame, did I?'

'You should have said! They wouldn't have whipped a girl.'

'That would have just looked ridiculous. Paulus and Otto had already given different stories. I don't think a third would have helped, would it? They'd still have been beaten. Besides, the boys wanted to help me, isn't that what the Saturday Club's about? I think it was very noble.'

Silke's fists clenched. She was red-faced. Angry but also embarrassed and ill-at-ease, a scruffy kid amongst so many little rich girls, all dressed in the same identical, beautiful bathing costumes that Dagmar was wearing.

'Who is this child?' a stern female voice snapped as Dagmar's forbidding-looking teacher approached. 'She should be with her own school. Girl, why have you left your group?'

'I came to talk to Dagmar, miss,' Silke mumbled at the ground.

'Chin up and speak out, girl! We are not at home to Mrs Mumble here,' the teacher snapped, provoking much giggling from the posh girls, which turned Silke positively crimson.

'I came to see Dagmar Fischer,' Silke said, raising her head a little.

The school mistress gave Dagmar a dubious look.

'Do you know this little girl, Fräulein Fischer?'

'Yes, Frau Sinzheim. She is the daughter of the woman who cleans the apartment where I have my music lessons.'

Silke's jaw dropped to hear herself so dismissively described.

'We're friends!' Silke asserted.

This caused further giggling amongst Dagmar's classmates and it was Dagmar's turn to go red.

'Well, she must run along now,' Frau Sinzheim said with a dubious look at Silke, 'as the finals are upon us and you need to concentrate, Dagmar. Under-tens freestyle, breaststroke and the relay. I look to you to deliver Gold in all three.'

'Yes, Frau Sinzheim.'

The mistress turned back to Silke.

'Get away now, little girl. You have no business here.'

Frau Sinzheim moved on, leaving Silke staring at Dagmar with blazing eyes and poking out her tongue.

'Come on, Silke,' Dagmar said. 'You're just jealous. You wouldn't have minded one bit if it had been *you* the boys took a whipping for. But do you think they would have done?'

Silke looked as if she was about to reply but then didn't. It seemed that perhaps Dagmar's observation had hit the mark.

Two Parties and a Crash

Munich, Berlin and New York, 1929

Twenty-fourth of February.

Two birthday parties.

One in an apartment in Friedrichshain, Berlin.

The other in Munich in a house at Schellingstrasse 50.

Paulus, Otto and the *Nationalsozialistische Deutsche Arbeiterpartei.*

All nine years old that day.

Only one of them would live to beyond the age of twenty-five.

The other two, like countless millions of other youngsters around the world, were doomed.

The Munich nine-year-old would murder them before perishing itself.

The birthday party in Berlin was a very jolly affair.

There were games and cake and American soda. The awkwardness of the meeting up of Paulus and Otto's school friends with Dagmar and Silke from the Saturday Club was soon overcome. Dagmar even let her hair down sufficiently to take her turn with the blindfold in Blind Man's Bluff.

There was much to celebrate, as the boys' grandfather pointed out in a rather lengthy toast that he insisted on being allowed to make during tea and which the children largely ignored, not unnaturally preferring to concentrate on the rolls and cold chicken.

'These lucky boys will achieve more than we ever have,' Herr Tauber said, 'for Germany's long nightmare is over and every opportunity is open to them.'

It was in fact for this very reason that the Munich celebration was not such a happy event. Germany's increasing success might have been good for the Stengel boys but it had left the National Socialist German Workers' Party thin and ailing.

Its message of violent, uncompromising outrage and hatred had begun to sound somewhat hollow as life in the Fatherland continued to improve. In the Reichstag elections of 1924 they had gained 3 per cent of the national vote. In 1928, after four more years of screaming, shouting, marching and fist-banging up and down the country, they were down to just 2.6 per cent.

The brown-shirted men were at a loss.

Their brown-shirted leader was at a loss also. Although of course he hid his confusion behind the stern face of an 'implacable' and 'unalterable' will.

What was going wrong?

Their message was clear enough. Despite the confusing and self-contradictory 'twenty-five points' with which Hitler had launched the party, it really boiled down to just one thing: 'Blame the Jews for everything.'

What could be simpler? And yet this message was proving increasingly difficult to either explain or sustain.

Should the Jews be blamed for the increasingly stable money?

The improving employment situation?

The efficient social services?

Membership of the League of Nations?

People liked all of those things. They were the very reason that in Berlin old Herr Tauber felt able to state that the country's nightmare was over.

Even the great outrage of November 1918, the so-called 'stab in the back' theory which had long been a Nazi Party favourite, was beginning to sound like a paranoid obsession. Over and over again throughout the 1920s Hitler had railed against the 'November Criminals', those rich and cowardly Jews skulking in Berlin who had deliberately, maliciously (and for no apparent reason that Hitler cared to explain) conspired to organize the defeat of the Imperial German Army.

People had used to lap that one up but now nobody seemed to give a damn.

Germany had moved on.

The Munich Baby was dying.

And yet unbeknownst to those glum brown-shirted men sitting around the table at the house in Munich, everything was about to change. The Nazi Party would have to wait eight months for its birthday present, but when it came, it was the best they could possibly have hoped for.

Chaos.

On 24 October 1929, six and a half thousand kilometres from Schelling Street. On another street. An infinitely more famous one, called Wall Street, there began the greatest collapse in market confidence in all history and with it a global depression.

Germany's economic recovery had been the most fragile, the abyss from which it had hauled itself the darkest and most deep. Its vulnerability to this new financial madness was therefore all the greater.

The Munich Baby was about to get its chance.

Fighting over Dagmar

Berlin, 1932

Otto was very surprised. What had got into Paulus?

Otto was a fighter, a two-fisted scrapper who never bothered with words when a blow could be more articulate, but Paulus was the opposite.

Paulus never fought unless he absolutely had to. He never lost control of his emotions either. He was passionate, certainly, but he always tempered his passion with reason.

Reason should therefore have told him that in a fist fight against Otto he was bound to get pounded.

He was taller, but he was thinner.

He had the reach but Otto had the grunt.

He was a rapier, Otto was a Howitzer.

Which was why it had come as such a shock to Otto to feel the knuckles of Paulus's left upper cut smashing into his mouth and rattling his teeth. What was more, the sharp pain of that first unexpected blow was followed swiftly by a deep intestinal ache as Paulus buried his right into Otto's guts.

Otto doubled forward involuntarily, as had of course been the purpose of the carefully placed blow, and shortly thereafter he found himself knocked sprawling on to the ground by a pile driver of a left hook to the side of his bowed head which split open the skin on his ear and made his vision double.

A perfect three-blow combination.

Proving just what can be achieved with surprise and cool, forensic determination. Exactly as the boys' boxing instructor had always told them it could. Paulus had clearly been paying more attention than Otto had supposed.

The boxing classes were Wolfgang's idea. Frieda had been dead against them.

'Teaching them to fight might actually get them *into* trouble,' she had protested. 'It might make them think they can handle something they can't.'

'They already think they can handle things they can't,' Wolfgang argued, 'so we might as well try and even the odds a bit.'

That had been two years before in 1930 when almost overnight Berlin had begun once more to resemble the lunatic asylum it had been when the twins were born. Those old familiar sounds had returned to the city, breaking glass, running boots, screams and gunfire. To Frieda and Wolfgang it was as if they'd never gone away. There were the same daily battles between the same old factions. Except on the right the Nazi *Sturmabteilung* had replaced the late and unlamented *Freikorps*.

'Just like old times,' Wolfgang remarked.

'Not quite,' Frieda remarked grimly. 'This time it's worse for us.'

She was right and Wolfgang knew it. The anti-Semitism was more pronounced than it had ever been before. Josef Goebbels, Hitler's *Gauleiter* of Berlin, did not let a day go by without appearing on some street corner to accuse the Jews of power and influence that corrupted and controlled every aspect of society.

'If we really had as much influence as that bastard says,' Wolfgang commented, 'we'd have had him fucking killed long ago.'

But the Jews of Germany were none of the things they were supposed to be. They were neither organized nor focused; the only thing that united them was the accident of genealogy that named them Jews. Accused of a collective conspiratorial aggression, they were incapable of collective defence, and all Wolfgang could do for his own family was put bars on the windows, keep a blackjack in his pocket and make sure his boys knew how to box.

Of course he had not expected them to start using their skills on each other.

Looking back, neither Paulus nor Otto could quite remember which of them it was who first admitted to being in love with Dagmar. A confession which sparked the bloodiest battle they had ever fought.

It was Silke who provoked it.

They'd been playing horse shoes with her in a muddy little patch of public gardens near the Stengel apartment, and Silke had taken the opportunity as she often did to complain about 'Princess' Dagmar and how more and more 'up herself' she had become.

'She thinks she's better than us because she's so rich and so pretty,' Silke said grumpily. 'Just because her dad's a millionaire.'

Stung by Silke's contempt, one twin had told her to keep quiet, that Dagmar was OK.

Then the other volunteered that she was more than OK, she was in fact rather wonderful. Gorgeous even. Stunning.

A total goddess might be one way of putting it.

And suddenly the truth was out. The Stengel boys were in love.

With the same girl.

Silke actually stamped the ground she was so angry and frustrated. She had long sensed that such emotions were gathering within her beloved twins, but was nonetheless shocked at how comprehensive they had turned out to be.

'You can't *both* love her!' she cried. 'It's just stupid.'

This was one thing on which the boys could certainly agree.

'Of course we can't!' Paulus snarled. 'Because actually I've already told her I love her and she's agreed to go around with me.'

'It's a lie!' Otto shouted back. '*I've* already told her *I* love her and she said she'd go around with me.'

Despite her fury Silke couldn't help but laugh at that one.

'Haha! She's tricked you both!' she cried. 'More fool you. She probably doesn't give a shit about either of you.'

'Yes she does!' Otto shouted, advancing on his brother and pushing him backwards. 'She loves me and you'd better back off and keep away or you'll regret it!'

That was when Paulus had surprised Otto by laying him out with his beautiful triple combination.

'She's mine!' Paulus shouted down at his astonished and slightly woozy brother. 'She told me she loved me!'

'Like hell she did, you wanker!' Otto shouted back, directing his cry to the space between the two images of his brother which were floating before his eyes. 'She said she loved me!'

Otto had never seen his brother's face red like that, his eyes wild with emotion. Paulus was supposed to be the calm one.

'She's making arseholes of both of you,' Silke called out from the tree stump on which she had perched herself to watch the fun. 'It's obvious she's told you both the same thing. She's having a laugh.'

'You keep out of it, Silks!'

Otto had been caught unawares. When he'd pushed his brother backwards towards the bike shed, a heavy palm banging against his twin's chest, he hadn't expected to be answered with this flurry of finely delivered blows. But he was ready now. He had discovered that there was one subject on which Paulus's usual calm and reason deserted him.

'Yes, you keep out of it, Silks,' Paulus said. 'This is between Otts and me and you'd better back off, Otts, OK? Or you'll be sorry.'

'Yeah?' Otto replied, raising himself from the ground. 'You

think 'cos you landed a lucky punch or two you're a fighter, do you? Well now I'm going to beat the shit out of you, Paulo, until you admit that Dagmar's mine.'

Otto got to his feet, put his head down and piled in with a flurry of body punches, right and left hooks banging into Paulus's floating lower ribs. Otto was not the clever one at school and Paulus got better marks in human biology but Otto knew where a man's liver and kidneys were, and he was seeking out his brother's with deadly accuracy, twisting his fists slightly, screwing the blows into Paulus's body as he'd been taught to do.

Paulus reeled backwards, gagging heavily as he tried to draw in breath and stop himself from puking.

'Admit it,' Otto shouted, 'just admit it!'

It was Paulus's turn to be bent double now, gasping, holding on to his injured sides.

'Fuck you!'

Otto stood over his wheezing brother. 'I reckon you've learnt your lesson now, so admit she loves me.'

Otto never should have dropped his guard.

Paulus straightened himself up, throwing a wild cross, a classic sucker punch, and Otto was the sucker for imagining his brother beaten. Otto had reckoned it would be ten minutes before Paulus could form a proper sentence, let alone deliver a haymaker of a right hook that swung up from out of nowhere and caught Otto in the eye, sending him once more sprawling to the ground.

In all the club bouts Otto had fought he had never once been knocked down, and now his brother, his thoughtful, cautious, calculating brother, had decked him twice in no time at all.

'Otto, are you all right?' Silke cried out. She'd seen the boys fight before many times but never like this. Paulus and Otto fought all the time, but just whacks and scuffles. This kind of brutality they reserved for common enemies, not each other.

Silke knelt beside Otto, dabbing at his bleeding ear with the hem of her dress.

'Get up,' Paulus shouted, 'get up and swear to me you'll leave Dagmar alone. Otherwise you'll get some more.'

'God, you're both pathetic. She's just a stuck-up bitch anyway.'

'Shut up, Silke!' Otto said, brushing her away. 'This hasn't got anything to do with you!'

'Yes it has! She lied to you both! She's trying to break up the Saturday Club!'

'Clear out of it, Silks,' Paulus shouted, 'this is between me and Otts.'

Now it was Paulus's turn to be caught off guard. He really should have been paying attention to Otto, not Silke, because just then Otto seized the opportunity of Paulus's momentary distraction to jump to his feet and commence another assault. This time he did not intend to underestimate his brother. Squinting through his rapidly closing eye, he put up his guard and steamed back into the fight. No flurry of punches now but a properly executed combination. By the book. Left jab, straight right, left hook, straight right again. Paulus tried to protect himself by going into a clinch but Otto saw it coming, feinting a hook and, when Paulus turned away from it, hitting him with a final cross before flattening him with a bone-crunching head butt, which was not out of any book but his own.

The fight was over and although technically Otto won with a knockout, it was evens on points, and both boys were probably equally dazed and bloodied at its conclusion.

'Cor,' Silke said, somewhat stunned, 'you two really went for it.'

Paulus had been very slightly concussed by Otto's final head butt but after a moment or two he raised himself up to a sitting position and wiped blood from his mouth.

'Dagmar Fischer's mine,' he said quietly. 'Just keep your bloody hands off her.'

'What?' Otto exclaimed fiercely. 'I just whipped you! I won her! *You* keep your hands off.'

'That's not how it works with girls,' Paulus grunted. 'You can't just win them in a fight.'

'Well, what the hell were we fighting *for* then?' Otto enquired, reaching out a hand to help Paulus up.

'Because you're both idiots!' Silke exclaimed angrily. 'And she's just a lying, hoity-toity cow. I can't believe either of you are interested.'

'Yeah, well, you're jealous of her,' Otto said.

'Am not.'

'Yes you are!'

'Why? Why would I be jealous of her?'

'Because we like her, that's why,' Paulus said, laughing.

'Huh! As if I care *who* you like,' Silke shouted, but she was going red beneath her golden tan. 'She's a stupid bean pole *and* I don't believe those tits are real. She's putting tissues under her vest, I bet. But anyway you can have her if you like. I'm going home.'

Both boys were laughing now. Their fight forgotten in shared merriment at their old friend's discomfort.

Silke turned on her heel and stomped off, leaving the boys to compare wounds.

The Saturday Club had suffered its first true division.

That Man

Berlin, 30 January 1933

It was stunning. Unbelievable. Incomprehensible. Incredible. Impossible.

Only yesterday, *yesterday*, everything had been fine.

And now out of the blue, *that man* had suddenly become Chancellor.

'He hasn't even got a majority!' Wolfgang kept saying, over and over again as the Stengels sat down for supper that dreadful night. 'The bastard was *losing ground*.'

It was true. They'd recently even begun to relax. All through the previous year he'd stalked them. *That man.* For month after month throughout 1932 every newspaper headline had seemed to bring him a little closer to their door. Louring over them like some murderous medieval golem. But just recently he'd been slipping. His vote had peaked. It was falling. Goebbels had begun to sound desperate. The crisis was passing.

'And now just because of a bunch of cowardly fucking *Junkers* and that senile old *cunt* Hindenburg, he's got his chance. Fuck them! *Fuck* them to hell!'

The boys looked up, their faces half shocked, half amused.

'Please, Wolf!' Frieda said, banging her water glass down in protest, trying to keep the fear from her voice, 'not at the supper table! The children . . .'

Wolfgang mumbled an apology, biting his lip, his knuckles white around the schnapps glass which he had just refilled.

'I don't care, Mum,' Otto said, stuffing his mouth full of food. 'I think Hindenburg's a cunt too.'

'Otto!'

Frieda actually reached over and slapped him, something she had never done before in her life. 'Don't you *dare* use that disgusting language in front of me! Don't you *dare* . . .'

She couldn't continue, there were tears in her eyes now.

'I'm sorry, Mum,' Otto said, as shocked as his mother was. 'I deserved it.'

'No, Otto. I'm sorry. I can't believe I hit you.'

'It's all right.'

Frieda got up and went around the table to hug Otto.

'See what he's done to us already, *that terrible man*.'

The four of them sat and ate for a few moments in silence. Bean soup and bread. There were cold cuts and beetroot to follow.

'They think they can do a *deal*,' Wolfgang muttered, unable to keep his frustration to himself, tearing at the bread as if it was a Nazi neck. 'A deal! With *Hitler*!'

'Please, Wolf,' Frieda said, 'let's leave it alone while we eat.'

Paulus had been looking at the evening newspaper, the one announcing the formation of Hitler's cabinet.

'The Nazis still only have a couple of seats,' Paulus said. 'The paper says he can't do anything without the other party's agreement. Perhaps Herr von Papen can—'

'Oh they're all bloody *vons*,' Wolfgang said. '*Von* Hindenburg and *Von* Papen and *Von* bloody Schleicher and they think that means they'll be able to tell him what to do. Like he was still a corporal and them all generals and field marshals . . . *Oh thank you for letting me be Chancellor, now I'll do what I'm told like a good little Nazi!* Haven't they heard him speak? Haven't they seen his private army? Like *fuck* he'll let them tell him what to do!'

'Wolf, *please*, this isn't helping.'

Later on, after supper, the family watched from their apartment window as the night sky flickered red and yellow from the light of the torch-lit victory procession that was stamping and shouting its way across the city.

Through the Brandenburg Gate.

That same crooked cross parading beneath it as had first appeared scrawled on the helmets of the *Freikorps* in 1920. Except this time the swastikas were not scribbled in chalk but flying red, black and crimson from a thousand banners. And the crowd that had gathered were not silent in protest but hysterical with joy.

Frieda struggled to remain calm and matter-of-fact as she cleared away the supper things.

'Don't forget your homework,' she told the boys, 'and scrape your football boots into one of the window boxes.'

Wolfgang just sat at the window and looked at the sky, cursing quietly under his breath. Slowly picking out the recent American hit *Happy Days Are Here Again* on his ukulele. Until Frieda told him to stop.

Not because she didn't appreciate the irony. But because she was scared. Since noon that day when the announcement had been made and *that man* had appeared, smiling, almost for the first time in his public career, it had been unsafe for Jews to draw attention to themselves. The ukulele was a penetrating instrument. And the walls of the apartment were thin.

The Penny Dropped

London, 1956

Stone woke up from his Wannsee dream.

He had been back on the little beach beside the lake. His brother was there, as he always was. And Dagmar. Just as it had been on that day.

Except in the dream, of course, Dagmar chose him. And it had been him who brushed his lips on her rain-dappled shoulders.

And, unconscious on his pillow, Stone's sleeping soul had soared.

Now he was awake, experiencing the same deflation that he always suffered when awakening from that beautiful Wannsee dream. And there was something more.

Somehow in his sleep, while he dreamt, his mind had been working. Trying to make sense of what he had been told on the previous day, in the bare room in Kensington. And now, eyes wide open, suddenly completely awake, it was as if a veil of emotion had been lifted and he was able to see things clearly for the first time since he had received his letter from Berlin.

The story he had been given wouldn't do.

It simply did not add up.

Essentially those men from MI6 had told him two things. The first, that Dagmar was alive. The second, that somehow her ruptured life journey had led her to the Stasi.

Stone now saw that in his eagerness to believe the first, he had accepted the second at face value.

He got out of bed and went to put the kettle on. The lino was cold against his feet. The pre-dawn air was chilly.

He struck a match in the darkened kitchen and the gas ring popped into life, the flickering blue flame casting faint shadows across the room. Stone fumbled for his jacket and found his smokes. He didn't switch on the light, somehow he felt he could focus better in the dark. He bent forward and lit his cigarette from the gas. No point wasting a second match.

He smoked hungrily. Watching the glowing tip grow bright and then subside as he drew deep and then exhaled. Bright. Then dim. Bright. Then dim. And with each new spark he sensed his thoughts becoming clearer. Almost as if that throbbing red tip was flashing out a warning. A silent alarm.

The whistle on the kettle shrieked.

It was a siren. Like the thousands he had heard before. Police sirens. Air-raid sirens. All meaning one thing. Trouble was coming. Danger was near.

He let the kettle keep boiling. The screaming seemed to focus his thoughts. Its ugly, jarring whine pushing him towards the conclusion he was dreading.

That the men from MI6 were wrong.

That Dagmar was dead, as for so long he had believed her to be.

The precious letter was a forgery. Cobbled together from other, older material, genuine letters, diaries perhaps. Long-buried memories. The Stasi were good at that sort of thing.

He was being lured back to Berlin.

Final Match

Berlin, 1933

Paulus and Otto were cornered.

They never should have come, of course.

How could they have imagined it would be the same as before? That they could just turn up in their footie kit at the old field, the way they had done for years and years, and play?

Paulus had been worrying about it all week. He'd even pinned a map of the local area to their bedroom wall the better to consider escape routes.

'If we get chased,' he said, 'we don't want to end up in a blind alley. There's two near the recreation ground plus a walled building site. We need to know the best way out from every corner of the field and how to make for the *U-Bahn* station, OK?'

'If we get chased,' Otto said grimly, 'we fight. There's only four fucking Nazis on the team.'

'Otts, they're all Nazis now.'

'Look, it's our team. We've been OK at school, haven't we?'

'So far.'

It was true, they had. There had been a few murmurs and angry mutterings, not least from a couple of the teachers, but so far nothing worse. Maybe things would be all right at soccer too.

Even Frieda and Wolfgang had agreed that they should go. The boys had been on the team since they were eight. Five years playing with the same lads had to mean something.

But now as Paulus and Otto found themselves cornered in the changing shed they knew it didn't.

Quite without warning their former team-mates had turned into a snarling, vengeful mob and the Stengel boys were in big trouble.

'*Jude! Jude!*'

The big lad, Emil, began to formalize the chant, ominously beating the wooden walls of the little changing hut with a rounders bat. 'Jew! Jew!'

The brothers stood side by side. Paulus had hold of a chair and Otto was preparing to use a dustbin lid and a broken corner flag as a sword and shield. The Stengel twins were formidable when they stood side by side and their assailants knew that, which was why for a moment at least they held back.

'Filthy fucking Jews,' Emil shouted, breaking the rhythm he had been banging out and taking a step towards the boys. 'Now you're going to pay for everything you've done to Germany.'

Paulus and Otto looked at the angry faces ranged against them. Emil had of course always hated them, he was the sort of boy who hated everybody, particularly the ones who stood up to him. But many others in the team had been their friends. Only a *fortnight* before, Otto had been sitting atop their shoulders having scored a direct goal from a corner kick in an important youth league match. But Hitler had been Chancellor for over a week now and the speed with which Paulus and Otto's world had changed had been breathtaking.

Emil Braas had grabbed his first chance to avenge himself on the Stengel boys. For being better footballers than him.

For being popular and easy-going while he was sullen and had a reputation for spite.

For being attractive to girls while he was laughed at and teased by even quite ugly ones for being dull and lumbering.

This was Emil's chance, as it was that month for every embittered, failed and inadequate fool in Germany. To be the big man at last.

Otto knew the score. He knew boys like Emil and as far as he was concerned there was only one course of action available to him.

Hit first and hit hardest.

That was his rule.

But Paulus hated that rule. He had a different one. Never confront if you could negotiate. That was the clever way. Yes, hit hard if you had to, but first, try not to hit at all.

Otto had already raised his weapon hand, the muscles on his bare arms and chest taut and prone. He was not quite yet even thirteen but already he had the physical definition of an athletic young man, of a fighter.

Paulus was in good shape too, Wolfgang had made sure of that. But he did not raise his weapon. Instead he laughed.

As a tactic, it had the benefit of surprise, if nothing else.

The crowd of adversaries looked taken aback, but they didn't lower their fists.

'What are you laughing at, Jew boy?' Emil sneered.

'Well, your face for one,' Paulus replied, 'but I ain't talking to you.'

Paulus then turned to one of the boys standing a little back from the main mob.

'Come on, Tommy,' Paulus said. 'We've been mates since kindergarten.'

Beside him Otto growled. What was the point of appealing to their better nature? Clearly things had gone way beyond that.

But that wasn't Paulus's idea at all.

He had a bolder plan. As Goebbels had said, if you're going to lie, make it a big one.

'We're not Jews,' Paulus said

It was the last defence anybody had expected, flying as it did in the face of accepted knowledge, and it certainly took the attacking mob aback.

'Come on, Tommy,' Paulus said, using the pause to press his advantage. 'When did you see me with silly sideburns and a big black hat on?'

Tommy had indeed known the twins since preschool and they had certainly always been friends. But Tommy also knew that the Stengel twins were Jews. Subhumans, according to the Chancellor of Germany. Vermin. A filthy cancerous parasitic disease festering on the nation's flesh. Sucking its blood.

'You are Jews, you bastards,' Tommy said. 'You hide it. That's what you swine do. You skulk and hide.'

'We're not bloody Jews, Tom,' Paulus laughed. 'Wankers like Emil may say we are but he doesn't know his arse from his elbow, does he? He certainly doesn't know which way to kick a football.'

A few of the boys laughed at that. Tommy smiled too.

Moments before when Emil had been marshalling them for the attack, blaming the Stengel boys for every possible injury that Germany had ever suffered, they had all been with him.

They had quickly overcome the unease they felt about attacking old friends (and good players) in the face of Emil's blood-curdling rhetoric. The Stengels were Jews and as such there was nothing for it but to give them a bloody good hiding and cast them out for ever. Nobody who valued their own safety was going to stick up for a Jew in Berlin in February 1933.

But then nobody had expected them to deny it either and Paulus's surprising position had stopped the assault in its tracks.

If they were Jews then they deserved everything they were going to get, but if they weren't Jews, then brilliant, they were back on the team, best mates again.

Even Otto was taken aback, although he tried not to show it. He'd learnt to trust his brother where planning and scheming was concerned, but this was a bold lie. Everyone knew the Stengels were a Jewish family, secular certainly, no worship, no special holidays, no funny hats or diet, Otto would have happily lived off bacon sandwiches and fried pork rinds for the rest of his life, but they were Jews nonetheless, everybody knew it, why try to deny it?

But Paulus had an ace up his sleeve.

Or, as he was later to tell his horrified mum, in his pants.

He had been thinking about it all week.

A foreskin wouldn't stand up against a proper search of family history, of course. But it might do in an alleyway, in a cellar. When the wolves were in your face.

If you waved it about a bit and shouted. Loud and clear and furious and certain. They seemed to respond to that sort of thing.

And now the time had come to test the idea.

With his ex-friends and old enemies closing in, nine against two, it was time to try the big bluff.

'Take a look at little Paulus, Emil,' Paulus shouted, pulling up the leg of his football shorts with the hand that did not hold a broken chair. 'What do you think of this big boy?'

Paulus reached up into his groin and pulled out his penis, shaking it at his surprised assailants.

'Ever see a Jew boy with foreskin?' Paulus crowed, putting down his chair leg and pulling down his pants. 'So how about you suck on this, arsehole! Come on, Otto, show the twat what a real German dick looks like.'

Otto didn't like it. Exposing himself in public seemed like black humiliation to him. On the other hand, they were so heavily outnumbered.

Slowly Otto laid down his corner flag and dustbin lid and pulled down his trousers.

The rest of the team loved it. They howled with laughter as Paulus waved his dick at Emil, who just stood there looking witless, unable to think of a rejoinder.

'Tell your old man next time he insults decent Germans he'll have to deal with the Stengel boys!' Paulus shouted.

Otto just snarled and pulled up his pants.

Outside the hut a whistle blew. The opposing team would be waiting. The ref getting impatient.

'So are we going to play football or what?' Paulus shouted. 'Let's beat these bastards, eh?'

The incident was over. Emil turned away, confused. One or two of the other lads slapped Otto on the shoulder. He told them to piss off.

Paulus and Otto played the game. Giving it everything they had as always. Occasionally exchanging glances, mutually acknowledging their lucky escape. Both aware of the doubtful confused looks they were getting from Emil and the other openly Nazi members of the team.

It was of course their last game.

Football was over for them. Years of fun, sport and comradeship, stopped dead.

They both knew they could never risk going back.

They left the field the moment the final whistle blew. Their team had won and Otto had scored twice but the Stengels didn't hang around to celebrate. There were no songs or scuffles or wild cheers. Otto was not hoisted high on shoulders as previously he would have been. They'd won but they had nothing to celebrate. Their entire world had collapsed.

'I think we should have fought,' said Otto as they stood waiting for their train.

'Don't be bloody stupid, we'd have been killed.'

'Yeah. But we had to show them our dicks.'

'So what? Who cares?' Paulus asked, genuinely surprised.

'I care. I suppose you and me are just different, that's all,' Otto said.

After that there was silence until the boys got home.

To face another humiliation.

From now on such things would be a daily occurrence.

Edeltraud was there, with Silke. And Edeltraud's boyfriend, Jürgen, now her fiancé. The respectful young man who had come cap in hand to the children's first concert recital five years earlier. The boys had seen him many times since then, although less so in the last year or two.

And never in the brown uniform of the SA.

'Say goodbye to Edeltraud, boys,' Frieda said. 'She won't be coming around any more.'

'Of course she won't!' Jürgen snapped. 'It is not fitting that a German woman should be a servant to Jews. You must know that.'

The boys looked at Edeltraud. Her face was hard, her chin set.

And at Silke, whose eyes were red with tears. Her chest heaving, weeping silently.

'Tell me, Jürgen,' Frieda asked quietly, 'was it fitting, ten years ago, for a Jew to take in a seventeen-year-old street kid with an infant in her arms?'

'You exploited her! You made her work for you!'

Frieda looked at Edeltraud.

'Edeltraud, you can't believe that's true.'

Edeltraud avoided Frieda's eye. 'You're Jews' was all she would say.

'Whatever we are, it's what we've always been. All these years, together in this apartment. So much laughter, so many tears. You and Silke and us. What's changed?'

'What's *changed*, Frau Stengel,' Jürgen barked, 'is that Germany has awoken. We have *all* awoken. We know now *who you are and what you've done*. And now it is *our* turn. Now give Edeltraud her money.'

'Money?' Frieda asked. 'What money? She has been paid as always. More than most girls would have got.'

'Her notice. We want a month's notice.'

'But she is resigning, Jürgen,' Frieda said quietly. 'Surely you know that she is not entitled to notice.'

'She is not resigning. You are *forcing* her to leave.'

'How? How am I forcing her to leave?'

'By being Jews,' Jürgen said. 'This is a racial dismissal. Give her the money and be grateful I do not demand more!'

Frieda went into the kitchen. To the biscuit barrel, where she kept her household supply of cash.

'You know, Edeltraud,' Frieda said quietly, 'I've always known that sometimes you took a little from here when I wasn't looking. A few extra marks here and there. I never said anything.'

The boys looked at Edeltraud in astonishment. Such a thing would never have occurred to them. Silke stared hard at her mother. Edeltraud went red-faced but said nothing.

Wolfgang had been sitting at his piano, not facing his ex-maid and her storm-trooper boyfriend.

'Would you like a schnapps, Jürgen?' Wolfgang asked, turning around for the first time. 'You've been happy to take one in the past.'

The young SA man remained silent standing beside Edeltraud on the blue rug where Silke and the boys had played happily so many times when they were small.

Frieda held out her hand to Edeltraud with some money.

'Goodbye, Edeltraud,' Frieda said. 'For more than ten years, you've been family. I shall remember you that way.'

'You're Jews,' Edeltraud repeated. It seemed to be all that she could say. The shield with which she kept her conscience at bay.

She snatched at the money and stuffed it into the pocket of her apron.

'Edeltraud! Silke! Come!' Jürgen ordered.

Edeltraud turned to go but Silke hesitated.

'Paulus, Otto,' she said, speaking for the first time. 'I am still a member of the Saturday Club and I always will be.'

'I said come!' Jürgen shouted.

And they were gone.

Thirteenth Birthdays

Munich and Berlin, 1933

The Stengel twins and the Nazi Party shared another birthday that February but this time it was the Munich celebration that was raucous and joyful while the mood at the party in Berlin was a little more subdued than usual, all the regular guests from previous years having declined their invitations.

'The problem is we just don't know enough Jews,' Wolfgang observed dryly.

'I hardly even knew I *was* a bloody Jew until a couple of weeks ago,' Paulus remarked moodily. 'I certainly don't think I look like one.'

'What does a damn Jew look like?' Wolfgang demanded.

'*Please* can we stop all this swearing,' Frieda pleaded. 'Just because they have no standards doesn't mean we can forget ours.'

Even Silke wasn't at the birthday party, having managed the previous day to send a card explaining that she was to be locked in her room for the day by her mum's SA boyfriend.

Dagmar was in fact the only non-family guest.

Although, if they were honest, the twins were actually perfectly happy with that. They were both so completely in love with Dagmar they would have had eyes for no one else anyway.

Dagmar didn't mind either. The Stengel twins were both growing up into fine, handsome boys. Very different from each other but both attractive in their way. Paulus was perhaps the more handsome by conventional standards, with thick, copper-black hair, deep ebony eyes and fine, sensitive cheekbones. Otto was a little shorter, with sandy hair, pale grey eyes and a tendency to freckles. But there was a fiery intensity about him which made people take notice and he was also extremely strong.

Dagmar had no objection at all to being the absolute centre of their combined attention.

Also, although it was their birthday, both twins had prepared gifts for her. Paulus had composed an extravagant epic love poem in which Dagmar was the heroine and he the hero (Otto had a minor role as Paulus's squire). He'd written it in High German and had inscribed it with great care in Gothic script. He'd even aged the leaves of paper with cold coffee to make them look like parchment.

Otto had made Dagmar a miniature chest of drawers in his school woodwork class. He was becoming a skilled craftsman and the tiny piece of furniture was beautifully finished, sanded and varnished with little pearl buttons for drawer handles.

'To go on your dressing table,' he said shyly, 'you know, to put stuff in, little stuff, like rings you know . . . and stuff.'

Dagmar was delighted with her gifts and both boys got a kiss, which turned them crimson, while their parents and grandparents smiled indulgently.

'Anyone would think it was Dagmar's birthday,' Frieda said, pouring out the lemonade, 'so come on, let's cut this wonderful cake she's brought. I see Fischer's bakers are as skilled as ever.'

But of course before the cake could be cut, Herr Tauber insisted on being allowed to make his customary speech. The old policeman had aged noticeably even in the three weeks since Hitler had become Chancellor, but now he addressed the table with his old robust authority.

'Otto, Paulus, I am proud of you,' he said sternly. 'You are thirteen now and fine young men. This is fortunate. Because Germany will soon be in need of fine young men. Good Germans who will step forward and take up the challenge of rebuilding our Fatherland's reputation in the civilized world. This is why today, on your birthday, I beg you boys to be careful. I see you with bruises and scratches on your faces and know that you have been fighting. Of course you have, you are brave and proud and these are intolerable times. But we *must* tolerate them, for mark my words, this current aberration will pass, and it will pass soon. There are fresh elections in March and until then, despite everything *that man* may say, the law and the constitution still protect us. They are bigger than any one government. I know that the scum of the beer halls are marauding in the streets at present, but the law is the law and even that man cannot just wish it away. I am still a captain of police, you know. If you find yourself in danger, you come to me. As long as we don't go getting ourselves murdered by stray SA men drunk on their success we will come through all this, you'll see. The greatest and most advanced nation in Europe will not allow itself to be ruled by street hooligans for long. The law will prevail. Mark my words. And now let us cut the cake.'

Three days later, on 27 February, the adolescent Nazi Party got another of its belated birthday gifts.

Somebody burnt down the Reichstag and the delinquent thirteen-year-old used the so-called 'provocation' to throw the birthday party of its dreams.

With mass arrests, countless killings and beatings, thousands of 'disappearances' and the outlawing of all but the most token political opposition.

Herr Tauber's beloved law was no protection now as three million brown-shirted SA hooligans were drafted into the regular police.

The newly empowered Nazi Party, a baby no more but a vicious, cunning teenage psychopath, issued *carte blanche* for robbery, rape and murder. Its Leader announced that crimes committed against the party's 'enemies' were not crimes at all but legitimate services to the German state.

The criminals were sitting in judgement and the law was dead.

Visitors to the Surgery
Berlin, 1933

Boom boom. Boom boom. Boom boom.

Frieda listened to the tiny heartbeat and smiled at the anxious face of the expectant mother at whose belly she had placed her stethoscope.

'All well I think, Frau Schmidt,' she said with a smile, 'just like the previous six.'

'Well, let's hope it's a quiet one,' the large, round-faced woman replied happily, 'I can't stand another like the last. Nor can anybody else in my building for that matter! When the idiots below us found out I was knocked up again they actually complained to the block management committee. As if *they* could do anything about it. It gets cold in bed in the winter and things happen, don't they? Can't stop that.'

'Well you *can* try and control the consequences of course, Frau Schmidt,' Frieda said, probing gently at her patient's belly with delicate fingers. 'No woman need feel obliged to have a child these days, you know, or at least you can considerably reduce the risk. In the past I have mentioned to you the idea of birth control—'

'Hush, doctor! That's treason!' The woman laughed, her big, stretched, purple-streaked, tired old tummy wobbling with merriment. 'Never mind *obliged*, haven't you heard? These days it's our duty! All these years I've been thinking I was an idiot for letting the old fella bother me when he's been on the beer and it turns out I'm a hero! How about that, eh? Mind you, I actually thought I was a bit of a hero at the time, to be honest – he's not getting any thinner or any easier on the eye.'

They laughed together, a shared moment of female solidarity in a man's world.

'Besides which, doctor, this one's going to turn a profit. How about that, eh?'

Frieda smiled, she knew that the woman was referring to the

government plans to 'reward' motherhood. Repayment of state family loans could be offset against the number of children that were produced. *Abgekindert*, as the joke went: borrow money and then 'child it off'.

'That's a good thing though, isn't it?' Frau Schmidt went on. 'I mean, you can't deny that.'

The jolly, red-faced woman looked slightly uncomfortable. In recent weeks Frieda had got used to people avoiding her eye as they self-consciously encouraged her to acknowledge the 'good' things that 'they' were doing for the nation. She had even noticed some irritation amongst non-Jewish acquaintances about the way Jews seemed fixated with their own situation. As if anti-Semitism was the *only* relevant feature of the new government. After all, everyone was making sacrifices for Germany's reawakening, weren't they? Why shouldn't the Jews?

'I don't think quite all of us will be eligible for the payment,' Frieda replied quietly. 'I'm not sure Herr Hitler is anxious for people like myself to procreate.'

'Mister' Hitler. It was how Frieda and all her Jewish friends referred to the Leader, in the desperate, unspoken hope that somehow referring to him in a civilized manner might actually make him civilized himself. That perhaps even after everything he'd said, beneath the surface he was a legitimate politician who recognized some sort of rules and norms of behaviour, rather than a deranged psychopath, the stuff of gothic nightmares.

Once more Frau Schmidt avoided Frieda's eye. Concentrating instead on buttoning up the front of her dress.

'No,' she said brightly, 'I suppose not. But then you never wanted a large family anyway, Frau Stengel. You after all are a *doctor*.'

'I am at the moment, Frau Schmidt.'

Frieda put away her stethoscope. She took the Schmidt family medical file from the bulging filing system that covered an entire wall of her surgery and went to her desk to write down the conclusions of her examination.

Frieda had worked in that same office, at that same community clinic, since graduating from medical school in 1923. Ten years of long, tough days and many many disturbed nights. Endless hours of hard and emotionally draining work on a small civil service grade salary.

This was a sacrifice that she had not made alone. Her family had made it with her. The boys had often missed their mum at supper time and even bedtime, while Wolfgang's dreams of spending long days writing jazz symphonies had been sacrificed to child care and bread and butter engagements.

'When are you going to finally stop being a martyr, put up a brass plate on your door and make some proper money, girl,' Wolfgang had often begged, only half joking. 'Help some fat society mommas with their hot flushes. Charge them a fortune to loosen their corsets and give them an aspirin.'

But Frieda loved her work, she was passionately committed to the Weimar Government's public health policies, which were the most advanced in the world, and she felt huge responsibility to her patients. After her family, the Friedrichshain community clinic was the centre of Frieda's life.

'If we don't look after these people,' she'd tell her husband as they struggled to balance their own family budget, 'who else will?'

'Well, I'm with your dad on this one,' Wolfgang would reply. 'Fuck 'em,' and Frieda hoped he was joking.

Flicking through the Schmidt file in search of the right card, Frieda found herself reflecting how badly her handwriting had deteriorated over her decade of practice. In that file were some of the first notes she had made as a junior doctor, when Frau Schmidt's husband had registered with the clinic as a young single man. He had come to her with a case of gonorrhoea picked up in an army brothel in Belgium. She had noted down the details in a clear youthful hand. The writing she added to the file now was, as with most doctors, legible only to herself and the local chemist.

'You will still be coming to see me, Frau Schmidt?' Frieda enquired, without looking up from her desk. 'You still wish me to deliver your baby?'

'Of course, *Frau Doktor*. You've delivered all the others, one a year since 1927, all ship-shape and screaming blue murder. Why stop now?'

'Well, Frau Schmidt, I think perhaps you know why. These are changing times.'

Now Frieda looked up. Frau Schmidt was putting on her coat, on the collar of which was a small swastika badge. Women were not allowed to be actual members of the Nazi Party but that did not stop them buying brooches to show their support.

'You mean because you are Jewish?' Schmidt said, once more a little embarrassed. 'Well, yes, of course it is . . . unfortunate . . . for you I mean. It must be a very worrying time. But really you mustn't fret, everybody knows that you are not one of *them*, *Frau Doktor* Stengel. The Jews in Berlin are different, aren't they? I know two or three SA men with Jewish girlfriends.'

Frieda tried to smile. She encountered this same attitude all the time. She was not one of *those* Jews, the ones Herr Hitler was talking about. The ones depicted weekly in the million-selling *Der Stürmer* magazine, who drank the blood of Christian virgins to fuel their dark Satanic rituals. *Those* Jews were somewhere else, out in the countryside perhaps, where the *Herrenvolk* were already putting banners across the entrances to their villages, saying Jews should keep out or risk the consequences. Here in Berlin people *knew* Jews. They worked with them, banked with them, bought cakes from them. They knew that it could not be those Jews who spent their time, as Herr Hitler had written, lying in wait for hour after hour in darkened streets stalking pure young Aryan girls in pursuance of a deliberate policy of corrupting their blood through rape.

If Herr Webber the baker or Herr Simeon the jeweller or Wolfgang Stengel the music teacher and jazz trumpeter had been doing that sort of thing, surely people would have noticed.

'You're not *that* sort of Jew,' Frau Schmidt assured Frieda, clearly under the impression she was being kind. 'I can't see how the Führer would object to *you*.'

'Well, we shall have to wait and see,' Frieda replied.

Frieda Stengel did not to have to wait long.

One thing that could not be said of Adolf Hitler was that he did not give the world fair warning. From his very first speeches and writings he had made it absolutely clear what treatment he had in mind for the Jews. On 31 March 1933, having been Chancellor for just sixty days, Hitler showed them that he meant what he said.

Frieda was just completing her notes on Frau Schmidt's condition when there was a knock at the door.

It was Meyer, Frieda's co-worker and her least favourite colleague. He was a Communist who believed the clinic should have a political as well as a medical mission and considered it his duty to attempt to indoctrinate his patients. An idea Frieda found both presumptuous and immoral. It was Meyer who had objected to her employing Edeltraud when she was in distress, because it was an action guided by sentiment and not political activism.

Doctor Meyer's face usually wore a smile. A patronizing, supercilious one which suggested that sooner or later it was historically inevitable that whoever he happened to be talking to would come to understand the wisdom of what he said. This morning, however, Meyer's face was dark. He was carrying a newspaper that he put down on Frieda's desk without saying a word. He did not need to, the headline was quite loud and clear enough, announcing as it did 'necessary' measures which were to be taken against Jews forthwith. These included an order that Jewish doctors were no longer to be allowed to treat non-Jewish patients.

'Well, Frau Schmidt,' Frieda said having read with mounting horror the first few paragraphs of the story, 'it seems you will have to find another doctor.' There was a moment's silence before Frieda added gently, 'Unless of course you choose to defy these criminals. Obviously I would appreciate it if you did.'

'Criminals?' Frau Schmidt replied, her jolly face becoming almost imperceptibly harder. 'They are the government, *Frau Doktor*. They cannot be criminals.'

'The Communists govern in Russia,' Meyer exclaimed, 'but your Hitler calls *them* criminals.'

For a moment there was silence. Frau Schmidt and Meyer glaring at each other, and Frieda, having sunk slowly into her seat, simply staring down at the file to which only a moment before she had been adding case notes.

'Ten years I have served this community,' she said quietly, almost to herself. 'In all that time I knew no Jew nor Gentile, only patients.'

Frau Schmidt began hurrying to finish buttoning her coat and gather up her things. 'I am sorry for you, *Frau Doktor*. Truly I am,' she said, but she was looking anywhere except at Frieda.

'Have I enriched myself, Frau Schmidt?' Frieda demanded with sudden passion. 'Did I put up my doctor's plate in the Wilhelmstrasse and cheat honest Germans out of fat fees as apparently all Jew doctors have been doing?'

Frieda knew that haranguing this embarrassed, insignificant, working-class woman was pointless, but then what was the point of anything? If a few million like her chose simply to defy the decree then everything would be all right again. Frieda's anger was rising, the injustice of what was happening was so overwhelming.

'Or, instead, did I work fifty or sixty hours a week for a government clerk's pay in this very building, during which time amongst many other things I delivered *your* bloody babies, Frau Schmidt! Vaccinated them! Saw them through measles and whooping cough and God knows what else!'

'Your people,' Frau Schmidt stammered, grabbing up the newspaper from the desk and pointing to its leading article, 'have been spreading lies abroad. Slandering the Fatherland. See, it says so, it's a proven fact.'

'My people? *My* people? Forgive me, Frau Schmidt, but I had been under the impression that the residents of Friedrichshain were *my* people or else why have I gone out to them at all hours of the night when they were sick? Was it in order to secretly drink the blood of their children, Frau Schmidt, as I am accused of doing? Have I ever drunk your children's blood? Please tell me that?'

The woman was embarrassed but neither was she to be cowed. She held the newspaper in her hands as evidence.

'I know you have not done these things, *Frau Doktor*, but many of your race have and if you yourselves can't stop them then Herr Hitler must. Surely you see that. He has been very patient. I know it isn't you, *Frau Doktor*, but those others, *they* must be stopped. They have been slandering Germany abroad and our Jews must be punished so that those Jews will not do it again. We are victims too you know. We have also suffered!'

The victims. Of course. That was how Hitler couched it every time. He and his followers were the injured party. Even as they set up their private concentration camps and torture chambers, they were *victims*. Acting with heavy heart and in self-defence, having been 'provoked beyond endurance'.

Frieda wanted to reply but no words came. What could she possibly say? That was the dreadful thing about these incredible lies that were now spouted daily in the national press. Even to deny them gave them credence. To *deny* to this woman, who had known her for *ten years* and whom she had seen through six pregnancies, that she was somehow part of a global conspiracy to destroy Frau Schmidt's 'race' and rule the world? What was there to say?

What would there ever again be to say?

Frau Schmidt took up her bag, red faced and unhappy but determined none the less.

'*Herr Doktor* Meyer,' she said, 'I shall be pleased to be seen by another doctor on my next appointment. As regrettably *Frau Doktor* Stengel is no longer allowed to treat me.'

Meyer took the newspaper from the woman and pointed to a paragraph buried deep in the article.

'In fact, Frau Schmidt,' he said, 'as you can see, for the time being this boycott is voluntary. It is true that the government has made it clear that it will shortly introduce a law banning Doctor Stengel from practising, but for the time being it remains *your* decision if she treats you.'

Frieda almost smiled. Funny old Meyer, still the pedantic

committee room politician debating subclauses. As if 'voluntary' meant anything any more.

It was clear from Frau Schmidt's face that it did not mean anything to her. She took her leave and waddled from the room as quickly as she could.

After she had left Frieda slumped further into the chair behind the desk that she no longer had any right to use.

'So it's really true? I'm to be banned from practising?' she said.

'Yes,' Meyer said, his lip quivering with anger. 'In fact it seems you're not to be allowed to do anything at all. From tomorrow there is to be a boycott of *all* Jewish businesses.'

Frieda looked once more at the paper: 'massed popular demonstrations announced'.

She almost laughed. 'Funny, eh? How can you announce a popular demonstration? They have to order their protestors to demonstrate spontaneously.'

'Well, Dr Stengel,' Meyer began, unable even now to resist the temptation to score a political point, 'perhaps now you can see why we Communists have always—'

'You Communists!' Frieda interrupted furiously. 'Yes, what about you Communists! Where are you now? A month ago you had *millions* of members. A hundred deputies in the Reichstag. You had a bloody thug army just like they do. You weren't much smaller than they are. What happened? Where are they? Where are *you*? Isn't anybody going to fight?'

Meyer looked at her coldly. 'Our leaders have—' he began.

'Your leaders have run away to Moscow, looking after themselves while their followers are murdered! Why don't *they* "announce" a "popular" demonstration? Why don't the Social Democrats? The Church? The Army? Why doesn't *anybody*! Those fucking Nazi bastards don't even have a majority.'

Frieda *never* swore. And even on this desperate morning she felt wrong in doing so. After all, the one thing Hitler should not be able to take away from her was her own personal standards. Only she could give those up.

And in any case her passion served no point. Battering as it did at the deaf ears of a closed mind.

'I cannot speak for the Capitalist lackeys of the so-called Democratic Socialists, *Frau Doktor*,' Meyer replied primly, 'however, in the case of the KPD, the theoretical position of the Soviet International proscribes that . . .'

But for once Frieda was to be spared the endless, dry, dialectical parroting of her earnest colleague. The pompous excuses for the Communist Party's craven inactivity and its blind commitment to the whims of Stalin.

For just then there was a commotion in the outer office.

There were bangs, angry voices. A guttural cry of fear. Then the door burst open and quite suddenly they were there. The unthinkable, the unimaginable. In *her* surgery.

That sanctuary of care in which Frieda had toiled daily for ten years was in a single moment corrupted and polluted.

Invaded. Violated.

Three men stood before her. Three men in black boots and brown uniforms.

The SA.

Frieda had seen them so many times on street corners, rattling their collection tins. Snarling at those who did not give. Their faces angry, bullying and stupid, playing the poor victim and the superman all at once. She had long since learnt to avoid their gaze and scurry past.

Now the impossible had happened.

They were *in her surgery*, standing before her desk, faces flushed and triumphant, thumbs stuck in leather belts. Boots spread far apart on the carpet, bellies pushed out in a manner so strutting and so brutish as to be almost a pantomime.

And yet, curiously, for all their swagger, for a moment at least they seemed hesitant, as if they too were aware of the newness of the situation. Aware of how incongruous their huge and brutal presence was in the small room with its various delicate scales and instruments, its anatomical wall charts and posters encouraging women to consider condoms for birth control and also as a barrier to disease. A small, female doctor sitting behind a desk, an open file before her, a pen still in her hand.

They were so terribly out of place. Like a tank in a small garden.

'This is a doctors' surgery,' Dr Meyer protested. 'A place of healing!'

Frieda admired him for finding his voice although it was clear to her that he was trying to keep from it the terror he felt.

'The boycott doesn't commence till tomorrow. What's more, it's voluntary. You have no business here. I shall call the police.' He had broken the spell, but not in the manner in which he would have liked. The SA men openly laughed, it was just what they needed, a good joke to overcome their embarrassment.

'*Herr Doktor*,' the leading trooper said, 'we *are* the police.'

Frieda got to her feet. 'What are you going to do with me?' she enquired. 'Am I to be killed?'

'We aren't going to do anything with you *at the moment*,' the lead man said. 'You have permission to leave.'

'*Permission* to leave my own office?'

'That's right, you can get yourself home. It's him we want.'

The three men turned suddenly towards Meyer.

His face an instant mask of abject terror. He had been so certain they'd come for Frieda.

'You are the Communist Party Member Meyer.'

'No! I mean, well yes, I *was* . . .' Meyer stuttered, 'but the party is banned, therefore of course I am no longer a—'

He got no further. The truncheon smashed across his face and he fell unconscious to the floor.

'Stick him in the truck,' the lead SA man ordered.

The other two men each took an arm of the unconscious ex-Communist and began dragging him from the room, leaving a long smear of blood on the floor as they did so.

'*Heil Hitler*,' said the lead trooper, clicking his heels and giving the German salute.

Then they were gone.

Frieda sank back into her seat. Gulping, fearful that she

would be sick. Trying to comprehend what had just happened.

Adolf Hitler, the subject of that ridiculous, ubiquitous salute, had been in power for sixty days.

And during that time it had become possible for an entirely innocent and defenceless man to be clubbed unconscious in a doctor's surgery and then abducted. Not just with impunity but as a matter of state policy.

In sixty days.

And Hitler intended his Reich to last for a *thousand years*.

Tears began to fall on the notes Frieda had been making. Blue ink dissolving in the splashes, mixing up the sentences concerning Frau Schmidt's pregnancy. Tiny, salty tributaries to an ocean of sorrow that awaited the world.

Hope Lost

London, 1956

Dagmar was dead.

As Stone lit a second cigarette at the blue flame beneath the screeching kettle he felt sure of it.

The brief idyll during which he had imagined his life might be about to begin again had been a cruel illusion. Long grey nothingness stretched out before him once more.

The story he wanted so desperately to believe was simply not credible. Escape from Birkenau? A soldier with the Partisans? Enslavement in a gulag? These things were possible. *Just*. But that they had led eventually to a post with the East German secret police, as MI6 insisted they had, that was *not* possible.

But at least now he would know. Whoever had written that letter knew a great deal about Dagmar. He would go to Berlin and find out the truth about what had happened to her.

In that there was some grim comfort.

What had happened during those terrible years after the perfume-scented kiss they had shared standing by the café table at the Lehrter Bahnhof in 1939? How long had she survived? The Jews had not been finally cleared out of Berlin until 1943. Had she lasted that long?

And what had happened then? To which charnel house did they send her? How did she die? Dagmar Fischer, loveliest girl in all of Germany.

By starvation? Disease? Gas? Was her body burned in an oven? Or did she nearly survive the camps only to fall, exhausted beyond endurance, into a ditch as the SS force-marched their victims towards Germany ahead of the oncoming Red Army? Did she die a slave in an underground factory? One of those hundreds of thousands of human beasts of whom Speer had apparently known nothing? Was her naked, skeletal cadaver heaped high amongst a thousand others, pushed into the pile by an American bulldozer with a weeping GI at the wheel? Were the local German population of Dachau or Bergen the last to lay eyes on her fly-blown remains having been forced there to bear witness by the horrified American troops? Did those German villagers stand staring with sullen stupefaction on that flesh for which every day he had longed and of which every night he had dreamt since he was a boy of twelve?

There was someone working for the Stasi in Berlin who knew the answer. Someone who knew enough about Stone and his love for Dagmar to forge the letter that had purported to be from her.

As Stone studied the glowing end of his cigarette throbbing in the darkness he struggled against the obvious conclusion as to who that person must be.

Trying somehow to avoid the dawning certainty that the dark and solemn oaths which once had bound the brave young members of the Saturday Club together had been broken in the most cruel and terrible manner.

Opening up Shop

Berlin, 1 April 1933

Dagmar Fischer stared at her face in the mirror. Normally she rather enjoyed looking at herself. She was beautiful and she knew it, so why shouldn't she appreciate her own reflection? What was it Otto Stengel had said in that silly note he wrote? Her eyes were like dark and sparkling pools? Or had it been Paulus? They both said such sweet things. But Paulus's notes were usually in French.

And her eyes *were* rather lovely, it would be foolish to deny it. Rather like Norma Shearer's, Dagmar thought, or perhaps Dietrich's, or the English star Mary Astor. They slanted slightly downwards at the edges which gave them, she fancied, an expression of great mystery with perhaps a touch of melancholy too. The eyebrows were all wrong of course, thick schoolgirl eyebrows which she hated but was absolutely forbidden to pluck. She had tried to do it by stealth, taking exactly three a day from above each eye, but it had seemed to make no difference at all, and when out of impatience she upped her daily quota to ten her father was on to it immediately and harangued her over breakfast. He had told the maid to remove the honey from the table and not to return it for a week, which had been mortifying. Not the loss of the honey but the shame of being scolded publicly. In front of the maid.

She turned away from the mirror and considered the dress that had been laid out for her. It was *awful* of course, almost as bad as school uniform, which was the only other option her parents had been prepared to consider.

A sailor dress for heaven's sake! She wasn't a child.

Her figure was developing. She had a bosom.

You couldn't wear a sailor dress with a bosom, it looked ridiculous. And socks! White socks, as if she were starting kindergarten. Dagmar considered a rebellion. After all, this was Father's plan, not hers. She could hold on to the banister and refuse to cooperate.

But of course she couldn't.

Her father was not a man to be disobeyed. He had given his orders and they would be followed to the letter.

'Above all, we must show a brave face,' he had said.

Easy for him, Dagmar thought, he didn't have to face the world dressed as a ten-year-old.

She turned once more to her reflection.

Her face did not *look* very brave.

If only she could have worn a little make-up. Some of her friends at the expensive school she attended had already begun secretly to wear it when they went out. They said it made them feel smart and confident. Dagmar would have liked very much to be feeling smart and confident that morning.

She wondered whether if she sneaked some eye shadow and blusher from her mother's dressing table it might pass unnoticed. Except she knew it wouldn't be. If she applied enough to make her feel smart and confident then it would be enough to make her father call for a flannel and wipe it off in front of the servants.

There was no getting round it. The brave face that she put on would have to be her own, plain and unadorned. She must thrust her chest forward and her shoulders back as Fräulein Schneider her swimming mistress always insisted, and put from her mind the fact that she was dreading what her father expected her to do that morning with all of her heart.

She took up the blue and white sailor dress, put it over her head and pulled it down over her silk slip. Then she sat on the bed, lifted her long elegant legs and reached forward to put on the despised white ankle socks.

Her mother's head appeared around the door.

'Are you ready, dear?' she asked. 'Hurry with your shoes. You know how angry Father is about lateness.'

'I look like a schoolgirl.'

'You *are* a schoolgirl, dear.'

'Why can't we just close for the day like everybody else.'

'Because, dear, we are *not* everybody else. We are the Fischer family. And as such are expected to set an example with our behaviour. With privilege comes responsibility, you must understand that. People expect us to lead by example and we shall not disappoint them. Now hurry up and put on your shoes. No, not the ones with the heels, the flat ones.'

Fischer's department store had been a part of Berlin life for fifty years. It was founded by Dagmar's grandfather who had begun (as most great shopkeepers do) with only a hand barrow. That tiny street business had since grown into one of the great shops of Berlin, patronized by office girls and movie stars alike. It was a symbol of stability, offering quality products at competitive prices through war and peace.

Through prosperity and disaster.

It had never once failed to open for trade.

'And we shall open for trade today,' Herr Fischer had said over breakfast before calmly returning to his newspaper, a newspaper which made grim reading indeed.

It was 1 April 1933 and the previous day it had been announced out of the blue that all Jewish-owned businesses were to be 'voluntarily' boycotted by all 'true' Germans from the following morning and until further notice.

The edict was shockingly comprehensive in its detail. Non-Jewish employees of Jewish-owned businesses were expected to boycott their own places of work while the 'law' insisted that the Jewish owners would be required to pay the absent workers in full for not attending.

That morning all over the country hundreds of thousands of Nazi Party storm troopers with the full backing and cooperation of the police were to turn out to stand 'guard' at the entrance to every Jewish-owned business in the country. This was in order to ensure that the population observed the spontaneous demonstration which their leaders had announced on their behalf. Paint was to be daubed on every window announcing that German citizens were committing a traitorous act if they shopped or did business there. Also to be daubed on walls and windows was the boycott slogan, coined by the notorious Nazi *Gauleiter* Julius Streicher, a man who was now a senior government official but who up until a few weeks before had been known to the authorities as a mentally imbalanced pervert and rapist. What Streicher's slogan lacked in elegance it made up for in brevity.

Death to Jews.

Most of the businesses thus picketed by the all-powerful Brown Army elected simply to close up shop for the time being in the hope that this momentary 'punishment' for their global crimes would pass.

Herr Fischer, however, famous proprietor of Fischer's department store, had other ideas.

'The people of Berlin know our opening hours and they expect us to be open *during* those hours. We will not let them down,' Herr Fischer told his staff on the previous evening (having 'granted' his non-Jewish employees a paid day off). 'The Empress Augusta Viktoria herself visited us only a month before the Kaiser abdicated. She purchased gloves as a present for one of her ladies-in-waiting on the occasion of the girl's engagement. Should her Imperial Highness be visiting from Holland tomorrow and wish to purchase gloves again, she will find us open, eager to serve and offering the most competitively priced and comprehensive selection of ladies' gloves in Berlin. As usual.'

This speech was met with considerable applause and, thus buoyed up with the support of his workers ringing in his ears, Herr Fischer instructed his maintenance department to prepare two signs with which to counter the messages that had already begun to be daubed across the great plate-glass windows of his shop. The first sign was a copy of the store's war memorial, the original of which was mounted beneath the clock in the splendid central gallery of the building. This memorial listed those employees of Fischer's stores who had given their lives for the Fatherland in the Great War, of whom several had been Jews. Fischer ordered that those names were to be underlined and marked with a six-pointed star.

The second sign was a huge banner that was to be hung directly across the grand entrance, announcing that Fischer's welcomed all its many regular and loyal customers, adding that in respect of that loyalty there was to be a 25 per cent discount on all purchases made on the first of April. This sale would last for one day only.

Despite the nightmare situation, Herr Fischer almost chuckled when he announced his plan to his wife that evening. 'Let's see if we can't turn this nonsense into a business opportunity,' he said. 'If I know Berliners the offer of twenty-five pfennigs in the mark off all goods will be too much to resist.'

Fischer's plans for passive resistance, however, were not confined to banners. They included Dagmar, who to her dismay had been called to the drawing room after supper and informed that she would be excused school on the following morning and was to attend the shop instead.

'You and your mother will stand together with me at the doors of our building and we will personally welcome every single customer who graces our premises. The Fischers of Berlin will show these hooligans and the world what a respectable German family looks like.'

Later, before getting ready for bed, Dagmar phoned Paulus and Otto. She had a telephone in her own bedroom (a refinement the Stengel boys found almost bewilderingly grand) and she often chatted to the boys after she had finished with her homework.

Paulus and Otto usually fought over the phone when Dagmar called, sometimes quarrelling so hard about who would speak first that she got bored and hung up. Tonight, however, understanding the seriousness of the situation, the boys didn't fight but clustered together around the receiver trying to offer comfort to their friend.

'It won't be so bad,' Paulus said. 'And a day off school's pretty good news, isn't it?'

'Maybe you'll get something from the cake department for lunch,' Otto added. 'See if you can grab any stales and keep them for us at the weekend.'

It was a very one-sided conversation and after a little while Dagmar said she'd better go because she wasn't supposed to use her bedroom phone after eight o'clock.

She put the little pearly white-handled receiver back into its polished brass cradle and prepared for bed, holding tight to the frayed woollen monkey that she had held tight to every night of her conscious life.

And then it was morning and breakfast which she was allowed to take in her room as a special treat but which she couldn't touch a crumb of, and then the hated sailor dress and the white socks and her mother's insistence on flat shoes. And suddenly it was time to go.

Her parents were waiting for her downstairs in the large entrance hall of their beautiful town house.

Father trying hard to look as if this was a day like any other.

Mother looking noble but nervous.

Dagmar took her hat and coat from the butler and went outside to where the great shiny black Mercedes car was waiting.

'Ten past eight,' her father said to the waiting chauffeur. 'I wish to draw up in front of the store at precisely 8.29 that I may personally open the doors exactly on time.'

'Of course, sir.'

The chauffeur held the door open as the proud, elegant family got into the car. Dagmar first and then Frau Fischer, who paused in front of the impassive, uniformed servant.

'Thank you, Klaus,' she said.

'Ma'am?'

'For working for us today.'

'I am *not* working for you today, madam,' the chauffeur replied. 'As you know, I am instructed by the Leader not to do so. I have already informed Herr Fischer that today's pay must be deducted from my monthly salary.'

'But—' Frau Fischer began.

'I am, however, honoured to *serve* you today,' the chauffeur continued, 'in my own free time and of my own free will.'

There were tears suddenly in Frau Fischer's eyes.

'Thank you very much,' she said, getting in beside Dagmar, who was also struggling not to cry.

Then Herr Fischer joined them and their short journey began.

'Such a lovely day,' Herr Fischer observed. 'Perhaps we might later ride together in the park, dear, if the evening remains clement. The horses will forget who is their master if they only ever exercise with the grooms.'

Frau Fischer attempted a smile in reply but could do no better than that.

Herr Fischer was right, it was a lovely day, one of the first fine mornings of spring and Dagmar found that her spirits, while not exactly rising, at least ceased to plummet as their splendid car purred its way through the expensive district of Charlottenburg-Wilmersdorf. The buds were beginning to show on the great parallel lines of plane trees that graced the grand old Kurfürstendamm as the Fischer family drove along it, and all the splendid shops and cafés so familiar to Dagmar and her rich school friends looked as normal and as exciting as ever.

Except not quite normal. There were exceptions to the familiar atmosphere of bustling well-being. A few of the businesses were closed, their beautiful plate glass, polished wood and brass facings disfigured with dripping paint, and outside their doors were standing young men in brown uniforms clustered around swastika banners.

'Mandelbaum, Rosebaum,' Fischer muttered as he stared out of the window. 'Even Samuel Belzfreund, I thought he'd have more nerve the way he struts about and throws his weight at the Chamber of Commerce, but every one of them has stayed at home.'

'Perhaps we too should rethink this, darling,' Frau Fischer said gently, 'if everyone else has—'

'As I have already explained, we are not *everyone else*. We are the Fischers, of Fischer's of Berlin,' was all her husband would say, grim-faced and tight-lipped.

'Don't you know, Mother,' Dagmar said, trying so hard to sound cheerful, 'the empress might come from exile in Holland requiring gloves for her ladies-in-waiting.'

'Exactly,' said Herr Fischer. 'Imagine if the empress found us closed.'

And for the first time that morning all three of them managed to smile at once.

Then suddenly the time had come. The limousine was drawing up alongside the famous Fischer's department store on the Kurfürstendamm, a shop often compared with Harrods of Knightsbridge or Macy's of Manhattan. Not this morning, however. This morning Fischer's store bore no resemblance to those other splendid emporiums. This morning Fischer's was on its own, in the middle of a unique and terrible nightmare.

Dagmar gasped in horror as she saw that every single one of the splendid plate-glass windows which she had always so adored with their ever-changing tableaux of fashion and luxury had been daubed and disfigured. Stars of David, crude insults and everywhere Streicher's leaden, doltish, spite-ridden slogan for the day: *Death to Jews*.

There were also at least twenty SA men gathered beneath the coloured-glass canopy which stretched out over the pavement from the shop's entrance. They were clearly surprised to see the great Mercedes pulling up directly in front of them. Some even gave the German salute, obviously under the impression that this must be some Nazi bigwig come down to check on the progress of the day's 'action'.

This impression remained for a moment longer as the uniformed chauffeur got out of the car and, without a glance at the arrogant brown figures, opened the passenger door. Many arms were raised in anticipation of who might get out, only to be dropped again in angry astonishment as the family Fischer, recognizable from numerous slanderous articles in the Nazi press, emerged from the car. Herr Fischer was first, and stepping out behind him Dagmar could see that beyond the SA men the shop staff were already in the shop, looking out through the big central doors in terror. Doors that had been barricaded from without with rubbish bins. There were, as far as she could see, no customers attempting to get in.

There was certainly no sign of the ex-Empress Augusta Viktoria.

'Good morning,' she heard her father saying, 'my name is Isaac Fischer and this is my shop. Where is my banner?'

Now Dagmar noticed that there was no sign advertising discounts hung above the door as Herr Fischer had promised there would be. Nor was there a large and prominent memorial to the war dead.

'What have you done with my banner, please?' Fischer asked again.

The Brownshirts began to snigger, one or two of them mimicking Herr Fischer's cultured accent: *What have you done with my banner, please?* Others were glancing down gleefully at the pavement. Dagmar saw why they were laughing: at their feet was a great quantity of rope and painted cloth. Her father's proud banners, a war memorial and the notice of a discount sale, torn and shredded amongst the rough hobnailed boots.

'Oh,' said one of the thugs, a man who by the badges on his sleeve affected the rank of some kind of sergeant, a *Truppführer*, as the Nazis styled it. 'So this is *your* banner, is it? Well, I must say, that's very unfortunate.'

'Stand out of my way,' Fischer demanded, 'all of you. I wish to open my store.'

'Stand out of your way?' the *Truppführer* roared in sudden, spitting fury. '*Stand out of your fucking way! Who the FUCK do you think you are, you Jew cunt!*'

Fischer stepped backwards as if he had been struck. Dagmar reached out for her mother, who was shaking violently.

To be spoken to in such a manner.

On the *Kurfürstendamm* – outside their own shop.

It was impossible. Unheard of. It could not be happening.

But it was.

The Fischer family of Fischer's department store of Berlin were discovering that not one single rule of civilization applied to them any more. Their wealth, their accomplishments, their cultured and educated ways counted for nothing. They were without rights and utterly defenceless.

The lead SA man spoke again, or screamed, in fact, in fair imitation of his leader.

'How *dare* you give orders to a *Truppführer* of the *Sturmabteilung*! You fucking rodent! You fucking *germ*. How about this, Jew boy! How about some of *this*!'

And with that, the young man, who was no more than twenty-two or twenty-three years of age, took a step forward and knocked Isaac Fischer, a slight man in his late forties, to the ground. In a single moment he had taken a knuckle-duster from his pocket, slipped it into his clenched fist and slammed it into the side of Fischer's head, collapsing him, semi-concussed, to the floor. Then the *Truppführer* kicked him, burying his great jack-boots into Fischer's prostrate and undefended body several times.

It was all so sudden, so utterly out of proportion.

Such violence. From *nowhere*, for *nothing*. In *seconds*.

For a moment Dagmar and her mother stood motionless, their reluctant minds struggling to catch up with the evidence of their eyes and ears. Then with guttural screams they both stepped towards the fallen head of their family, the husband, the father. The protector. The man on whom they relied utterly and who they trusted without question.

But they could offer him no comfort or support. Before they could help him they were seized and pulled roughly away by other members of the brown troop. The chauffeur had also leapt in, perhaps hoping to get Herr Fischer back into the car, but he too was grabbed and blows were raining down on him.

As Dagmar struggled in the arms of the laughing SA men, feeling their hands upon her, pulling, it seemed to her, at her coat, their hands everywhere, she saw that across the traffic, in the middle of the wide boulevard, on the central reservation, beneath the row of plane trees, two policemen had stopped to watch. For a moment she imagined that their ordeal was over. She knew the Berlin Police, Paulus and Otto's grandfather was one. Her father made regular contributions to their benevolent fund. They had kept the peace in Berlin through all the violent years without fear or favour. Surely they must keep the peace now.

'Are they Jews?' one of the officers shouted.

'Yes,' a trooper replied. 'Dirty Jews who thought they could order National Socialist comrades around.'

At this the policeman smiled and waved. He and his colleague watched for a moment or two more and then moved on.

Now the SA attackers dragged Fischer to his feet.

The chauffeur they dismissed with a few further kicks but they had not yet finished with the Fischer family.

'So now,' the *Truppführer* snarled into Fischer's face, on the right cheek of which a great swelling was rising. 'Let's start again, shall we? You say that this is your banner, is that right, Mr Yid?'

The scene spun and rocked before Dagmar's eyes. Her ears were ringing, an orchestra seemed to be playing inside her head, an orchestra whose instruments were broken glass and blaring horns, harsh cries and the crunch of steel on stone. She saw a hand thrust forward at her father's chest. She saw him fall to the pavement for a second time. Then she felt a blow herself, a violent shove in the small of the back, her knees buckling, and then she also was on the pavement, her mother beside her, sprawling amongst the black and the brown boots.

'If it's your banner, *cunt*, then you and your bitches need to clean it up,' she heard the troop leader saying through the strange cacophony that was pounding in her head. 'It's littering the street, if you hadn't noticed.'

Had he said it?

Was it real?

In that moment Dagmar truly felt she had gone mad. She was on the *pavement* on the Kurfürstendamm outside her father's store. That great castle of commerce of which *she* was the princess. Not *standing* on the pavement, but *sprawled on it*. The breath knocked from her body. Her beloved parents, those symbols of strength and authority to whom she had always looked for comfort and *certainty*, were helpless on their knees beside her. Her father's face swollen and bruised. His blood was on the stones.

On the Kurfürstendamm.

Minutes earlier, not even as many as three, they had all been driving together in the family Mercedes. In *one* of the family Mercedes. These were the stones across which she had stepped a thousand times. Alone. With her friends. With her parents. Occasionally (and discreetly) with Paulus and Otto, who simply could not believe it when she had been saluted at the door by a smiling doorman.

This was her kingdom. It had been so only yesterday.

'You're not cleaning up your dad's banner, Fräulein Fischer,' a voice called out, half shout, half sneer. 'Maybe we should teach you some respect for a German pavement.'

Mechanically Dagmar began to reach out and collect a piece or two of the torn and shredded banners.

She heard a cry beside her. It was her mother, who, having collected a number of scraps, had then had them kicked from her hand.

'I thought you were told to pick up your rubbish,' a brown-shirted thug shouted at her. '*Pick it fucking up, Jew bitch.*'

They were speaking to her *mother*.

In Berlin.

On the Kurfürstendamm.

Dagmar looked up. She could see that beyond the circle of SA men people were hurrying by. Heads down, faces turned away, seeing no evil. Others stopped, not many but enough, and they had smiles on their faces, one or two held small children up to watch as they shouted encouragement to the troopers.

Make them pay.

Make them crawl.

Make those rich fat Jew bastards pay for what they've done to us.

What they've done? What *had* she done?

Dagmar felt that she would faint. She *wished* that she would faint.

Die, in fact, that would be a relief.

But she did not faint or die. She remained stubbornly conscious of the fact that she was on her hands and knees, head bowed searching for scraps to pick up. Praying that they would not crush her fingers on the pavement with their boots.

A voice rose above the general hubbub.

It was a passer-by, one of those who had stopped to gloat. A woman, quite smartly dressed.

'Make them lick it,' she shouted. 'Make them lick the pavement.'

And the Nazi young men thought that was a wonderful idea. They must have wondered how it had not occurred to them before.

And so, under threat of further blows, the Fischer family, mother, father and daughter, bowed their heads to the flagstones and putting out their tongues began to lick.

Laughter mingled now with the jeers. Horrible, triumphant, mocking laughter. Somebody tried to start a song, the *Horst Wessel Lied*, of course, ubiquitous marching anthem of the SA. It was inevitable. Did they only know one song?

But the singing did not catch on this time. People were having too much fun to bother singing.

Suddenly Dagmar could bear it no longer. She leapt to her feet, blind with tears, screaming at the top of her voice, and began to run. To her surprise the storm troopers didn't stop her, perhaps her revolt had been so sudden and her condition so hysterical that they were taken by surprise.

The crowd parted too. She was not yet fourteen, a girl in a sailor dress, wild with terror, possibly they felt pity for her. Possibly they did not wish to be infected by the progeny of subhumans. Either way, she found herself suddenly outside the crowd and running along the wide pavement past the great display windows of the store.

She could hear the sound of her shoes on the pavement. They were beautiful shoes of shiny patent leather.

It was lucky her mother had made her wear flatties. She could never have run so fast in the heels she had begged to wear.

The store was huge. It spanned a whole block along the

Ku'damm and stretched back nearly a block behind. It had many entrances, all of which were picketed by SA men.

She was running blindly. Looking down at her shoes, focusing on the black shining uppers as they rose and fell, disappearing under the hem of her dress and then re-emerging.

Had she not been stopped she would undoubtedly have careered into something or somebody or run off the kerb into traffic. But instead brown-shirted arms reached out, gathering her up as once more Dagmar found herself in the clutches of her mortal enemies.

'Not so fast, little miss,' a rough voice said. 'We saw you run. Aren't you supposed to be helping Daddy clean the street?'

'Please,' Dagmar whispered, 'please.'

But the man did not reply.

Because suddenly and without warning she was back on the ground.

How had it happened?

At first she thought her SA tormentor had pushed her.

But he was on the ground too. Lying beside her, gasping for breath.

Gasping beneath the weight of a boy.

It was Otto Stengel.

The moment that the Stengel twins had put down the phone to Dagmar on the previous evening they had known that she wanted their support. A member of the Saturday Club had been reaching out to them and it was their duty to go to her. Although of course in truth their decision had nothing to do with those solemn weekend oaths of solidarity taken after their music lessons when they were little kids. Dagmar was an obsession for them both, an object of both reverence and desire. They certainly were not going to pass up this excellent and legitimate excuse to seek her out and perhaps do her service.

Therefore, on the following morning, the moment that they had left the Stengel apartment, ostensibly to go to school, Paulus and Otto rushed to the *U-Bahn* and jumped on a train to Bahnhof Zoo. From there they ran the rest of the way and emerged on to the Ku'damm just in time to see what was happening at the entrance to the department store. And Dagmar forcing her way through the crowd that had gathered to watch.

Instantly the twins gave chase, skirting the terrible scene where Herr and Frau Fischer were still on their knees, their heads to the pavement, and charging along after Dagmar, catching up with her just as the SA man took hold of her.

Otto, who always acted on instinct, simply launched himself at Dagmar's attacker, hurling his body against the man at a full run, cannoning into him with all the force that a muscular thirteen-year-old boy travelling at speed could deliver. All three of them, Otto, Dagmar and the SA man, hit the pavement together. Otto on top of the large, pot-bellied, heavily winded thug, and Dagmar sprawling beside them both, her legs in the air and her pretty sailor dress torn and spoiled.

Paulus, who always acted on intellect, had been a step or two behind in the chase. As he brought himself to a skidding halt, barely avoiding tripping over the prostrate threesome, he knew he had perhaps a second and a half at most to consider his plan. After that there could be no doubt that the other Brownshirts would overcome their surprise, pull Otto off their comrade and beat him, very possibly to death.

The trick must be, Paulus thought, in the flash of time available to him, to get his story in first.

'Bastard!' he shouted, reaching down and hauling his brother to his feet and putting him into a vicious neck lock. 'Got you now, haven't I? You're mine!'

Then with the arm that was not around his brother's neck he delivered a rabbit punch to the side of Otto's head (with what, Otto was later to complain, was unnecessary force).

Paulus then looked up at the Brownshirts who surrounded him.

'Jews! Jews!' he shouted in affected semi-panic. 'Dirty Jews! A pack of them! With a German girl! Round the corner! They have her, it's revenge! They're pulling off her clothes! Please. I've got this guy, I won't let him get away, run! You have to help.'

Young though he was and with almost no time in which to

think, Paulus had made his pitch brilliantly, appealing to the very heart and soul of the Nazis' pathological anti-Semitism. That most favourite and well-rehearsed part. The crude and salacious sexual fantasies that made up the majority of the accusations peddled against Jews in *Der Stürmer* and other Nazi papers.

The men didn't hesitate. The prospect of being able to intervene violently in a pack rape appealed to so many of their natural instincts and secret fantasies at once that they clattered off immediately in the direction in which Paulus was pointing. This left just their winded comrade who was now beginning to pull himself together, sitting up on the pavement, chin on chest, catching his breath.

This man, Paulus realized, would be highly unlikely to give up his opportunity to avenge himself on Otto, even for the opportunity of seeing a girl having her clothes torn off by Jews. Besides which, it would only be moments before the other Brownshirts reached the corner and realized that they had been tricked. Again Paulus had less than seconds in which to consider his next move and again he was able to find the most promising point of psychological weakness in his still groggy opponent.

'I'll get these two across the street!' Paulus shouted urgently, dragging a dazed Dagmar to her feet with his free arm. 'My father is a *Hauptsturmführer*. He is collecting prisoners. He will be very pleased you stopped this swine. I'll send him over to speak to you personally.'

As a sentence it did not make a lot of sense but what it did do was invoke authority. And if there was one thing that Paulus knew Nazis liked, it was to be told what to do. Nothing seemed to make them more comfortable than following a leader, and if there was a *Hauptsturmführer* in the vicinity then his will must of course be obeyed.

Paulus did not hang around to find out how long it would take the trooper to ask himself why a thirteen-year-old boy who was not even in a Hitler Youth uniform would be running around the streets collecting prisoners for a *Hauptsturmführer* SA. Instead he dragged his brother and Dagmar off the kerb and into the road, oblivious to the beeping horns and screeching tyres as he headed for the central reservation where the trams ran constantly up and down the street.

The folding middle doors of an east-bound carriage were just closing as Paulus reached it, but (much to the annoyance of the passengers already on board) he was able to get an arm in and force the doors wide again.

Once they were seated on the tram, Otto took his chance to protest.

'Shit, Pauly, you didn't have to whack me in the side of the head!'

'Never mind that, you arsehole,' Paulus replied. 'Are you OK, Dag? What happened?'

But for the time being at least Dagmar was incapable of speech. She simply stared ahead of her, unable even to cry. Simply trying to breathe.

The Banks of the Red Sea

Berlin, 1 April 1933

'Everyone is looking for Moses.'

Frieda smiled as she said it. She felt she had to smile.

The horror and the shock on the faces that surrounded her was so absolute that some show of spirit seemed to her essential. For if Frieda Stengel knew nothing else on that dreadful day, that awful, ill-starred day when the Nazis began truly to show their hand, truly began to give some glimpse of the limitless darkness into which they would be prepared to take their crazed philosophy, she knew that from that point on in all their lives, spirit would be the only thing that could possibly sustain them.

If they were to be sustained at all.

She looked around at the faces assembled in her living room.

Faces that had only recently been familiar but which seemed now to stare back at her as if belonging to new and different people. Blank, bewildered people, lost and helpless. Babies, it seemed to Frieda, born that very morning, ejected screaming from the warmth and comfort of the womb of their previous lives to find themselves blinking and struggling for breath in the harsh and unforgiving glare of a totally alien and entirely brutal new world.

New and different people. Quite literally.

Previously respectable citizens of the German Republic. Parents, workers, taxpayers, war veterans. Human beings.

Now *Untermensch*. Subhumans. Despised outcasts. *Officially* despised. *Legally* outcast. Barred from their businesses. Ejected from their work. Beaten and bewildered, they had come to her, to Frieda Stengel. The good doctor.

Fear twitching in their nostrils. Standing red wet in their eyes.

Wringing, pulling and twisting at their fingers until the knuckles turned white with the effort of self-control.

Katz the Chemist, with his wife and grown-up daughter. The Loebs, who ran the little tobacco and newspaper kiosk at the steps to the *U-Bahn*. Morgenstern the book dealer. Schmulewitz, a broker of insurance. The Leibovitzes, who owned the little restaurant on Grünberger Strasse. A garbage man. An employee of the wire factory. A brewer's assistant. Two men currently looking for work. Wives. One or two children too scared to go to school.

The Jews of Friedrichshain.

Citizens yesterday. Today just Jews.

They had gravitated to the Stengels' apartment in search of some comfort, some meaning. Frieda was a community lynchpin. Loved for her kindness, respected for her intelligence and her tireless energy. Perhaps she would have an answer. Some crumb of comfort to offer, some semblance of an explanation. After all, the good *Frau Doktor* had always had answers in the past.

But Frieda had no answers this time.

For there were none.

All she could do was smile and find herself, to her surprise, taking refuge in imagery from legends in which she neither believed nor had a spiritual interest and yet which were without doubt appropriate.

'I guess the poor old tribe is on the move again,' she said, trying to impose some brightness on her tone. 'We're standing on the shores of the Red Sea, chucked out of Egypt for the umpteenth time. Hitler's just another pharaoh, isn't he, really? The question is how to save our skins this time? *Everybody is looking for Moses.*'

But no one knew of a Moses at that point and so, with nowhere to go on a day when their own streets were occupied by the Brown Army, they sat. Strange and stilted. Counting the seconds that led to nowhere.

Coffee was served, there were various cakes and small treats which people had brought. Sweet pretzels, *Butterstollen*, *Streuselkuchen*. More coffee.

Wolfgang played a little quiet piano. Nothing too mournful, gentle show-tunes mostly.

'This is rather like how I imagine it was in the last hour on the *Titanic*,' he said. 'Always admired the boys in that band. Never thought I'd be a member myself.'

Frau Katz began to cry at this.

'Wolfgang, please,' Frieda admonished.

Wolfgang apologized and returned to his playing.

Occasionally there were exclamations of anger and frustration.

They pushed me.

They spat at me.

Frau So-and-So said nothing.

Herr So-and-So turned away.

I've known them years. I gave them credit after the crash. They did nothing when those thugs broke my window. When they shoved the dog's mess through. Nothing.

But for the most part they made polite conversation. Papering over the chasmic, vault-like, hellish darkness lying just below the surface of every word they spoke.

How are your children?

Is Frau So-and-So recovered from her flu?

Hasn't the blossom come early in the Tiergarten this year?

While all the time the strained voices and nervous rattle of Frieda's best china coffee cups screamed WHY? WHY! WHY!

Why us?

And, of course, what next?

Once or twice, non-Jewish friends did drop by to show their support. The chairman of the housing collective. The man who swept the street and who every morning for ten years had stood by his dusty hand barrow as Frieda emerged from her building, leant on his broom and told her how lovely she looked. Wolfgang had always thought this was a bit creepy but he was grateful to the man now.

'And you look lovely today, *Frau Doktor*,' the man said, standing shyly in the doorway, holding his cap and staring at his feet. He had brought flowers which he left on the little table by the door as he hurried away.

Doctor Schwarzschild, a colleague of Frieda's from the surgery, came in his lunch break. He explained that they had thought about closing the medical centre in solidarity but had decided it would be a counterproductive gesture. Frieda agreed.

'People still need doctors,' she said.

'Just be sure to treat the Jews too, eh?' Wolfgang added.

Schwarzschild looked confused. 'Of course,' he stammered. 'How could you think otherwise, Wolfgang?'

'Oh I don't know, mate,' Wolfgang replied with a hint of angry sarcasm. 'Can't imagine.'

'Stop it, Wolf,' Frieda said for the second time. 'It isn't Rudi's fault.'

'Whose fault is it then?' Wolfgang asked.

Already a gap was opening up.

And the gap was wide. As wide as that universe that lies between life and death.

And those on the death side, those who now knew themselves to be Jews, could not help but be bitter, angry and resentful of the status of those on the life side. Those people now called Aryans. And since no Nazi or even silent fellow traveller would speak to them or look them in the eye, they found themselves taking out their feelings on the only 'Aryans' who would still acknowledge them, their remaining non-Jewish friends.

So this is what your Mr Hitler thinks, is it?

What will your people decide to do to us next?

Do you really believe we have stolen your homes and jobs?

Schwarzschild did not stay long. He had patients to see, Frieda's as well as his own. Patients about whom Frieda was already worrying, feeling guilty, despite herself, that she was suddenly absent from their care. A hundred half-finished stories sprang suddenly to her mind as she showed Schwarzschild to the door.

'I'm concerned about Frau Oppenheim's boil. I lanced it but it isn't healing properly and I suspect she's not cleaning the wound as I instructed. The little Rosenberg boy is still not walking after his accident and it's because he is not doing his physiotherapy, you must be very firm with his parents . . . I will write notes for them all. Can you bring me my files? I'm sure that is still allowed. We can go through them. You know that I'm fearful old Bloch might be turning diabetic; you must test his blood sugar.'

Perhaps it helped her. Taking refuge in the responsibilities of a life that was over. Trying vicariously to impose her attentions on people who were now obliged by government decree to shun them.

Wolfgang had watched her from his place at the piano.

'Why do you still care about those people, Frieda?' he asked. 'Do they care about you?'

'Wolf, I'm a doctor. I do not require my commitment to be reciprocal.'

Wolfgang smiled, a smile and a shrug.

'OK,' he said, 'fair enough. You're a better person than any of them but we didn't need the bloody Nazi Party to know that. I, however, am not and if it was up to me I'd say let them rot.'

In defiance or frustration he began to play some Kurt Weill, *The Ballad of Pirate Jenny*.

'Wolfgang! Please!' Frieda said.

He looked up. There was fear on every face.

'Oh sorry,' he said bitterly. 'Not happy with Jew music?'

'Come on, Wolf,' Frieda said. 'The walls aren't thick and there's no point provoking them.'

'That's what I thought too,' Wolfgang said. 'But now I wonder whether it makes any difference.'

'If we provoke them they'll kill us,' Herr Loeb the tobacconist said. 'We are few and they are many.'

'They won't kill us!' Frau Leibovitz almost pleaded. 'This is Germany, it's an aberration, it must be. It *must* be an aberration.'

Some others agreed. This could *not* be real. It was simply unimaginable that the National Socialist Government intended to keep this onslaught up.

Again, the formal description. The *National Socialist Government*. As if somehow, using the Nazi Party's full name, treating them with formality and politeness, might cause the Nazis to somehow reciprocate.

Other voices took a grimmer view.

'My son thinks they will keep it up till we are all dead,' the bookseller Morgenstern observed. 'He is leaving. He and his fiancée. He has a friend in Zurich who will put them up for a while.'

'But what will he do? How will he work? Has he a Swiss work permit?' came the enquiries.

Morgenstern admitted that his son did not.

'But he's leaving anyway. He will go on a holiday and then refuse to leave; he says they can shoot him if they wish. His girl agrees. They intend to go within a week.'

This news of course depressed the little gathering further.

Clinging to hope as they were it was terrible to realize that some people had already forsaken it. But everyone knew someone who had already decided the situation was now impossible. The young in particular, those who had least to leave behind, were all making plans to go.

Then the Hirsches, a retired couple from two floors down,

arrived with the first edition of the afternoon newspaper. Amongst the crowing lead story reporting the 'success' of the 'spontaneous' boycott was another headline:

'Exit Visas Introduced'.

Anybody who wanted to leave Germany had first to get police permission to do so. It was stated that Jews in particular were not simply to be allowed to wander around hostile foreign countries spreading their lies. If they wanted to get out they would have to beg and only then would the authorities take a view.

'They want to trap us,' Wolfgang observed and defiantly banged out a few chords of *Mack the Knife*.

Morgenstern asked if he could use the telephone to discuss the news with his son.

Frieda's parents arrived.

It almost broke Frieda's heart to see the old man's face, a combination of suppressed fury and utter confusion that she'd never seen in him before. Only weeks earlier Captain Konstantin Tauber had been an important senior officer in the Berlin Police. He was a decorated war veteran. A deeply conservative German patriot and champion of the rule of law.

Now he was a non-person. Without status, without a job and without rights.

'The *Sturmabteilung* came to our station yesterday afternoon,' Tauber explained.

Again, the refuge in formality. *The Sturmabteilung*.

The National Socialist Government.

Herr Hitler.

As if somehow they were dealing with something recognizable and relatable to their previous experience of the world. And not an entirely new, completely alien force, more brutal and more primevally cruel and ignorant than anything they could possibly contain within their understanding.

'Simply marched in,' Herr Tauber went on. 'They have been coming and going as they pleased since Herr Hitler became Chancellor but yesterday they came for me. It's only *weeks* since I was arresting these actual same men for violent disturbances.

For intimidation. For all sorts of squalid thuggery. Throwing them into the cells night after night. Now they are in charge! They wanted my desk! They took my cap, my side arm. They told me I was not a good enough German to be a policeman. I was a good enough German to be gassed at Verdun, was I not? To sit for three years in a hole in the ground for the Kaiser?'

Herr Tauber lapsed into silence, accepted a cup of coffee and held his wife's hand.

'We came over because we read about the decree regarding Jewish doctors,' Frau Tauber explained. 'It's a terrible thing. To stop you caring for your patients.'

'From two respected professional people in the family to none,' Captain Tauber growled.

'Come off it, Pa,' Frieda said. 'You never even wanted me to be a doctor.'

'That was a long time ago. I changed my view. I've been very proud of you. Did I never say?'

'As a matter of fact, no you didn't.'

Wolfgang broke the silence that followed this.

'Cheer up, Pop. You've still got a musician in the family.'

Tauber merely glared.

Morgenstern, who had been on the phone to his son, approached Herr Tauber to ask a favour.

'Excuse me, *Herr Kapitän*,' he said, 'but perhaps you still have friends and colleagues at your old station.'

'Fewer than I might have hoped,' Tauber said.

'This business of exit visas, the announcement was only made today. I cannot imagine they could implement it at once.'

'No, they are not supermen, whatever they might say. Even in these extraordinary times, if they want the border to function as a border they cannot just "will" it, they must have due process.'

'Would you be kind enough, *Herr Kapitän*, to be so good as to make an enquiry to find out when these exit visas will be required from?'

'I'll try,' Tauber replied. 'And it's just "mister" now, I'm not a captain any more.'

Tauber got up, crossed the blue rug and went out into the hallway to the telephone. Frieda watched as he went. His gait stooped at first, the walk of an old and defeated man. After a few steps, though, he seemed to realize it and straightened himself up. Putting back his shoulders and holding his head a little higher.

That's right, Frieda thought. We must all keep trying to walk upright. It was what Wolfgang told the boys. If you want to feel tall, you have to walk tall.

The phone rang as Herr Tauber reached for it.

'Stengel residence,' he said. 'Tauber speaking.'

After a moment he turned back into the room.

'It is Herr Fischer,' he said, 'of Fischer's department store. He is enquiring after his daughter Dagmar.'

A Quiet Day at the Store

Berlin, 1933

After their daughter's flight from the front of the department store, Herr and Frau Fischer were forced by the SA gang to remain on their knees on the pavement for some ten minutes longer.

Collecting torn shreds of Herr Fischer's vandalized 'discount' banner and licking the paving stones until both of them thought they would choke to death.

'Some water please,' Frau Fischer croaked, looking upwards at the boys standing over her, who were young enough to have been her sons.

'What was that, old sow?' one laughed. 'Can't you speak German? I can't understand you.'

Frau Fischer's tongue was swollen up and her mouth was filled with grit and dust. She struggled once more to speak.

'Water, please, for pity's sake.'

But there was no pity to be had. Her tormentors would have argued that it was not that they lacked heart or conscience, but simply that Jews did not deserve pity. Their crimes were too terrible and their natures too sly. Heartless cruelty towards such *Untermenschen* was the stern duty of a German patriot.

Only that week in an editorial in the *Völkischer Beobachter* Herr Goebbels had warned *specifically* against the temptation to show pity, reminding decent Germans that such weakness was in fact not just weak foolishness, but treason. The Minister of Propaganda pointed out that the cousins of the poor old Jew granny appealing for help in Berlin were sitting in Washington and Moscow, rubbing their hands together with glee and plotting the annihilation of European civilization.

Therefore Frau Fischer simply could not be shown pity for fear of the global threat her blood posed for Germany.

Which was fortunate for the young men towering over her, because there could be no doubt that tormenting helpless creatures was also the best fun.

It was not pity that brought the Fischers' ordeal to an end but pragmatism. Word of the scene taking place outside the famous department store had spread to the offices on the Wilhelmstrasse, where there were those who understood that such incidents would not look well abroad. And for the time being at least the new German Government, anxious for its voice to be heard in the world, still considered that to be an issue.

As Frau Fischer was begging for water, a second Mercedes pulled up.

Roaring to a halt behind the splendid empty vehicle that had delivered the proud Fischer family to their fate.

From this second car stepped a man in a gabardine coat and wearing a homburg hat, the inevitable 'tough guy' look favoured by the Prussian Political and Intelligence Police, who were shortly to be renamed the *Geheime Staatspolizei* or Gestapo. This gangster-like policeman was followed by another, less stern-looking individual in a lounge suit.

'You!' the Gestapo man shouted, flashing his police identification at the SA troop leader.

'*Heil Hitler!*' the SA man shouted back, springing to attention and delivering his stiff-armed salute all at the same time.

'This necessary action is over. Get these two to their feet.'

The SA man looked a little put out at having his sport curtailed. The official police and the SS to whom they were now attached were much resented by the rank and file of the SA, who considered themselves to be the true inheritors of the Nazi revolution. But orders were orders and that was something that could never be ignored. The troop leader therefore swallowed his disappointment and shouted at his men to pull the Fischers to their feet.

'That man with the camera,' the Gestapo officer snapped, 'bring him to me.'

A man in the crowd who had been taking photographs saw himself pointed out and turned on his heel. He was clearly hoping to be able to get away but wisely chose to stop when ordered to and waited while two troopers pushed their way through the crowd in order to escort him back.

Meanwhile Herr Fischer had shaken himself free from the SA men and now approached the Gestapo officer. Despite his ordeal, the bruising on his face and the disarray of his clothing, Isaac Fischer still managed to carry himself with some dignity.

'My name . . .' he said, speaking with great difficulty. His lips were bleeding, his tongue dry and swollen, and like his wife he was in desperate need of water. 'My name,' he repeated, 'is Isaac Fischer.'

'I know who you are,' the Gestapo officer replied curtly. 'Why are you addressing me?'

Herr Fischer was forced to cough and clear his throat several times before attempting another sentence. A function which provoked a look of utter offence and contempt from the policeman.

'Because,' Herr Fischer began, his voice like sandpaper on stone, 'because you clearly have some authority and I wish to make a complaint.'

There was something of a gasp amongst the crowd. Some

surprised at the man's bravery, others shocked at his effrontery. This was followed by much angry murmuring as word of the Jew's whining spread.

'A complaint?' the officer enquired coldly. 'What have you to complain about?'

Fischer's eyes widened. It was a shock. Even in his dazed and battered state he had not expected quite such brutal indifference to his obvious plight. And to that of his wife, a middle-aged woman publicly assaulted by a large gang of young men.

What had he to complain about? He attempted to gather his thoughts to frame an answer to such a question.

Only *eight weeks* before, the thugs standing behind him would be facing years in prison for what they had done.

'I have been prevented,' he said finally, 'from entering my store by these men.'

'One moment.' The Gestapo man turned to the photographer whom the SA troopers had brought from the crowd.

'But—' Fischer found himself protesting.

'You will address me when I give you permission and not otherwise!' the Gestapo officer snapped, his rising tone giving warning that despite his pretence at formality he was every bit as unpredictable and as dangerous as Fischer's previous thug tormentors.

Fischer fell silent.

'Who are you please?' the officer asked the man with the camera.

'I am an American citizen,' the photographer replied in poor German. 'I am an American citizen, I work for Reuters and these men have no right to be holding on to me.'

'The camera please,' the Gestapo officer demanded, holding out a black gloved hand.

'Absolutely not! I am an accredited news photog—'

At a nod from the Gestapo, one of the SA troopers snatched the man's camera, which had been hanging around his neck on a leather strap, and handed it over to the officer.

'That camera is the property of . . .' the American protested, but then did not bother to complete his sentence, there being no point because even as he spoke the Gestapo officer took the film from the camera and exposed every frame of it. He then returned both the camera and the ruined film to their owner.

'And here is your property returned to you. Everything is in order, is it not?' the officer said. 'My colleague from the Ministry of Enlightenment and Propaganda will be happy to answer any further questions you might have regarding the necessary police action you have just witnessed.'

The American was led protesting from the scene, the civilian who had arrived in the same car as the Gestapo man following him, already firing off a series of rapid excuses and qualifications.

'Jewish provocation,' the man from the Propaganda Ministry could be heard saying. 'An essential containment action in order to maintain public order . . . Jews required to clean up results of their own vandalism.'

The Gestapo officer turned back to the Fischers.

'So, you will now get inside your shop,' he said.

'Sir,' Herr Fischer began, 'you are clearly a policeman. These troopers have acted illegally. The boycott is voluntary . . .'

'Herr Fischer.' The Gestapo man spoke quietly now. Leaning forward, bringing his face quite close to Fischer's, conveying more menace than ever mere shouting would have done. 'You have been given an order by an officer of the Prussian Political Police. I suggest you follow it immediately. Otherwise I will have you arrested for a breach of public order and, believe me, you do not wish these men to take you into their custody. Now, Jew, take your Jew wife and get inside your Jew shop.'

Frau Fischer tugged gently at her husband's arm.

'Come, Isaac,' she croaked, 'please, they are releasing us. And I must have water.'

Herr Fischer made a small bow, then taking his wife's hand turned away from his tormentor. With stumbling step and aching knees weakened by their ordeal on the pavement, they made their way towards the multiple glass-front doors of their store.

It was 9.05.

Thirty-five minutes late.

Thirty-five minutes later than the Fischer department store had ever been opened in all its history.

The doors swung open as the Fischers approached them.

Shocked, white faces awaited them, cowering behind the glass. Such familiar faces, made strange with fear.

The doorman.

A store detective.

The senior under-manager, due to retire in only two weeks' time after forty years of service. His gift was already at the engraver's.

All the Jewish members of the Fischer's staff were there. Making do to cover the numerous tills, waiting behind their counters, as they had all been waiting since 8.15 that morning, in theoretical anticipation of a visit from the Empress Augusta Viktoria.

Lovely young people. Fine, upstanding young people. Smartly turned out in their matching outfits. The girls with little caps that Frau Fischer had designed herself.

But no customers. A ghost shop. Silent during business hours for the first time in its history.

The beautiful, sparkling, tastefully sumptuous store was like a film set just before the extras were ordered to their places. As if some unseen director was about to shout 'action' and flood the aisles and counters with hundreds of eager shoppers.

Herr Fischer attempted to smile and even found his voice, or at least a croaking semblance of it.

'Thank you all for coming,' he said. 'I hope that you will stay at your positions in expectation of later trade.'

Then, still holding his wife's hand, he began to make his way across the floor.

Some of the girls gave way to tears as the injured couple passed. The young men too looked shaken and close to breaking. The Fischers seemed to notice this and attempted to hold their heads up a little, giving a small nod or the hint of a smile to various of the longer-serving employees.

On they walked through the tension and the silence. Their footsteps ringing on the polished marble floor. The sole sound in that great and splendid room.

Past porcelain and china. Perfumery.

Cosmetics. Small leather goods. Luggage. Stationery. Sticks, canes and umbrellas.

Through the glass central arcade where stood the food hall and restaurant. The very *Konditorei* from which Dagmar had chosen her chocolate cake to take to the Stengels, seven years before, and again just weeks ago on their birthday.

Past the famous escalators. Those mighty moving stairways which all Berlin had marvelled at and admired when the old Herr Fischer had installed them. Which Crown Prince Willy himself had opened and which every day since had thronged with shoppers, but which were empty now.

Empty but running.

Making their rumbling, vacant progress, up and down, up and down from 8.30 till 6.00, with only ghosts to ride them.

Finally Herr and Frau Fischer arrived at the elevators in the far wall of the building.

Herr Fischer turned to his wife, addressing her for the first time since they had been assaulted. 'We must go to the office and begin telephoning, my dear. We must find Dagmar.'

'Begging your pardon, Herr Fischer,' the under-manager interjected softly, 'but Fräulein Fischer was seen by the staff members who were assembled at the south doors. She'd been running from the disgraceful scene at the main entrance when she once more found herself in the grip of those villains. However, it seems that two boys got her away. Only young lads but somehow they were able to extricate the Fräulein from the *Sturmabteilung* and get her on to an east-bound street car, sir.'

'Ah,' Herr Fischer nodded and it seemed as if the ghost of a smile might be playing on his scabbed and bloodied lips, 'then, my dear, I think we may know where she is gone.'

That night, alone in their bedroom, Paulus and Otto made a pact.

They swore to themselves and to each other that no matter

what happened, no matter what Hitler tried to do to them, they would protect Dagmar.

It would be their mission in life.

They would be her brave knights in shining armour, she their damsel in distress.

Their own lives meant nothing, their only value was that they be placed in the service of the girl they loved. Somehow or other the Stengel boys would protect their princess and see that she survived this fire-breathing dragon which threatened to devour them all.

Hitler wouldn't get her.

They would be her shield.

Law Student
London, 1956

Stone turned off the gas beneath the kettle and made a pot of tea.

He lit the grill for toast and went into the living room to gather up his law books.

The following summer he would be taking his Bar exams via correspondence course. It would be his third attempt to pass but recently he had been ignoring his studies. The letter which purported to have come from Dagmar had chased such things from his mind. Taking his tea and toast, Stone spread the books across the kitchen table and tried to focus.

The words swam before his eyes: *torts, jurisprudence, criminal, civil, family, property, commercial.*

Amazing how much law it took to run a civilized country.

Hitler had always despised the law. And lawyers too.

Stone swore he would be a lawyer yet.

A Party Is Announced

Berlin, August 1933

Midway through the first of the thousand summers that Adolf Hitler had planned for his Reich, the Stengel family were breathing a sigh of relief. Tentative and highly qualified, but relief nonetheless.

'Basically we're still alive,' Wolfgang said, spreading sardines in the boys' sandwiches for their lunch. 'I wouldn't have put money on that two months ago.'

'I would, Dad,' Otto said. He had finished his breakfast oats and was lifting dumbbells in the corner of the room as was now his regular habit, both morning and evening. 'I'd like to see them try and kill me.'

'They *would* have flipping killed you, Otts,' Paulus said, 'if I hadn't told Dad what you were up to.'

'Like a bloody snitch.'

'Saving your life, mate,' Paulus said, through a mouthful of porridge.

Otto did not reply, concentrating instead on curling the weights up his body, his biceps bulging under the strain.

Frieda sank down on the couch.

'It still makes me weak to think about it.'

'Yeah, well, I'm sorry, Mum,' Otto snapped, 'but I just reckon it's time somebody let these pigs know they can't push us Jews around. We're strong. We're proud. We'll settle them in the end.'

'Us Jews?' Paulus laughed. 'Suddenly you're such a Jew! You never gave a damn about being a Jew before.'

'Yeah, well, I do now and if it hadn't been for you being a snitch, I'd be Jew with a gun!'

'Otto be quiet!' Wolfgang hissed. 'And please let's not go over it again, eh? The thing's at the bottom of the Spree now. Which by the look of it was where the guy you bought it from got it in the first place. But just be damned certain, Otts, that a Jew found with a gun, even a rusty old relic which probably hadn't been fired since the Franco-Prussian war, would without doubt be hung on the spot, child or not. Do you hear me? They'd execute you on the spot.'

Otto just rolled his eyes and continued lifting his weights.

'Listen to your father, Otto!' Frieda demanded, fear making her voice harsh. 'You know what these people are capable of.'

Only the week before a well-known local family of Social Democrats had been lynched in their own back garden for brandishing a hunting rifle when their house was attacked by drunken SA. A father and two sons, all hanged from the same tree in five minutes for defending their home.

'I just wanted to *do* something.'

'Getting killed isn't doing something,' Paulus said. 'It's doing nothing.'

'Hitler says we're cowards,' Otto insisted. 'One day I'll show him just how brave a Jew can be. What are you going to do, smart arse?'

'I don't know what I'll do, but, believe me, Otts, when I do do whatever it is I'm going to do, I'll be ready to do it.'

'Pardon?' Otto asked, somewhat confused.

'I'll be prepared.'

'Prepared? How? By *studying*? What's the point of that any more? They won't let you have a job no matter how many exams you pass.'

'Who knows? We might have law again one day. And if we do we'll need lawyers.'

'That's right, Pauly,' Frieda agreed. 'You should listen to your brother, Ottsy.'

'Mummy's boy!' Otto sneered.

'What's more,' Pauly went on, ignoring the insult, 'if we have to leave Germany and I'm qualified, then perhaps I'll be able to support us. What will *you* say on your immigration form, Otts? "Please give me a visa, I've got big muscles"? They've got plenty of people who can lift weights in America, you know.'

'And plenty of trumpeters,' Wolfgang said ruefully.

'Who knows?' Frieda said, putting on a brave face. 'It might not come to any of that. As Papa says, we're all still alive, aren't we? Now go and have a flannel, Otto. You can't go to school all hot and sweaty like that.'

There was no doubt that from the Stengels' point of view August 1933 was a distinct improvement on the previous spring and the legally sanctioned orgy of brutality that had culminated in the first Jewish boycott.

'They don't want to scare their new chums in industry and the banks,' Wolfgang said.

Jewish businesses were no longer picketed, arbitrary public beatings and robberies were no longer tolerated on the streets and the number of people abducted from their homes and spirited away to ad hoc concentration camps had also declined dramatically.

With care, and treading softly, Jews felt safe to go about the city once again.

This is not to say that life was any fun. It may have become a little less dangerous but it was no less demeaning or irksome. The various bans and exclusions on Jews and gypsies remained in place. Access to the professions was closed to them. There would be no more Jewish judges or lawyers. Jews were banned also from the army, the police and most commerce. University places were restricted to a tiny quota and books written by Jews were not merely banned but publicly burned.

But life was not impossible.

Frieda had, to her immense surprise, even been able to resume her work at the Friedrichshain Clinic, now called the Horst Wessel Medical Centre, the whole district having been renamed after the SA's favourite 'martyr', who had been a local boy. It was true that Frieda was only allowed to treat Jews, but there were plenty of them to keep her busy as Jews were no longer allowed to be treated by Aryans. Even wealthy Jews who previously would not have been seen dead in a public surgery came to her now. Sadly this did not enrich Frieda or the centre since private medical insurers were excused from reimbursing Jewish doctors, and so effectively every premium any Jew had ever paid was stolen by the state overnight.

However, to Frieda's astonishment she herself was still paid her salary. She was discovering that the vast pre-Nazi German bureaucracy would continue to function until told otherwise, and told not just once but in writing and in triplicate. It was going to take the State a long time to get round to officially de-Jewing everything and in the meantime she remained on the public pay roll, which enabled life in the Stengel household, for the time being at least, to return to something vaguely resembling the pattern it had followed before.

Paulus and Otto still attended the same school they had during the days of the Weimar Republic, although they now had to be constantly ready to defend themselves against attack from bully gangs, and lessons had acquired a more sinister tone. The law required that each school day now begin with the National Anthem followed by the Horst Wessel song and that every classroom display a picture of the Leader. Teachers were expected to greet their classes with the 'German greeting', which had to be returned *en masse* on pain of beating. The children of Jewish families, though still tolerated, were 'excused' History classes during which their 'blood race' was systematically blamed for every wrong that had ever beset the Fatherland.

But despite the deeply unpleasant nature of all of these pressures, none of them were, for either Paulus or Otto, the principal frustration of that summer. What really bothered them was that they had not seen Dagmar for months.

The object of their mutual obsession had almost completely disappeared since her terrible experience at the hands of the SA. The boys had heard that she scarcely attended school now and she had certainly not turned up for her Saturday music lessons at the Stengel apartment. Apart from the occasional note in response to the boys' regular letters, poems and gifts, the twins heard nothing from Dagmar at all.

'I'm afraid that poor girl will never entirely get over what happened to her on that dreadful morning,' Frieda said.

'But she wasn't badly hurt, Mum,' Otto protested. 'We saved her before they could do anything.'

'It's not the physical violence, dear. It's the *shock* of it. It's what a man called Freud calls *trauma*, which is something that affects the *psyche*. Something so powerful as to actually change it. Perhaps damage it permanently.'

'Psyche, Mum,' Paulus asked, 'what's that?'

'Well, I suppose you might say it's the soul.'

'Soul!' Otto gasped with deep concern. 'You think Dags has got a damaged soul?'

'Yes, in a way. Certainly a very badly bruised one and it's going to take a long long time and a lot of love and care for it to be better again.'

The two boys exchanged glances. Instinctively aware of what the other was thinking. If Dagmar needed love and care then it must be they who supplied it. If her soul was bruised and damaged then the brave and noble Stengel twins would make it better.

Then quite suddenly, on the last Saturday in August, the very girl herself arrived at Paulus and Otto's door in a state of breathless excitement.

'We're going to America!' she told the twins with a little shriek. 'New York! Mama has a cousin there! We leave from Bremerhaven on the SS *Bremen* in a fortnight. Imagine it, boys! I shall have my own cabin on the voyage next to Mama and Papa's! *My own cabin!* Just think of it, with a steward!'

Dagmar gave another squeal and clapped her hands together. It was as if all the accumulated misery of the previous seven months had been transformed into a single moment of pure joy.

'My goodness, Dagmar,' Frieda said from the hallway. 'Come in and tell us all about it. Have you got the visas then? Is everything in order?'

'Yes! Daddy's been working on it since . . .' Dagmar did not say since when. Even in her relieved and happy state she could not bring herself to speak of what had happened to her. 'Well, he's been working on it for months anyway and it's all come through. Exit and entrance. Getting into America doesn't seem to have been half as hard as people are saying it is.'

'Well, Dagmar,' Wolfgang said with a smile, 'I think it might have something to do with money. It's not as if you're going to be a burden on the American State, is it?'

'Gosh I hope not!' Dagmar laughed. 'I don't think I'd do very well in a hobo city like on the news reels.'

Frieda and Wolfgang could not help but exchange rueful glances. They too had been looking into the possibility of emigration but it was not so easy if you weren't Isaac Fischer of Fischer's of the Kurfürstendamm. The Great Depression was showing no signs of easing and foreign countries were far from anxious to encourage immigration when millions of their own people were already out of work. As a doctor Frieda certainly had a skill to offer but she came encumbered with two school-age sons, a husband with no 'practical' skills and two ageing parents who would certainly not be able to find work. Therefore, while the Nazis were allowing Jews to leave (having first taken a substantial portion of their assets), it was only possible to do so if you could find somewhere to go.

'How exciting, Dagmar,' Frieda said, putting on a brave face for the excited girl's benefit. 'America! I've always so wanted to visit.'

'Well, now you can!' Dagmar gushed. 'You can all come and visit us. Father is arranging for us to have an apartment in Manhattan but I'm sure we will have somewhere out of town as well so there'll be plenty of room. Anyway, never mind that for now. The *first* thing is that I'm having a party! Well, my parents are but it's my party too and of course you absolutely *have* to come. It's to be a ball! We've taken the grand room at Kempinski's and I'm allowed to invite whomever I like, so of course I'm inviting absolutely *everybody*. Well, I have so many people to say goodbye to and this way I can do it all at once. Although of course it's really just *auf Wiedersehen*, not goodbye, because I'm sure everything will be all right in the end.'

Dagmar was actually slightly hysterical with excitement and relief and gabbled on and on about the arrangements, assuring the boys that there would be more delicious food at the party than either of them had ever dreamt of.

'And of course since it's mainly a grown-up party there'll be gallons of champagne too and I'm going to sneak some! You wouldn't mind, would you, Herr Stengel? Frau Stengel? If I give the boys a taste?'

'Not as long as you leave some for me,' Wolfgang replied. 'Now since you're here, do you think we should try a bit of music? The band's been a bit thin lately what with you not coming and losing our singer to the League of German Maidens.'

'Is Silke in the BDM?' Dagmar gasped. 'The bitch!'

'That's not a nice word to use about anyone, Dagmar,' Frieda said. 'I don't think your mother would like it.'

'And come on, Dags,' Paulus insisted. 'You know Silke's step-dad forces her. She sneaks off all the time.'

'Yes, well, that's as may be,' Dagmar observed tartly. 'But she's still marching around with a swastika on her arm, isn't she? I'll bet all that Aryan blonde hair looks lovely under the black beret.'

Otto and Paulus let it go. They knew that Silke was no Nazi but were far too caught up in the joy of seeing Dagmar again to waste any more time defending the fourth but absent member of the club.

And Dagmar was far too full of her party and the glamorous new life that beckoned in the USA to waste any more time talking about Silke either, or to do any music for that matter, so Wolfgang gave it up, poured himself a schnapps and announced that school was out.

'There's a few marks,' he said giving some money to Paulus. 'Go and get me a pack of Lucky Strikes and don't smoke more than half on the way home.'

Delighted at this unexpected pass out, the three thirteen-year-olds tumbled out of the apartment into the lift and then out into the local streets. Just as they had done so often during happier times.

Although Dagmar in fact had probably never been happier than she was that very afternoon. And as the three of them wandered the streets together, she held the boys' hands and almost danced for joy.

The boys, however, were not dancing.

They wanted to look happy for her but could not prevent themselves from kicking moodily at the kerbstones as they walked and even Dagmar's offer to stand them each a Coca-Cola to go with the cigarettes didn't seem to raise their spirits.

'So you're really going then,' Paulus asked. 'I mean all the way to America?'

'Of course I am. What possible reason could anyone have for wanting to stay here?'

'No,' Paulus conceded sadly, 'I suppose that's true.'

They had wandered as far as the Volkspark and were standing beneath a favourite tree. A great plane around which they had chased each other a hundred times. Paulus picked up a stick and threw it angrily at a squirrel. Otto picked up another and snapped it over his knee, thus giving him two shots, both of which were as futile as Paulus's effort had been.

'Are you jealous, boys?' Dagmar asked, her tone no longer gleeful but quieter now, almost gentle. 'I'd understand if you were. I know I'd be terribly *terribly* jealous if it was you that had got your visas and not me.'

'Of course we're not jealous,' Paulus replied angrily. 'How could we ever mind anything that made you so happy?'

'We only want you to be safe,' Otto added. 'It's all we care about.'

'We love you,' Paulus muttered. 'You know that, we've told you often enough.'

'I do know that, boys,' Dagmar said, her eyes glistening wet, 'and you must promise to always love me because I couldn't bear it if you didn't. You saved me after all. You risked everything for me.'

Standing between them now she took their hands.

'That was nothing!' Otto said, reddening fiercely and staring at the ground. 'We'd do it ten times . . . a hundred.'

'Except now we won't need to,' Paulus added, 'because you're going to be safe, which is really brilliant and just the best thing . . . It's only that we're going to miss you, that's all.'

'Oh, boys,' Dagmar said, squeezing their hands, the glistening in her eyes turning to two single tears, one for each cheek, one for each of them. 'Dear darling boys, I shall miss you too. Every single day. And I'll write, I promise, every day if I can and send you lots of chewing gum.'

'Yes, but the thing is . . .' Paulus said and then hesitated.

'Yes?' Dagmar asked.

'The thing is . . .'

'What?'

Paulus was also red in the face now, a rare sight indeed, his colouring being so much darker than Otto's. He kicked at the dry grass and stuck the hand that wasn't held by Dagmar deep into his pocket.

'Just so long as you know . . . That one day . . .'

'Yes, Pauly,' Dagmar said, smiling again now. 'One day what?'

'One day you're going to marry me, that's all.'

'He means me,' said Otto quickly.

'Yes, all right,' Paulus conceded. 'One day you're going to marry me or Otto. That is, one or the other of us. We've talked about it. Lots as a matter of fact and we've decided.'

'Yeah,' Otto added. 'We've decided. We need that to be clear.'

Dagmar's face spread into the broadest smile. She plonked herself down beneath the tree pulling both boys down beside her. Her skirt billowed out around her on the grass. She let go of their hands and drew her bare legs up to her chest, throwing her arms around her knees. Her shiny painted toenails twinkled through her open sandals.

'Oh *Pauly, Ottsy*! You are *silly*. Of *course* I'll marry you. Both of you! At once if you like. You're my best friends and you always will be. And of course I shan't even *look* at any American boys!'

'Good,' the boys grunted.

'Unless of course they're Clark Gable. Have you *seen Red Dust*? God he is *so* dishy! But other than Clark Gable I absolutely promise.'

The boys' mood lightened now. They had said what they needed to say and the principle had been established.

The Fischers Throw a Party

Berlin, 1933

Frieda, Wolfgang and the twins got out of their cab at the entrance to the famous old Kempinski hotel. That splendid portal which had in the past regularly welcomed royalty and heads of state and which had for so long bustled with the richest and most elegant people in Berlin.

Being Jewish-owned the hotel had of course been much defaced with paint in recent months, but much to Wolfgang and Frieda's relief there was no gauntlet of SA pickets to run on the night of the party. The Fischers had not announced the event in the social papers as they would have done in previous years, and the only evidence that the police were aware of the celebration at all was the two black-leather-coated figures in Homburg hats who stood at the entrance just behind the doorman with notebooks and pencils in hand.

Unfortunately, however, it was not just the SA who were absent from the party that night.

There was no sign of other guests either. From hearing Dagmar talk about the extent of the invitation list, the Stengels had been expecting a jam of cars and a merry throng at the hotel doors, but for the moment at least they had the red carpet which stretched across the pavement to the street to themselves.

'Perhaps people will come along later,' Frieda said brightly. 'After all, we're bang on time, which everybody knows is not the fashionable time to arrive. I'm sure it'll fill up. Come on, at least there won't be a queue for drinks.'

The four of them entered the lobby of the hotel and were politely directed to the grand ballroom which was situated at the rear of the building along a number of thickly carpeted corridors.

'I know what it is!' Frieda said. 'Of course! The ballroom has a separate entrance, I remember now. I came to some doctors' do here years ago and we all entered from the street behind.'

But whether or not they had got the right entrance, when finally they arrived at the gilded doors to the ballroom there was still no throng of people bustling to get in. Just the Fishers themselves, waiting to greet their guests.

They made a handsome threesome. Magnificent in a way.

The very cream of rich Berlin society.

Herr Fischer upright in formal evening dress, a service medal at his chest and a sash representing the Berlin Chamber of Commerce across his shoulder. Frau Fischer in a full-length gown, cut low at the bosom to accommodate a fabulous diamond necklace that was surely worth a fortune.

And then there was Dagmar.

The boys' jaws almost dropped to the level of the carpet with self-conscious admiration when they saw her. She was suddenly a young woman, while they two still felt like little boys. Little boys, shuffling their feet, tongue-tied and pole-axed with ill-concealed longing. She had on a silken gown with a full-length skirt and a tight, strapless bodice which left them in no doubt that the figure Silke had once pronounced a fake was certainly nothing of the sort any more. The boys were struck dumb with admiration.

So mesmerized were they that at first they did not notice the tension on their friend's lovely face and the sadness in her eyes.

They were, after all, thirteen-year-old boys and at that moment, speechless with longing, they weren't looking at her face.

'Welcome, Herr Stengel, Frau Stengel,' Herr Fischer said. 'You met my wife of course on that dreadful day when we collected Dagmar from your apartment, after these two fine lads had been her saviour, for which we will always be grateful . . . You are very welcome. Please. Do go on through.'

Herr Fischer then turned to his daughter.

'Dagmar, you must greet your guests.'

Dagmar had seemed in something of a daze.

'Yes, of course, Papa. Hello, Paulus. Hello, Otto.'

'Wow, Dagmar!' Paulus stammered.

'Yeah. Wow,' Otto echoed.

'You look . . .' Paulus began. He was trying hard to keep his focus on Dagmar's face but was having a lot of trouble preventing his eyes from flicking downwards.

'You've got . . .' Otto was not even trying.

'They look . . .'

'They're just . . .'

Dagmar went red. 'Stop staring!' she hissed.

'I wasn't!' Paulus protested, going red himself.

'Nor me!' Otto lied too.

'You were!' Dagmar whispered ferociously. 'Anyone would think you'd never *seen* me before.'

'Not so *much* of you, we haven't,' Otto said.

At which Paulus kicked him.

'Well, it's very rude to gawp like that but I don't care because this evening is absolutely horrible anyway! Now go through and get some ice cream which is all you probably care about anyway and I have to stand here with my parents and I just want to *die*!'

Then Dagmar turned away from them, sniffing loudly and dabbing at her eyes.

Somewhat at a loss, Paulus and Otto did as they were told and followed their parents through into the ballroom where even they, who had never attended an event remotely like it before, realized at once that things were not going the way they were supposed to.

The ballroom was empty save for them, their parents and twenty waiters.

'Keep smiling, boys,' Frieda muttered through a fixed grin. 'I'm afraid we're the first.'

Wolfgang's smile at least was genuine. It was such a ridiculous situation. The four of them standing alone in the huge ballroom beneath the light of ten enormous crystal chandeliers outnumbered five to one by the waiters.

'Well, I must say, that's a lovely carpet, isn't it?' Frieda said bravely attempting to fill the emptiness with small talk. 'I imagine it took absolutely *for ever* to weave. And the champagne *is* delicious, isn't it! How is the fruit cup, boys? What a *treat* this is.'

Slowly as the minutes ticked by a few more guests drifted in until eventually there were perhaps forty or so people in a room that could comfortably have held two hundred.

People skirted around the obvious embarrassment.

'There has been a flu of some kind going around,' they assured each other. 'Perhaps that has put some people off.'

Finally the hosts themselves entered the ballroom, having clearly concluded that they could expect no further arrivals to join the party, no matter how long they stood at the doorway. Canapés were brought out by yet more members of staff and soon after that a buffet appeared. Some ten metres of white linen-clad table, laden with food for two hundred.

Paulus and Otto did their best.

Time and again they returned to the sumptuous spread, enjoying more fresh meat in one evening than they'd eaten in the previous three months. Followed by bowl after bowl of the various desserts, fiercely determined to try them all.

Dagmar sat with them, picking sadly at a single chicken leg and staring at all the empty tables around her.

'*None* of my friends came,' she said. 'Not one. I'll never forgive them. Any of them.'

'We came, Dags,' Paulus said, through a mouthful of strawberries whipped in cream and sugar.

'Yeah, we're here,' Otto added, looking at her over a fork loaded with rare roast beef. Otto had decided to return to the savoury tables in order to start the whole meal again.

'You don't count, Otto. I *knew* you and Paulus would be here. But no one else, not one, not even the *Jewish* ones. Why wouldn't the Jewish ones come?'

'I expect they were worried that the SA would give them a kicking at the door,' Paulus said. 'I don't mind admitting I was.'

'Me too,' Otto said darkly. 'Which is why I came prepared.'

'What do you mean?' Dagmar asked.

Otto attempted an enigmatic smile. Somewhat spoilt by the layer of cream that surrounded his mouth.

'Leave it, Otto,' Paulus said.

'No,' Dagmar insisted, 'what do you mean, Otts?'

Otto glanced about himself and then, putting his hand into his breast pocket, pulled out a flick-knife. A neatly executed twist of his fingers snapped out the blade which he then used to impale a new potato from his plate and put it in his mouth.

Dagmar's sad eyes gleamed momentarily with excitement.

'Wow, Otts! You look like a gangster in a movie!' she gasped.

'Put that away!' Paulus snarled. 'How many times, Otto! It's one thing taking precautions, it's another bragging about them. If you got found with that they'd show no mercy, you know that.'

'Yeah,' Otto replied grimly, 'and neither would I.'

Then Otto stuck his knife into a blood-red slice of roast beef on his plate and offered it to Dagmar, who took it from the vicious-looking point, with an excited giggle.

Paulus wasn't giggling. 'Don't be such a bloody prick! Put it away. Fuck, Otto, you can't go flashing a knife around. The cops are bound to have spies in a big Jewish business like this. I've seen some of the waiters sneering behind their bow ties. If one of them sees that and reports you, you're dead. There's Gestapo outside, you know.'

Reluctantly Otto closed the blade and put it back in his pocket.

'Yeah, well, maybe you're right,' he said. 'But whoever does catch me had better watch out because I'll tell you this, Pauly, this is one bad Jew boy who won't be going quietly.'

'Good for you, Otto,' Dagmar said angrily. 'You stick it in one of those pigs. I hope you kill a hundred!'

'A hundred's not enough,' Otto snarled. 'One Jew is worth at least a thousand of them and that's how many I'm going to kill. Just you wait.'

'Yeah, and what about Mum if it's *you* that gets killed?' Paulus snarled back. 'As if she doesn't have enough to worry about.'

For a moment the three of them ate in silence.

'At least now I know who my real friends are,' Dagmar said. 'I shan't need to bother writing to anyone else from America but you.'

'Well, *that's* certainly something to celebrate,' Paulus grinned. 'Come on, let's get some more of that strawberry cream stuff.'

'Why don't you get me a plate too, Pauly,' Dagmar said. 'I'd like to try some now.'

'At your service, ma'am,' Paulus said leaping to his feet, delighted at having been the one selected to do her bidding.

When he had gone Dagmar turned to Otto.

'Show me again,' she whispered.

'What?'

'Show me your knife.'

'Yeah, right. OK,' Otto said, taken aback but also delighted. 'It is pretty hard, isn't it?'

He took it out and discreetly flipped it open once more.

Dagmar leant forward and put her finger against its wicked point.

'Do you really think you could do it?' she said, her voice a little unsteady. 'Really stick it into a Nazi?'

'Of course I could,' Otto replied, 'if I had to. I reckon it'd feel great. I'd enjoy it.'

A spasm of excitement passed across Dagmar's beautiful face.

'I know you could, Otts,' she breathed. 'And I *love* it.'

Otto's fingers tightened around the hilt of the knife.

'But you mustn't, of course,' she added quickly. 'Paulus is right, it's too risky . . . I'm just glad you could, that's all.'

Then with a glance across the room to see that Paulus was fully occupied at the dessert table, Dagmar took up a napkin and, under the guise of pretending to wipe something from Otto's cheek, leant forward and kissed him.

Not a little girl's kiss. But something older and more knowing, something closer to how Jean Harlow had kissed Clark Gable in *Red Dust*.

'That's to remember me by,' she said. 'Now, quick, put that knife away before someone sees.'

Otto was so surprised and flustered that he almost cut his fingers off as he closed the blade and slipped it back into his pocket.

Paulus returned with the plates of dessert.

'What's up?' Paulus said to Otto. 'You've gone bright red.'

'Bit of food,' Otto said quickly, 'went down the wrong way.'

In the centre of the sparsely occupied ballroom, the Fischers, who had been making the rounds of their few guests, had arrived at Wolfgang and Frieda.

'I must say,' Herr Fischer remarked, 'I had expected better of Berlin. To think that people are so craven, it is astonishing.'

Fischer was swaying slightly, having clearly had a number of glasses of wine.

'You mustn't blame them, Herr Fischer,' Frieda said. 'People know that their names will be taken, you saw the Gestapo outside.'

'But that is exactly why those with a position in society should show themselves. And lead by example. Otherwise they're cowards!' Herr Fischer said. 'This government rules not by law but by fear!'

The drink was making him indiscreet, his voice was slightly raised.

'Hush, dear,' Frau Fischer said, looking at the hovering waiters with concern, 'we must remember where we are.'

'And again, that is the point,' Herr Fischer went on defiantly, although lowering his voice slightly. 'Everyone is terrified to speak the truth. Well, I am done with this country now and may say what I like. In fact –' Herr Fischer leant forward conspiratorially – 'I gave a valedictory interview to the Berlin correspondent of the *New York Times* this afternoon. The man was witness to what happened outside my store on April the first. He himself was manhandled.'

'I wish you'd left it, dear,' Frau Fischer said. 'Talking about it can't do any good now.'

'I will not leave the land of my fathers with my tail between my legs, my dear. We are not running, we have been *driven* out and I'm damned if I'll make a secret of it.'

Once more Frau Fischer looked nervously about her.

'I think they're serving coffee, dear,' she said.

'Yes, and we really should be going,' Frieda added. 'The boys have school in the morning and I must be at the clinic.'

'Then before you go,' Herr Fischer went on, taking Wolfgang by the hand and speaking carefully like a man who knows he's had too much to drink and wishes to disguise it, 'there is something else I must say. My wife and I owe those splendid boys of yours a great deal.'

'Please, forget it,' Wolfgang interrupted, 'you gave them each a hundred marks at the time, they couldn't believe their luck.'

'It's quite possible that they saved Dagmar's life that day,' Herr Fischer went on, 'or at least saved her from the most terrible sort of attack. I can never repay them for that.'

'Dagmar's their friend,' Frieda interjected. 'You really mustn't—'

'All I'm saying is I won't forget,' Herr Fischer said. 'Dagmar, Frau Fischer and I will be Americans soon and I have friends who have friends in Congress. I beg you to write to me . . . if things become . . . well, if they . . . if you ever feel you are in need.'

Wolfgang looked Herr Fischer in the eye.

'Thanks very much,' he said. 'I hope you mean it, Herr Fischer, because I think there's a very good chance we'll be taking you up on that offer.'

'I mean it most sincerely,' Herr Fischer replied, squeezing and shaking Wolfgang's hand. 'You and *Frau Doktor* Stengel are fine, fine people and those are two very precious boys you have there. My wife and I will never forget them.'

Auf Wiedersehen

Berlin, 1933

Dagmar never got the chance to be the American girl she dreamed of becoming because she and her family never left Berlin.

Later, looking at the photographs of the arrest in the newspaper, it was pretty obvious to Frieda and Wolfgang that the

Gestapo had held back deliberately. They could have taken Herr Fischer into custody as he had left his house, but by catching the famous store owner with his feet on the very steps of a first-class carriage, they made him look all the more like a sneaky, pampered fugitive attempting to make his getaway. The caption underneath it in the *Völkischer Beobachter* read: *Not so fast, Jew! The German people want a word with you!*

The expression of surprise on Isaac Fischer's face, captured forever by the photographer (whom the police had conveniently alerted to the arrest), showed that he had no inkling of what was coming. It was a cruel and terrible blow.

The Fischers had driven to the station from Charlottenburg in their gleaming Mercedes, confident in the knowledge that soon they would once more be living in a country where they were safe from robbery and assault.

It is true that the journey had been made somewhat unpleasant by an article in the morning paper, reporting on the party that had been held at Kempinski's on the previous night. The article was not in the social pages as it would have been had it been published just a year before, a gushing description by a female fashion correspondent of the gorgeous gowns and wealthy elite dancing till dawn. This report was in the news section and it was a damning and violent attack headlined *Food for two hundred gorged by scarcely forty Jews*. The article went to great length to describe dish by dish how a handful of rich, spoiled Jews had arranged for themselves quantities of food which they could not possibly consume while true Berliners tightened their belts against the hard economic times and stern tasks the nation faced.

Fischer had bitten his lip with anger at the outrageous twisting of the truth, screwed the paper up and thrown it on the floor of the car. Nothing, however, could dampen Dagmar's rising spirits. In fact in a way the vicious article (which had named her specifically as a disgusting and spoiled Jewish princess) served only to strengthen her resolve and steel her soul to emigration.

'They will have to lie about someone else now, Papa!' she said, squeezing her father's hand. 'We are sailing away from all this!

Thank you, Papa. Thank you so much for making sure that we would be safe after all.'

At the station the Fischers dismissed their car and hired a porter. The Mercedes was to be sold along with everything else the Fischers owned in Germany, Herr Fischer having left it in the hands of his bank to liquefy his assets. He was aware of course that the state would claim a large part of his fortune but at this early stage of the Nazi administration he was confident of getting something out. Besides, he had substantial assets overseas, and the main thing was they would be free from further persecution.

Herr Fischer bought a button-hole carnation at the station flower stall, a lilac corsage for his wife and a posy of primroses for Dagmar. Dagmar herself bought a bag of sugar-coated pretzels.

'If they don't have these in New York, Papa,' she said, 'we should set up a bakery and sell them.'

'Darling,' Frau Fischer remarked, 'they have *everything* in New York.'

'They will have once they've got me!' Dagmar replied and she even skipped for a few steps until she recalled that she was a grown-up now. She was after all wearing actual proper stockings instead of her usual ankle socks. And young ladies in stockings did not skip.

They made an elegant-looking threesome on their way to the boat-train platform, dressed in their fashionable travel clothes, the ladies in splendid hats and with their beautiful matching luggage trundling behind them on a cart.

They were certainly not difficult for the Stengel twins to spot as they emerged from the *U-Bahn* entrance.

'Dagmar! Dagmar!' came the shout as Paulus and Otto rushed across the station to intercept them just as the Fischers arrived at the ticket barrier.

'Boys!' Herr Fischer said with stern surprise. 'Why aren't you at school?'

'Oh, it's one of their festival days, sir, no lessons,' Paulus explained.

'We bunked off, sir!' Otto said at exactly the same time.

Dagmar laughed as Paulus punched Otto. Same old twins.

Herr Fischer pretended to frown. 'One useful lesson in life, boys,' he said, 'is to always get your stories straight,' at which Paulus cast a further angry glance at Otto. 'Anyway, it's very nice to see you.'

'We wanted to say goodbye to Dagmar,' Paulus said.

'Well,' Frau Fischer said, 'that's very sweet. Dagmar, it is time to say goodbye again.'

'And I'm afraid we must hurry along a bit,' Herr Fischer added. 'We depart in twenty minutes and I like to be settled before the train begins to move.'

Dagmar looked from one twin to another.

'I'm so glad you came, boys,' she said. Then she gave them each a kiss and a hug.

'We're glad too!' Paulus said.

'Yeah!' added Otto.

Dagmar pushed her bag of sugar-coated pretzels into Otto's hands.

'To *share*,' she said, and turned away.

'We'll be waiting right here at the ticket barrier till you're gone!' Paulus shouted after her.

'In fact, we may just stay here till one day you come back!' Otto called out.

'Be sure to lean out of the window,' Paulus added.

They watched wistfully as Dagmar's elegant figure made its way along the platform, hoping she would turn once more and wave, which of course she did, every few steps. They saw Herr Fischer consulting with a guard and being shown towards the carriage with their reserved seats.

They watched as Dagmar boarded the train.

In later years Dagmar often thought back to that cosy carriage. She was only in it for a minute at most but she felt she could remember every detail of its deep plush upholstery. The little lamps on the tables. The face of the smiling attendant who showed her to her seat. The feeling of security and comfort as she contemplated the happy journey to Bremerhaven. The coffee. The magazines. Lunch in the first-class dining car.

She had not quite sat down when she heard her father's voice raised in anger.

'What is the meaning of this!' Herr Fischer was demanding of someone on the platform. 'I have committed no crime.'

But he had. He had defamed the German state. He had libelled the SA. He had invented the most dreadful lies about the Berlin police force, saying that they were indifferent to the law.

He had told the truth to the *New York Times* but neglected to ensure that it was only published after he had left Germany. In fact, quite the opposite, he'd intended the story as a parting shot.

They had so nearly made it too.

It had been nine a.m. in Berlin when the telegraphed transcripts of the first edition of the *New York Times* had landed on various desks in the offices on the Wilhelmstrasse.

Nine a.m. in Berlin. Three a.m. on the east coast of the US.

Somebody had been up either very early or very late at the German embassy. And bad news always travels fast.

If the German attaché had slept later, or if the Fischers had been on an earlier train, they would have been out of Berlin by the time the Minister of Propaganda caught sight of what Herr Fischer had done. But then they would probably just have been stopped at the docks or even intercepted at sea. They were after all travelling on a German ship.

But then at least Dagmar would have got her coffee and her lunch. An hour or two of extra happiness before the darkness closed in.

Josef Goebbels liked to boast that he read all of the foreign press but that morning he must have stopped short at the *New York Times*. With its front page article about the famous Jewish store owner beaten up at the entrance to his own shop. His wife and young daughter terrorized and abused. About how one of Germany's foremost families was being forced to leave what had become a 'gangster' nation for safety in the USA.

Such a slur could not go unanswered. This after all was *exactly* what the Leader had accused the Jews of doing. Slandering the Fatherland abroad.

In no way did the fact that the minister and his staff knew perfectly well that the article was true diminish their genuine righteous indignation. Theirs was a world in which it was *always* possible to have things both ways. To be both bully and victim.

And so the Gestapo were despatched and an arrest staged.

Later, Isaac Fischer was to ask himself the bitter question whether his catastrophic lapse of judgement had been a genuine mistake or suicidal vanity.

Was it pride that had led him to speak out before he had reached safety? He had known in his heart that it was a risk. Why had he taken it?

Lying on the bare floor of his cell, his legs and arms broken, blood seeping from his face, he tried to take comfort in his anguish from the thought that his intemperate interview had simply given them a convenient excuse.

That they would have stopped him anyway.

But in the darkness that engulfed him Fischer knew that it wasn't true. That had he not insisted on speaking out on what he had believed was to be his last day in Germany, he would almost certainly have got away.

Other rich and prominent Jews had got out. Plenty of them. But they had had the sense to leave quietly.

He had condemned himself. He had condemned his family. He had deliberately provoked them. Like a fool he had wanted the last word. How could he have ignored what the world knew? That the Nazis were nothing if not vengeful. That spite and wicked pride motivated their every action. That they *never* forgave.

Watching from the ticket barrier, Paulus and Otto saw it all.

They watched in horror as the men in black coats and Homburg hats appeared as if from nowhere and laid a hand on Herr Fischer's shoulder.

They looked on as Frau Fischer tried to grab on to her husband and pull him towards the carriage door.

They saw Herr Fischer pointing at the train, gesticulating furiously for his wife to board it. Ordering Dagmar who was leaning out of the window to stay where she was.

They watched as Frau Fischer shook her head and beckoned Dagmar to get off.

They saw Dagmar emerge from the first-class carriage once more and step back down on to the platform, her face white with shock and fear, her brief American dream turned back into a German nightmare.

The Gestapo frogmarched Herr Fischer back down the platform and out through the barrier. As he passed them Herr Fischer saw the boys and Otto thought he briefly tried to mask the terror on his face for their benefit.

Then he was gone.

Along the platform his wife and daughter stood there still as if frozen in shock and grief.

A whistle blew. The train compressed its steam.

Paulus cried out from behind the barrier.

'Dagmar! Frau Fischer! Get on the train! Go!'

Heads turned. Some openly hostile. Others just surprised.

Otto was surprised too. In the selfishness of youth, a part of him had rejoiced to see the beloved girl remain. But even at thirteen, Paulus understood much more.

'Otto, you know what happens. They *always* punish the family too! If Dags doesn't get out now she'll never get out.'

Otto wasn't stupid, he knew his brother was right.

'Get on the train, Dags!' he shouted suddenly. 'Take it to the top of the Empire State building!'

A whack around the head interrupted him. The ticket collector had had enough.

'Shut your face, kid. You don't go shouting about and making a scene at *my* barrier! Particularly over a Jew.'

'Fuck you!' Otto said before shouting once again, 'Dagmar! Get on the train!'

But the train was moving now and the two figures were still, standing motionless in the smoke and steam as their carriage pulled away from them. And then the next and then the next until they were alone on the empty platform.

Together they turned and walked slowly back to the barrier. There were sneers from onlookers as mother and daughter emerged back on to the station. The ticket man's face wore a look of stern and pompous authority as if by dint of the fact that he wore a uniform he had somehow been a part of the police action.

'Get along there, you two,' he ordered pointlessly. 'Your train's gone, you've missed it. Move along.'

But for a moment at least Frau Fischer did not move along, she paused just outside the barrier seemingly at a loss, her eyes staring but seeing nothing. Dagmar looked up at her mother and gave way to tears.

Paulus took charge.

'We should go to the taxi rank,' he said, taking her arm. 'You should go home, Frau Fischer.'

His voice helped her pull herself together. 'Yes,' she agreed. 'Thank you, Paulus. You're right. We should go home.'

Paulus led Frau Fischer towards the front of the station, leaving Otto to walk with Dagmar.

'You look great, Dags,' he said after a few steps. 'I've never seen you in stockings before.'

Dagmar smiled momentarily through her tears.

'You have to protect me now, Otto,' she said, her voice shaking. 'You know that, don't you? You and Paulus. You have to protect me.'

'Well, *obviously*,' Otto replied.

Isaac Fischer was tried the following month on charges of libelling the German State and its servants. There was only one witness for the defence, an American photographer who, it was gleefully reported in Goebbels' press, had no actual photographs with which to back up his scurrilous claims. The man did, however, have a Jewish grandmother, a point which was raised in court as if it were evidence for the prosecution.

Two other potential defence witnesses did attempt to put themselves forward. The Stengel twins visited Frau Fischer in her big house in *Charlottenburg-Wilmersdorf* and volunteered to go to court and describe what they had seen on the Kurfürstendamm on the day of the first Jewish boycott. Frau Fischer had been very grateful but declined the offer.

'You're such good boys,' she said, sitting in her still splendid sitting room, the trappings of her previous life not yet having been stolen from her, 'but I doubt that the word of two Jewish boys would make a lot of difference, and standing up like that would certainly get you and your parents into a lot of trouble.'

The prosecution was much better represented. Twenty members of the SA testified that Fischer had merely been cautioned having refused to clear up an unauthorized and offensive banner which the authorities had caused to be removed from Fischer's store front. A Gestapo officer and member of the Ministry of Enlightenment and Propaganda who had arrived later on the scene also testified that there had been no assault and the accusations were thus exposed as disgusting Jew lies which a Jewish-dominated American press had peddled as fact. As a result of the trial, the American ambassador was called to the Wilhelmstrasse to receive an official complaint from the Foreign Minister.

Herr Fischer himself received ten years' hard labour, to be served at the new SA concentration camp at Dachau. He was, however, dead in three months. According to the official story he was shot while trying to escape, but Frau Fischer was not allowed to see the body.

Further Briefings

London, 1956

Once more Stone was sitting at the table with the teacups and the 1930s telephone, staring at the short plump man sitting opposite him, while the thin, quiet one in the corner looked on. True to form the short one had already started on the biscuits.

'We are here to brief you in elementary spy craft,' Peter Lorre said. 'Principally codes and communications protocol. They're going to be watching you, of course. They watch everybody from the West, but as a member of the Foreign Office you'll be of special interest to them. The moment you attempt to establish contact with Dagmar Stengel they're going to know about it.'

'They know already,' Stone replied, quietly but emphatically. 'I'm being set up. Dagmar's dead. It wasn't her that sent me the letter.'

'Well,' Bogart conceded, 'of course that *is* possible.'

'It's more than possible. It's probable. A damn sight more probable than Dagmar being an East German agent. You know as well as I do that the Stasi are even more anti-Semitic than the KGB. They don't take Jews. Particularly Jews with no training or aptitude who have spent their whole adult life either hiding in a Berlin apartment or incarcerated in a gulag.'

'So,' Bogart replied, 'you think that somebody in the Stasi has communicated with you in the name of your dead sister-in-law.'

'Yes. I think that's exactly what has happened.'

'Well, it's an interesting theory,' Bogart conceded.

Stone looked hard at his two interrogators.

'Yes, isn't it?' he said. 'And the thing is, I find it difficult to credit that it never occurred to you.'

Bogart smiled, a kind of cheerful shrug. 'Well, we might have considered it,' he said pleasantly.

'*Might have done!* You damn well know it! You think the Stasi are luring me to Berlin, don't you?'

'It's a possibility.'

'It's a bloody certainty!'

'For what purpose?' Peter Lorre enquired. 'Since you seem to know more about them than we do.'

'Same purpose as yours obviously. Dirty spying. You said you were sending me to Berlin to persuade a Stasi officer to turn traitor and work for you. I think they have exactly the same idea except the target is me. I don't flatter myself that I'm much of a catch. I'm just a translator, but I'm in the Foreign Office and what's more I'm attached to the East German desk. That's got to be of interest to them.'

For the first time Bogart left his corner and joined the party. He even reached over and helped himself to a biscuit.

'You're absolutely right, of course,' he admitted in his soft Yorkshire burr, 'it may very well be that you are being targeted. Which is why we must be getting along with your briefing. We don't want to lose you to some stupid mistake on elementary protocol.'

'Not so damned fast,' Stone snapped. 'I want to get this clear. You're admitting that you were happy to send me into East Berlin even though you knew I was being set up for some kind of Stasi entrapment?'

'We don't *know* that,' Lorre replied. 'We don't *know* anything. One never does in our game. We think you *might* be being set up.'

'You told me you knew she was alive, you bastards!'

'Perhaps we should have said that we knew somebody using her *name* was alive,' Bogart conceded gently. 'Somebody who may or may not be entitled to use it.

'Either way works for us,' he went on cheerfully, pouring Stone another cup of tea. 'Whether we end up trying to recruit her or they end up trying to recruit you, it's a very promising situation for HM Government.'

Stone lit a cigarette, trying to take it all in.

'So right from the start you've had it in mind that I might return to Britain having been recruited by the Stasi?'

'That is one possible scenario,' Lorre admitted.

'Were you going to warn me?'

'We find it is generally a useful policy to refrain from divulging anything that we do not absolutely have to.'

'So you would have sat back and watched to see if I turned traitor? Content that you could use me either way?'

'We were content to keep the various options open for as long as possible.'

Stone smoked and sipped his tea and thought about it. 'Well,' he said finally, 'at least now we understand each other a little better. So let's get on with it, shall we? What do I need to know to be a spy?'

'Oh, nothing too taxing,' Peter Lorre said, once more adopting his vaguely patronizing tone. 'Some addresses, a safe house if you need to run. Sources of money. Embassy codes and a bit of diplomatic law in case you have to try and claim immunity.'

'I hate studying law,' Stone said grimly.

'Yes, we noticed you've been trying to pass your Bar exams,' Lorre said. 'Not happy at the Foreign Office?'

'I'm not happy anywhere.'

'There is just one thing, Mr Stone,' Bogart said quietly. He had returned to his corner and was once more considering Stone with his enigmatic, faraway gaze.

'Yes?'

'The letter that first alerted you to the possibility that Frau Stengel might still be alive.'

'Yes.'

'That letter was sufficiently detailed and intimate to give you real hope. It was only when we told you that whoever wrote that letter was a Stasi agent that you began to doubt its credibility.'

'That is true.'

'So *if* Dagmar Fischer didn't write it, who did? I can't believe you haven't thought about it. Who could still be alive today who had sufficiently intimate knowledge of your youthful relationship with Dagmar Fischer to be able to forge that letter?'

Stone waited a moment before replying.

'I find it is generally a useful policy,' he said finally, 'to refrain from divulging anything that I do not absolutely have to.'

A Friendly Nazi

Berlin, 1934

Wolfgang was playing piano in a bar down by the river.

It was not yet completely illegal for Jews to perform in front of non-Jews but Wolfgang did not make a point of admitting his racial status if he could avoid it. He was only playing for drinks and tips anyway and since the landlord, who was a jazz fan, didn't ask, Wolfgang did not tell.

He kept his dirty little secret. A secret of which he was supposed to be ashamed. And because of that, in a vague, difficult to define sort of a way, he *was* ashamed.

Scarcely a year after Hitler had been handed power, something of what he had always claimed about the Jews had actually come to pass.

He said they were different.

And they had *become* different.

He had accused them of being furtive and sneaky.

And they had *become* furtive and sneaky. Covering up. Lying low. Watching the door. Hiding away. Survival rats. Constantly nervous, trying to blend in, avoiding people's eyes, keeping out of people's way. Attempting wherever possible to conceal the fundamental truth about themselves.

Exactly as Goebbels and Streicher said they did.

'It's a kind of ghettoization of the soul,' Frieda said.

Wolfgang sat in the little bar with the smoke-blackened ceiling and played. Eyes closed, his mind transported far away by the music.

Yes, sir! That's my baby. No, sir, I don't mean maybe.

Slow and rolling, not like Lee Morse had immortalized it back in '25, but soulful, like a blues. A faraway blues. Far away in America.

'Hello, Wolfgang.'

The voice came from behind him. It was quiet, gentle even, but it shattered his reverie just as surely as if it had been the voice of the Leader himself. Wolfgang was, after all, vermin. A rat or a cockroach, startled, terrified, looking for a skirting board to scuttle under.

Warily he opened his eyes and glanced around. A handsome blond man in his late twenties or early thirties was standing just behind him, elegantly dressed, with a rakish pencil-thin moustache and a sardonic, knowing smile.

And a Gold Nazi Party badge on his lapel.

Wolfgang turned back to his piano, his fingers stumbling on the keys, clumsy with fear.

Gold party members were *real* Nazis.

Only the first hundred thousand members owned such a badge. People who'd joined when the rest of the nation were dismissing Hitler as a lunatic. These were true believers who despised the so-called *Septemberlinge* who had begun to flock to the swastika after Hitler's first electoral breakthrough in September 1930.

And this Gold Party member knew his name. And if he knew his name, he knew he was a Jew. And if he knew he was a Jew then Wolfgang was at the mercy of his slightest whim.

'I'm not sure I ever heard you play piano before,' the man said, still from behind Wolfgang's back.

'Well, you're hearing me now, mister,' Wolfgang replied, concentrating on his keyboard, 'and if you've been listening, then a few coins or maybe a beer would be much appreciated.'

'Oh absolutely. Always a pleasure to drink with an old friend. Single malt's your tipple, if I recall. Am I right, Mr Trumpet?'

Wolfgang remembered now. It was the use of that old nickname that did it. 'Mr Trumpet' had been Kurt's invention but all his gang had used it.

'Hello, Helmut,' Wolfgang said, stopping playing and turning around on his stool.

'Ah. That's better,' Helmut said with what appeared to be a genuinely friendly smile, pressing a tumbler of scotch into Wolfgang's hand.

It had been eleven years but, apart from the moustache, the slim, handsome, somewhat effete young man Wolfgang had known in another life had not really changed all that much.

'Long time since the Joplin Club.'

'Indeed. Eleven years,' Helmut replied cheerfully.

'Eleven years for you. Eternity for me.'

'Ah yes,' Helmut said with a nod but nothing more.

Wolfgang raised his glass. 'How about we drink to Kurt?'

'Yes. Why not? To Kurt. I still miss him. I remember warning him at the time: if you can't afford *decent* drugs, *don't take any*. Such a shame. Mind you, perhaps it was for the best. I don't think he'd have fared very well in our brave new Fatherland.'

'Unlike you, Helmut,' Wolfgang said, nodding at the badge on his companion's lapel. 'You seem to be faring all right.'

'Ah yes. Bend with the wind, that's me. And I saw the way it was blowing earlier than most. Drink up.' Helmut ordered another round of drinks. 'You're still playing music, I see, and I'm very glad, I might add.'

'Well, things are a little more difficult these days of course,' Wolfgang answered warily. 'I play when I'm allowed. This isn't a job, you know. I do it for tips, that's all. I'm not employed here.'

'Please, Wolfgang,' Helmut said. 'I wear this badge because it is practical to do so. It has nothing to do with who my friends are.'

Wolfgang sipped at his second whisky, focusing on that brief, now unfamiliar luxury rather than the demeaning fact that whatever Helmut might say, Wolfgang was still a Jew and so they were *not* friends. Their relationship, such as it was, existed only on sufferance. It was simply impossible to ignore the fact that socially they were polar opposites. One the master, the other the dog. And no matter what kindnesses a master might show a dog, the dog was still a dog.

'And you?' Wolfgang said finally. 'Are you still—'

'A queer pimp? Oh yes, very much so. More than ever. My brown-shirted comrades have *tremendous* appetites, some of them *most* exotic. Funny really, the more they rail against depravity the more they seem to want it. Perhaps they're just checking that it really *is* as bad as they say it is. You know, for purposes of research. For how can one *really* know how wicked it is to batter open the arse of a penniless unemployed youth who only wanted bread and a uniform until you've actually done it?'

Wolfgang tried to smile at Helmut's levity, his newly acquired dog instincts prompting him to want to be ingratiating, despite seeing no humour in what was being discussed. 'Well, you know what they say about power corrupting,' he observed, gratefully accepting one of Helmut's American Camel cigarettes. Wolfgang himself could now only afford to smoke cheap local brands, and not even as many of those as he would have liked.

'Yes and *absolute* power corrupts absolutely,' Helmut said, grinning, 'which of course is what we Nazis have got, so absolute it's positively tasteless. Hey ho. 'Twas ever thus, and in the meantime the standard-bearers of New Europe are fucking themselves senseless and there are more shivering little girls and boys working the pavements of Schöneberg and the Potsdamer Strasse than ever there were under decadent old Weimar. Ain't life a scream?'

'You said brown-shirted "comrades" a moment ago,' Wolfgang said, looking his companion properly in the eye for the first time. 'Are you in the SA, Helmut?'

'Oh absolutely. Since 1927 in fact . . . almost an *Alter Kämpfer*, don't you know. Not that I've ever been in a fight in my life, you understand. No, I went straight to the top. Pimp-in-chief to Röhm himself. Funny, don't you think? That a man who commands three million devotedly obedient young men needs a chap like me to fix him up. I suppose it avoids small talk, although I can't imagine dear Ernst's small talk consists of much more than "Get your trousers off, lad, turn around and bend over".'

Wolfgang was most surprised at Helmut's indiscretion. Of course everyone in Germany had heard the rumours that the SA's all-powerful leader was a homosexual and one with a brutal and rapacious appetite, but Wolfgang could not imagine anyone being so open about it.

'Funny, isn't it?' Helmut laughed. 'In a way me and old Ernst are a bit like you, in so much as we're officially blood enemies of National Socialism. The party's *terribly* down on us homos, you know. There's talk of having us sterilized, which is hilarious, don't you think? I mean, what would be the point of *sterilizing* a queer? But that's my dear party colleagues for you. Never let an inconsistency get in the way of brutality. Thick as two short planks every one of them. My dear, you won't *believe* the ignorance.'

Helmut was making no effort to lower his tone and one or two of the other drinkers in the bar were beginning to shift about, casting aggressive glances in his direction. They looked away again, however, when Helmut ostentatiously displayed the black and red badge ringed with gold that was pinned on his lapel.

'Come on,' Helmut said. 'If you're not officially working here, you can take the evening off, can't you? Let me buy you dinner. There's no one here I'm interested in anyway. Did you ever *see* an uglier bunch?'

'Dinner? You want to *eat* with *me*?'

'That's right, a Jew and queer, eh? The SS would love that, wouldn't they? Perhaps we can plot an assassination attempt.'

At first Wolfgang was astonished at Helmut's provocative behaviour, but he soon recognized that it was not so very surprising and certainly not brave. The Nazis respected nothing more than authority, and as a senior SA man close to Ernst Röhm, Helmut was invulnerable. Wolfgang decided therefore to try and relax for an hour or two and enjoy a free dinner.

After all, he could be in no safer company in all of Berlin.

And besides, there was something he very much wanted to ask Helmut. He raised it the moment they had sat down in a cosy little restaurant and ordered their drinks and food.

'Do you ever see Katharina?' Wolfgang asked.

A shadow of sadness passed across Helmut's habitually amused countenance.

'Ah,' he said, 'you were rather in love with her, weren't you?'

'Was it that obvious?'

'Glaring, my dear. Glaring. And who can blame you? Katharina, lovely Katharina, she was such a very exquisite creature. Loveliest of them all.'

'Was?' Wolfgang asked, the shadow passing from Helmut's face to his own.

'Yes – was, I'm afraid,' Helmut replied, staring sadly into his Martini.

'Helmut. Please don't tell me she's dead.'

'No. Not dead. Not yet. I don't think so anyway. But she's been very ill for years. Not a nice condition at all; sad to say, she has syphilis.'

'Oh my God. Not Katharina.'

'It's quite advanced and so of course she's rather disfigured. Such terrible luck. You know how reserved she was, never loose at all, not like most of us that year. She told me it was one mistake. A film producer. She wanted to be an actress, you recall.'

'Yes, I recall.'

Wolfgang felt such pain. Real physical pain. Katharina was his secret. The funny, wistful little might-have-been that he kept hidden in a box somewhere deep in his heart. He scarcely even looked into the box any more. He had plenty else to worry about, after all. But it was always there, a sweet memory of something beautiful that had passed him by.

'I'm sorry, Wolfgang,' Helmut said, sniffing the wine the waiter had offered him. 'I know how much she meant to you . . . you didn't ever . . . did you?'

'No, no, we didn't,' Wolfgang said, 'but not for want of desire on my part. I tried one night, when I was drunk, but she put me in my place. She didn't sleep with married men.'

'For which you should be very grateful. You may have had a lucky escape. Life is undoubtedly unfair and cruel and swinish.'

The waiter brought the soup and they ate for a few moments in silence.

'What more can I tell you?' Helmut went on. 'She pretty much retired from everything and went to live with her mother. I saw her about a year or two ago. The symptoms were in remission but she was very scarred.'

'I should like to see her.'

'I very very much doubt she would want that, Wolfgang. Besides . . .'

Helmut left the sentence hanging where it was while he studied the diamond on his cigarette case. He didn't need to say more. It was pretty obvious that the last thing any distressed girl needed was a Jew trying to befriend her.

Wolfgang could be of no help to anyone. Not Katharina, not his family, not himself.

'Best to remember her as she was, don't you think?' Helmut said. 'Beautiful, captivating Katharina.'

They ate their meal together. Sharing happier memories of the great and glorious Joplin Club, memories which for Wolfgang were destined always now to be suffused with an intolerable sadness.

It was certainly no consolation that all the other members of Kurt's old gang were doing very well in the newly awoken Germany. Dorf the bookish money launderer was now with Schacht at the Reichsbank.

'Still juggling debt,' Helmut laughed. 'The only difference is that now he does it while he's sober. And you remember Hans? Believe it or not, he's also at *exactly* the same game as he was in 1923. Acquiring expensive motor cars on the cheap from those who find they have to liquidate their assets urgently.'

Wolfgang nodded. Wondering how many of those fine cars that had pulled up outside the Kempinski hotel for the Fischers' 'farewell' party a year before had since been bought short and sold long by his old friend Hans. The Fischer Mercedes probably amongst them.

'And Helene, of course,' Helmut went on. 'You remember dear sparkling Helene? She is the star of us all, still passing out at the end of parties but now she does it in the homes of ambassadors and in ballrooms on the Wilhelmstrasse. A friend of Goering, no less. Who as we all know does love a pretty girl.'

'Helene's a Nazi?' Wolfgang replied.

'Oh yes,' said Helmut, 'and not from convenience either. She's not like me, I'm just a fair weather National Socialist, but she's the real thing. She's *besotted* with the whole business. Loves it. The flags, the uniforms. The power. She honestly believes that Germany's woken up. From what and *to* what she never really explains. It's just woken up that's all, new dawn, young nation, pure blood. The lot. She's hysterically in love with Adolf, of course, but then so many otherwise perfectly sensible women are. They dream of him marching into their boudoirs and ordering them sternly to bed where they will lie back rigidly to attention with right arm outstretched while he tells them that it's his unalterable will that he ravishes them. Honestly, I bow to no one in my appreciation of male beauty but that one I really can*not* see.'

Wolfgang thought back to the Helene he had known. Young and bright and intelligent. In love with fashion and fun. And now she was in love with Hitler.

'She was a fashion buyer for Isaac Fischer,' Wolfgang said.

'Well, the Jews enslaved us all before the awakening, don't you know,' Helmut said with a smile.

Wolfgang almost smiled too. Helmut didn't care what he joked about; he never had.

'She was such a free spirit,' Wolfgang went on. 'And a good heart, too, I know she was. We laughed together all the time. She loved *The Sheik of Araby* and *Avalon*. Doesn't she *mind*? I mean about all the hatred and violence.'

'She doesn't *think* about it, dear. And if she did, she'd think it was all lies, just Jewish moaning and a few sweet, over-excited SA boys getting carried away. People like Helene are having too much *fun* to want any of this to stop. *Everyone* is having too much fun. Every day another parade assuring us that we're better than everyone else in the *whole* world, *so* invigorating. You can see why people love it, surely? I mean if Adolf had decided to pick on, say, left-handed people and let Jews join his gang, you'd be strutting about with everybody else, wouldn't you?'

'I hope not. Not me. But I'm sure plenty would. Of course it wouldn't happen though. It's always the Jews who get it. It's why we're here.'

'Apropos of which, Wolfgang,' Helmut said, producing a pen and a little leather notebook on which a swastika was embossed, 'I'm going to write down my telephone number for you. If you need help, and of course you will, you may call me. Be discreet, of course, when you explain yourself, but I promise that I will do what I can for you, for friendship, you know, for old times' sake.' Helmut tore the piece of paper from his book and got to his feet. 'And now I'm afraid I must go. I fear I have a long long night on the train ahead. I'd only popped into your little bar to see if I could pick up a bit of company for the journey. Love a bit of fresh trade, you know, can never resist the lure of the new, but now I fear I shall just have to read a book.'

'Where are you off to?' Wolfgang said. 'Somewhere nice?'

'Munich! Heart of the movement, my friend! Home of big bellies and small minds. Thank God I'm just passing through. Off to Bad Wiessee, a charming little spa resort. Have you been?'

'No. I've never had a holiday, as it happens. We had our kids too young, never had the time, never had the money.'

'And of course when we were young Berlin *was* a holiday. Why would one have gone anywhere else?'

'That's true.'

A wistful shared moment hung between them. Then Helmut drained his wineglass and his Cognac and called for the bill.

'Anyway, you certainly aren't missing much on this trip. Bad Wiessee itself is beautiful but the company won't be. Hey ho! Duty beckons, all work and no play makes Chief of Staff SA Röhm a dull boy and I must go and line up his playmates.'

As they parted Helmut took Wolfgang's hand.

'Don't forget,' he said, 'I can help you. I'm SA and we can do what we like. Pretty soon there won't be an army, or a police, or even a government in Germany, just us, the SA. We *are* the party, and we are the nation. Even Adolf is scared of Röhm, you know. Well, who wouldn't be? Three million troops? The SA is the biggest army in Europe and it answers to Queen Ernst, not King Adolf.'

'I'm grateful, Helmut. Thank you.'

They emerged from the restaurant and parted, Helmut in a

black Mercedes that had been waiting for him, Wolfgang to make his way home on foot.

As he did so his thoughts were far away and long ago. Back in the Berlin of 1923, at a bar, talking theatre and art with an intoxicating girl.

He didn't love Katharina any more. He had never loved her in the truest sense. He loved Frieda and Frieda alone, Katharina had been a crush, an infatuation. But a beautiful and sincere one nonetheless, based as much on a meeting of minds as it had been on her sexual allure, and his heart ached to think of her in such abject misery. If he *had* ever loved another woman it would certainly have been beautiful, thrilling Katharina.

All those nights talking art and theatre. All that style. That captivating beauty.

And now.

Wolfgang had seen the faces of those ravaged by that cruel disease.

Forcing such images from his mind he focused once more on the beautiful nineteen-year-old with the severest shining black bobbed hair he had ever seen. The smoky stare. The purple lips. Chattering about Erwin Piscator and Bertolt Brecht. Stealing Lucky after Lucky from the packet on the bar between them.

Lost as he was in 1923, Wolfgang wasn't concentrating on the present.

Had he been, he might perhaps have noticed the large black van parked opposite their apartment building. He might have seen the little gang of kids standing nearby, as if waiting for something to happen, throwing glances his way and giggling. He might have sensed the nervous excitement with which the concierge grunted her *guten Abend*, her manner even ruder and more abrupt than usual, her door closing quickly as he passed.

But preoccupied and half drunk, the first inkling Wolfgang had that something was wrong was when the creaking, clanking old lift began to settle as it arrived at his floor. That was when he noticed through the metal diamonds of the cage that the front door to their apartment was wide open.

That was certainly unusual.

Then a moment later as he was pulling back the concertinaed door and stepping out, Wolfgang heard Paulus's voice shouting out. Shouting out a warning. 'Run, Dad, run!'

But it was too late.

He turned but they were already all around him, reaching hold and dragging him into his own apartment, where Frieda was standing in silent terror, her arms around her sons.

There were half a dozen men present, one in plain clothes, the others dressed in a uniform that Wolfgang had only seen in news reels. A terrifying, all black affair, on the caps of which was a skull and crossbones.

One of the black-clad figures was holding the print that for ten years had hung above Wolfgang's piano. The one by Georg Grosz depicting an army medical team from 1918 passing a skeleton fit for active service.

The man holding the print had put his leather-gloved fist through it, glass and all. The jagged shards lay broken at his feet.

'You admire this decadent?' the man said with a superior sneer.

Decadent? Even in that moment of dawning horror Wolfgang's mind recoiled at the strange outrage of a thug who, having invaded a private home, ripped a picture from the wall and smashed it with his fist, then had the effrontery to call the *artist* decadent.

'Yes,' was all Wolfgang could think of in reply. Knowing very well that from this point of complete disaster onwards what he said was irrelevant anyway. They had come for him, that was all. He did not know why, but no one ever did. He had lost enough friends over the previous year to know that once these people had you in their sights there was no hope . . .

Another officer spoke up. He had hold of Wolfgang's beloved trumpet.

'You play nigger music?' the man asked.

The same casual sneer. These people genuinely seemed to feel that *they* were the civilized ones.

'Well . . . I did play jazz . . . but now I . . .'

The plain-clothed officer spoke up. Obviously a Gestapo man, dressed as ever in the inevitable gabardine coat and Homburg which every German, even the most fervent Nazi, had come to dread.

'We have received intelligence that you are a dangerous subversive. A dangerous *Jewish* subversive. You will come with us.'

'Dangerous? I play music.'

'Nigger music.'

'How is that dangerous?'

'It is morally corrupting. Germany protects itself from decadent and inferior culture. You will come now.'

Frieda cried out in desperate protest.

'But, sir, officer, I've explained!' she pleaded. 'It must be a mistake, he's just a poor musician. A harmless nobody. I am a doctor, I'm known in the neighbourhood, many Aryans of my acquaintance can vouch that my husband is of no consequence. The local Lutheran minister, he will speak for us, I know it . . . Please, let me call him!'

'Stengel,' the plain-clothed figure commanded, pointing at Wolfgang, 'come quietly or we will subdue you. I presume you would not wish your children to see that.'

Wolfgang glanced across at his family.

Frieda scrabbling in her address book for the pastor's number.

Otto looking ferocious, ready to kill . . . His hand playing with something in his pocket.

Paulus glancing about, his eyes darting from one black-clad figure to another, trying to think of something, anything.

Wolfgang knew that the longer he drew this out, the more chance there was of his boys doing something very stupid. Particularly Otto.

'Very well,' he said. 'I will come. Boys, be calm. For Mum's sake. Be calm.'

'No! Take me!' Otto shouted. 'I'm the subversive. Whoever called you must have meant me! Look, I've got a—'

Otto's hand was emerging from his pocket but Paulus, seeing

what Otto intended to do, stepped forward, holding Otto's arm and positioning himself in front of his brother. 'Wait,' he said, trying to smile, 'I've got it! I know what this is about. There's been a mix up. Your informant must have meant those *other* Stengels! The Communist ones. They live on – oh, where is it? – that's right, Boxhagener Strasse! We're always getting mixed up with them. If you just . . .'

It was a good effort but the home-invaders weren't listening. The Gestapo man barked a command and two of the black-clad figures took hold of Wolfgang. Frieda screamed in terror, leaping forward and holding on to him, struggling in the grasp of his tormentors.

During the moment of confusion when the room seemed to have twice as many bodies in it as a moment before, Wolfgang was able to grab at his wallet and press it into his wife's hand.

'Here, take what I have, there's a little money – for the boys,' he said, before leaning forward into her desperate embrace and whispering, 'The number. Call it, ask for Helmut, tell him.'

Then the SS men dragged Wolfgang away.

As the last one, the Gestapo man, was leaving, his figure framed in the doorway, Otto pulled his knife from his pocket. There was a click and the blade sprung open. A vicious gleaming spike. Otto raised the weapon, blind hatred in his eyes, poised to spring. Paulus saw the danger just in time and shoulder-charged his brother, sending him sprawling on the floor as the door to their apartment closed.

'You lunatic!' Paulus snarled. 'You stupid bloody lunatic. Do you want to get Mum killed as well?'

Otto turned on his brother, furious for a moment, then blank, and then, quite suddenly, he began to cry. Perhaps it was the words 'as well' which set him off. Had their father been dragged away to be killed? Both boys knew it was possible. Probable.

Paulus cried also. Perhaps Frieda would have done so too but she was too busy searching in Wolfgang's wallet.

Outside they heard the groan and clank of the lift as it began its descent.

Unfriendly Nazi

Berlin, 1934

For an hour or so after Wolfgang's arrest, Frieda tried continuously to call the phone number that she had found in Wolfgang's wallet, but received no answer.

Paulus and Otto sat on the couch, scarcely able to speak. So sudden and absolute had been the disaster that had befallen them. They knew precisely what sort of danger Wolfgang was now in. This had not been an arrest in the way such a thing was recognized in other countries. With the reading of rights and the arrival of lawyers. The possibility of a defence, even of innocence. Too many husbands and fathers had been arbitrarily abducted over the previous eighteen months for the Stengel boys to be under any illusions that their father would be given a chance to defend himself. It was perfectly possible that Wolfgang was already dead.

'Just like Dagmar's dad. At the station,' Otto said finally. 'One minute you see him, a second later he's gone.'

Paulus glared at Otto. 'It's not going to be like Dagmar's dad,' he said, and then repeated it, quietly, almost to himself. 'It's just not.'

Frieda put down the phone.

'I'll wait fifteen minutes and then call again. Have either of you boys ever heard your father mention anyone called Helmut?'

But the boys had not.

Frieda tried to pass the time by making herself some tea and hot chocolate for the boys.

Then they heard the noise of the lift approaching their floor once more and dared for one moment to hope.

But it was Silke.

She had come around intent on rehearsing her own grievances. Her relationship with her mother's Nazi boyfriend had gone from bad to worse. Right from the start Silke had refused to accept his authority in the house and for that reason he had taken to slapping and spanking her. She was fourteen years old and was of course deeply outraged at this and so became all the more defiant, which in turn outraged the SA man. And also astonished him. He had clearly imagined that by living with Silke's mother he had acquired for himself two servants for the price of one. He expected his clothes laundered, his food cooked and his cigarettes and beer brought to him while he sat hogging the gas heater. Edeltraud herself was completely cowed and terrified of losing him. As the fiancée of an SA man she was a 'somebody' in her block for the first time in her life. The SA were all powerful, they did what they liked, and if anybody objected there were three million more of them around the corner spoiling for an uneven fight. Edeltraud simply adored going about knowing that all the old bitches who used to sneer at her and call her a whore must now be pleasant to her, and so she always sided with Jürgen against her daughter. Silke had therefore taken to keeping out of the way as much as she could, and often took refuge at the Stengels' apartment, where she was always welcome.

She had come there now, nursing a swelling ear and a sore backside courtesy of the newly awoken German man, but she soon realized her troubles were as nothing compared to those that had befallen her old friends. And befallen her also, for Wolfgang and Frieda were as much family as she'd ever known.

'Is there anything your Brownshirt stepdad could do, do you think?' Otto asked but without any hope at all.

'Are you kidding? He has no idea I still come here,' Silke replied, 'and if he did he'd probably actually kill me. Besides, those guys were SS, that's different. Jürgen's only a stupid little prick of a corporal in a street gang really. He's a big man in our block or when he's hitting me but out in the real world he's just a scared little rat. The only Nazis that listen to him are the other apes on our street corner.'

Frieda brought some hot chocolate for Silke and together they tried to think. Frieda noticed that there was still broken glass on the floor from the destruction of Wolfgang's Georg Grosz print and began to clear it up. Paulus went and got some parcel tape and carefully repaired the torn picture. Despite the SS man having put his fist through it, no pieces had actually come away and so it was possible to make it look almost new, from the front at least.

Paulus hung the now glassless print back up where it had been. A small act of defiance.

Then once more they heard the lift creaking and clanking outside in the well of the building, followed by a heavy footfall outside, and again for a tiny moment they dared to hope.

But the figure who a moment later was standing there in the shadows was not their father. The boys did not know who it was at all, but Frieda did. Even if she had not seen him for eleven years. Not since that day at the market during the Great Inflation when he had been selling his works for a pittance.

'Good evening, Frau Stengel,' the man said, remaining in the dark. 'I hope I do not intrude.'

'Well, no,' Frieda stammered, 'no, of course not . . . Herr Karlsruhen . . . what a very unexpected surprise. Boys, go to your room please and shut the door, take Silke.'

The surge of hope that Frieda had felt on hearing footsteps had been replaced by complete astonishment at the utterly unexpected appearance of this figure from her distant past. Now, however, as the youngsters retreated with many a wary glance at the shadowy figure in the doorway, hope rose within her once more. This man had once been infatuated with her but he had wronged her. Could it be that his conscience was troubling him? Had he come finally to make amends?

Could it be that somehow his sudden reappearance could be of assistance to Wolfgang?

From what detail she could make out, Karlsruhen certainly looked like a man of influence. A very different figure to the lean and angry stallholder who had been peddling his work for peanuts during the inflation. Clearly he was once more a person of substance. More so even than when Frieda had first known him. More portly and more expensively dressed in his big cashmere coat and holding his silver-topped cane.

Frieda did notice that the collar of his coat was turned up high and his wide-brimmed hat had been pulled low. As if he had not wished to be recognized when he entered the building.

After all, he knew what she was. She had once spat the fact in his face.

'Goodness, Herr Karlsruhen,' Frieda said, 'this is a surprise. Won't you have some tea?'

He stood looking at her for a moment, his eyes flicking from her feet to her head and back down again. She was standing in the middle of the room on the big blue rug. He still hovered close to the door.

'Or coffee perhaps? Or I have some chocolate I made for the children – it's a chilly night. Please, come in. Sit down?'

But he just kept staring. Or at least Frieda presumed he was staring, his eyes were hidden in the shadow cast by the broad brim of his hat.

'Turn around,' he said finally.

'Excuse me?'

'Ten years is a long time, thirteen in fact,' Karlsruhen went on. 'You were twenty or twenty-one as I recall when you modelled in my studio. Now of course you are in your thirties. Most women lose their bloom and their shape during those years. I knew you wouldn't, though. Yours is a beauty that will take many more years to fade. Won't you turn around?'

Frieda swallowed once or twice but then did as she was asked, rotating a single turn on the carpet where she stood and ending with a desperate, self-conscious little flourish.

She had decided she must humour him. At least until she knew more. Any hope, no matter how tenuous, was worth grasping at. This man wore the party badge. If he wanted her to turn around and to pay her ridiculous compliments as he had done when she was young, then of course he could.

Karlsruhen breathed deeply, sucking in air in a kind of reverse sigh. Frieda felt almost as if he was trying to *smell* her.

'You are still beautiful, my dear,' he said.

'Thank you,' she said, forcing a smile. 'That's very sweet.'

'You haven't changed so much you know,' Karlsruhen said.

'Your figure is still beautiful, at least, I think it is. One cannot tell for *sure* of course until . . .'

He left the unfinished sentence hanging in the air. Frieda knew that she was going red and hot and flustered and fought against it. It was obvious that for whatever reason he still desired her. Perhaps somehow she could play that to her advantage.

He was a party member after all.

'I have come,' Karlsruhen said majestically, 'to ask you to take up modelling for me again.'

'Modelling? But why? Can't you find younger girls than me?'

'I have never forgotten you, Frieda, my dear. Despite the – difficulty – of our parting I have never forgotten how you – inspired – me and often since then I have longed to be inspired again . . . I see you have one of our pieces still,' he said, turning to the little statuette that stood on top of the piano. 'Your father acquired it. For a fraction of its worth, as I recall. But then he is a Jew and so one shouldn't be surprised at that. It is the way of your people.'

Despite still being prepared to try to ingratiate herself, Frieda found herself protesting the slur.

'He paid what you and your wife were asking,' she said. 'You were offering the same prices to anyone in the market.'

Karlsruhen studied the end of his cane for a moment. He clearly did not wish to discuss the statuette. He flicked some invisible speck from the moulded silver knob while clearly considering what best to say next.

'Let us not fall out, my dear,' he said finally.

'Have you come here after dark to offer me employment, Herr Karlsruhen?' Frieda asked. 'Wouldn't a note have been a better beginning to our reacquaintance?'

'I will speak plainly. I have never forgotten our last, ahem . . . encounter. Not at the market . . . I mean at my studio.'

'No, Herr Karlsruhen, nor have I,' Frieda replied, 'but let's not dwell on the past, you had been drinking and—'

'By rights I should be angry with you, and in many ways I am.'

Frieda had been trying to appear forgiving but now her mouth gaped wide in astonishment. '*You*, angry with me!'

'You deceived me,' Karlsruhen whined piously. 'I thought you were a German girl.'

'I was a German girl! Herr Karlsruhen. I am a German girl. It's only this last year or so that anyone has presumed to say I'm not and they have no right.'

'You are *not* German, Frau Stengel, and you know it. You are a Jew. Shortly there will be new laws at Nuremberg and you will lose your citizenship as all Jews will . . .'

'Herr Karlsruhen, have you come here to tell me what I can read every day in the *Völkischer Beobachter*?'

'I have come here to tell you that I still desire you, Frau Stengel! I wish to finish the business I began in 1920. It has stayed with me all these years like no other need. You denied me then but I hope you will not deny me now. There, I have said it. I know that it is wrong but—'

'Of course it's wrong—'

'You are a Jew, so such things are rightly forbidden. Your blood is not my blood, your race inferior. And yet you bewitch me. You always did and I have never forgotten the feel of your body when I laid my hands upon it.'

Frieda knew that she would have to decide.

It was a dreadful, impossible prospect, one which would have been unimaginable, even an hour before. But Wolfgang was in the hands of the SA. She knew that she would do anything to save him. *Anything*.

'Well . . . that's very . . . flattering, Herr Karlsruhen,' Frieda said, trying to keep her voice steady, 'and perhaps I was a little *brusque* with you all those years ago. But now, well, the thing is, my husband—'

'Ah yes, your husband,' Karlsruhen said with triumphant malice. 'Once there was a time when you told me your husband would kill me for what I would like to do to you. But he can't help you now, can he, Frau Stengel? He can't even help himself. For where is he? Do you know, Frau Stengel? I don't think so.'

And the dreadful truth dawned on her. Incredible that it took so long for the devilish penny to drop. It was so obvious.

Him turning up that very night. Scarcely an hour after . . .

'What do you know about my husband? Tell me!'

'I know that he is a decadent and a purveyor of corrupt Jew filth and he has been rightly taken into custody and—'

'It was you! You reported him!' Frieda hissed. 'You evil bastard, you had them get him out of the way so you could force yourself on me!'

'Your husband has been arrested, Frau Stengel, that is all we know. Meanwhile, there is the matter of you and your children to consider. I have influence. I am highly regarded in official circles. You may in fact have read that I have recently been elected to the Prussian Academy of Arts . . . I am perhaps not quite an Arno Breker but nonetheless I have been told even the Führer has—'

'Can you help my husband? If I do what you want, can you help him?'

She had decided. She would let his plan work out the way he wanted if only he would bring back Wolfgang.

But of course he couldn't.

'Your husband is gone, Frau Stengel. Into the abyss,' Karlsruhen said. 'His fate is now beyond you or me to influence. It is now for you to consider your own position and that of your children. If you will agree to meet me in secret from time to time I can help you. I can protect you and gain you privileges. Believe me, your kind will be in need of such things quite soon now. I can make sure that your sons are allowed to complete their studies. I can see that the local SA are warned off.'

'Herr Karlsruhen, can you help my husband? He has only just been taken! Surely it is not too late!'

'That Jew is gone!' Karlsruhen said angrily. 'Forget him. Think only of yourself. Do as I say and I will help you. Deny me and I swear I will do the opposite. How old are your boys now? Fourteen? Old enough to go to Dachau I can assure you . . . You *must* succumb to me. You have no choice. You must finally allow me to do to you what you deserve, you little Jewish slut! You whore! Do you think you can deny me? You are *Untermensch*. You must crawl or die. I'll break your Jew pride. I'll show you how a beast should be tamed. You will let me use you as I wish or your boys will follow your husband to Dachau!'

He had taken hold of her now, all pretence at civilized manners gone. And she was utterly at his mercy. Legally without protection, socially without position or influence. Completely defenceless.

He would take her boys. They'd be sent to a camp.

She had no choice.

Frieda kissed him. Hard on the mouth.

Reaching down she took a hold of him for a moment through his thick woollen trousers. He squirmed against the pressure of her hand.

'At last,' he gasped. 'I will take what I want.'

'But not here,' she begged, breaking away. 'The children—'

She did not finish her sentence.

And that unfinished sentence was the last Karlsruhen ever heard. The words 'the children' the final two words ever to enter his consciousness.

Which was fitting, for it was the children who killed him.

Otto struck the blow.

He, Paulus and Silke had been listening from the boys' bedroom and when they heard the sinister conversation degenerate into scuffling sounds they had opened the door and entered the living room.

Karlsruhen had been too preoccupied to notice movement behind him and Frieda could see nothing but the sculptor's huge face and body pressing down on her.

Otto acted, as ever, on instinct. He scooped up the nearest weapon, which happened to be the little bronze statuette of his mother that stood upon Wolfgang's piano, and, leaping forward, smashed its heavy marble plinth into the back of Karlsruhen's head. Splitting open the man's skull.

Karlsruhen simply crumpled up. Pole-axed, slumping down on to the thick blue rug.

Frieda found herself facing the three young people over his prostrate form.

For a moment they all remained motionless.

Otto, breathing hard, holding the statue by the head, Paulus and Silke just behind him. Karlsruhen slumped on his side. Blood seeping from the back of his head. Frieda, eyes wide with shock, for once at her wits' end.

'What . . . ? What do we do?'

It was all simply too overwhelming.

For her, but not for Paulus, who stepped forward, kneeling down beside the unconscious man and feeling his pulse.

'Is the bastard dead?' Silke asked from behind him.

'No,' said Paulus. 'He's still breathing.'

Without saying a world Otto raised the statuette in his hand, clearly about to bring it smashing down for a second time.

Frieda gasped in horror. Paulus raised his hand.

'Stop it, Otto!' he hissed. 'We don't want any more blood than there is already. Thank God he fell on the carpet and thank God it's such a thick one. If he'd gone down on the floorboards we'd be in trouble. Can't get blood out of wood.'

The news that Karlsruhen was alive cleared Frieda's muddled thoughts, her natural instincts forcing her to focus.

'If he's alive then I should help him.'

'What?' Otto said.

'Yeah. What?' Silke echoed.

'He's injured, I'm a doctor.'

'Mum,' Paulus said quietly, 'he's injured because Otto hit him. You can't help this man.'

Frieda paused. It was obvious he was right.

But it was hard for her nonetheless. For the first time in her life she must fail to help someone in need. Deny her Hippocratic oath. To most people, Paulus, Otto and Silke included, there would be no question. They would gladly let the swine die, even without the enormous threat that he posed to them if he survived. Simply because he deserved to.

But Frieda was not most people. She was that rare thing, a truly altruistic individual, and in that moment a part of her was lost. It was not the worst thing for which she would never forgive Adolf Hitler, but it was terrible to her nonetheless.

On the rug Karlsruhen began to stir. Paulus reached into the injured man's top pocket and pulled out his handkerchief. A huge square of purple silk. The perfect affectation to complement the wide-brimmed hat and silver-topped cane that went to make up the man's absurdly self-conscious 'artistic' image.

'What the . . .' Otto exclaimed, perhaps under the impression that Paulus was intending to use the cloth to try to bind Karlsruhen's wound. The protest died on his lips, however, as Paulus began stuffing the handkerchief into the semi-conscious man's mouth.

Perhaps some dream-like notion of the danger he was in jolted Karlsruhen out of his stupor and he began to writhe. Otto dropped down beside his brother and held the flailing arms while Paulus stuffed the last of the cloth deep into the gaping gullet, using the fountain pen he always carried in his breast pocket so as to avoid losing his fingers.

Then Paulus held Karlsruhen's nose.

The dying man was big and heavy and desperation lent brute strength to his final convulsions. But the boys were strong too, particularly Otto, strong in arm and strong in hate, and they held him down till he was dead.

'Paulus, Otto,' Frieda murmured.

But she knew that what they did they had to do.

The Nazis had made killers of her boys.

Paulus stood up. His voice shook a little as he spoke but nonetheless he was calm. Even commanding.

'We have to get rid of him,' he said. 'It's night time and we can do this . . .' He paused. Thinking. *Willing* himself to make a plan.

'How, Pauly?' Otto asked quietly. 'Tell us how.'

Once more there was silence.

Paulus stood over the corpse, his fists clenched, his eyes closed. His features contorted with the effort of concentration.

Frieda looked down at the dreadful sight on the floor. The blood seeping from the fractured skull, spreading, creeping, *soaking* into the thick blue of the carpet.

'Oh, Pauly, Pauly,' she whispered, 'how can we ever—'

'Right,' Paulus said abruptly, interrupting his mother, perhaps unaware even that she had spoken. 'Otto, you run to old Sommer and borrow his cart. Tell him Mum's selling some stuff. Park the cart by the bikes in the courtyard and come straight back up. All right?'

Frieda wiped a tear from her eye.

'It's no good, Paulus,' she said. 'Even if you got him out. When they find he's missing they'll retrace his movements.'

'They'll try, Mum,' Paulus replied, 'but I don't think the trail will lead them here. Remember how he turned up? After dark. Collar up, hat down – he didn't want to be seen, did he? Good Nazis don't consort with Jews, they certainly don't pay them house calls. Do you think he could afford for people to know he was trying to force a Jewess to be his mistress? And him a party member? No chance. Nobody knows he's here and if we don't panic and we make a proper plan, nobody ever will.'

Paulus turned to Silke.

'You don't need to be a part of this, Silks,' he said, 'you should get out now.'

Silke didn't speak, she couldn't, she was swallowing hard to keep from gagging, but she looked at Paulus and shook her head.

'All right,' Paulus said. 'If you want to help you can. We've got to roll him up.'

Still without a word Silke knelt down on the floor.

Paulus turned to his brother. 'What are you hanging round for, Otto? Go and get the cart!'

Otto had also seemed in something of a state of shock but Paulus's words snapped him out of it.

'Right,' he said, making for the door, 'the cart.'

Paulus got down beside Silke and began to go through Karlsruhen's pockets.

'Pauly!' Frieda gasped. 'You aren't *robbing* that man.'

Paulus looked up at his mother. His face grimmer and more determined than she had ever seen it.

'He's not a man, Mum. He's a corpse,' Paulus said. 'Me and Otto killed him. And the only chance we have of getting away with it is to stay absolutely calm and make the best plan we can. Money's useful stuff when you're in trouble and we have very little. The sensible thing to do is to take his. We *have* to do the sensible thing, Mum. No mistakes, not one. It's the only way we'll survive this.'

Silke had already found the dead man's wallet, which contained more money than Frieda earned in three months.

'We killed him in self-defence,' Frieda said, 'but if we rob him and you're caught—'

'If we're caught, Mum, it won't make any difference whether we've robbed him or not,' Paulus said, heaving the heavy carpet over the body and beginning to roll it up. 'But we won't *get caught*. The only people who knew he was here tonight are us and him. He's dead and we're not telling. You can be bloody sure that when he made his complaint about Dad he did it anonymously. They always do.'

This last comment made Paulus pause. In all the horror of the situation he had forgotten about Wolfgang's arrest. For a moment the fight and spirit seemed to drain out of him, but then drawing a deep breath he steeled himself once more.

'Got to concentrate on the *plan*,' he said, speaking, it seemed, to himself. 'If we can just get him out of the flat and dump him, I reckon we're safe.'

By the time Paulus and Silke had the body rolled up and tied with parcel string, Otto had returned. Then he and Paulus wrestled the rolled-up carpet with the body in it into the lift and got it downstairs, with Silke scouting ahead to ensure the coast was clear. The three of them then carried the heavy roll outside and wrestled it on to the cart. They were very lucky that nobody else in the block came or went during the time it took to do this but they were also ready to brazen it out with a sob story about having to sell everything to buy food. Of course with a man of Karlsruhen's bulk inside the rolled-up carpet it did look strange but once they had brought other rugs and cushions from the flat and loaded them on to the cart all around the concealed corpse, it gave a pretty good impression of an impoverished

Jewish family forced to sell off all their meagre possessions.

'It's only nine o'clock, Pauly,' Otto whispered as they arranged the cart. 'The streets will still be pretty crowded. Don't you think we should wait till later? Till the middle of the night?'

'Absolutely not,' Paulus replied, 'it's better this way. Crowds are good. I wish it was lunchtime.'

'What?' Otto hissed. 'Are you crazy?'

'Otto,' Paulus replied, 'the only way to get away with something like this is to brazen it out. If we go sneaking around at dead of night then we'll be stopped for sure. This way we're just one of a hundred carts. Now come on.'

As the boys began to push the cart away, Frieda appeared in the doorway of the building.

'Funny,' she said, her voice strange and leaden, 'I rode on this cart once myself, you know. You boys did too in a way. Your father was taking me to hospital to . . . to . . .' Frieda could not finish the sentence. She simply stood there gulping down her tears.

'We know, Mum,' Paulus said gently, 'you've told us about it lots of times. Don't worry, Dad'll be back. Some people do come back, you know. Especially now this bloke's not in a position any more to keep Dad out of the way.'

Frieda returned to the apartment and Paulus, Otto and Silke began to push the cart away.

'Where are we going?' Silke said. It was the first time she had spoken since the murder.

Otto, who had been growing in confidence with his brother's surety, went suddenly white with alarm. 'Christ, Paulus! I hadn't thought! Where *are* we going?'

'To the river obviously,' Paulus replied, already beginning to push. 'With such a heavy carpet tied around him he'll sink like a stone. All we have to do is get it in without anyone seeing. Or at least anybody caring.' Paulus turned once more to Silke. 'Silks,' he said, 'you've been so incredible helping us like this, but really, you shouldn't come now. There's only two cart handles and there's no point you risking your life too.'

'I think you'll do better with a girl along,' she said quietly. 'It'll just look more innocent somehow. Two lads on their own are much more likely to attract trouble.'

Paulus just smiled and once more put his weight to the cart.

As they made their way along the streets, they attracted the odd glance but nothing more. For the previous twenty years Berlin's cobbles had rung constantly to the sound of metal cartwheels as desperate people traded and bartered what little they had to survive. The boys' main fear was that somebody might take it into their mind to try and rob them and for that reason Otto kept his hand on his knife.

Fortunately he had no occasion to use it and after an hour or so of heavy work they found themselves down amongst the wharfs where Paulus pointed the cart towards a lonely jetty.

'We do it quick and we do it bold,' Paulus said. 'No creeping, no skulking. That's the way to get away with stuff. In my experience if you front people up they tend to mind their own business.'

'They'd fucking better,' Otto said grimly.

'Right. Let's do it,' Paulus said.

'That drunk's watching us,' Silke whispered in panic.

'It doesn't matter. There'll always be someone watching. What will they do? Call the cops? People down by the river at night don't like cops. Now's as good a time as it's ever going to be.'

And so the three of them pushed the cart to the end of their chosen jetty and simply tipped its bloody burden into the river. Then, having put the other pillows and blankets back into the cart, they turned around and pushed it away.

'Don't look back,' Paulus warned. 'Walk steady. Don't hesitate but don't run either.'

Paulus was right in his cool analysis. Nobody bothered them. The tramp just shrugged and looked away. As did a drunken sailor smoking with a whore on the next jetty along.

Shadowy figures had been disposing of bodies in Berlin on a nightly basis since November 1918 and every morning the river disgorged its dead. It was not such an exceptional thing. If you knew what was good for you, you tended not to confront the people doing the dumping, no matter how young they looked.

Party Interrupted
Bad Wiessee, 1934

All day and all evening the quaint little spa town had resounded to the sound of raucous celebration. Bands played, beer flowed in rivers and vast quantities of food had either been consumed or thrown about in fun. Ernst Röhm and the senior leadership of the Nazi *Sturmabteilung*, along with a large supply of teenage storm troopers, were having a 'conference' and seldom had so little business been mixed with so much pleasure.

The only jarring notes in the general mood of excess and celebration came when conversation turned to how slowly the fruits of the National Socialist Revolution were being distributed amongst those who deserved them most. It had after all been the knuckle-dusters and steel-capped boots of the SA that had brought Hitler to power and now the Brown Army wanted its reward.

'We *are* the police! We *are* the army!' Röhm roared, pushing his face close to Helmut's in order to make himself heard above the din. Beer foam around his mouth, pork grease on his chin. 'Don't talk to me about the *Reichswehr*, a hundred thousand snobbish little *Junkers* kissing that senile old fool Hindenburg's arse. Let me assure you, my dear friend,' Röhm went on, wiping the beer and spit from his mouth, 'that if our fine *Leader* does not proceed sharply to place we SA at the very centre of the state, then there will be a *second* German revolution and at the end of it nobody will be in any doubt about who is running this country.'

'Quite right too!' Helmut replied, beckoning to a young trooper to come and squeeze in beside Röhm. 'And, in the meantime, Ernst, you deserve a little relaxation!'

Even as Helmut spoke, even as Röhm took possession of the youth that Helmut was offering him, out on the country roads Nemesis was approaching.

A fleet of Mercedes was gliding through the night.

Jet black Mercedes. Black like the uniforms of the men who drove them. And the darkness that cloaked their grim purpose.

By the time the motorcade drew into the spa town, the SA leadership had all retired to pursue their various private pleasures. Only the cleaners and night porters were witness to the extraordinary sight of the dictator of all Germany getting out of the leading car and marching into the hotel with a revolver in his hand.

Hitler was accompanied by a chinless man with small wire glasses. He wore the black uniform with the skull and crossbones badge of the rest of the gang and he too was armed with a pistol. The soldiers that followed carried machine guns.

Helmut was lying in bed in a room on the first floor of the hotel, preoccupied with the attentions of a young SA *Sturmmann* whom he had picked up in Munich the day before.

But Helmut's heart wasn't really in it.

The evening had been such a dreadful bore, with nothing but the prospect of more of the same to come in the morning.

He'd never liked forced bonhomie; the idea of a boys' camp filled him with loathing. Sing-alongs and ridiculous drinking games were no substitute for the joys of subtle seduction in his opinion. He really could see no point in drinking oneself stupid before attempting to make love and the ritual humiliation of newly initiated young recruits turned his stomach. At dinner a couple of downy-cheeked youths had been forced to stand naked to attention giving the Hitler salute while Röhm and his cohorts threw food at them.

Helmut, however, was destined never have to endure the second day of Röhm's SA conference because there would be no second day. For once those survival instincts which had served him so well through Germany's various insanities had failed him. He had backed the wrong horse. He should have been seeking out pliant starlets and society girls for Goebbels and Goering rather than lining up boys for Röhm. Because Röhm's days as the second man in the Reich were about to end. The vast hooligan organization he had built was shortly to be tamed by a darker, even more sinister force. This was the night the world would come to know as the Night of the Long Knives.

It was all over so very quickly.

Perhaps Helmut and his lover heard some commotion outside but they would have ignored it. There was always some commotion when Röhm's clique took a holiday. The corridors banged, shrieked and thudded all night as boys were chased from room to room. Had anyone told Helmut that Adolf Hitler himself was in the building, prowling the darkened corridors gun in hand, followed by a company of SS, he would not have believed them.

All Helmut ever knew was the door of his bedroom bursting open, the young SA *Sturmmann* raising his head from Helmut's lap as black-clad figures rushed in and levelled their machine pistols.

The guttural snarled accusation of 'Pervert' and then . . .

Oblivion. Helmut's brains exploded on his pillow. Those of his lover spread across his lap.

All that evening far away in Berlin Frieda had been dialling the number that Wolfgang had left her – as she had been for the previous twenty-four hours – but, as ever, it simply rang and rang. By the following morning when she tried again, the telephone had been disconnected.

Aryan-free Zone

Berlin, 1935

One day Paulus and Otto arrived at school to be informed that their classroom was to be segregated. The form-master made the announcement in the gravest and most self-important of tones, standing at the head of the room in front of the photograph of Hitler. Both the master and Führer looked stern and resolute as together they shouldered the heavy and heroic burden of belittling and terrorizing defenceless juveniles.

'It has been declared intolerable,' the master pronounced, 'that any German child should be forced into association with Jews in our public schools. The Jew children will therefore be put apart, sitting only amongst their own kind in those seats which have been generously allocated for their use.'

Then the teacher read out the names of the six boys in the class who were Jews, even though everybody was already well aware who they were. He read the names slowly, pausing between each in order to frame his face into a nasty sneer and to shake his head. Making the boys stand up as their names were called.

'You Jews,' he solemnly intoned, evoking a phrase which was used daily in every classroom in the country, 'are Germany's misfortune. You *six* standing amongst us now are Germany's misfortune. You are *poisonous mushrooms*.'

It was a brutal and deliberately demeaning slur. He was quoting from a kindergarten book called *The Poisonous Mushroom*, which was the first book every child in Germany, including Jewish children, encountered when starting school.

'We know,' the teacher continued, 'from our classes in Racial Science that just as in a field there are good and bad "races" of mushroom, so it is with the various human "races". Some human "races" are poisonous and some are not. Jewish humans are, of course, the most poisonous race of all. And remember, boys, just as with mushrooms, sometimes the most poisonous of all look the most harmless. Many an innocent woodsman has died having believed a mushroom that he picked was safe. And the body of our nation has for too long thought the Jews were harmless. Just as these six who have studied amongst us all these years have always seemed so.'

The teacher paused in his lecture while the six boys stood and waited.

'And what of you? Hartmann?' the teacher added, turning to a nervous-looking lad sitting at a desk amongst his friends. 'Do you know what a *hybrid* is? Of course you do. You will have learnt in your biology class that in the animal world creatures stick to their own species. A herd of chamois never allows itself to be led by a deer. A cock starling only mates with a hen starling. When creatures cross-breed, unnatural, mongrel hybrids are produced which combine in themselves only the worst qualities of each species. This is science, boys! Pure and simple science and in you, Hartmann, we have a scientific example of just such a species hybrid. A half-breed. A mongrel. Stand up.'

The boy Hartmann rose to his feet. Face blazing red with shame. His friends sitting around him looked puzzled and embarrassed. Most looked away.

'The mother of this half-breed is a Jewess,' the teacher went on, 'and so the German blood of the father is corrupted in this boy. *Irredeemably* corrupted. Hartmann is a *Mischling*. A mongrel child of mixed races. And he will sit with the Jews until his status has been clarified in law. From today all these seven boys are to be separate. Their presence in the classroom will be tolerated but no more. German pupils are forbidden to associate with them. They are the *poisonous mushrooms*.'

It was quite a shock. The class had been together since kindergarten and such a division went across numerous relationships and a lot of shared history. However, the vilification of the Jews had been so constant and all-pervasive over the previous two years that many old friendships had long since been severed and it was already a brave boy who maintained a foot in both camps.

The six Jewish boys and the single *Mischling* took up their books and went to their corner. Heads bowed, understanding very well that another step was being taken towards a time when their lives would become unliveable. Six of the boys sat down at their desks. One, however, remained standing.

'Sit down, Otto Stengel,' the master ordered.

Otto did not sit down, but instead stood foursquare with his hands on his hips.

'I have something to say,' he announced.

'Then say it at break-time. Sit down and open your books.'

'I'll say it now.'

Paulus tugged at Otto's blazer.

'Otts, sit *down*,' he hissed. '*Please*.'

But Paulus knew he could not stop Otto. Whatever his brother wanted to do he would do and damn the consequences. The killing of Karlsruhen (about which they rarely spoke but often thought) had of course affected both boys deeply but in opposite ways. For Paulus the memory of that desperate, horrifying action and its aftermath had made him even more careful, more calculating. Determined always to have a plan, to take the path of least resistance towards the most beneficial result. It was not that he lacked passion; he hated the enemy no less than Otto and felt every humiliation just as deeply. But he also understood that pride and hot-headedness were not only the enemy of survival but also the enemy of revenge.

'The trick to beating them,' he often told his brother, 'is not to try and kill them but to stop them killing us.'

Otto, on the other hand, had drawn an angry strength from their victory over their mother's attacker. His family had been attacked and they had successfully defended themselves. That was the lesson. If he had been reckless before he was more so now. He had killed one. He had tasted their blood. He knew that if you fought them you could hurt them.

The brutal imprisonment of their father had also affected the boys differently. Paulus tried very hard not to think about it, because when he did he was so overcome by fear and misery that he could scarcely function at all. He knew that the best and only way he could support his father was by helping his mother. By keeping going. Working hard at school and hard at the practical task of day-to-day survival.

Otto instead dwelt constantly on his father's plight and it constantly enraged him. Filling him with an overwhelming fury that made him fearless.

And so now, empowered by the blood on his hands and the misery of his father, Otto faced down his teacher and his classmates.

'This,' Otto said, making a sweeping gesture to the seven Jewish seats, 'is an Aryan-free zone! You are all *prohibited* from entering it since no Jewish boy should be forced to associate with you. This order,' Otto barked, in impersonation of the man in the photograph that hung on the wall, 'is my unalterable *will*!'

The stunned silence that followed such shocking insolence lasted perhaps two seconds. Just long enough for Paulus to manoeuvre his chair so that his back was to the wall.

Then mayhem ensued.

It is true that some of the 'German' boys found Otto's protest funny and had laughed, one or two even banged their desklids. But a sufficient number were outraged and formed an instant squad of retribution. Eight boys in all leapt to their feet and piled on to Otto. Even with such weighted odds the attackers didn't have it all their own way. Otto was solid muscle and due to his boxing lessons knew how to use it. Also the space was limited and obstructed by desks so the full force of the attackers could not be brought to bear. The first two boys were knocked down before the others were able to close on Otto and drag him to the floor. Meanwhile Paulus had leapt to his feet and was attempting to fend off other boys who had made their way around the desks in order to attack the twins from the flank. Paulus knew of course that there was no way of his keeping out of the fight. Since kindergarten everyone in the school had recognized that the Stengel boys came as a pair.

It took the master and two more teachers from next-door classrooms to break up the mêlée and then only by wading in and flailing about themselves wildly with their canes. When some order had been restored Otto was hauled to the front of the class, where he stood, wiping blood from his face and staring down his attackers through swollen eyes with fierce belligerence.

'You will attend the headmaster's office immediately, Stengel,' the master shouted, 'where I have no doubt you will be beaten and then expelled.'

'Too late,' Otto spat back through his bloody lips, 'I quit! Otto *erwacht*!' he shouted in imitation of the Germany Awake slogan so beloved of the Nazis. 'You stole my father! You're not keeping me.'

And with that Otto walked out of the classroom, never to return.

The master turned to Paulus, his lip trembling with fury at this Jewish affront.

'Well, Paulus Stengel?' he said. 'Have you anything to add?'

'No, sir, absolutely not, sir!' Paulus replied, snapping to attention. 'I am very happy to sit in whichever seat the school chooses in its generosity to allow me, sir! Also I apologize unreservedly for my brother's disgraceful display. He is stupid and hot-headed but he will learn his place, I swear, and until then I beg that you forgive him his foolishness.'

'Well then, Jew,' the master said, pleased as ever to be grovelled to, 'you may return to your books.'

Beached Dolphin

Berlin, 1935

Shortly after the edict was issued segregating school classrooms, Jews were banned from using public swimming pools.

This was a particularly cruel blow for Dagmar Fischer. Swimming had always been central to her life, and since her father's death she had taken refuge in the isolation and anonymity of the water more and more. The beautiful public pool at Charlottenburg and the vast swimming lake at Wannsee had become her sanctuary. Here she found peace and solace. Churning through the cool water at race-winning speeds she could for a moment blot out the agony of her father's arrest and murder. Diving, dipping and scissor-kicking in elegant precise balletic display for no one but herself, she could briefly wash the taste of the Ku'damm pavement from her memory.

'In a way I'm glad that Papa isn't here to see us banned from pools,' she said to the Stengel boys, fighting back tears as ever when thinking of her murdered father. 'He taught me to swim almost before I could walk. I was two, we were at Lake Como in Italy. He used to call me Dagmar the Dolphin. He was so proud of me.'

Dagmar was far and away the best swimmer in her school. A true athlete, slim and strong, and as she grew into adolescence her coaches had felt that she had real potential.

'When they announced that the Olympics would be coming to Berlin, Papa and I actually danced together! We did, you know. I know it seems funny to think of, he was normally so stern and formal. But that day he grabbed me and we danced. He already had me winning gold for Germany! Of course that was before the Nazis. Now I'm not even allowed to train, let alone compete. What do they think? That somehow a bit of my Jewishness will dissolve in the water and get up their precious pure German noses?'

Then the tears came properly and the boys looked at each other helplessly as they always did when Dagmar cried.

'They should be so lucky,' Otto growled. 'Don't forget, Dags, they're only doing this because they *know* we're so much better than them. It's why they hate us.'

'That is so *stupid*!' Paulus gasped in frustration. 'Just *listen* to yourself. *They* think they're the bloody master race, *we* think we're the chosen people. Fuck the lot of them, I say. I'm me. That's all. Just me.'

'Yeah and you're a twat,' Otto replied.

He was communicating in breathless grunts while doing sit-ups on Dagmar's pink fluffy rug. Otto rarely let any moment pass in physical repose; he was always exercising. Training for the battles to come.

It was a Sunday afternoon, the most boring time of the week. Paulus and Otto were sitting with Dagmar in her bedroom, one of the few places in Berlin from which they weren't barred.

'I don't see why we shouldn't think ourselves special, Pauly,' Dagmar interjected, stretching out on the bed and blowing cigarette smoke at the ceiling. 'After all, we have to put up with enough because of it.'

'Because, Dags,' Paulus replied, 'going on about being the chosen people is just the same elitist racial bullshit that they spout. People are people and we all started out as monkeys anyway. Otto'd probably have been a Nazi if he wasn't Jewish.'

'Fuck you,' Otto grunted, hands behind his head, red-faced and bulging-veined.

'Oh, very erudite, I must say,' Paulus sneered. '"You're a twat." "Fuck you." Brilliant argument, Ottsy. I can see how *you* got to be one of the *chosen* people. It must have been your language skills.'

'*Ninety-two. Ninety-three*,' Otto gasped.

'Whoopee, the ape can count,' Paulus said.

'One hundred!' Otto gasped triumphantly, lying back, chest heaving, staring at the ceiling. 'I'm just *saying*, Pauly,' he went on, 'that the reason they won't let Dag swim is because they're scared she'd win.'

'Of course I'd win!' Dagmar said angrily. 'I always do . . . Or I always did. Now what do I do? I can't run at the track, I can't swim at the pool or the lakes. I'll just get fat and old sitting in this bloody house!'

Dagmar and her mother still occupied the same big house in Charlottenburg-Wilmersdorf that they had lived in before the Nazis, although now many of the rooms were shut up and Frau Fischer employed a much reduced staff, Jews being no longer allowed to employ Aryans.

The big house had become a prison. Ever since her husband's death, Frau Fischer had been trying desperately to get their aborted immigration back on track. But while they still had an entry visa for the USA, their German exit visas had been withdrawn. The Nazis were nothing if not vindictive and they had decided that, for Isaac Fischer, paying with his life was not a sufficient punishment for telling the truth about the German state, his family would have to suffer also. Only the previous week Frau Fischer had received another rejection to her application to leave the country. A rejection made all the more sad and wearisome because she had queued for six hours at the offices on the Wilhelmstrasse to make her application.

'They say we'll spread lies about them so they're not going to let us go,' Dagmar explained miserably.

'Well, maybe it'll work out for the best in the end, eh?' Otto said, still lying on his back while bench-pressing Dagmar's dressing-table chair, 'because you can come with me to Palestine.'

'Palestine?' Dagmar asked in some surprise, having never heard Otto even mention the place before.

'Oh yes,' Paulus said with heavy sarcasm, 'haven't you heard? Otto's a *Zionist* now. Fuck, Otts, you don't even know where Palestine is!'

'Yes I do!' Otto protested. 'It's the next one down after Turkey – sort of. Isn't it?'

'It's in the Middle East and it's already full of Arabs,' Paulus said.

Otto's recent announcement that he had decided to become a Zionist had both amused and frustrated his brother. Lots of Jews in Berlin had begun talking about trying to get to Palestine. The Nazis themselves even raised the idea as a possible way of dealing with their 'problem'.

'It's our homeland,' Otto continued defiantly, 'that's all I need to know about it. Next year in Jerusalem!'

Even Dagmar giggled at this. In the past there could have been no less political individual than Otto Stengel. And no less a religious or spiritual one either for that matter. Otto was an archetypal teenage boy. His interests were sports, machines, food, music and Dagmar. At school the only classes he had ever enjoyed were woodwork and art, and the only remotely reflective pursuit he indulged in was music. Now, having picked up a few illegal pamphlets in Jewish coffee shops, Otto had suddenly begun using the language of Zionist politics.

'Homeland!' Paulus protested. 'Homeland? *Two thousand* years ago, Otts! Believe it or not, mate, things have moved on. *Palestine* is now the homeland of – who? Oh, let me see. Oh yes, I remember: the *Palestinians*. Get it? The Palestinians live in *Palestine*. There's a clue in the names. And I don't think they will take very kindly to a fifteen-year-old German Jew boy turning up and saying he owns the place.'

'We'll take it back,' Otto said darkly. 'We have no choice.'

'Great!' Paulus snapped. 'And when you do maybe you can ban all the Arabs from using the parks and swimming pools.'

This point reminded Dagmar of her own more immediate distress.

'Ten years I've been using our local pool,' she said bitterly. 'Since I was five. I know every attendant, most of them have made passes at me. And then yesterday they told me I couldn't swim. It was a school trip too. I had to wait in an office with two other Jewish girls while my class all went in. It was so *humiliating*. Girls used to beg to be on my squad. *And* the school got all the team cossies from Daddy's store at cost. They're still wearing them!'

And she cried once more. Desperate helpless tears.

Even aside from the dreadful blow of her father's death, the change in Dagmar's circumstances had been steeper and more brutal than it had been for most of Berlin's Jews. They, like any ordinary people, had at least some experience of the petty restrictions, humiliations and disappointments of existence. Dagmar's life, however, up until 30 January 1933, had been almost uniquely fabulous and blessed. The beloved only daughter of enormously wealthy and doting parents living at the very heart of the most exciting city in Europe. Few girls on earth were so cosseted and few could look forward to a future more exciting or glamorous. Now the glittering memory of that life taunted Dagmar. Every day she encountered someone or other who had once fawned upon her and whom she now suspected of gloating at her distress.

Dagmar wiped the tears from her eyes, looking for a handkerchief and pretending to sneeze.

'You see,' Otto muttered, casting a dark glance at Paulus. 'You see what's happening? They're grinding us down. We need to *do* something.'

'I *am* doing something,' Paulus said.

'What? *Studying?*'

'Yes. Studying.'

'Ha! What bloody good is that? Jews have always studied! *Study study study!* Mum never shuts up about it. Why? What good has it done us? Fuck that. You want to be a lawyer? What a joke! What's the *law* to us? It's the *law* that's fucking us. Besides, Jews aren't allowed to *be* lawyers, are they? Or any sort of decent job. You're just going to end up a really really well-qualified beggar!'

'Yeah, well, let me tell you this,' Paulus replied. 'When I get out of this country, whether it's Palestine, London or Timbuktu, I'll be ready. I'll have skills to offer. It's all very well you lifting weights and going about with a knife in your pocket, but you can't fight them all. You need to *plan*.'

Paulus might have continued his lecture but he was sitting on the floor with his back against the end of Dagmar's bed. She had stretched out her long legs so that her bare feet were hanging over the edge, quite close to Paulus's face, and even his analytical mind was incapable of remaining focused while in such proximity to any part of Dagmar's naked skin.

'I *hate* school now,' she said kicking her feet and wiggling her toes in frustration, 'now that they've started making us sit separately.'

Paulus wasn't listening. He was drinking in the sight of her pretty painted toes and shapely ankles dangling so close. Otto was staring too.

Both boys simply aching to kiss those feet.

'Me and the two other Jewish girls,' Dagmar went on, addressing the ceiling, for once oblivious to the stupefying effect that any part of her exposed self had on the Stengel boys, 'stuck in a shameful little corner. We weren't even friends before. They're scholarship kids who don't pay fees. I used to secretly look down on them, which seems funny now. Now that I'm getting looked down on myself.'

'Personally I don't give a stuff about sitting apart,' Paulus said, sliding away from the end of the bed, unable to take the pressure and frustration of Dagmar's crimson-tipped toes any longer. 'Why would I care? I'm there to work, not talk. Sod 'em, I say. If they stop being my friends because of a law then they were crap friends anyway. I just don't let it bother me.'

Dagmar swung her legs off the side of the bed, four hungry eyes following her every move. She took a packet of cigarettes from the little drawer in her bedside table.

'Blimey, Dags, you're chaining it,' Paulus said. 'Won't your mum smell it?'

'She will, but so what? I used to do what she said but now that Daddy's gone it's all different. I don't even bother to open a window any more. To be honest I don't think she cares anyway.'

The boys nodded but they did not really understand. The ongoing misery of their own father's incarceration in a concentration camp had of course hugely affected their family life but it had not changed their basic attitude to their mother's authority. Perhaps it was because she had always been more of a boss in the home than Wolfgang had anyway.

Dagmar offered the boys cigarettes.

'They're French,' Dagmar said. 'Gitanes. I have a French pen pal who sends me them.'

The three of them smoked for a little while in silence.

'I think I'll do what you did, Otts,' Dagmar said with sudden venom. 'Chuck in school. I just *hate* it now. The way they all look at me. It's like, it's like I'm *sick* or something. Most of them are trying to be nice but actually that just makes it worse. I'm the poor little kid with the incurable Jew disease. And then there's *him*. *He's* there, always there.'

'Who?'

'*Him*, of course. That man! Everywhere, hanging up in every single classroom. Staring out like the complete bloody nutcase that he is. The man who killed my dad. The man who won't even let me go swimming. What is *wrong* with him? Why does he *care* if I go swimming or not!'

Dagmar smoked ferociously in an effort not to begin crying again.

Paulus and Otto looked at each other, helpless in the face of her distress.

'Don't chuck in school,' Paulus said gently. 'Don't let them beat you.'

'Bollocks,' Otto snorted, 'give it up. Screw them, why should you sit there while they sing the bloody Horst Wessel song? I know why Pauly studies all the time. It's so he can write you those stupid letters in Latin that he thinks are so clever!'

Paulus was aghast. 'You've been looking in my notebook, you bastard!'

'Yeah, and what a load of crap! *Pulchra es amo te* – I looked it up. Oh you're *so* beautiful, Dags and he *loves* you! *Oculi tui sicut vasa pretiosa* – your eyes are like precious jewels! Ha ha! What a lot of big hairy balls!'

Paulus was crimson with fury, his fists clenched.

'Fuck you, Otts!' he said, leaping to his feet.

'And fuck you double,' Otto replied, getting up from the little pink and gold dressing-table chair on which he'd just sat down and squaring up to his brother.

'You're *not* to fight in here, boys!' Dagmar cried but with a rare smile – the rivalry between the twins for her affections always cheered her up a little. 'I have all my special things and you're such great big lumps these days you'll break everything. Anyway, Ottsy, I *like* Pauly's Latin letters.'

'I wanted to do something for you that was difficult,' Paulus muttered defensively, crimson with embarrassment, 'so you'd know I'd made an effort and be impressed.'

'Why don't you chisel her a letter on the Brandenburg Gate? That'd be an effort.'

'I *am* impressed, Pauly,' Dagmar said. 'I love your letters. For one thing they make me pay attention in class so that I can actually read them. My friends can't believe I have a boy who writes to me in Latin . . . *Or* a boy who writes me songs, Ottsy.'

'*Songs?*' Paulus exclaimed. 'Has he been writing you songs?'

'Yes, didn't you know?' Dagmar grinned. 'They're *so* sweet.'

'You sneaky bastard! When have you been doing that then?'

'While you're at school being an idiot and studying, mate.'

'You mean he's snuck round here without me and been playing you songs?'

'Well, just once or twice,' Dagmar admitted coyly.

'You see, Pauly,' Otto crowed. 'Just because you study hardest doesn't mean you're cleverest.'

'No need to be jealous, Pauly,' Dagmar said soothingly. 'You know I love you both.'

'Yes, well, one day you're going to have to choose, you know,' Paulus blurted. 'You know we've always told you that.'

'Yeah. That's the one thing him and I agree on, Dags. You'll have to choose some time.'

'Well, maybe I'll choose the one who can get me out of this country,' Dagmar said.

She said it jokingly but there was an uncomfortable amount of truth in the jest. The pressing challenge of survival was never far from any of their minds.

'I'll get you out, Dags,' Paulus said firmly.

'No, Dags, I'll get you out.'

'Well then?' Dagmar said cheerfully. 'It looks like the three of us will be leaving together. Won't *that* be fun?'

New Laws

Berlin and Nuremberg, 1935

Wolfgang did not die in Nazi captivity.

The concentration camps the SA set up in such haste during their first orgy of power were not yet the death factories that they would later become under the SS. Wolfgang came home, just as Paulus had said that he would.

'It's the Olympics next year,' a guard sneered, as Wolfgang and a group of other prisoners hobbled, limped and even crawled through the wood and wire gate. 'Got to look dainty for the world, haven't we? Maybe you lot can form a relay team.'

The joke was not lost on the hollow-faced skeletal figures as they staggered towards a kind of freedom. The health of anyone who had survived a year or so in the care of the *Sturmabteilung* was certain to have been completely broken and Wolfgang was no exception. The starvation diet, harsh physical labour and exposure to the elements had brought his primary organs to the point of near collapse. He had become rheumatic and his liver and kidneys were weak; he had also contracted TB. This last of course meant that he could no longer play his beloved trumpet for more than a few minutes at a time.

'Like cutting off a footballer's feet,' he said.

He could, however, still play violin and piano, having done everything in his power to protect his hands during captivity.

'I used to clench my fists when they beat me,' he told Frieda, 'and when they knocked me down I kept my hands under me. The guards used to like to stamp on people's fingers, so I kept mine out of the way. Most blokes protected their balls, I looked after my fingers.'

'Thanks a lot!' Frieda tried to joke. 'Not thinking of me then!'

'Don't worry, baby,' Wolfgang smiled. A hollow-cheeked, gap-toothed smile. 'My balls are made of steel, you know that. The SA used to break their toes on them.'

Wolfgang liked this joke and he made it often in the weeks after his return, always causing Paulus and Otto to grimace, Silke also, who continued to spend as much time at the Stengel apartment as she could.

'We don't really want to hear about you and Mum and that sort of thing,' Paulus said.

'Yeah,' Silke agreed, 'it is pretty yucky hearing old people talk about sex and stuff.'

Wolfgang smiled. 'It's hard to think of you kids being squeamish about anything any more,' he said, 'not now.'

Wolfgang glanced at the floor.

At the space where previously the thick blue rug had been.

Of course one of the first things Wolfgang had learnt on his return from prison camp had been about what had taken place in the apartment on the night of his arrest. How his wife had nearly been raped and his two thirteen-year-old sons aided by Silke had bludgeoned and then suffocated Frieda's attacker to death on the very floor on which they were now standing.

'Please, Wolf,' Frieda said, a shadow passing across her face, 'I try never to think of that.'

'I know, Freddy,' Wolfgang replied. 'It's a terrible thing but I'm still so proud of the boys and Silke. I only hope I'd have the guts to do what they did.'

'You would have, Dad,' Otto assured him.

'Yeah,' Paulus agreed. 'You wouldn't have thought about it. We didn't.'

The three young people exchanged glances. They rarely spoke of, or even referred to what had happened on that dreadful night, but it was always with them and often in their dreams.

If the subject was broached openly it tended to be on the occasions when Dagmar was making one of her increasingly rare visits. The fact that the other three members of the Saturday Club had gone through such a brutal and life-changing experience together was something of which she always seemed a little jealous. For all the fact that the twins loved her and her alone, she understood that Silke still shared one thing with them that she did not.

'I'd have done it,' she always insisted. 'I'd have killed him, or at least I'd have done as much as Silke did.'

'I helped roll him up!' Silke would snap back defiantly. 'And I helped chuck him in the river!'

'Maybe you should tell your friends in the BDM about it,' Dagmar remarked one day when, despite Frieda's protests, the subject had arisen once more. 'It could be one of your cosy campfire stories.'

Silke reddened; she was wearing her *Bund Deutscher Mädel* uniform. She always felt self-conscious when visiting the Stengels in her Nazi regalia but she had little choice. Like many working-class girls, her BDM uniform was by far the smartest and most serviceable outfit she owned. Besides which, on this occasion she was on duty, having come around to say goodbye before departing for the 1935 Nuremberg Rally.

'I can't believe they're making you leave now, Silke,' Frieda said, happy to find a way to change the subject. 'The rally isn't for another month.'

'I know. But guess what? We're *walking* there. It's true! From Berlin to Munich. Kids are expected to do it from all over the country. Apparently it shows how tough and united we all are.'

'They're taking children away from their families for a month?'

'Haven't you heard the joke? What with the HJ and the BDM and the SA and the Women's League, the only time a good German family meets up these days is at the Nuremberg Rally.'

Frieda smiled a sad smile. 'And what about school?'

'The party doesn't care about education. Only loyalty.'

'I do think,' Dagmar sniffed, 'that you might at least take off the armband when you visit. This is, after all, one of the few places in Berlin where we don't have to look at swastikas.'

Silke certainly cut an incongruous figure in the Stengel living room, her thick blonde pigtails clamped beneath a jet black beret and a swastika emblazoned on the arm of her brown blouse.

'It's stitched on,' Silke protested, 'and don't sneer like that. It isn't my fault.'

'No, of *course* it isn't. None of this is anybody's fault except the Jews themselves, is it?'

'Come on, Dags,' Paulus said. 'Just because she's in the League of Nazi Maidens doesn't mean she's a Nazi.'

'I doubt she's a maiden either,' Dagmar observed.

'Dagmar!' Frieda protested.

'I'm not a Nazi,' Silke claimed hotly. 'I'm a Communist, you know that.'

'They're the same thing,' said Dagmar.

'That is just a pig ignorant thing to say,' Silke replied. 'We Communists hate the Nazis.'

'You don't know anything about Communism,' Dagmar replied loftily.

'I know a lot more than you,' Silke said. 'I've been reading. We did a book burning and I pinched some Marx and Lenin. Lots of kids stole books. A friend of mine grabbed something called *The Well of Loneliness* because it's about lesbians and she thinks she is one. Not all the BDM girls are Nazis, you know. Lots of us just have a laugh.'

'What? Marching about?' Dagmar snapped. 'Sounds *hilarious*.'

'We don't do so much marching,' Silke replied, her usual good humour returning. She rarely allowed Dagmar's snootiness to irritate her for long. Partly out of sympathy for everything Dagmar had lost, and also because she had long since realized that the twins, whose approval she craved, would always take Dagmar's side in the end. 'There's a fair bit of chucking medicine balls and jumping through hoops in your knickers and waving scarves about,' Silke went on, 'but it's not like the *Hitler Jugend*. They're not trying to turn us into soldiers. It's much looser in the BDM because basically the party doesn't really care about girls.'

'You sound as if you actually *like* being in the BDM.'

'Well, as a matter of fact I do. We do lots of camps and trips and I've learned to knit too.'

'Yes, well, lucky for some,' Dagmar commented dryly. 'I must say it would be nice to go on a camp or an outing some time but you see *we're* not allowed to go anywhere.'

'Yeah, I know that, Dags,' Silke said hotly. 'And I'm sorry and all that but don't forget you went on plenty of holidays before. I never went on one, not one. I got my first *ever* holiday with the BDM. Working-class people didn't get that chance before . . .' She stopped, slightly embarrassed. 'I mean, not that I'm saying it's *better* now. You know I don't think that . . . It's just, actually, it's better for *me*, that's all.'

'I'm thrilled for you,' Dagmar replied.

Frieda interjected, ever the peace-maker.

'Well,' she said gently, 'I'm sure you'll have a lovely time on your walk, Silke, and the rally will be very . . . interesting. The newspapers keep saying it's going to be even bigger than last year, although I really don't see how it can be. There were seven hundred thousand at the last one.'

The 1934 rally had been made into a hit movie called *Triumph of the Will* chronicling for the entire world the incredible scale of Nazi triumphalism. Frieda had gone to see the film out of a sort of grim fascination. No identification was required to buy a ticket. Nobody imagined a Jew would want to attend.

'All those hundreds and thousands of rows of people,' she said, 'standing in perfect lines. Where did they all go to the toilet?'

'You just pee where you can,' Silke explained, 'round the edges, sometimes even where you stand. In your pants if you're up the front, those poor people were waiting for eight hours and more. The stink in the latrine areas was just awful but of course you don't get that on the film. It might have been a triumph of will but it wasn't a triumph of plumbing. This year I'm going to make sure I don't drink anything on the morning of the parade.'

As it turned out the 1935 rally was bigger than its famous predecessor and for Germany's Jews at least it was much more significant.

There were to be new laws. Laws that would formalize the anti-Semitic discrimination that was already central to German National life.

The Nuremberg Laws, as they came to be known.

Silke, who was there, could not understand what was being said, standing as she was eighty rows back and squirming for the toilet. To her the blurred rasping voice echoing across the vast parade ground sounded like a dog yapping from inside a barrel.

But listening on the radio in Berlin Frieda could make out the Leader's voice very clearly and understood what it meant for her family.

For her sons.

'Wolfgang,' she whispered, 'we have to tell the boys.'

Wolfgang had been struggling to avoid drawing the same conclusion.

'Are you sure?' he said. 'These laws don't seem to be much different to what's been going on already.'

'I know, Wolf,' Frieda replied, 'but don't you see? They're making it all legal now. Slowly but surely they're putting us in a position where the law not only won't protect us but it will actually destroy us . . . *legally*. It's like they're building a gallows bit by bit, plank by plank, so that by the time they come to stand us on the trapdoor and put our heads in the noose it will seem inevitable, proper, the *correct* thing to do. Finishing us off will be a *legal* requirement. An administrative matter. Beyond their control. Sorry and all that but it's the law!'

'Bastards,' was all Wolfgang could find to say.

'But of course,' Frieda went on, her voice filled with emotion, 'it's only the law for three of us.'

For a moment there was silence between them.

A mutual acknowledgement of the secret they had shared for fifteen years.

A secret that had once been just a family affair.

A matter of private feelings. Something they knew they would one day have to address but which they intended to do in such a manner that the four members of the Stengel family might continue as before.

In fact, in earlier years, when Frieda and Wolfgang had

discussed how they would eventually tell the boys about the adoption, they had fixed upon the plan that at first they would only tell them that *one* of them had been adopted and not reveal which of them it was. Saying that it was a matter of no consequence and that they might or might not tell them the full story later.

Because it really was impossible to tell.

Neither boy seemed any more or any less a child of their parents than the other. Paulus was studious and dedicated like his mother. Otto wilder and less diligent like his father. Otto was the musical one, taking after Wolfgang, while Paulus was planning a career, a career in which he hoped one day to be able to help people, just as his mother did. He was darker coloured like Frieda while Otto shared the same sandy hair and tendency to freckle like his father.

'If ever there was an interesting experiment in nurture over nature,' Frieda had frequently observed during the carefree years, 'it's our boys. I may write a paper on it one day.'

But in Hitler's Germany, the nature and nurture debate was long since dead. Something called 'blood' was everything.

'Blood' *that man* screamed over the radio.

German 'blood' which must be protected at all costs.

Every person in the country was to have their 'blood' categorized to determine how much 'German' blood they possessed and how much 'Jew'.

The secret which had begun at the Berliner Buch medical school in 1920 could be a secret no longer.

Romantic Gesture
Berlin, 1935

Up until the age of fourteen and a half, Otto and Paulus had done pretty much everything together. Laughed together. Fought together.

Fallen in love with the same girl together.

And killed together.

The last and most terrible of these bonds had of course been born of urgent necessity; they had had no choice. When Otto decided to attack again, forming what he called his retribution squad with a view to mugging a storm trooper, the brothers parted company.

'We've done worse before,' Otto said darkly when Paulus expressed his complete opposition to the plan. 'You've done worse, you know that.'

'Shut up about that, you stupid bastard!' Paulus hissed. 'We should *never* talk about that outside, do you hear?'

'I'll talk about what I like,' Otto replied, 'and I'll do what I like. And I'm going to do this.'

'Then you're completely crazy,' Paulus said. 'You'll be killed and it'll break Mum's heart.'

But Otto was adamant. The time had come to fight back. A line had to be drawn, a counter-attack mounted. No matter how minor or insignificant a gesture it was, somebody had to *do* something.

Dagmar loved the idea.

In fact, her eyes positively gleamed with excitement when Otto revealed his plan on one of the many evenings the three of them spent smoking cigarettes together in Dagmar's pastel pink bedroom. The thought of action, *vengeful* action, was like a tiny spark in the darkness of her nightmare existence.

'But what do you mean, "retribution squad"?' she asked.

'Exactly that,' Otto said, trying to seem casual and matter-of-fact. 'Me and a bunch of other Jewish lads from around our way are going to beat up a Nazi. There's even a couple of non-Jew kids who want to be in on it, Commies and the like,' he went on, 'but we won't let them. This is our fight.'

'Exactly,' Paulus replied. 'Which is what the police will think too when they come to get us.'

'They won't know Jews did it,' Otto said. 'I've thought it through. We'll take the bloke's money so it just looks like a robbery. Anyway, even if they do blame us, what more can they do to us?'

'Are you crazy? Haven't you seen what they did to Dad in their camp? What they did to Herr Fischer?'

Invoking the fate of Dagmar's father had the opposite effect to what Paulus had wanted. It fired up Dagmar to further encouragement, which was of course all Otto needed to hear.

'That's right, Pauly,' Dagmar exclaimed with bitter venom, 'they killed my dad. They *killed him*, Pauly. And now Otto's going to give one of them a good hiding. If there was any justice in the world, Otto would kill the bastard.'

'No!' Paulus protested.

'I will if you want me to, Dags,' Otto said eagerly. 'I really will. I'll stick my fucking knife in his throat.'

'No,' Dagmar said, quietening down. 'No, I don't want you to kill one. Not for me. Pauly's right about that. They'd come after us all for sure. There'd be a riot. But if you mug one you can make it look like a robbery.'

'Well,' Otto muttered, 'OK. I'll kill one next time, eh?'

'Yeah,' Dagmar said, her mouth set hard, her eyes cold, 'and in the meantime just give him something to think about. Do it for me. In fact, I want a souvenir. How about bringing me the buttons off his shirt?'

Paulus looked up in alarm. He knew that nothing on earth could be more calculated to spur Otto to action than that.

'Dags!' he gasped. 'You're talking like some gangster. What's happened to you?'

'What's happened to me?' Dagmar asked, her voice cold as ice. 'You ask me that, Pauly? What's *happened* to me?'

Pauly could not meet her gaze. He looked away.

'I'm just worried you'll get Otts killed,' he muttered.

'I won't get killed,' Otto said firmly.

Then solemnly, menacingly, he laid out his collection of weaponry on Dagmar's dressing table. His flick-knife, a cosh and a knuckle-duster. They looked strange and incongruous amongst the brushes and powder pots and little girlish trinkets.

And the beautiful miniature chest of drawers which Otto himself made for Dagmar on the occasion of his own thirteenth birthday. When he had still been a boy.

Dagmar went and stood before the dressing table, staring down at the weapons. Brushing her hand across them. She was wearing shorts and white tennis shoes without socks, showing off her long olive-toned legs. Her blouse was knotted beneath her bust revealing a band of soft, delicate skin between it and her shorts. Both boys stared in rapt fascination but for once she seemed not to notice their adoring glances. She was staring at the weapons.

'Do it, Otto,' she whispered. 'Give one of them something to think about.'

'I promise I will,' Otto replied.

'I'm telling you you're crazy,' Paulus said again, sullenly.

'Nobody's asking you to come,' Otto said.

'Don't worry, I won't.'

Paulus caught Dagmar's reflection in the dressing-table mirror. He could see the disappointment in her eyes.

'I'll find better battles to fight,' was all he could say and he knew how weak it sounded.

The following night Otto fulfilled his promise. He and four other boys ambushed two uniformed SA men and beat them up in an alleyway. It was a horrible mêlée, with kicks and blows and slashing knives. The troopers were bigger and stronger than the fifteen-year-old boys and were also used to street thuggery but, in the end, numbers and vengeful passion prevailed. The SA men went down and were kicked unconscious in the gutter. Then, while the other attackers went through the men's pockets for their money, Otto knelt beside one of them and snapped open his flick-knife.

For a moment the gleaming blade hovered over the prostrate victim's neck. One slash would do it. Otto glanced up into the faces of his comrades standing over him. Fear and exhilaration seemed to shine in equal measure in their eyes.

'Next time, you fucking Nazi cunt,' Otto whispered, 'next time.'

Then he cut the buttons from the man's shirt.

Two hours later, having scurried across the city imagining at every moment that the Gestapo were upon him, Otto presented himself at the Fischers' front door. He cut a wild and dishevelled figure but Frau Fischer let him in without comment. Frau Fischer commented on very little these days, having begun to withdraw into herself more and more. She seemed so distracted that perhaps she did not even notice the cuts and bruises on Otto's face and the splashes of blood on his shirt which he had concealed beneath his coat.

Dagmar noticed them.

'My God, Ottsy,' she gasped, leaning over the balcony of the first stair landing.

Otto looked up at her, standing like Juliet in the famous English play they had been made to read in translation at school. Her luxurious auburn hair framing such perfectly proportioned features. The huge dark eyes enchanting, bewitching.

'Come up to my room,' she said.

Frau Fischer turned away, returning to her shuttered drawing room and to the memories of her gilded past, leaving Otto to run up the stairs, two at a time.

Once safely ensconced in Dagmar's bedroom he held out his clenched fist towards her, turned it upwards and opened his fingers.

'For you,' he said.

There lying in the palm of his hand were the SA man's shirt buttons.

Dagmar looked down at them and gave a little gasp.

'You got them,' she said. 'You did it.'

'Yeah. I did it . . . I did it for you.'

She looked at him and smiled.

Otto felt weak at the knees.

'It's nice to see you smile, Dags,' he stammered. 'You don't seem to very much these days.'

'Whenever I try to smile,' she said, 'before long I see the pavement. And the boots all around me. And Mother and Father, with their tongues out . . .'

'Don't, Dags.'

'Sometimes I see the station platform and those men pulling at Daddy but mainly I see that pavement outside the shop. And my face is pressed against the paving stone. In my dreams I can actually *smell* it.'

Otto didn't attempt to answer; he and Paulus had long since come to understand that there was a place where Dagmar had been and where a part of her would always remain, which was beyond any comfort they could offer.

Except perhaps that was not quite true tonight. Perhaps in doing the wild and stupid thing he'd done he'd helped her just a little. Given her a momentary respite from her own pain and bereavement.

She played with the buttons in her hand for a moment, then let them fall one by one on to the glass surface of her dressing table, *clack – clack – clack*.

'Someone else is the victim for once,' she whispered. 'Someone else was lying on the ground with boots all around them.'

Then she gave Otto a cigarette, a Gitane.

She had done the same thing many times. But this was different. Spine-tinglingly different. She lit the cigarette for him. Putting her full, soft lips around the end and taking the first puff before handing it to him.

What touched her lips then touched his.

Otto was literally quivering with desire. His hands were shaking despite his every effort to still them.

After he had taken a drag or two, she reached over and plucked it from his lips, took another deep draw herself and then put it back in Otto's mouth. Her lipstick was red on the white paper, he could taste it along with the smoke.

Otto had never dreamt that having a ciggie could be so sexy or so sophisticated. He felt as if he'd grown up a whole decade between puffs.

When the cigarette was nearly burnt down, Dagmar took it from Otto's lips for the final time and ground it out in the crystal ashtray that sat beside her dolls on the dressing table. Then she drew Otto towards her and kissed him, full on the mouth. This was no furtive, stolen moment, like it had been at the Kempinski hotel, but slow and rich and generous.

Her lips opened beneath his and then he felt her tongue brush against his.

Otto's mind spun cartwheels in almost blind delirium. This was ecstasy pure and simple. He tried to concentrate; he was, after all, living through the most important and most ecstatic moment of his life.

The kiss lasted a moment longer before Dagmar stepped back and smiled at him.

Otto imagined the ecstatic moment was over but he had no complaints. Had he dropped dead then and there he would have died a happy boy.

But then he felt her soft lips against his ear.

'You can put your hand in my blouse if you like,' she whispered.

No dream had ever come more true.

For three long years Otto had wanted nothing so much on earth as to put his hand in Dagmar's blouse and now quite suddenly that sublime moment had arrived.

She kissed him as he pulled at the sweet-smelling cotton, dragging the hem from beneath the waist of her skirt. Then he put his hand underneath, moving it upwards, across the soft skin of her ribs. He felt one of her breasts, first through her brassiere and then, slipping his fingers inside the wired garment, touched the nipple beneath.

He was shivering with excitement. And it seemed to Otto that so was Dagmar.

This was an unexpected development. It had never even *occurred* to Otto that she might feel passion too. He would never have flattered himself to imagine that a goddess such as she could reciprocate his desire. All he had ever dared hope was that she might *tolerate* it in return for undying devotion and lifelong service.

And yet she seemed to shiver too.

For a moment they stood together, pressed against the dressing table, lips working at each other's mouths. Otto trying simultaneously to both lose himself in and yet also remember forever the extraordinary ecstasy of actually *touching* Dagmar's breasts.

Then she pushed him away.

'No more,' she gasped. 'We should stop before . . . Not because I don't want to . . . but because I *do* . . .'

Dagmar reddened as the sentences trailed away.

Otto grinned a grin so broad it seemed to split his face in two. He had come so much further than ever he had dared to hope.

'This is the best night of my life,' he stuttered. 'I mean literally. Honest. Just the best . . . literally.'

Dagmar smiled too. A true and genuine smile, a smile that for a moment seemed free of pain. The smile not of a hunted and a haunted Jew who was celebrating the mugging of an enemy, but simply of a young girl just turned fifteen who was growing up and had properly kissed a boy for the first time.

'Thanks for my buttons,' she said, tucking her blouse back into her skirt. 'Although I don't really think I want to keep them. Do you mind?'

'No, I don't think you should either,' Otto replied, still red-faced with delight. 'I'll take them and chuck 'em, shall I?'

'Only if you absolutely promise to throw them down the first gutter. If you kept them and they were ever found . . .'

'Don't worry.' Otto smiled. 'Paulus may be the clever one but I'm not *completely* thick you know.'

The mention of Paulus made them both think for a moment. Looking into each other's eyes in silent acknowledgement that the dynamics of all their lives had changed.

'I'd better go,' Otto said.

He scooped up the buttons and made for the door, stumbling over the thick rug and nearly upsetting a little table crowded with stuffed toys and ornaments.

'Ottsy,' Dagmar said, 'you know you and Pauly always tell me that one day I'll have to choose?'

'Yeah,' Otto gulped.

'Well, I have. I love Pauly but . . . I've chosen you.'

The Adopted Son

Berlin, 1935

It was very late when Otto returned home having, it seemed to him, almost floated across Berlin on a cloud of happiness, descending to earth only once in order to dispose of the buttons in a great mound of horse shit on Köpenicker Strasse.

It was late but to Otto's surprise, Wolfgang, Frieda and Paulus were still up.

They were waiting for him.

His family.

'About bloody time,' Paulus snapped. 'Mum and Dad want to talk to us and they won't tell me what it's about on my own so we've had to wait for you and I haven't been able to study all evening.'

'I'm heartbroken, mate,' Otto said. 'Oh, by the way, Dagmar's agreed to be my girl. Sorry but that's how it goes.'

Whatever Paulus had been thinking about his mother's strange behaviour he forgot it at once in the face of this terrible pronouncement.

'You're lying!'

'Ask her if you like,' Otto replied. 'Ring her, she'll be up.'

The devastation on Paulus's face made Otto wish he hadn't put it so bluntly, but then he knew there was never going to be any easy way to say it.

Paulus got out of his chair; he looked close to tears.

'Sorry, Mum,' he said, trying to sound calm. 'Whatever it is you want to say will have to keep. I'm tired, I'm going to bed.'

Frieda smiled. A sad smile.

'No, Pauly,' she said, 'you have to stay. I want to talk to you both. You'll have to fight about Dagmar another time.'

'Fight's over,' Otto said smugly. 'I've won.'

Perhaps it was the word 'fight' that gave Frieda pause for thought. She had been so intent on what she needed to say that she had not noticed Otto's dishevelled appearance.

'Where have you been, Ottsy?'

'Out,' Otto replied.

'Is that blood on your shirt?' Frieda asked, fear starting in her eyes.

'I don't know. Maybe.'

Paulus knew. 'You've done it, haven't you?'

Otto merely shrugged.

'Done what, Otto!' Frieda asked with rising alarm. 'Tell me what you've done.'

Otto did not reply but instead went and grabbed some bread and put the kettle on the gas. Frieda turned to Paulus.

'What's he done, Pauly?' she said. 'You obviously know.'

Now it was Paulus's turn to shrug.

'Him and his mates said they were going to mug a storm trooper. I suppose they must have done it.'

'Thanks,' Otto said, putting beef dripping on his bread. 'Big mouth, eh?'

'You'd have boasted about it in the end anyway,' Paulus replied. 'Just like you've obviously been boasting to Dagmar.'

'Oh, Ottsy,' Frieda said.

'Well what if I did! I'm proud of it! We slapped those bastards about a bit and made them squeal like the cowards they are. And next time I'm going to do one on my own. Man to man. I'll kill him too. I only didn't kill one tonight because Paulus bloody begged me—'

'I didn't *beg* you, mate!' Paulus snapped. 'I *told* you you'll make it worse for all of us!'

'How? How can it be any worse? We're not even citizens any more. We get spat at on buses! Pushed out of shops. Kicked and punched every day. Our girls are insulted and worse. We can't join anything, we can't go anywhere! They're taking everything away from us! Everything!'

'Keep your voice down, you stupid bastard,' Paulus hissed.

Wolfgang and Frieda were sitting at the table in silence as Otto and Paulus traded harsh words.

'Yeah that's right, Pauly, whisper! Whisper in your own home! Don't you see? We're crawling! They are making us Jews crawl. Well this Jew ain't crawling any more! I made Dagmar smile tonight because I took a bit of revenge for her dad. When did you last see her smile? We have to stand up for ourselves. Nobody's going to help us Jews. Everybody hates us even in the countries that pretend they don't! Only Jews can help Jews!'

Otto had taken his flick-knife from his pocket. He was brandishing it as he spoke. 'I'm sick of this,' he said. 'I'm going out.'

'Otto!' Frieda said, her tone demanding silence. 'Don't you dare leave this house. You have to listen to me. We have to talk.'

Otto stopped. The boys glanced at each other and then looked at their mother. Something was up. They fell silent.

'Yes, Mum?' Otto said almost contritely.

Frieda looked at him steadily. The time had come.

'Ottsy, baby. Darling boy . . . darling son. You're not a Jew.'

Both boys stared at her for a moment.

Paulus was the first to speak.

'What?' he said. 'What's that supposed to mean, Mum?' Then his voice brightened. 'Hey! Have you found us a goy in the family records! Wow, Mum, are we *Mischlinge*? Some *Mischlinge* can still use the swimming pools!'

Frieda shook her head sadly. 'I'm not talking about you, Pauly.

Or your father and me. I'm talking about Ottsy. I'm sorry, darling. I never wanted it to come out like this.'

'What? What to come out?' Again it was Paulus who asked. Otto was still silent.

'Otto. Darling. Daddy and I love you more than life itself. You know that, don't you? Paulus and you are our darling boys and . . .'

Now Otto spoke.

'What are you trying to tell me, Mum?'

Frieda tried to speak. Words she had been preparing in her mind for so long. Trying to think of a way to show her son that she loved him with all her heart and that what she had to tell him was good news. That unlike the rest of the family, Otto had a chance, a chance for a normal life. A life without fear.

But she knew that Otto would not *want* that chance.

He loved his family. His mother, his father, and his grandparents. He was inseparable from his twin brother no matter how much they might fight. And in a strange way Otto had even decided that he loved being a Jew. Because Otto was the fighter of the family, fiercely loyal and worryingly reckless. He loved a cause and Hitler had given him the cause of all causes. And now along with everything else in Otto's life it was to be pulled from under him.

Frieda could not speak.

'What, Mum?' Otto asked again. 'What are you trying to tell me?'

It was Wolfgang who said it. Wolfgang spoke less and less these days. Preferring to smoke in silence when his lungs permitted and drink whatever he could find. But he spoke now. Briefly strong again for Frieda.

'You're adopted, Otts,' he said gently, his hollow cheekbones casting deep shadows across his thin, prematurely aged face. 'Mum had twins but one of them was stillborn. Your natural mother died in childbirth and you had no father. We took you as our own. Right there and then on the day you were both born. Neither you nor Pauly had been alive an hour when we first put you together. And that's how it's been ever since.'

'You're our twins,' Frieda said softly, 'our beloved boys. But you didn't start life inside me, Otts. Though I love you like you did.'

Both boys simply stared open-mouthed.

'We never gave it a thought,' Frieda continued quickly, 'it didn't matter to us. You're our boys, that's all. But then Hitler came and suddenly it mattered. *Blood* mattered. Blood, blood, bloody blood! They never shut up about blood! It's a fetish, a perversion. It's insane. I've referred patients for a hundred transfusions. We never once used to ask what the donor's damned religion was!'

Frieda tailed off. Both boys were still staring in silent shock. It was Wolfgang who tried to be practical, tried to move past the emotion by bringing the conversation back to specifics.

'The thing is, Ottsy,' he said, 'with these new laws, everybody's family history is going to be investigated by law. They are going to decide once and for all who is a Jew in their eyes, and who isn't. Mum, Paulus and me are Jews, Otts. And you aren't.'

Still Otto could not reply; he had sunk into a chair, the knife still in his hand.

'Blimey, Otts, mate,' Paulus said, forcing a laugh into his voice. 'That's good news, eh? Who'd have thought it? Looks like you're off the hook. We should celebrate.'

Now Otto found his voice, turning to his brother. His blank, drained face suddenly vivid red with anger.

'You think I want that! You stupid bastard! You think I want to be off the fucking hook?'

'Otto, *please*,' Frieda said.

'You can't tell me off,' Otto said rounding on her, 'you're not my mum!'

'Don't say that, Otto,' Frieda gasped. 'Never say that. Not ever! I am your mum.'

'You just said I wasn't your son! Pauly's your son. I'm not. I come from God knows where! I'm not even a Jew. Who am I? I'm no one!'

'That's not true, Otts,' Wolfgang said. 'You're one of us. Our family. It's only the Nazis who are doing this to us. I—'

'Why didn't you tell me before! All these years you've known that I'm not your son!'

'You *are*. You are our son!'

'Hey, Otto!' Paulus said sharply, and now his face was angry too. 'Don't attack Mum! This is a shock to me too you know. But really, what does it matter? Like Mum says, blood is crap. Race is crap.'

'Family isn't!' Otto replied.

'Exactly, and that's what we are!' Paulus said. 'What happened when we were born happened, that's all. Lots of kids got adopted after the war. Personally if I were you I'd be pleased.'

'Pleased?' Otto gasped. 'Are you crazy?'

'Of course I'd be pleased!' Paulus was as angry as Otto. 'Because I'd know I was no less your brother and Mum and Dad were no less my parents. The only difference would be that I wouldn't have an entire country wishing I was dead . . .'

'*I* wish I was dead!'

'No!' Frieda wailed.

'That's just stupid!' Paulus said. 'So what if you're not a Jew?'

'I am a Jew,' Otto protested. 'I don't *want* to be one of them. I nearly killed one tonight. Why are you telling me this now? I'm a Jew!'

'Because you were going to find out anyway,' Frieda said. 'You have to see that, Otts. The Gestapo is going to go through every detail of every single person in Germany. Everyone is going to be categorized. Your history is documented. The adoption forms are at the hospital. Your birth certificate is at the town hall. We had to tell you and we have to make a plan . . .'

'Plan! What plan?' Otto said through tears. 'There is no plan! Because there's no me! There's no Otto Stengel. He never existed. I don't exist.'

Otto grabbed his coat and once more made for the door.

'Otto! Please!' Frieda cried, tears running down her face.

'Otto, stop,' Paulus demanded, 'you have to stop.'

'Who are you shouting at?' Otto said with a wild and angry snarl. 'Who are you giving orders to? You're not my brother!'

Family Trees

Berlin, 1935

Otto spent the night on a bench in the People's Park amongst the fairy-tale statues but the following morning, as dawn broke over the city, he went home. He was cold and stiff and his heart still ached but his tears had dried. He knew that the pain and the confusion he was feeling, the fear of rejection, the isolation and the loneliness, were not his parents' fault. They were Hitler's, and the Nazis were now more his enemy than ever.

He climbed the six sets of stairs in order to avoid using the creaking lift at so early an hour, and let himself into the darkened flat. Inside he found his mother sitting exactly where he had left her and where she had clearly sat all night. He rushed forward and threw his arms around her.

'I'm sorry, Mum,' he said. 'I'm so sorry.'

'Don't be, Ottsy. Don't be,' Frieda whispered. 'Goodness, look at me, crying again. I didn't think I had any tears left in me.'

She hugged him tight.

'I've been so worried. Pauly looked for you till one in the morning. Wolfgang tried too but he got tired. We called your friends. They all thought you'd been picked up for . . . for what you did yesterday evening.'

'I'm so sorry,' Otto repeated. 'I shouldn't have run. I just wasn't thinking straight.'

'You know that we love you both just the same,' Frieda went on. 'You and Paulus, our two boys.'

'Yeah, I know, Mum. They can't break us apart,' Otto said. 'They never will.'

Silent tears were running in streams down Frieda's cheeks.

'Not in our hearts, baby,' she whispered. 'Not in our hearts.'

Otto felt the wet tears against his own face as he hugged her. He knew what she was saying, the salty agony glistening on her cheeks confirmed it.

'Are they going to take me away, Mum?' he asked.

Frieda could not bring herself to reply.

Wolfgang had appeared at the door of his and Frieda's bedroom and had been listening.

'We think so, Otts,' he croaked through his tobacco- and TB-ravaged voice. 'We have to presume so. The newspapers say the police are supposed to identify "racially valuable stock". The SS have been setting up orphanages. Himmler's collecting kids.'

'God. What *are* these people?' Frieda said under her breath. 'Can they truly be *human*?'

Fear replaced grief on Otto's countenance. His face shining white in the pale dawn that was creeping in at the windows. It was a rare sight for his parents to see. Otto had become so adept at disguising terror over the years that they had imagined him fearless. But the prospect of being put into the care of the SS seemed for a moment at least to overwhelm even him.

'I'll hide,' Otto said finally. 'If they come for me I won't be here, I'll go underground. I'll hide.'

'Then they'll take us.' It was Paulus who spoke from the twins' bedroom door.

'Always the voice of reason, eh, bro?' Otto replied with a bitter smile.

'You know it's true, Otts,' Paulus said. 'I don't like saying it any more than you like hearing it but if they come for you and don't find you they'll punish us. I don't mind. I'll run, I'll fight, just like you would. But Dad can't go back into that camp.'

Otto nodded. He knew that was true.

Wolfgang turned away, ashamed to be identified as the most vulnerable member of the family.

'You're right, Pauly,' Otto said. '*Obviously*. You always bloody are. I'll let them take me. *Then* I'll run.'

'Well,' said Frieda, 'I imagine we have a few weeks to consider things. Let's try to do it calmly, eh? Hope for the best, plan for the worst as they say. You've been out all night, Otts. I'll make you some toasted bread and cheese and a mug of chocolate.'

'Thanks, Mum,' Otto said. 'Best mum in the world.'

The Stengels were not the only people hoping for the best in the weeks that followed the announcement of the Nuremberg Laws. As the long summer of 1935 turned finally to autumn it seemed as if the whole country could speak of nothing else but family history.

The new rules officially defining what constituted a Jew sparked a frenzy of genealogical research. Everybody in Germany was to be racially classified and even the most proudly Aryan types began referring nervously to their family trees in terror that they might find a Jew lurking somewhere on a branch. All across the Reich, church records, parish lists, gravestones, bible inscriptions, ancient deeds and transactions were consulted minutely by both individuals and the police in an effort to establish the racial credentials of the whole population.

Credentials which, as Wolfgang dryly observed, were supposed to be self-evident anyway.

'I don't know why they have to go through this fuss,' he said bitterly, 'surely all they need to do is look for the hunched figures with sloping foreheads, noses like grappling hooks and dripping knives in their hands and that'll be the Jews!'

'It's horrible,' Frieda said. 'All the Aryans are terrified of finding a Jew in their line and all the Jews are desperate to find an Aryan. I've been having people come in all day at the surgery asking me for medical records. People are going about praying that their grandma was raped by some bacon butcher because it's actually better to be descended from an Aryan sex criminal than a Jewish charity worker.'

It was this remark of Frieda's that led Otto to announce he had had an idea.

The four of them had been discussing the new laws over dinner, as they had done on every evening since the night that Otto and Paulus learnt the truth about their family history.

'*You* had an idea, Ottsy,' Paulus gasped with mock wonder. 'Is this a first? Should we celebrate?'

Otto punched Paulus. Whatever fears the future might hold for them, the twins were still the twins.

'Yes, I've had an idea,' Otto said. 'Why should I wait for the Gestapo to investigate my history? I should do it myself. If I can find a Jew somewhere way back, then they won't take me away.'

'Oh, Otto,' Frieda murmured, 'that is such a brave and lovely thought.'

Wolfgang stretched his thin bony hand across the table to squeeze Otto's.

'Thanks, son,' he whispered. 'You've got nerve, I'll give you that.'

Paulus, however, was having none of it.

'You're crazy!' he said, tearing angrily at a piece of black bread as if it was Otto's head and then drowning it in his plate of goulash. 'Completely crazy. Every Jew in Germany wants a couple of Gentile grandparents and you're trying to find a Jew?'

'That's right,' Otto replied, clearly pleased at having for once wrong-footed his know-it-all brother. 'As far as I'm concerned I *am* a Jew. I just need a convenient relative to prove it.'

'You're *not* a Jew, Otts!' Paulus protested. 'That's the point! Can't you see you're safe?'

'I don't *want* to be safe!' Otto said. 'I want to be a Stengel and the Stengels are Jews.'

'Please tell me this is a joke, Otts,' Paulus said. 'It's perverse. It's also potentially suicidal. Nobody wants to be a Jew in Germany.'

'What a shame, eh, Mum,' Otto said, 'that it wasn't the other way around back in 1920 in the hospital. Then we'd have all been happy, wouldn't we?'

This remark brought Paulus up short. Otto could see that his point had hit home.

'Well, Pauly?' Otto pressed on. '*Would* you have liked that? Do you really wish it was *you* who didn't have to be a Jew any more? Even if it meant having to leave home and go and live with foster Nazis?'

'Yes,' Paulus said firmly. 'And not because I'd be able to go swimming and study properly again. But because if I had proper rights as a citizen I could help Mum and Dad and Pops and Grandma. And *you* come to think of it. Things are going to get a lot worse, you know, and having a tame German in the family might be pretty useful. I'd be happy to take the job.'

'I think that's a very sensible answer, Pauly,' Frieda said.

'Yeah, Mum?' Otto said, with a touch of a sneer. 'Well I think Pauly's famous brain might not be working so well today. Tame Germans! Come on, Pauly, they're *all* tame. That's the bloody problem. We know *lots* of them, whispering to us that they don't approve of what's happening. Apologizing with their eyes for not saying hello to us in the street. What good do they do? Nothing. Bugger all. Just like Silke's precious bloody Commies! I keep telling you, when things *do* get worse, the only people who will be able to help us is us. We're going to need to stick together. Which is why I need to find a kike in my tree.'

'Well,' Frieda said, 'you can have a go, Otto, but I'd be surprised if you'll find one. I only ever met your birth grandparents once but they looked pretty *völkisch* to me.'

'I have to look. I'm going to find some Jew in my blood if it kills me.'

'Otto, if you *do* find any,' Paulus said solemnly, 'it probably will.'

'Thanks a lot, Pauly,' Wolfgang said, refilling his glass with spirits, 'that *really* cheers us up.'

A Country Excursion

Saxony, September 1935

The following day Paulus and Otto went to Friedrichshain town hall in search of the names and addresses of Otto's natural grandparents.

'If it wasn't a matter of life and death it'd actually be quite funny,' Paulus said on their return. 'The place was absolutely packed. Jews, gypsies, Nazis, all scrabbling at the town records. They've got this big chart on the wall with all these different family tree models, white circles for Germans, black circles for Jews . . .'

'Surprise surprise,' Wolfgang remarked from his piano stool.

'And then mixed circles for the *Mischlinge*. The idea is you put your great-grandparents in the various circles and that way you can work out whether you qualify to sit on park benches or not.'

'And did you find anything out,' Frieda asked, 'about Otto's family?'

'Only on his mother's side,' Paulus said, 'and then only their names and their home village. It's in Saxony.'

'I'm going to find them,' Otto said firmly. 'I'll cycle – it's only a hundred and twenty kilometres.'

When Silke heard about the trip she insisted immediately on going along for the ride. She had only just got back from her epic march to Nuremberg and having tasted the freedom of the open road and nights out camping under stars had no desire to return to the drudgery of life in her mother's apartment where her step-father treated her as an unpaid servant.

'It'll be easy to get off school,' she said. 'I'll just say it's BDM business. I am Youth and I belong to the Führer, don't you know!' she added, quoting party rhetoric with a wicked laugh. 'I have a special place in his heart and in his plans so my teachers can go screw themselves! Ha ha! It'll be a good thing to have me along in my uniform anyway, Otts. A lad on his own out there with a bike and backpack who's not in the Hitler Youth is a dead set target. They've banned all the other youth clubs, even the Catholic bird-watchers. The country's swarming with HJ and believe me there's plenty of them looking for a fight. They go for any kid who isn't in the gang. If you're with me, it'll just look like you're in civvies.'

And so the very next morning Otto and Silke set out together with their sandwiches and apple juice, a blanket each, a little canvas tent and a few marks to buy food along the way.

The first part of the journey meant cycling all the way across Berlin from the south-east to the north-west, a dirty, sweaty business on what was a warm late September morning. Soon, however, they picked up the old Hamburg road and found themselves rolling happily along an almost empty country road which meandered its way through the glorious countryside of Brandenburg towards Saxony and would eventually lose itself in the beautiful Elbe valley, where they planned to camp that night.

It was a wonderful day bathed in perfect sunshine, and Otto found himself forgetting all his terror for the future as he revelled in the simple unfettered freedom of the open road.

'Hitler weather', people called it, and it was true that the summers since the Leader had seized power did seem to have been longer and more pleasant than those under the Weimar.

'Bloody hot, eh, Otts!' Silke said as she laboured at her pedals, leaning forward over the handlebar in order to lend more power to each pumping motion of her legs.

Good legs too, Otto could not stop himself from thinking, as he glanced across the dusty lane at his travelling companion. The skirts of the BDM uniform were fully calf-length but Silke had tucked the hem of hers up into her knickers to make it easier to ride. Her legs were thus fully displayed, and the flexing and unflexing of her muscles cast nice shadows across her tanned thighs and calves as she rode.

How strange, Otto mused, that scrappy little Silke should end up having nice legs. He rubbed the sweat from his eyes and took in the pleasant sight. Who would ever have thought it?

Firm, shapely legs. *Girl's* legs. Not spectacular like Dagmar's, but then no girl had legs like Dagmar's. Hers were endless, slim and delicate, like some fabulous, human gazelle. Silke's legs were not long at all and certainly not skinny. But nice nonetheless. Friendly and strong. No longer covered in grazes and sticking plasters either. Otto did not think he'd ever seen Silke's knees before without the scabs and plasters and as often as not some dirty inky scribble. Now they were clear and smooth. The only evidence that remained of a thousand fights and falls were one or two little scars that stood white against the copper skin.

Amazing. Silke had been 'one of the boys' for so long that it was quite a shock to realize she'd ended up turning into a girl after all. She even had curves. When had that happened? Skinny little Silke with curves? They seemed simply to have arrived overnight.

'Isn't Silke growing up?' Frieda had remarked recently. 'I always thought she'd turn out pretty.'

And she had.

An old friend with a big smile and a disposition as sunny as the reflections that sparkled in the corn-blonde hair blowing in the breeze behind her as she panted over her handlebar.

Good old Silke.

Such a dear, old friend.

'Poor Pauly, eh?' Silke shouted. 'Bet he wishes he was here.'

'Yeah!' Otto called back. 'Sitting in school surrounded by the enemy studying for a job they won't let him have. And he thinks *he's* the clever one! Ha!'

Side by side they rode. Up and down hills, past streams, through fields and sweet-smelling forests. Stopping occasionally for draughts of apple juice.

Both of them knew that they would remember that wonderful day's ride all their lives. Their spirits rising with every kilometre passed. With the scent of the forests and the freshly made hay and sweet meadow flowers, all wafted to them on a warm and gentle breeze through pure and pristine air.

'It really is a lovely world,' Silke said.

'Yes it is,' Otto agreed. 'Shame about the people in it.'

He said this as yet another labourer in a field paused in his work to greet them as they passed, not with a wave or a simple '*Guten Tag*' but with the 'German' salute and a loud '*Heil Hitler*'.

'I almost *resent* the sun for shining on them,' Otto went on. 'It makes everything look so wonderful, even them with their stupid outstretched arms.'

'Well, of course there never was any sun before Hitler,' Silke joked.

It was the time of the September Solstice. A pagan festival beloved of the Nazis. Every village they passed through was bedecked with flowers and swastikas. Every little green or square was filled with dancers.

Girls in traditional country dress with garlands in their hair. Boys stamping about in HJ uniforms with wooden rifles on their shoulders. Marching bands playing and children's choirs singing songs.

Songs Otto recognized as he cycled past returning the friendly waves of the singers. The same songs that were sung at his school, at assemblies and during music lessons.

Das Judenblut vom Messer spritzt, geht's uns nochmal so gut.

'The Jews' blood spurting from the knife makes us feel especially good.'

All day they cycled, alternately delighted to be free and in the countryside and depressed to be so continuously confronted with evidence of the Nazi occupation of it. Village after village had a banner strung across the road at its entrance saying 'No Jews' and 'Jew Beware'.

And then there were the shouts.

'Death to Jews,' peasants called out cheerfully as Otto and Silke passed. Just as if they were shouting, 'Good morning! Good luck! Enjoy your ride.'

Time and again they cycled past marching groups of boys and girls with happy, smiling faces, calling down death on their fellow man. The countryside was alive with them. Off to the rivers and forests intent on developing the 'steel hard' bodies that Hitler had demanded of 'his youth'.

That night, exhausted, they made camp together in a little copse of trees beside a stream. Or a small river, as Otto insisted it should be ranked, having pronounced it as one from the map.

They didn't bother pitching the tent because the night was warm and there was no chance of rain. It was too warm even for a fire, which Otto thought was a great shame but Silke said was fortunate.

'Fires attract all sorts of nasty insects,' she said. 'Gnats, mosquitoes and *Hitler Jugend*. You can bet your shirt that if there was a troop around they'd feel honour-bound to scout us out. It's an obsession with them, they are the "eyes of the Führer". It's not like we have anything to hide, particularly now it seems you aren't even a Jew any more! But all the same we don't want company.'

Otto agreed. 'Smart girl,' he said. 'Paulus would be proud of you.'

'And there was you thinking I was just a pretty face.'

She laughed self-consciously as she said it. Otto laughed too.

'Good old Silke! One of the lads, eh?'

A compliment which did not seem particularly to please its recipient.

They ate their supper of cheese and bread and some fruit and then each curled up in their blankets beside each other. Lying staring up at the stars, which they could see twinkling through the canopy of trees.

Otto couldn't remember the last time he'd talked to Silke. Talked *properly*, just her and him. If indeed he ever *had* talked to her. He'd *laughed* with her countless times, fought with her, run from irate shopkeepers with her and teased her endlessly. But never actually simply *talked* to her. Why would he have done? She was just one of the boys. A mate. You didn't go rabbiting on to your mates.

'What do you think will happen, Otts?' Silke asked. 'I mean to Pauly and you and your mum and dad?'

'Well, hopefully Mum'll manage to get the family out,' Otto replied. 'I know her and Dad talk about it quite a lot, but of course Dad's basically unemployable these days and then there's Pops and Grandma to think about. It would be hard for them to move even if they wanted to.'

'Don't they want to?' Silke asked.

'Come on, Silks, you know them better than that. They're Germans! They don't know how to be anything else. Pops always says he's been German since 1870, while Hitler the Austrian has only been German since 1932, so why should Pops be the one to leave?'

Silke laughed. 'Yeah, that's Herr Tauber all right. He always used to scare the crap out of me.'

'He still does scare me,' Otto said.

'So do you think your mum will leave them behind?'

'I think in the end she might have to. But I'll tell you one thing, Silks, if Mum and Dad do manage to get the family out, I won't be going with them.'

Silke raised herself up on one elbow and looked down at Otto's face, faint and pale in the shadowy moonlight.

'Because of Dagmar?' she said quietly.

'Of course,' Otto said. 'Unless Dagmar can get out herself I'm staying to look after her.'

'Saturday Club rules, eh?' Silke smiled.

'Yeah. That's it,' Otto replied.

But they both knew it had nothing to do with the Saturday Club.

Silke changed the subject.

'Have you ever heard of the *Rote Hilfe*?' she asked.

'The Red Help?' Otto repeated. 'No, I don't think so. What is it?'

'It's a sort of resistance thing,' Silke went on, 'in Berlin. It was attached to the Red Cross before Hitler but now of course it's underground. They try and help out families who've had their men stolen to camps. And also to let people abroad know what's really happening.'

'Are you a member then?'

'Well, I don't really know. It's all secret and you never know anybody's name, but I have a couple of contacts.'

'What do you do?'

'It seems a bit silly to me. They write a newsletter and it's my job to see that copies get out of Germany.'

'Wow, how do you do that?'

'Easy. I post them! Nobody suspects a teenage girl in a BDM uniform, you see. I buy a woman's magazine and slip the secret stuff between the pages. Then I go to the post office and send it as general printed matter to an address in Geneva.'

Otto thought about it for a little while.

'Good for you,' he said eventually.

'I just wanted you to know,' Silke said hesitantly, 'that the gang is still together. The Saturday Club. I may wear a BDM uniform but we believe in the same things.'

'I know that, Silks.'

'And,' Silke went on nervously, 'just like *you* want to look after Dagmar, I'd like to help look after you.'

'Well, we're all bound by oath, aren't we?' Otto laughed.

'Yes, that's right.'

'So you'd help Paulus too?'

'Of course I would! How can you even ask!'

'And Dagmar?' There was a pause. 'She's in the Saturday Club too, remember?'

'Yes. I *suppose* so,' Silke said.

Otto smiled in the darkness.

'I hope you will always try to help her if you can, Silks,' he said. 'If only for my sake.'

'Otto,' Silke said. 'We're all in the Saturday Club. We made a vow.'

After that there was nothing more to say and they went to sleep.

Or at least Otto did, almost immediately, dead beat from the ride. Silke lay awake for quite some time though. Listening to Otto breathe and watching his face in the moonlight.

Blood Family

Saxony, 1935

The following morning they rose with the sun.

Silke took a towel from her bag and a little galvanized tin box with soap in it.

'I'll just go and have a wash and stuff,' she said.

'Wow. Soap. You never bothered with that when we slept out as kids.'

'Yeah, well, I'm not a kid any more, am I?' Silke replied, not looking Otto in the eye.

'I didn't think to bring any myself,' Otto admitted.

'God! Boys!' Silke said with mock exasperation. 'Well, you can borrow mine . . . I mean after.'

'Yeah. Of course. That's right. You go first. I'll wait and go next.'

They smiled at each other. In the past they would have simply gone together. Free and unselfconscious. But now they both understood that the time of innocent intimacy had passed.

'Back in a minute,' Silke said.

'No rush.'

'I've got a little garden trowel and a roll of lavatory paper in my bag, too, if you want to use them.'

'You're a good camper, Silks. I didn't bring anything.'

'Ah they train us well in the BDM, you know. The Führer watches over us even when we're squatting in a bush!'

'Always thought he looked like a pervert.'

After their ablutions and a drink of stream water to wash down the remains of the bread and cheese, they mounted their bikes once more.

'Ouch!' Silke said.

'Me too,' Otto agreed, 'but only twenty-five K to go.'

'Yeah. And then all the way back.'

The hamlet that was their destination was scarcely large enough to even make it on to the map. It was reached by a deeply rutted, hard-to-cycle, unmetalled lane which ran through some small outlying farms and ended up amongst a little group of poor cottages clustered around an algae-covered duck pond.

There was a small wooden chapel and beside that a village pub of sorts which was really just the front parlour of one of the cottages with an old tin Bitburger beer sign hanging outside. This also doubled as a post office and tiny general store, offering a few tinned goods and some grey-looking chocolate. It was here that Otto enquired after the people he was looking for. Herr and Frau Hahn. His maternal grandparents by birth.

He had half feared that in the intervening fifteen years they might have moved on from the village where they had lived when their daughter died, but like most peasants of their generation and of all the many generations that had preceded them, Herr and Frau Hahn were born, lived and would no doubt die in the same few square kilometres of land. Their only trip to Berlin had in fact been for their daughter's confinement when they had hoped to bring her back and get her wed to a decent farm boy who would accept her bastard child.

That plan of course had never happened and the Hahns' daughter had never come home. But now her child had and he was standing in their little parlour.

'You are a fine-looking boy,' the man said, the deep lines of his weather-beaten old face creasing between tears and a smile.

The old woman was openly crying, dabbing at her eyes with an ancient, yellowing lace handkerchief.

'Are you truly our Inge's son?' she asked.

'Of course he is,' the man said, 'look at him, can't you see her in him? Can't you see her now? Standing here in her home as if she'd never left. He has her beautiful eyes.'

The old couple were clearly almost overcome and Otto shifted uneasily. Embarrassed to be the focus of such unbridled emotion from two people who were strangers to him and whom he intended should remain strangers.

'He is! He's Inge's boy!' the woman said.

'Please, Frau Hahn . . .' Otto began, but before he could finish the stooped little woman had scurried across the room to a dresser on which were arranged their few family treasures. One or two pieces of ornamental china, a music box and some framed family photos.

'Come see,' the old lady said, picking up various photographs. 'Here is your dear mother.'

Otto did not move to join Frau Hahn and view the photo. He was looking at a different picture, hanging on the wall above the display in pride of place, framed by a garland of dried flowers. A picture of Hitler.

'You are Nazis?' Otto asked.

Herr Hahn turned to Silke, who was sitting on the only cushioned chair, which the old couple had insisted she occupy, nodding at her BDM uniform.

'We all serve the Führer,' he said with a little bow. 'Just like your charming young friend.'

'Our Führer was sent to Germany by providence,' his wife added with an evangelical smile. 'He watches over us and makes all well.'

Otto was silent, his lip quivering slightly.

'Never mind that, Otts,' Silke said quickly. 'Everyone has that portrait on their wall. Forget about the Führer, come on! Take a look at the photo of your mum!'

Otto turned to Silke. 'You know who my mum is, Silke, and she's not in that photo.'

'Yes of course, Otto, I know that, but all the same you should look.'

Otto stepped forward and looked at the faded photograph of an attractive sandy-haired girl.

'It was taken in 1919,' the old farmer said with a touch of bitterness, 'the year before she met . . .'

'My father?' Otto said sharply, finishing the sentence that the old man had been reluctant to complete.

'He was a Communist!' the farmer said, still clearly very angry after sixteen years. 'He got her with child and then deserted her.'

'He was murdered,' Otto corrected. 'My parents told me. He

died in the massacre at Lichtenburg. Murdered by the *Freikorps*. By the same people who became the Nazis, Herr Hahn.'

The old couple looked confused.

'Please don't call me Herr Hahn, my boy,' the sad-looking peasant begged. 'I am your grandfather.'

Otto bit his lip.

'I've come to ask you about my family,' he said. 'I want to know if there is any Jewish blood in our line.'

The old couple looked shocked for a moment and then smiled. They of course completely misunderstood the purpose behind Otto's question.

'Oh you poor boy,' Frau Hahn exclaimed. 'Of course, as an adopted child you must be worried about your blood for fear that it isn't pure.'

'That some Jew crept over the back fence!' the farmer grunted.

'Of course! Of course, my child,' the woman said, 'you must be reassured. But look!'

Frau Hahn reached up to the single shelf that hung bracketed to the wall and on which stood just two books. An ancient family Bible and a copy of *Mein Kampf*. Frau Hahn brought down the Bible and displayed it to Otto. 'See,' the old wife said with great pride, 'our whole family tree laid out for six generations right back to 1790. All good Christian names and every one of them to be found on gravestones here and in nearby villages. None more than ten kilometres from the pure German soil on which we are standing right now. And you will also find every one of the names you see here inscribed in the records of the parish churches here and thereabouts. No Yids and no gyppos in our line, my dear, dear boy.'

Such a sweet-looking lady. And no doubt as kind as she looked. Except when it came to the treatment which she would happily see handed out to any 'Jews or gyppos' who dared to come near her exalted 'stock'.

Otto stared at the handwriting in the Bible. Reading the various names, the last of which was that of Inge Hahn. His mother.

'And my father?' Otto asked. 'What about him? He's not

entered here and there was no name on the adoption certificate either. Do you know who he was? Do you know his name?'

'Yes,' the farmer said, 'we know his name, although I won't speak it in this house or anywhere else.' He took some paper from a little drawer in the treasures table and slowly and carefully wrote down a name. 'But you mustn't fear, my boy,' Herr Hahn went on. 'I know that the man was of good stock for all he disgraced his own family and ours. Inge wrote and told us his father was a minister in the Lutheran Church in Prenzlauer Berg in Berlin, but he died in the war. His mother may live. We wouldn't know.'

Otto took the paper and thanked the old couple.

'We have to leave,' Otto added. 'We've got a long way to go on our bikes to get home.'

Herr and Frau Hahn were horrified, devastated even. Clearly Otto's sudden appearance had brought them such hope.

'But won't you stay?' they pleaded. 'You and your friend? We have food and apple juice. We are so pleased to see you and we have so much to talk about.'

Otto stared down at his boots.

'No, ma'am,' he murmured, 'we don't.'

'But yes! Of course we do,' the farmer's wife protested. 'You can't leave now that you have only just arrived.'

'I'm sorry, Frau Hahn. But I can't stay. I really am sorry but I have heard all I came to hear.' Otto went to the door. 'Come on, Silke, we need to get going.'

Frau Hahn began crying. Her husband took up the old leather-bound Bible and thrust it towards Otto.

'Won't you put your name in our Bible at least?' the old farmer said. 'Beneath your mother's? She is the last one of our family so inscribed.'

But Otto wouldn't do it.

'I wish you well, Herr Hahn,' he said politely. 'I really do. But you're not my grandfather and the people in this Bible aren't my family. I have no place in your book. My family began with the mum and dad you gave me to. And what's more, they're Jews. I am a Jew.'

The two old peasants looked dumbstruck.

'Jews?' Herr Hahn asked in genuine horror. 'That doctor gave you to Jews? *We* let you be taken by *Jews*?'

'That's right,' Otto replied, 'you left me with the finest people in Berlin and for that at least I will always be grateful to you. Goodbye.'

With that Otto left the tiny cottage with Silke scuttling after him, mumbling embarrassed farewells on both their behalf.

Otto didn't look back as they cycled away, but Silke did, and she saw the old couple standing in the doorway staring after them, their faces empty with loss.

When Otto got back to the city, the first thing he did before even going home was to ride to the Lutheran church at Prenzlauer Berg and enquire after the previous minister. The one who had died in the Great War and whose name the peasant farmer Hahn had written down for him.

It was just as old Herr Hahn had said it would be. There was no shadow of Jewry to be found in Otto's paternal line, any more than there had been in that of his mother.

That news for which every other German longed, to be classified officially as a genuine six-generation 'pure blood', left Otto devastated. He really wasn't a Jew and he could not turn himself into one no matter how much he might want to.

And so, like the Jews he could no longer claim to be, he must be exiled.

Fate Sealed

Berlin, 1935

Frieda and Wolfgang were summoned to the local Gestapo Office about a fortnight after Otto returned from his trip to Saxony.

They returned ashen-faced.

'They say that you are never to see us again, Ottsy,' Frieda said, trying with Herculean effort to pull herself together enough to speak.

'No!' Otto shouted. 'That can't be true. Why? What's the point of stopping us even seeing each other?'

'They said we've been a corrupting influence for too long,' Frieda explained through her tears.

Wolfgang took his bottle of cheap spirits and sank down on the piano stool, his head slumped forward.

'They say it will be a serious criminal offence if we try to maintain any kind of relationship with you at all,' he said, speaking into his chest.

'But what if it's me?' Otto almost pleaded. 'What if I'm the one who comes to you? They can't blame you for—'

'If you visit us,' Wolfgang interrupted, 'they'll treat it as if we've kidnapped you, and Mum, me and Paulus will be sent to a concentration camp.'

The four of them stared at each other.

'Tomorrow?' Otto said almost mechanically. 'They're coming tomorrow?'

'We'll see you, Otts,' Wolfgang went on, emboldened by the gulp of liquor he'd taken. 'Somehow we'll find a way. They can't just pretend our family doesn't exist.'

'Of course they can't and nor will we,' Frieda said, sniffling into a handkerchief and trying to collect herself. 'Somehow we will stay together.'

'But if you see me they'll punish you,' Otto said in despair. 'If I come around here they'll take you away.' He looked at Paulus.

'We've been together since our first day on earth, Pauly. Now they won't let us be brothers at all.'

Paulus was pulling himself together also, wiping the wet from his eyes with angry sweeps of his sleeve.

'Maybe they'd let us see each other if we promised to fight,' he said, trying to smile. 'We wouldn't find that too difficult, would we?'

Otto still did not cry but now he began to rage.

'I'll make them wish they never heard of me,' he said banging his fist down on the dining table. 'Any family that takes me in is going to regret it. I will make their lives hell. I'll make them hate me for the Jew I still am! I'll kill them if I have to.'

'Otto, please!' Frieda cried. 'Don't say that. You can't fight these people. They'll punish you.'

'Punish me! What more can they do to me? I'm telling you, Mum, I don't care!'

'But I *do* care, Otto. And I'm your mother. Whatever those mad men say, I'm *still* your mother and you are only fifteen and you will do what your mother tells you!'

Otto was brought up short. Frieda's tone was so incongruous and yet so very familiar. She'd used it so many countless thousands of times before. Almost by force of habit Otto cast his eyes to the floor, as if she'd been ticking him off for stealing biscuits from the treat tin or brandishing a dirty postcard that she'd found hidden in his bag. He almost found himself smiling.

'And don't grin like that when I'm talking to you!' Frieda snapped, dabbing at her eyes. 'You will wipe that smile off your face and listen to your mother! It is quite bad enough that you have to go away for a while, without me having to worry that you're going to get yourself into terrible trouble when I'm not there to look after you.' Frieda had regained her composure now. The issue of controlling Otto's behaviour being more urgent to her than her despair at his having to go. 'I *have* to know that you'll be good, Otts. That you'll do what they say, otherwise they'll punish you terribly. You're already marked, don't you see? You've been brought up by Jews, they'll be watching you. You have to toe the line. For my sake! Do you hear? Join the HJ, sing their songs, give their salutes. Swear death to the Jews, Ottsy! It's the *only* way I'll know you're safe.'

Otto stared at his mother, his expression a terrible cross between fierce determination and abject despair.

'All right, Mum,' he said quietly, 'I'll be good.'

'*Promise* me, Otto.'

'I promise,' Otto said.

Frieda smiled and held him to her.

Behind Otto's back his fingers were crossed.

Looking over his mother's shoulder, Otto caught Paulus's eye. He knew he could fool Frieda any time he wanted but he could never fool his brother.

'Well then,' Frieda whispered, 'at least I'll know you'll be safe. Now let's have no more quarrelling. Tomorrow you'll leave and we won't see you for a long time.'

'When?' Otto asked. 'When do you think I'll see you again?'

'When this madness somehow subsides,' Frieda replied. 'That time will come.'

Sitting at his silent piano, staring blankly at the sheets of music propped up on the stand, Wolfgang sighed. He couldn't help himself, perhaps he didn't even know he'd done it. But that sigh spoke volumes. Wolfgang for one no longer believed that the madness would ever subside.

'It will,' Frieda said in answer to his unspoken thought, 'and I'll tell you why it will, Wolf. Because otherwise the only possible conclusion to all of this is complete destruction for Germany. They keep saying they're rebuilding the nation but it's so damned obvious they're destroying it that even fools will soon see.'

Wolfgang shrugged.

'No, don't shrug at me like that, Wolf! I *will not* despair! *We* must not despair. This criminal state will end! You can't survive for ever sustained only by violence. No society ever did or ever will. If these people continue to ignore every basic moral code, every fundamental prerequisite for civilization, they'll *murder themselves* in the end and I think they're *far* too cunning to allow that to happen. They like their fat life and their uniforms and their big black cars too much to risk losing them. So in the end they'll compromise. Somehow they'll compromise if only to avoid their own destruction.'

Wolfgang shrugged again. He simply couldn't help himself, it seemed to be the only gesture he had left in him. 'I hope you're right, Freddy,' was all he would say.

That night Paulus and Otto went to bed in the room they had shared since they were tiny babies and would now almost certainly never share again.

'You had your fingers crossed, didn't you,' Paulus whispered, 'when you promised Mum you'd keep out of trouble?'

'Well, I didn't want her to worry, did I?' Otto hissed back defiantly. 'And if you don't want her to worry either you'll keep your mouth shut about it, eh?'

'So you're not going to keep out of trouble, then? You're going to fight the whole German state?'

'What do you think, mate?'

'I think you're crazy.'

'Hey, Pauly, you aren't the one who tomorrow morning has to go and live with some Nazi fucking strangers! You're still a Jew and even if you can't go to the pictures at least you can live with your family. I'm going to a foster home and then what's the betting some Nazi school, and you bloody well know they're going to expect me to join the Hitler Youth. Well, I can't face any of it, all right? None. I want to die, I want to bloody die right now. I'd be happy if they try to kill me because when they do I'm going to take one with me.'

'Ottsy—'

'I'm telling you, Paulus. The only way I can get through this is to hate them. Hate them and fight them and that's exactly what I'm going to do.'

'And if you get killed? What about Mum?'

'Well, maybe she'll never even know, Pauly,' Otto snarled. 'You think about that. She's wrong when she says the Nazis will be finished one day. She may be right about most things but she's wrong about that. They'll *never* be finished. They're going to last a thousand years, just like the bastard says. And they won't stop until they've killed us, Pauly.'

'Killed who?'

'The Jews.'

'But you're not—'

'I'm still a fucking Jew, you bastard, and I'll smash your face in if you say I'm not. They're going to kill every Jew they can in the end. It says it on the wall at school, *Death to Jews*. But you won't let that happen to our family. I know that, Pauly. You're too bloody clever and so's Mum. You'll find a way to get out. And I probably won't even know! I'll be left here, on my own, living with the enemy. I'm being exiled, Pauly, and I'd rather die.'

Paul went and sat beside his brother on Otto's bed.

'Ottsy, mate. We'd never leave you behind, you know that.'

'They won't let me out, Pauly, don't you see? They need me for their bloody army. That's all the HJ is about, military training. Hitler wants me for a soldier. But let me tell you, mate. By the time I've finished, they'll either have to let me go or kill me, and right now, I don't care which.'

'Ottsy, you've got to stop talking like that. We'll find a way out. I promise.'

'Maybe. But I doubt it,' Otto said.

Then he went and brushed his teeth. As he passed through the living room he saw his father, still slumped at the piano in the dark. The bottle, empty now, lying on the floor beside his stool.

'Dad,' Otto whispered, 'go to bed.'

'Later, son,' Wolfgang replied, without looking up.

'Dad, you've got to pull yourself together a bit,' Otto went on. 'Mum's going to need you now.'

'Yeah. That's right,' Wolfgang said but without conviction. 'I'm not being a lot of help, am I really?'

There was nothing more to say so Otto continued on to the bathroom. When he returned Wolfgang was still sitting, slumped in the darkness at his silent piano.

Later, after the lights in their room were out, Otto whispered once more to his brother.

'Pauly.'

'Yeah, mate?'

'I want you to do something for me.'

'Yeah. I know. You want me to tell Dagmar, don't you?'

Otto smiled to himself in the darkness. 'We might not be the same blood, bro, but you can still read my mind. The thing is, I don't think I can go to her myself even if I get the chance.'

'No, I don't think so either,' Paulus whispered. 'After what the Gestapo have said I think we have to presume they'll be watching you at least for a while and will go after any Jews you try to contact.'

'Yeah. I think that's true.'

'I'm sorry, mate,' Paulus said, trying to smile. 'Just when she'd let you have a bit as well. You lucky bastard. I *still* can't believe she let you feel her up! If I'd known she was going to go that far I'd have beaten up an SA man myself.'

'Yeah. Well, you get her all to yourself now, don't you? So who's the lucky bastard then?'

'You know I wouldn't have wanted it that way, Otts.'

'You *sure*?'

'Well . . . *almost* sure.'

They both laughed.

'Better go to sleep, I suppose,' Paulus said. 'If you're going to fight every Nazi in Germany you're going to need your strength.'

'Yeah . . . So this is it, eh? My last night at home.'

'Looks that way. Night, bro.'

But there was one last thing Otto wanted to ask.

'Pauly?'

'Yeah?'

'Have you wondered at all what he would have been like?'

'Who?'

'Him. Your twin. The real one. The one who was with you inside Mum, the one who died. If he had lived and I'd never turned up. What he would have been like?'

'Of course I haven't, Otts,' Paulus whispered. 'I don't need to, do I? I *know* what he would have been like. He'd have been *exactly* like you. Because he *is* you.'

A Spontaneous Drink
London, 1956

'That was the last night me and my brother ever spent together,' Stone said. 'The Gestapo arrived the following morning.'

Despite their previous arrangement not to meet up until after his return from Berlin, Stone had decided to call Billie and to ask if she could see him.

He knew that to do this was against the unspoken rules of their relationship. But sitting alone in his flat, after spending an entire day with the deeply irritating and unsettling MI6 double act, Stone had realized that he did not want to wait until he got back from Berlin to see Billie.

Not least because he was not at all sure that he ever *would* come back from Berlin. A trap was waiting for him there. Of that he had become quite certain.

He hadn't expected Billie to agree to come out. He had presumed she'd be busy. Busy with her young, carefree, potential-packed life. Busy associating with people who were not crippled by history.

Busy being properly alive.

'I know we said we wouldn't meet up in the week but . . .' he began over the phone.

'Baby, *you* said dat, not me,' Billie corrected him. 'Personally I don' like to make no rules. I like to be spontaneous.'

'Spontaneous?' Stone said. 'That sounds like a nice thing to be. I think I can just about remember what it is.'

'Well, let's be spontaneous now then. Let's go out for a drink on a school night. How's dat for wild and reckless?' Billie laughed. 'Do'an worry, baby, it do'an mean we be married nor nuttin.'

They agreed to meet on Piccadilly and chose a little pub halfway down St James Street from the Ritz. As they entered Stone noted the looks they got from the other clientele. He was used to it but it always irritated him. Black people were still pretty rare in pubs up West and a white man with a black woman always drew attention. Particularly a woman such as Billie who was young, beautiful and dressed as ever in as eye-catching a manner as she could contrive. That evening she had on white stiletto shoes, tight denim pedal-pusher jeans and an equally figure-hugging pink cashmere sweater which extended over her bottom and was tied off at the waist with a black patent leather belt. To top it all off she wore a rakish tweed trilby hat perched on top of her magnificent jet black bouffant.

'I know what they're all t'inking,' Billie whispered as Stone returned from the bar with their drinks.

'They're thinking "Lucky bastard". That's what they're thinking,' Stone replied.

'No, man. They're t'inking how much she chargin' 'im an' could I afford it meself.'

Stone set the drinks on the table. A pint of bitter and a port and lemonade on either side of their packs of cigarettes, hers French, his American.

'So you jus' felt like some company then?' Billie asked.

'Yes. I suppose. Something like that. This Berlin trip. It's got sort of complicated.'

'Everyt'ing about you is complicated,' Billie replied with a laugh. 'It's kind of interestin' an' sort of cute but you don' wanna overplay it. A girl could get bored only gettin' to meet ten per cent of a fella.'

'I thought you told me to keep my demons to myself,' Stone said, smiling.

'That was when I only knew you a week,' Billie replied. 'Now it's been t'ree months. Maybe it's time you let a couple out. You know, jus' one or two every now and den.'

'You'd really like me to?'

'I just said so, didn't I?'

And so Stone began to talk.

Talking about things he *never* talked about. Sharing something of the weight of history and emotion that he kept shut up in the locked suitcase of his mind.

Perhaps it was the cigarettes that set him off.

Billie was smoking Gitanes, the same brand Dagmar used to get from her French pen pal. The same brand that he and she had smoked together on the night when he'd brought her the buttons from the SA man's shirt and she had chosen him over his brother. Even the design of the packet was the same as it had been in the thirties.

'We mugged those guys,' Stone said, drinking deep on his beer. 'I can't say I regret it even now. I can see the bastard like it only happened this evening, right there, through the bottom of my beer glass. And I'd do it again too. When we jumped them they were strutting up the street like they owned it. Like they all strutted. Strutting and marching and stamping around like they'd done something brave and special by ganging up in their millions in order to persecute a few scared little individuals. That was what always annoyed me the most, the way they acted as if their "revolution" as they called it had been somehow heroic. Like they'd had some long, legendary struggle. Jesus, the Nazi Party was only as old as me. We were born on the same day. And heroic? The best they could come up with for a martyr was a pimp called Horst Wessel who got knifed over a girl three years before Hitler even came to power. They had all these festivals and celebrations, every week it seemed like, commemorating their "years of struggle" and their "martyrs". They'd parade around with their "Blood Banners" going on about what a fight they'd had saving Germany. Jesus, when you actually added it up they'd lost about ten yobs in pub fights, that was it. But every Nazi walked round like he'd been a Spartan on the bridge when all they'd actually done was push Jewish grannies off the pavement.'

'So you rolled dese guys,' Billie asked.

'That's right, we rolled them. Cornered them in an alleyway, me and four other kids, and kicked the shit out of them. You'd have done the same if your dad had been half crippled in a concentration camp like mine was.'

'Ha! Do'an give me dat! You wasn't doin' it fo' your dad, you was doin' it cos o' dis girl.'

Stone smiled.

'Well. Let's say I did it for various reasons,' he said.

'But you didn't kill dem?'

'No. Not that time. I'd killed a man before though.'

'What?' Billie said, quite horrified. 'Before you were fifteen?'

'Me and my brother did it. In our apartment. I knocked the guy out and then Paulus suffocated him. I used that little statuette that's in my flat. The one of my mother.'

Billie grimaced at the horror of it, but there was something else in Stone's story that also made her think.

'Paulus?' Billie asked looking quizzically at Stone. 'So that's your brudder den?'

'That's right.'

'But your name's Paul?'

'Yes,' Stone agreed warily.

'So you're called Paul an' your brudder was called Paulus?'

'So it would seem.'

'What the matter wit' your momma? She only know one name?'

Stone gave a noncommittal shrug and took another swig of his beer.

'Don't you want to know why we killed the guy?'

'I guess you must a' had a pretty good reason.'

'We killed him because he was about to rape our mum.'

'I s'pose they don't come much better than dat.'

Stone told the story. Surprising himself by taking pleasure in divulging information that had not even been sought. He, who for twenty years had made a habit of giving nothing away until forced to. He told Billie about killing Karlsruhen and about the buttons he'd cut off the SA man for Dagmar. About how triumphant she had been and how she'd kissed him and let him touch her.

'Sounds like a dangerous girl to be in love with if you ask me,' Billie observed.

'She was excited,' Stone replied defensively. 'We'd drawn blood. Stood up and fought back. Don't judge her – they made her lick pavements and they murdered her father.'

'I ain't judging her, Paul,' Billie replied. 'I don't judge anyone.'

Then he told her the rest of the story of that night.

About how he'd arrived home to discover the truth about his adoption.

'I just felt so completely alone. Deserted. They were my family, my whole life, and suddenly I was no longer a part of the single greatest element of their lives, the terrible danger they were in. I was alone. It was so strange. I'd decided so completely that I was a Jew, you see.'

'And suddenly you weren't?'

'No.'

'You told me you were.'

'Yes. That's what I've told people ever since I came to this country. But I'm not. Sorry about that.'

'Don' matter to me.' Billie shrugged. 'Jew or non-Jew is two exactly similar t'ings as far as I'm concerned.'

Stone drained his beer, took Billie's glass and was about to go to the bar for another round. Billie put her hand on his arm to stop him.

'What's your real name, Paul? Just so I know.'

Stone smiled.

'Otto,' he replied. 'My real name is Otto.'

Into Exile

Berlin, 1935

Otto was taken from his family by a female council official and a policeman. They informed him that as a 'racially valuable' individual he was to be housed with a decent Nazi family. They told him he must come immediately.

'Bring no money nor any significant possessions,' the council woman explained. 'You are coming home to the Reich and the Reich will support you. You need nothing from these Jews.'

'My family,' Otto said.

'You have been deceived,' the woman replied. 'The Jew will only look after his own. All else is trickery.'

Otto went meekly. He kissed Frieda briefly, ignoring the distaste on the face of the government woman and then shook Wolfgang and Paulus by the hand.

'Please, ma'am,' Frieda asked, 'are we not even to know where Otto will live?'

'That information is of no concern to you,' the woman replied sharply. 'Your parenthood of this boy is illegal under the law and you no longer have any rights or interest in him whatsoever. You are to have absolutely nothing to do with him from this moment forth. Come, Otto.'

'He is our son!' Frieda cried, finding it difficult to keep control. 'He has lived in this same apartment for all of his fifteen years.'

'That has been his misfortune,' the woman said, 'but his Jew nightmare is over. He is a German now.'

Otto went to the door without even glancing back. It had already been agreed between him and Paulus that he would show no regret or affection for fear of provoking the Gestapo.

As the door of their apartment closed behind Otto, Frieda literally sank to the floor. Her still lovely face, habitually lined with care. Now contorted with grief.

It occurred to Frieda that her heart had been broken in this same place before. Leaving a sadness so great and all-consuming that the empty space it made would remain empty all her days.

When had that been?

Of course she remembered. In the hospital, in 1920 when the old nurse had taken away the little shrivelled grey bundle. Then she had felt as she felt now.

And it had happened again. Once more she had lost a son, and for the second time Paulus had lost his twin.

Outside in the corridor Otto said nothing as he entered the familiar, creaking, clanking lift with the woman and policeman and descended to the ground floor. Still silent he walked with his captors out of the front door and into the well of the building.

'What about my bike?' he asked, speaking for the first time.

'Perhaps it will be sent for,' the woman said. 'I do not know.'

Otto got into the police car and allowed himself to be driven away.

He did not speak again as the car traversed the familiar streets through which the Saturday Club had roamed on so many happy yesterdays.

'Cheer up, son,' the policeman said. 'A year from now you'll have forgotten you ever knew those Jews.'

Otto waited until they were completely out of Friedrichshain before he acted but then he did so decisively. As the car pulled up at some lights, he simply opened the door and jumped out.

'*Auf Wiedersehen* and fuck you,' he said and ran.

He didn't know where he was going and he did not expect to get far. It was the principle of the thing. The first protest. From day one Otto wanted them to know that they had made a mistake. That they had caught a live one and that their lives would have been easier if they'd left him where he was.

As he ran a whistle blew behind him. The copper had leapt out of the car and was shouting that the boy should be stopped. Almost immediately Otto found himself confronted by diligent citizens responding to the policeman's call. Otto smashed his fist into the face of the biggest person blocking his way and as the man staggered back Otto buried his boot between the same unfortunate citizen's legs. By which time the policeman had caught up. As he reached out to grab at Otto he too got a fist in the face.

'Fuck you!' Otto shouted once more.

The other passers-by who had been intent on stopping Otto fell back. Anybody who was prepared to physically attack a police officer in broad daylight was clearly out of control and they did not want to be the next person in his line of fire. Otto may have been only fifteen but he was very strong and an experienced fighter. He was also motivated by a blind fury which was plain for all to see. People stood aside and let him pass.

Otto ran on, pushing his way through the busy street, turning blindly left and right. It could not last long of course. Pretty soon other local beat officers responding to the whistles and the hubbub had joined the pursuit and before long Otto was surrounded and subdued.

They took him to the cells of the local police station where they beat him up pretty badly, but when he was brought before a judge Otto was let off with a caution. The council woman explained the situation and it was decided that you could not expect a lad brought up by vermin to become civilized in a single morning.

There was, however, no question of Otto going to a foster home now. It was clear that the Jews had turned him into a savage beast and that no normal family could control him. The party, however, could and would, and it was decided between the court, the Friedrichshain council and the local SS that Otto would be sent to a *Nationalpolitische Erziehungsanstalt*, or Napola for short, an institute for National Political Education. This was a grouping of supposedly 'elite' boarding schools, the purpose of which was to educate the Nazi officials and administrators of the future.

These academies had been set up shortly after the Nazis came to power and had immediately gained for themselves a fearsome reputation for fitness and toughness. The court considered such a school would be the best means by which Otto would receive the discipline and indoctrination he needed in order to become a good German.

'He is of the purest Saxon peasant stock,' the SS officer attached to the court insisted. 'The most valuable type of German of all. This is one we can't afford to lose.'

When they told Otto the news in his cell, he was fearful that they would be sending him far away, but fortunately a Napola school had been established the previous year in the Spandau district of Berlin. The headmaster had already been contacted and had, Otto was assured, accepted 'with relish' the 'challenge' of making an elite German from a boy raised by Jews.

'This really is very fascinating,' the SS man explained when he visited Otto in his cell. 'It's the same as with these wolf boys one occasionally hears about. Feral children raised by a different species who must somehow be brought home to their race. A wonderful opportunity, lad, for which I am confident you will one day be truly grateful.'

Otto spent that night in the police cells before being taken directly to his new school the following morning. It was an intensely lonely night, an isolation of which he had no experience and for which he had prepared no strategy. It was almost the first time in his life that he had not gone to sleep to the sound of his brother breathing just a few feet away, and although the cells were noisy and the nearby traffic constant, to Otto the long hours seemed heart-breakingly silent and empty.

Still he did not cry. Some inner defence instinct told him that were he to give himself over to despair he would be lost. It was quite clear to Otto that this was only the beginning of the nightmare and young as he was he recognized that he must hoard jealously his store of emotional strength.

Hatred would be the staff on which he leant.

So instead of crying that night, Otto exercised. Performing push-ups and sit-ups in his little cell until exhaustion let him sleep. He knew he must stay fit because he was quite resolved that he would be in another fight within a very short time and would be fighting constantly after that. They thought their Napola could bend him to their will. Well, his fists would tell them a different story.

The school in Spandau had been set up in an institution that had until the previous year been the Prussian Academy of Gymnastics teacher training school.

'Good facilities,' the SS man assured his silent and sullen charge as they drove across the city. 'Plenty of sport. As the Führer has said so often, it is the body which must be trained first. Above all, he wants boys who are fit! Book learning is a lesser issue. We do not much trust those so-called "clever" gentlemen. Wasn't it them who ruined Germany?'

Otto did not reply but for the first time since being taken from his home he almost found himself smiling. How often had he wished for a school which didn't like books? Now that he'd found one it was run by bloody Nazis.

The first thing that Otto was subjected to after he had been delivered to his new school was a 'medical' examination to determine scientifically and mathematically the exact nature of his 'race'. It seemed that even amongst those of 'pure German' blood there was an enormous variation in blood 'value' and a strictly annotated pecking order of racial superiority.

Two other boys, a thirteen-year-old and an eleven-year-old, were taking the same tests as Otto, both hoping they possessed the correct shape of skull and right length of nose in order to be judged worthy of an elite education.

'Why would you want to come anyway?' Otto asked the older of the two as together they stripped to their underpants in a sports changing room.

'Why *wouldn't* you?' the thirteen-year-old replied. 'This is it! The elite. Have you *seen* the uniforms! The parade one's black. It looks amazing! And when we get out, we're the bosses. The future *Gauleiter*. My HJ leader says we get to rule Germany, and when Germany rules the world, we'll rule that too.'

The younger boy was trying to look brave but seemed a lot less sure this was all a good idea.

'I liked my old school,' he said, 'but the Napola are free and my mum and dad are a bit poor, you see. My dad's a miner and he doesn't want me to have to work like he does. They can't believe that I can get a private education in a top school and the Government pays. They really really want me to get in so I have to try hard to, I suppose.'

'No snobbery any more,' the first boy said with brash self-confidence. 'It doesn't matter if you're a lord or a peasant in Germany now. Not to the Führer. He knows it's not class that counts but blood! We're all Germans together.'

Otto wished the lad had been older so that he could have punched him.

The three boys were summoned into the gymnasium and told to sit on a bench that had been placed in front of a table on which lay a selection of strange and scary-looking objects: a pair of very long metal callipers, which looked like an insect's antennae, and a couple of instruments that reminded Otto of the sort of clamps he had used in woodwork at school. There were also a series of wooden sticks from which were hung many locks of hair of varying colours and textures. Most intimidating of all was a sinister-looking display box from which thirty or forty different coloured glass eyeballs stared blindly upwards, all laid out neatly in little compartments.

'Wow, creepy,' the older boy laughed. 'Looks like a morgue after the post-mortem's finished.'

'This is not a morgue, boy!' a voice barked as a white-coated figure entered the room. 'It is a *laboratory* dedicated to the science of racial truth. Stand up!'

The two other boys leapt to their feat. Otto rose more slowly. He had decided in his own mind that he must gauge his next protest in order to make the maximum impact. This he decided was not the right time. The only witnesses would be the white-coated figure and the two other boys who were much younger than him.

'Good morning,' the man in the white coat said. 'I am Doctor Huber of the SS Central Office for Race and Colonization. You are all three of good German lineage or you would not be here. However, the Napola require more than that. Only the best and noblest of blood can be educated here and I shall decide whether it flows in your veins or not. We recognize five Germanic types. The finest of which, the *Herrenmensch*, is of course Nordic. After that comes Falic, then Dinaric, West Germanic and finally Balto Slavic. Only the first two racial types are guaranteed places here. However, despair not, boys, if you have a Polish great-granny lurking in your line. The majority of the *Jungmannen* we see here are a mixture of the five types and we require only that applicants are *predominantly* Nordic. Step forward, Stengel!'

Otto stood up and stepped forward.

He was weighed and then measured and subjected to the various tests. The size of his ears and his skull was determined using the long callipers, and the distance from his chin to the bridge of his nose was measured with the clamp-like devices. Swatches of hair were held up and compared with Otto's thick, sandy thatch and various glass eyeballs were placed against his temples that a match might be found for his pale grey eyes. His pants were pulled to his knees and his penis was held and closely inspected. The foreskin which his mother had denied to Rabbi Jakobovitz during the Kapp Putsch of 1920 was rolled back and forth over Otto's glans.

All the while Dr Huber barked out a bewildering series of numbers and letters which an orderly with a clipboard diligently recorded on Otto's form.

When the examination was over, Otto was told to sit back down while Huber pored over the form, tallying up the columns of figures and applying them to various charts.

'Congratulations, lad,' Huber said finally and with much solemnity, 'you are of pure Falic blood.'

A term Otto had never before heard in his life.

'A rare and fine thing indeed,' the doctor went on. 'You are second only to pure Nordic and to Nordic/Falic in the great German family of races. You are truly a son of German soil and will be admitted to this academy this day.'

Otto absorbed this news in silence and was irritated to receive a slap of congratulation on the back from the older of his two fellow candidates.

Then it was the turn of the other boys. First, the younger one was subjected to the same bewildering series of measurements, comparisons and numerical diagnoses, before finally being graded as an acceptable mix of Falic and Dinaric. Like Otto, he was told he would be entering into the school, an honour Otto felt the little boy received with distinctly mixed emotions. The thirteen-year-old, however, the one who had been so enthusiastic about joining a Napola, was rejected. He was informed that his 'rounded' cranium was 'pure Balto Slavic' and hence he was racially unfit to study alongside the purer-blooded boys.

'Cheer up, lad,' the doctor said as it was clear the boy was fighting back tears. 'You're a good German, no doubt about that. Just not one of the best, that's all. The Wehrmacht will be delighted to have you when you are older and you may serve the Führer as a soldier.'

When the three boys returned to the changing room, Otto and the younger boy found that their civilian clothes had already been removed and replaced with a school uniform in which they were told to dress.

Otto felt as if he was in a dream as he buttoned up the brown shirt and knotted the brown tie, then pulled on the black trousers and lace-up boots. The jacket was also black with a swastika armband stitched to the sleeve, with a diamond-shaped design rather than the traditional circular motive. There was a shiny black belt, shoulder belt and epaulettes. There were white gloves and a little black forage cap with an eagle and swastika badge.

Apart from the cap and the boots, the whole ensemble looked exactly like the SS uniforms that Otto had first seen worn by the men who had come to take his father to a concentration camp. On the night he and Paulus had killed the would-be rapist Karlsruhen.

Otto looked at the little eleven-year-old. He was dressed in the same way except that his boots were knee-length, laced all the way up and had caused the little boy considerable trouble.

He looked ridiculous, like a little Nazi doll.

The other boy had already left. Hurried out by the school orderlies while still buttoning his shirt. He was a bad smell that could not be mentioned and must be quickly dispersed. Then the eleven-year-old was collected to join his year group and Otto was brought before the headmaster.

The principal of the school was a big, quite jolly-looking man who nodded with approval at Otto's uniform, even leaning forward to adjust Otto's tie.

'You wear it well,' the principal said. 'You're not tall, I admit, but you're strong. A fighter I'm told. Well there's no better uniform to fight in.'

'Where are my clothes?' Otto asked.

The principal flinched slightly to be so perfunctorily addressed, but then smiled indulgently.

'You won't be needing civilian clothes any more, boy,' he said. 'From this day forward you will wear only uniform. A school uniform to begin with but after that who knows? A party uniform in some important *Gau*? Or an SS one? A member of the black knighthood? Perhaps as an officer of the Wehrmacht if you choose a military career. Although I think that by the time you are of age the Waffen SS might well have seen off those old army *Junkers*, eh? No matter, army or party you will live your life in uniform, my boy, for you are now a servant of the state. Give thanks, boy! Give thanks! For from this day forward you belong to the Führer. He who knows all, sees all and loves all. All that is German.'

If the head teacher had imagined that this little speech would inspire Otto then he was immediately disappointed, for Otto had decided the time had come to make his feelings felt.

'Speaking of the Führer,' he said.

'I did not give you permission to speak, lad,' the head replied sternly. 'I forgave that once, but not a second time. Be quiet.'

'I was just wondering what sort of racial mix *he* is?' Otto went on, ignoring the headmaster's order. 'Some people say he looks Jewish but *we* wouldn't have him. I'd say he was about half prick and half arsehole – what do you reckon, sir?'

Otto knew exactly what he was doing.

He truly didn't care if they killed him. His life was over anyway.

Everything that he loved was lost to him. His home. His family. And his beloved Dagmar.

They were all that mattered in his life and they had been stolen from him. In exchange he had been given a *Nazi* uniform. An SS uniform in all but name. Had there ever been an irony so cruel? A fate so despicable and low? To be in amongst the Devil's own? Welcomed as a prodigal son?

Otto would quite happily have taken his own life but he did not want his enemies to be able to say that his Jewish family had turned him into a coward. Therefore he had resolved that he would see if he could force them to do the job for him.

'A half prick, half arsehole *Untermensch*, that's your Führer, *sir*.'

The principal didn't rant and rail as Otto had expected him to. He didn't beat him or shoot him on the spot. Instead, the big friendly-looking face broke into a smile.

'Well, I must say, lad,' he boomed good-humouredly, 'those Jews certainly didn't manage to knock the spirit out of you, did they? You've got balls, my fine young man. Big proud German balls.'

'Fuck you, sir,' Otto replied, 'and fuck Hitler too.'

'That's right. Get it all out. Fifteen years a kike is going to have an effect, isn't it? But I'm going to fix that. You see, young Otto my lad, you are my *project*. An experiment if you like. I'm going to show that your blood is stronger than any Jewish lie. I'm going to bring you back to the *Volk*, my son. Renew your membership of the *master race*, which some careless Commie doctor disregarded at your birth. So then, let's get to business. We know you've got guts all right. Tell me, can you box?'

Otto had resolved not to cooperate with this man but still could not resist the question.

'If I'm hitting Nazis,' he replied.

'Good. We have lots of those here. There's a senior class going on right now as it happens. Come with me.'

Otto was led back down to the same changing room that he

had just left and presented with a sports kit marked with the same triangular swastika badge that was switched to his arm. He could hear the sound of boxing going on in the gymnasium where he had just been examined and, sure enough, on being led back in he saw that a boxing ring had been set up and a group of seventeen- and eighteen-year-old boys were sparring.

'Lads,' the head teacher shouted as he entered the room, causing all the youths to spring to rigid attention. 'This is Otto. He's a new boy. He just insulted the Führer. Who wants to teach him a lesson?'

The clamour that this announcement caused produced the most likely candidate in short order, a hugely powerful young man who was three years older than Otto and twenty centimetres taller.

'If this *Jungmann* has insulted our Leader,' the powerful-looking boxer boomed, flexing his rock-like biceps, 'then it will be my honour to punish him.'

Otto shrugged and climbed into the ring.

As he did so the principal stepped forward and put a hand on his shoulder, whispering into his ear, 'Bet you can't last a single minute with him, little Jew boy.'

Otto wasn't stupid. He knew he was being goaded. But then he did not need goading. He was ready and happy to fight an opponent who looked quite capable of killing him. All he hoped for was to do some damage first and show those Nazis that a Jewish boy knew how to die. As they tied the gloves to his hands and pushed a gum guard between his teeth, Otto resolved that the only way he was leaving the ring was either unconscious or dead.

The fight was stopped after lasting almost three rounds, by which time Otto was not quite yet unconscious, but then neither was he fully conscious. He was a swollen, bleeding, staggering, gagging, punch-drunk wreck, hitting the canvas over and over again but refusing to stay down and somehow managing to drag himself back on to his feet.

For most of the first round he had even held his own, tucking in under the big man's reach and getting a couple of heavy hooks into his opponent's body. But as the older lad got his measure,

Otto quickly became nothing more than a tenacious punching bag, as bloody faced as he was bloody minded, careering about the ring, propelled by the massive blows that were raining down on him.

Eventually when one particularly vicious haymaker sent him spinning and tumbling through the ropes and in amongst the spectators, the principal called a halt.

'You see this wild boy,' Otto could hear the principal calling out, 'brought up by Jews! But within him flows the blood and beats the heart of Thor! This fight has been proof! If proof were needed that *blood* is everything. Take him to the hospital.'

As they dragged him to his feet, Otto attempted to bawl out a cry of defiance, but his mouth was too cut and swollen for him to speak. Both his eyes were also closing fast. He struggled feebly in the grip of the grinning youths who had hold of him, flailing weakly with his gloved fists, before staggering and falling once more. This time when he hit the floor the lights had truly gone out.

Making Contact

Berlin, 1936

For the first four months that Otto was at the school, he was kept closely watched and not allowed any contact or communication with the outside world whatsoever.

'Your body and your blood belong to the Führer,' the principal informed him many times, 'but it is clear that your mind still resides with your Jew abductors. Therefore, *Jungmann*, we will keep you close, eh?'

Incarcerated in the Spartan confines of a uniquely confident and self-satisfied institution, Otto soon realized that making his protest was not to be as easy as he'd hoped. His plan, such as it was, had been to fight the entire school until they either killed him or threw him out. The problem, he discovered, was that the more he fought, the more spirited and 'German' they considered him to be. Every blow he delivered and every beating he took confirmed the school in its belief that rare 'blood' flowed in his veins. They held that no Jew could ever show such courage or loyalty and therefore the fact that Otto had maintained these characteristics despite their malicious influence was further proof of Nazi racial theories. The principal saw his happy challenge as simply to redirect Otto's splendid fighting spirit back in its proper direction. What was more, the harder that task was, the further proof it provided of how wicked and manipulative the perfidious Jew family who had brought Otto up had been. In the principal's mind, the more Otto fought, the more noble he appeared and the more spitefully cunning his adoptive parents seemed.

Otto had also won for himself the amused respect of his peers, which of course made him angrier still. Right from the first boxing match when he had gone three rounds with the school champion he had been admired as a fighter, which was really the only quality the school thought worthy of respect. Otto's snarling aggression and willingness to mix it at any time and with anyone was regarded as magnificent, endearing almost. Otto had a pleasant, open sort of face (when it wasn't bruised and battered beyond recognition) and people had always been drawn to him, liking him on sight. It was the same at the Napola, and very soon the school began to treat him as a sort of pet. A valuable dog that had an impressive mean streak and killer instinct which, when tamed, would make him the best of his breed.

It made Otto almost crazy with frustration. He could not make them hate him the way he hated them. In fact, he began to realize, they felt *sorry* for him. A fine lad, ruined by Jews. Anti-Semitism was the number one subject at the school, it informed every lesson whatever the subject, and Otto became a living, breathing mascot for the school's creed. Brave, aggressive and headstrong because of his blood and misguided because of his upbringing.

Lying silently in his dormitory amongst boys with whom he refused to speak and with whom he fought every single day, Otto realized he must rethink his strategy. Clearly just fighting was not enough.

He almost smiled to think how Paulus would have laughed to hear him admit that.

He missed Paulus so much.

Paulus was the clever one, the thinker, the strategist. He would know the right way to behave. He would have a plan. He always did.

Thinking of Paulus reminded Otto of how wretchedly lonely he was. So lonely that he had occasionally even found himself considering making a friend or two amongst the other boys. They weren't such a bad lot, country lads mainly, farmers' sons and party kids. All bound together in common cause against the pathologically harsh discipline which the school clearly seemed to feel was the only way to educate future leaders. These *Jungmannen*, as they were called, were harassed constantly by often sadistic group leaders who were barely older than they were. This suffering of course formed a close bond in the dormitories and Otto would have liked very much to take some comfort in being part of the group. But he could not. Not ever. These same jolly boys chucking balls, laughing at farts, exchanging dirty postcards and comparing strap marks from the beatings they all regularly endured, these were the same boys who believed that his mother and the girl he loved were vermin.

He would not forget that just to make his life in this prison easier. He could not.

Nonetheless, as the days and weeks passed he found himself slowly compromising on his attitude towards his captors. His anger never subsided but he started trying to manage it. He could see that by behaving in such an openly combative manner he was really only hurting himself.

Besides which, he missed his parents and his brother so much that he resolved to try to behave at least well enough for them to allow him to go outside of the school occasionally. He knew that he could make no direct contact with his family but he longed at least to have news of them.

Desperately, gnawingly lonely as he was, he longed also for a friend. And so he set himself the task of earning a pass out. He kept on fighting, of course, but he began principally to do it within the rules, in boxing and military classes. He also began to give the Hitler salute, having perfected a way of giving it with two fingers very slightly crossed, which always made him feel closer to Paulus. And he began to make an effort on the playing field, which, along with fighting and soldiering, seemed to be the only area of achievement the staff were interested in. He even started to exchange the odd word or two with those hearty farmers' sons who tried sometimes to engage him in conversation.

By the middle of the spring of 1936, Otto finally managed to get through a week without being disciplined for insubordination and he decided that the time had come to approach the principal in the hope of being allowed out of the school.

The principal had of course been delighted to note the change in Otto's attitude, and slapped him on the back while Otto stood rigidly to attention before him.

'Well now, boy,' the principal said indulgently. 'Of course, I should be happy to let you have an afternoon free each week as the other boys have. The only thing is how can I trust you not to go and visit those Jews you once called family?'

'Because they *are* Jews, sir,' Otto replied, 'and I wear the uniform of a Napola *Jungmann*.'

The principal smiled but he was far from convinced.

'You are saying that you are done with them? That you have no family feelings left?'

Otto might not have been as clever as Paulus but he knew enough not to overplay his lie.

'No, sir. I still love my ex-mother and father because they were kind to me. However, I am a *Jungmann* of the Napola and I belong to the Führer. Therefore I cannot visit my ex-family because whatever I may feel for them personally they are still Jews.'

'Well, who do you wish to visit then?' the principal asked.

'A girl, sir.'

'Ahh!' The big man laughed. 'Now *that* I can believe. What girl?'

'A fine German girl, sir. She is the daughter of my ex-mother's ex-maid. She is a member of the BDM and her stepfather is in the *Sturmabteilung*.'

'Now that sounds more like it!' the principal said. 'I'll tell you what I'll do. To start with you can invite her here. Sundays are visiting days when older boys may entertain family or a friend to tea. You can invite this girl. Sit down at once, boy, and write her an invitation. I'll see that it is posted.'

And so the following Sunday Silke came.

She had scarcely been able to reply to the invitation fast enough. For once even she had the support of her stepfather, who had been hugely impressed when Silke received a letter from such a prestigious institution as a party academy.

When Otto first caught sight of Silke he nearly broke down and cried. He had had no word nor sight of anyone he loved in many months and when he saw his old friend smiling through the railings waiting to be admitted he was almost overcome. Then, when the moment came and the great iron gate was opened, they rushed to each other and hugged and hugged and actually jumped for joy in each other's arms before they had even spoken a word. It was only the awareness of grinning faces around them that made Otto let go of Silke at all.

'Hey watch out, miss,' one of Otto's dorm mates called out. 'He normally punches before he speaks.'

'Looks like now we know what makes him smile,' another laughed.

The faces and the voices were friendly. Everyone was pleased to see the wild boy of the school hugging someone. Especially a pretty girl in a BDM uniform. For once Otto did not resent their intrusion – he was too happy to be back in contact with at least one part of the life he loved and had lost.

Together Otto and Silke walked and talked in the school

grounds for the whole allotted two-hour visit; they missed tea but didn't care. Silke had made a point of going to the Stengel apartment the night before so she was able to give Otto recent news of his family.

'They're all well,' she said. 'Things are a bit easier at the moment for them. What with the Olympics coming up, some of the restrictions on Jews have been lifted. Even the signs on the park benches have gone, so your dad can go and sit in the Märchenbrunnen on nice afternoons.'

'How is my dad?' Otto asked.

'Oh he's fine, absolutely fine,' Silke replied, but the slight catch in her voice gave away the lie.

'Silks,' Otto said, 'you're my only friend now, you have to tell me the truth.'

'OK, Wolfgang's not so fine,' Silke admitted. 'He just seems to have lost hope. I think the problem is that there's simply nothing for him to *do*. He just sits around really, which is really hard for your mum. I think she finds his kind of *emptiness* pretty depressing to be around. I mean she hasn't said anything to me, but it's obvious really. He used to be such fun and now he just *sits* there. Drinking when he can get it and smoking too, which is so stupid because it makes him cough till it looks like his head's coming off. And of course since your Mum's at home most of the time now they're kind of bumping into each other a bit.'

'Mum's at home?' Otto asked in surprise.

'Oh God, yes,' Silke replied, her face falling. 'I forgot, you didn't know, did you? They finally got around to banning Jewish doctors from working in public health institutions. She can't go to the clinic any more.'

Otto gripped his fists tight.

'Jesus wept!' he hissed. 'Don't they ever stop? Haven't they got better things to do? She did *nothing* but good there, ever. They are fucking *crazy*!'

Otto and Silke both knew what a truly cruel and terrible blow losing the clinic would have been for Frieda. After her family it had been her life for sixteen years.

'She practises from home now,' Silke went on quickly. Otto's face was reddening and his anger rising and she didn't want the happy day ruined by him lashing out at a passing Nazi. 'Just Jews of course but there's certainly enough of them to keep her busy, let me tell you, and they pay her what they can, which means food's not a problem. The main thing is that she misses you so terribly, Ottsy. It's turned her grey and she's only thirty-six. But now we're back in contact again it's going to be *so* much better. Now at least she'll get news. That's the important thing, it was not knowing anything that was killing her. I can't tell you how thrilled she was when I told her I was going to see you. She grabbed hold of me and Pauly and we all did a little dance. Your dad even banged out a tune on the old piano. It's a while since we've heard that. Dust flew! Of course I'm going to go straight round there after I leave you to tell them all about it, so you'd better make sure I can give them a good report!'

Otto smiled. 'Good old Silke.'

Silke frowned slightly.

'Don't say that, Ottsy,' she said, pretending to make a joke out of it. 'You always do and it makes me sound like a dog.'

Otto just laughed. 'Tell me about Pauly. I miss him ever so much.'

'Do you now?' Silke teased. 'You actually *miss* the Paul Monster! Can I quote you on that?'

'No, you bloody well can't!' Otto said, grabbing hold of her. 'If you *dare* tell him you'll be sorry!'

He began tickling her as he'd done so often when they were kids, growling comically like a bear while Silke screamed with laughter.

But they weren't kids any more, of course, and as Silke struggled in his arms Otto was conscious of how close her face was to his. How white were her teeth. How red her lips.

'So tell me about that bastard Pauly,' he said, disengaging from her. 'Not that I care of course.'

'You boys are so *stupid*,' Silke said. 'Of course you care, and you won't be surprised to hear he's as strong and steady as ever.

He handles the budgeting and shopping for your mum these days and manages to get good stuff too, even though there's less cash around and fewer and fewer places where Jews are allowed to spend it. It's kind of like Pauly's taken over from your dad as man of the house. But he still studies, goes to school every single day. All the other Jews in his class dropped out in the end but Paulus has stayed on. Sitting on his own in the corner working away for his exams. I don't think they really notice him any more. He says he gets in hardly any fights now you've gone.'

'Ha!' Otto laughed. 'Bloody wimp.'

'Bloody clever, more like. He wants to go to graduate school.'

'Of course he does, the silly twat,' Otto snarled. 'What *is* the point of being a qualified Jew in Germany? For a clever bloke he can be pretty damned stupid.'

'He wants to get out, Otts,' Silke said, glancing around to be sure that the nearest other boys were out of earshot. 'You know that. He thinks he'll be a lawyer in England or America one day. He says he wants to defend the oppressed.'

'He *is* the bloody oppressed.'

'I think that's the point,' Silke replied gently. 'He wants to make something out of what's happening to him. It's the same as you in a way. Neither of you could ever give in. You just have different ways of dealing with it, that's all.'

'I fight, Pauly studies, eh?'

'No,' Silke scolded, 'not completely, Otts. You don't *just* fight. You need to remember there's more to you than that. You always loved your woodwork and your music.'

'Silks. These days I just fight.'

Otto was silent for a moment. Contemplating the possibility of his brother's departure. His mother and father too.

'Well,' he said finally. 'It's lucky it's me that got sent to this place and not him. He'd *hate* it and you can tell him that from me. They're all so bloody *thick*. And I'm talking about the *teachers*! Honest, I'm not joking, they call it an elite academy but the place even makes *me* feel sophisticated. The so-called lessons are just a joke. We do German folklore and pagan legends instead of proper history. And they keep going *on and on* about blood and soil and soil and blood. What's blood and soil got to do with the price of eggs, I'd like to know? They're bloody *obsessed* with it. And of course there's endless stuff about the Jews. They manage to get us into everything, with Negroes, Slavs, Chinks and gypsies thrown in behind us as fellow *Untermensch*. That's how Germany's going to conquer the world by the way, because Germans are best and everyone else is varying degrees of shit. It's that simple. It's actually what they *teach*. Science class is basically how to assemble a machine gun and the rest of the time we do sport and sadism. We're always doubling over some hill with a backpack full of rocks. Or running barefoot over broken stones or refolding all our kit in under a minute. Pauly would go mad.'

Silke laughed. 'Tell me everything. I want to know all the details of your day.'

'Do you want to know how to strip down, clean and reassemble a sub-machine gun?'

'Yes.'

The precious afternoon passed all too quickly and when they heard the 'five minute' bell ringing neither of them could believe the time had flown already. Otto was particularly devastated. Being with Silke had returned him so completely to his old life, his *actual* life, that the prospect of returning to the false one he now lived was a desperate and cruel one.

'Will you come next week, Silks?' he pleaded. 'I don't think they'll ever actually let me go out, so please say you'll come next week.'

'I'll come if you promise to try not to have too many new cuts and bruises on your face when I do,' she said with a smile, reaching up and putting a hand on his cheek. Otto may have been fighting less but he still had plenty of recent wounds to prove his belligerence remained undiminished.

'You're such a *handsome* boy, you know,' Silke said, gently touching his scars.

'I have to fight them, Silke,' Otto protested, 'sometimes at least. To show them I'm a Jew.'

'Bide your time, Otts,' Silke whispered. 'There are better ways. Look at me. I fight them too, you know, and my face is still *lovely*, don't you think?'

Otto smiled, but if Silke had been hoping that he'd take the opportunity to pay her a compliment, she was disappointed.

'Yes,' he laughed, 'you've still got the same old ugly mug as ever, Silks. You're talking about the *Rote Hilfe*, aren't you?' he added in a whisper. 'I couldn't join them, Silks.'

'Why not?'

'Dagmar wouldn't like it. She hates Commies.'

Silke's usually sunny smile darkened somewhat.

'Yeah. I find most millionaires' kids do,' she said.

'Dagmar isn't a millionaire's kid any more, Silke,' Otto said firmly. 'They executed her dad, remember.'

'Yeah. OK. She's had it very tough I admit,' Silke said, 'but once a princess . . .'

The bell rang for a second time.

'I'd better go,' Otto said. 'It's a ten-K run in full kit for lateness and I'm not kidding. You'd better hurry too or you'll get locked in.'

'I wouldn't mind, Otts!' she said rather too eagerly, grabbing at his hand.

'Believe me, you would. This place is hell. Promise you'll come back next week.'

'Only if you promise not to fight!'

'Can't promise that,' Otto shouted as he ran off. 'Cos I don't want to lie to you.'

'Promise!' she shouted. But he was gone.

Silke turned towards the gate, knowing that nothing on earth would stop her from visiting the following week.

Weekly Visits
Berlin, 1936

Otto didn't stop fighting but he fought less.

The fact that by behaving himself he had been able to open up a line of communication with his family was too precious a thing to put at risk, even at the price of buckling under to the Napola regime.

'I don't think he's any less angry,' Silke reported to Frieda after her third visit, 'but he's learning to bottle it up. The honest truth is I think that secretly he's starting to quite enjoy the stupid curriculum. All the sport and craft and guns and hardly any of what he calls "book learning". They mix up legends with real history and talk about mythical German heroes fighting evil dwarfs and trolls as if it had all been real.'

'Yes,' Paulus observed. 'And we all know who those trolls are supposed to represent, don't we?'

Frieda smiled. 'Well, I'm glad Otto's finding at least something to enjoy in that horrible place, and I'm also comforted to hear that this is how the Nazis educate their so-called "elite" because by the sound of it we'll only have to wait for twenty years or so before the whole damn system just dies of pure ignorance.'

'Well, from what I can see they're certainly not going to find a substitute for Einstein out of the boys at the Berlin Spandau Napola, that's for sure,' Silke said, laughing.

'Only the Jews could produce an Einstein,' Wolfgang observed from his habitual place at the silent piano. He was a little drunk, having been able to earn a few coins that day playing accordion outside local bars.

'What a stupid bloody thing to say, Dad!' Paulus snapped. 'Newton wasn't a Jew, was he? Faraday wasn't a Jew. Aristophanes wasn't a Jew! The whole basis of what's happening to us is that we're supposed to be a race apart and we're bloody *not*. Don't you know any thick Jews? I certainly do.'

Wolfgang looked chastened.

'No, Pauly,' he mumbled, 'you're right. It was a stupid thing to say.'

There was a moment's silence. The fact that Wolfgang was not merely losing his authority over his son, but also Paulus's respect, was clear for all to see. Silke, who had known Wolfgang as the funny, talented, enthusiastic man he had once been, looked away in embarrassment.

'Well, now,' said Frieda. 'These Sunday nights when we get news of Otto are the absolute highlight of our week, Silke. Truly they are. We are so grateful that you can do this for us, you do know that, don't you, dear?'

'Of course I do, Frieda, but you must know how much I love to do it. Sundays are my best day as well. Seeing Ottsy . . . And of course coming here.'

Silke smiled awkwardly and went a little red beneath her spring tan.

Frieda smiled back. 'Yes, Ottsy and all of us.'

A far less astute observer than Frieda could scarcely have missed how much Silke was relishing the special place she now held in Otto's life and also within the brotherhood of the Stengel twins. For the first time since that faraway day in 1926 when Herr Fischer had first brought his little princess for a music lesson, Silke was centre-stage with her beloved boys once more. Their only link. The glue that continued to bind them all together.

Silke had known for as many years as she could remember that Otto and Paulus loved Dagmar more than they loved her. She knew very well that while she was their 'mate', Dagmar was their *passion*. The person for whom both boys would gladly risk anything. At first the jealousy she had felt over this had just been that of a little girl who knew her place in the pecking order of childhood friendship. But in the previous two or three years her feelings had grown more painful and all-consuming.

And Silke also knew that those feelings were no longer as evenly placed as they had been when the three of them were children.

For while Silke was merely jealous and irritated that Paulus preferred Dagmar's company to hers, the fact that Otto did caused her that unique private agony that only unrequited love can inflict.

Silke knew now that she was in love with Otto. And while she also knew very well that Otto was in love with Dagmar, Otto could no longer see Dagmar.

He could only see her.

She was the *only* one he could talk to and confide in. Share his secrets and his pain. Even Paulus, his life companion, was barred to him, and any conversation Otto wished to have with his brother he had to conduct through her.

This was a new and exciting intimacy, which Silke in her tough, rough-and-ready life had never remotely experienced before. Her home life was cold, alienating and occasionally violent. Her school and BDM friendships were always suspect to her because unlike most of the girls she was not in love with Hitler. But now she had Otto.

Every week she would visit him and he was so very pleased to see her and actually *said* so, which he had certainly never done in the past.

And then they'd walk the grounds of the Napola together and he'd want to *talk* and she would gasp in suitable girlish admiration at his stories of winning races and being the sharpest shot and showing all those Nazi arseholes what a Jew could do. And then she'd tut and scold him over the cuts and bruises that he still sustained from all the fights he could not avoid. And she'd make him laugh with descriptions of all the silly leaping and jumping about and balletic scarf swirling she was required to do in the BDM.

'And you can bet those pervy party guys make sure to be around just to check our little white gym dresses are good and short,' she'd laugh. 'We know their game all right.'

Then, when they'd found the quietest possible place in the wooded parkland, they'd sit beneath a tree and Otto would listen in rapt silence while Silke told him all the news from his family.

And sometimes, particularly when she talked about his mother,

Silke would even find herself holding him. Just every now and then, when the hopeless loneliness of his new life all became too much for Otto. When he was even prepared to cry a little and to let her see. Which he would have died before doing in his previous life.

And sometimes after the tears came the anger, when he would swear vengeance on the whole Nazi state.

'One day I'll burn this fucking school down,' he'd say. 'Sometimes in the dorm at night I plan it out. How I'll steal the fuel and where I'll set the fires. I'll choose a time when the lads are out at sport because some of them aren't so bad for all the fact they think they're going to rule the world. But that fucking grinning, patronizing principal and all his master race of teachers, they'll have to take their chance. We'll see if they're such supermen then, eh? I might even lock the doors before I set the match.'

Otto scared Silke when he talked like that. But then when he was at his most angry and his face became violent and his voice was filled with hate, Silke would hold him closer and whisper, 'Ottsy, don't turn into them,' and then tears would come again and he'd put his head on her shoulder and she'd put her arms around him and tell him that in the end everything would be all right.

And in those times Silke dared to hope. As they sat together, beneath their favourite tree on the little grassy rise which overlooked the soccer pitch, she dared to hope that perhaps now she would have her chance to be more than Otto's friend. To actually be his girl. That perhaps today or next week or the week after that, he would turn to her, look deep into her eyes and kiss her.

It didn't seem as mad an idea as it had once been.

Silke knew that she had turned out quite pretty. Her looks were suited to the times. Girlish, youthful, blonde, blue-eyed and tanned. She looked like a not quite so perfect version of the girls shaking tins on the Nazi fundraising posters. Certainly the other Napola boys she and Otto encountered as they walked around the school grounds always grinned and nudged each other in evident approval as they passed. One or two had even whistled.

'Why don't you introduce us to your girlfriend, Stengel,' one boy called out, which made Silke flush red, as she always seemed to be doing these days.

But she was pleased all the same.

She certainly *felt* like she was his girlfriend. Visiting him each week and attending the formal tea with him to which most boys only brought their mothers.

Otto was the envy of plenty of jealous eyes as he escorted Silke to her place and she knew it. Many nice-looking boys, impeccably dressed in their smart uniforms, tried to smile at her but she turned haughtily away, making it clear that she was interested only in the handsome boy who had brought her.

She loved sitting down beside Otto at the beautifully laid out table and then leaping up again as the principal entered and welcomed the guests. She enjoyed the robust masculine atmosphere as every single boy in the room snapped to attention in one perfectly synchronized action and shouted 'Welcome, guests!' on cue.

She was one of the guests.

Otto's guest, and very proud to be so.

He was as smart and as disciplined as any boy in the school. Delivering his Hitler salute, stamping the floor and singing the Horst Wessel song with as much gusto as any of them. And he did those hated things because it was the only way he could maintain his privileges. The only way that he could continue to see *her*.

And then as Otto sat down having delivered the salute, Silke would nudge his hand in the shared knowledge that his fingers had been slightly crossed. And she would feel him smiling inwardly as he pressed his knee against hers beneath the table and grabbed the biggest slice of cake for *her*.

It was heady stuff for a girl like Silke.

A girl whose mother was a cleaner and whose stepdad was an occasionally employed SA thug.

A girl who had always thought herself a plain second best to every other girl in Berlin. Particularly to Dagmar.

A girl who was so hopelessly in love with Otto.

Rejected on Grounds of Race
London, 1956

Stone delivered a fourth round of drinks to the table and without prompting took up his story.

It had been so very, very long since he had talked about himself but now that he had started he found he didn't want to stop.

'Finally they let me out,' he said. 'The principal got me in his office and said I could leave the school for an evening between five and nine. It was what I'd been working towards. It was why I'd stopped fighting and swearing at the Führer.'

'An' I bet I know jus' exactly what you did when you *did* get out,' Billie said with a smile of her beautifully crimson lips, which seemed to remain perfectly covered with lipstick no matter how much of it she left on the rim of her glass.

'What do you think?' Stone asked.

'You went straight aroun' to this Dagmar's place of course. Bet your feet didn't even touch the ground.'

'Yes I did,' Stone said quietly, a faraway look in his eyes.

'An' so you broke little Silke's heart.'

'You think so?' Stone enquired. 'I really don't know if she liked me that much. Not in that way. We were mates. We'd always been mates.'

'Men *never* know. 'Specially when they don't want to. An' little sixteen-year-old men are worse. I *remember*. They are *dumb*!'

Stone smiled and shook yet another cigarette from his pack of Luckies.

'Well, if I did hurt Silke I certainly got paid out myself,' he said.

'Dagmar dumped you?'

'I suppose that's what happened. Although I hadn't really been her boyfriend except for that one night. She certainly rejected me. I turned up on her doorstep and at first her mum wouldn't even let me in and even when she did I only got as far as the entrance hall. I was in that terrible black uniform you see, covered in swastikas. I had to be, I didn't have any other clothes. You can imagine what it looked like to Frau Fischer. Me dressed up like a teenage SS officer. She went completely white. It took her a minute to even realize it was me. I think she'd thought I'd come to arrest her. She was completely hostile. Told me to go away at once. Said I was a German now and not a Jew. I never thought they'd reject me like that but of course she had a point. I was putting them in danger. If I'd got caught visiting them it would have been them that got punished, not me. The authorities wouldn't have needed much of a reason to have another go at the Fischer family.'

'Well, like you say, it's a fair poin',' Billie said.

'I know. But I was still completely devastated. I pleaded with her. Swore that I'd sneak around and that nobody would find out but she asked me if I'd visited my own family, which of course I hadn't, so she said I should show the same consideration to her and Dagmar.'

Billie sipped at her drink for a while. 'Amazing situation. I guess there's a lot of mixed-up stories dat got lost in the Holocaust.'

'I've never talked about it before.'

'I *know dat*,' Billie said with the smallest touch of irritation. 'You don' have to be telling me all the time. You've *said*. You're an uptight, wrung-out, buttoned-up, emotionally empty guy who's in love with a dead girl and doesn' deserve to be happy. I *know* the rules, OK?'

Stone smiled. 'Sorry,' he said.

'Well, it's *borin*',' Billie scolded. 'Now, even though you *never* tell an' even though it's *all* a secret, what happen'd next? What about Dagmar? The amazin', curvy, sultry, long-legged Dagmar who you an' your brother be wet-dreamin' about every night since you was twelve. Did you see her?'

'Yes, for a minute,' Stone admitted, staring sadly at the soggy beer mats on the table. 'She came down the stairs and stood behind her mother. I tried to say something to her but she just shook her head.'

'Didn't she say anyt'ing at all?' Billie asked.

'Yeah. I'm afraid she did. The very worst thing she *could* have said. She said I wasn't a Jew any more. That hurt so much. It was the one thing I was dreading. And for it to come from Dagmar was just devastating.'

'If you want my opinion, baby,' Billie said, snapping her Gitane alight with an elegant flick of her beautiful Dunhill cigarette lighter, 'I t'ink your Dagmar girl is a little bit of a bitch.'

'No,' Stone said firmly, 'don't say that, Billie. Please don't. I can't have you say that.'

'You really do still love her, don't you? After all these years you're still leapin' to her defence.'

'Yes I am. Because, you see, she wasn't a bitch. She was a lovely girl. Funny and beautiful and proud and clever. That's how she was before the madness anyway. I'm not saying she was an angel but believe me she was a *good person.* A decent person. Just try to imagine what she'd been through, what she was *going* through. Her whole life had been stolen from her. Her whole wonderful world had turned into this brutally cruel and terrifying torture.'

'Yeah. Of course,' Billie conceded. 'I said I didn't judge people and there's me doin' jus' that. I have no right.'

'She felt betrayed, you see,' Stone went on.

'By you?'

'Yes. I could see it in her eyes as she stood there on the stairs. Of course it was unfair and I'm sure she knew it was. But she still felt it and I understood. We were living on different planets now. I had a future and she didn't. I can see her now, looking so beautiful. Thinner and more careworn but just as lovely as she ever was. And then she told me to go. She said that even without the risk she didn't want to see me. She just didn't want to be around a boy who still had a life when she was slowly . . . slowly dying.'

For the first time since he had begun his story, words failed him.

Billie put her hand on his knee and squeezed it.

Then the barman approached their table.

'Excuse me,' he said, 'but could you kindly finish your drinks and leave.'

Stone, who had been in the act of taking a sip of his pint, put it down and looked up at the man.

'What?' he asked quietly, his fingers already closing into fists.

'I'm sorry,' the barman said. 'I don't mind myself so I haven't said nothing, but the landlord's come back from being out and he's seen your friend. He won't have no blacks in his pub, see. It's policy, so you'll have to go.'

Stone picked up his glass again and took a slow deliberate swig of beer. Billie was already putting her cigarettes and lighter into her little purse.

'You tell the landlord—' Stone said slowly.

'Paul, please,' Billie interrupted angrily, 'let's go. I don't wanna drink in dis boozer anyway. With such people? No thanks. It's beneath me.'

Stone put an arm out to stop her getting up.

'You tell your landlord,' he repeated to the barman, 'that he's a Nazi *cunt*. Do you hear me? And that goes for you too, by the way, and you're a coward besides.'

'Now listen here!' the barman protested. 'This ain't me, I just work here—'

'Just obeying orders?' Stone sneered. 'Now where have I heard that before?'

'Paul . . . Otto . . . please. I wanna go,' Billie said.

The landlord appeared. A large, arrogant-looking man with Brylcreemed hair and a bristling moustache. He wore a military blazer, shiny at the elbows with a regimental crest on the pocket. 'Right,' the man said, 'this is my pub and I say who drinks here so you hop it and take this black slut with you.'

Billie was already on her feet, having shaken off Stone's arm.

'We're going anyway, you sorry and disgustin' person,' she said, looking like a queen addressing a peasant. 'The air done started stinkin' in here. Maybe it's the drains but personally I t'ink it's da management.'

But still Stone did not move.

'I'm going to count to five,' he said menacingly, 'by which time I suggest you'll have apologized to this lady. One . . . two . . .'

Billie tried once more to interject but it was no use. Stone completed his count and then, rising from his seat with his upper cut already in motion, brought his fist up under the landlord's chin and knocked the man sprawling to the floor. The sickening crack his knuckles made on connection suggested the landlord's jaw may have been broken. Stone spun around, ready to deal with the barman, but the frightened man was already backing away, cannoning into the table behind him and upsetting the drinks. No one else in the pub seemed minded to get involved.

'Now we can go,' Stone said, draining his glass and getting up.

'I t'ink we'd better,' Billie replied, hurrying to the door. 'There ain't never a call for violence, by da way.'

'That's what Chamberlain said,' Stone replied as he followed her.

Together they hurried out of the pub and hailed a passing cab.

Personal Sacrifices

Berlin, 1936

When Dagmar returned to her bedroom, her face was stony cold.

'Thanks for not coming out,' she said.

Paulus was standing by the window.

'I wanted to,' he replied, 'more than anything.'

He was looking out. Watching the black-clad figure retreating through the gate.

Dagmar's mask of indifference lasted only a moment. Her voice was already cracking.

'I had to send him away,' she said, tears starting in her eyes. 'It would have been even harder if he'd seen you. I sent him away, Pauly. Our Otto.'

'He shouldn't have come,' Paulus said, trying to speak sensibly for her sake. 'I knew he would, though, the first chance he got. I don't blame him. I would have done the same.'

'You should have seen him,' Dagmar said, crying now. 'His uniform! It was horrible. He was dressed . . . dressed as one of *them*!'

'It's the same Otto inside, Dags,' Paulus said. 'It's just a uniform. You know that.'

'No it isn't,' Dagmar sniffed. 'That uniform can never be *just* a uniform.'

Paulus and Dagmar had been spending the evening together as they often did. In Dagmar's bedroom. Drinking acorn coffee and smoking cigarettes. Paulus visited Dagmar at least three or four times a week. She was always home, having continued to cut herself off from her old life, from life in general.

'Well, we're not allowed to *do* anything if we *do* go out,' she often lamented, 'so what's the point?'

Paulus was now Dagmar's only friend and he was not ashamed to admit to himself how selfishly happy this made him. His love for her was undiminished and he took great pleasure in the knowledge of how much she needed him and appreciated him coming round. She had started to rely on him. Leaning on him more and more.

Her mother was no help to her at all. She now spent all of her time living in the past. Sitting in her drawing room, the shutters permanently closed, reading old letters and pasting photographs into albums.

'It's so depressing,' Dagmar often complained. 'Sometimes I think I'm going to go mad.'

She had been dwelling on the subject before Otto's surprise arrival. Lying on the bed as she always did. Paulus sitting on the rug at her feet, always feeling the absence of his brother on the empty dressing-table chair. Paulus and Otto had occupied those two places in Dagmar's room for so long that even though Otto had not been there for many months his absence still sometimes took Paulus by surprise.

'The boredom is going to actually physically kill me,' Dagmar had been saying. 'I'm serious, if only I could just go *swimming*. I would give anything to just go swimming.'

Otto's unexpected arrival at the front door had interrupted her thoughts and once he was gone neither she nor Paulus felt like resuming their conversation.

Seeing him and rejecting him had been too traumatic.

'I broke the sacred bond of the Saturday Club,' Dagmar lamented with a sad smile, having dried her eyes.

'The Saturday Club rules were made for a civilized society,' Paulus said. 'Nobody should have to deal with the sort of dilemmas we do. It just isn't fair.'

Paulus offered to go and make some more pretend coffee but Dagmar didn't want any.

'It's repulsive anyway,' she said. 'I don't know why we drink it. *Boredom* again of course. Something to do.'

The conversation became stilted.

They were both thinking about Otto.

Soon Dagmar said she was tired and thought she'd go to bed.

For perhaps the first time in his life Paulus was actually pleased to leave. It had been devastating for him to have been so close to Otto and then to have to watch from a window as he disappeared into the night alone. He had tried to be strong about it for Dagmar's sake but now, like her, he needed a moment for himself.

As he went downstairs Frau Fischer appeared at the sitting room door and asked him to come in for a moment.

Paulus had imagined that she would want to talk about Otto. Ask him to try and exert some influence in persuading his brother not to return. But Frau Fischer brushed over the subject of Otto. It was Dagmar she wished to talk about.

'You're her only visitor now,' Frau Fischer continued. 'One or two of her old friends have tried, but she won't see them. It's her pride, you see, she used to be such a golden girl, so much the centre of attention, and now she can't bear being an object of sympathy. She never really had any Jewish friends, I'm afraid, apart from you and . . . well. Apart from you. She went to the very *best* school, you see, and we never really saw ourselves as Jewish anyway.'

'So she's lonely?' Paulus asked. 'Of course I know that.'

'I don't think it's so much the loneliness as the *inactivity* that's really killing her. It's all right for me. I've had a life but she's only sixteen and she's going crazy. She used to love teas and parties and dances and all sorts of lovely jolly things. And of course she was such an athletic girl too. With her gymnastics and her swimming, which meant everything to her. Now all of that's been taken away and I feel like . . . I feel like I'm watching her *fade*.'

Paulus looked at his feet, he didn't know what to say. Frau Fischer had never been one to unburden herself, even before her retreat into herself.

'I don't really know why I'm speaking to you about this, Pauly,' Frau Fischer went on. 'You're a Jew too and of course subject to the same restrictions as she is. There's not much you can do to help, I know. I just . . . I just wish somehow I could get her *out of the house*.'

'Well some restrictions are being lifted for the Olympics,' Paulus said, attempting a positivity he didn't feel. 'Not the swimming pools I don't think but I reckon we'd be OK going to a park.'

The mention of the Olympics brought a look of angry despair to Frau Fischer's face.

'Those games will break Dagmar's heart,' she said. 'I remember when Berlin won the right to stage them back before the Hitler time. Dagmar danced around the room and made her daddy book her extra swimming lessons right there and then. She might have competed you know. Even at sixteen it's possible she could have qualified. And if not for Berlin perhaps for Tokyo in 1940. But that's a fantasy now, she hasn't trained properly for two years, and anyway no German selection committee would choose a Jew. We're not even Germans any more, not since Nuremberg. Those damned games will be a torture for Dagmar every day they are on. She had always said she would attend every event.'

Paulus was silent. There really was nothing he could say.

'I'm sorry, Paulus,' Frau Fischer said. 'It's quite late and I'm keeping you from getting home and it isn't safe out there. Run along, dear. There's nothing you can do. There's nothing any of us can do.'

Paulus left the Stengel house with a heavy heart. He knew that Frau Fischer was right. Dagmar was changing. Getting listless and depressed. *Fading,* Frau Fischer had said, and horrible though it was Paulus knew the description was a good one. He wanted more than anything else to be able to help. To be able to give Dagmar something of her life back. To be the cause of bringing a bloom back to her cheek. But he could not. He was a Jew like her and a Jew in Germany was powerless.

Paulus did not mention Otto's appearance at the Fischers' house to Frieda and Wolfgang when he got home. However, when Silke came to the Stengel apartment the following Sunday to give her weekly report, Paulus was privately not surprised to hear that Otto's growing tolerance of his situation had been interrupted.

'I'm worried about him,' Silke admitted. 'He was really different today. I thought he was settling down but now he's back to being as angry as he was when he first left.'

'Has he been fighting?' Frieda asked anxiously. 'Is he in trouble?'

'No,' Silke replied, 'but I think it's coming. He was so bitter today. He hardly spoke on our walk and he wouldn't take me in to tea. He said he didn't want to eat with the bastards. Lately he's been so relaxed about it too. We've been laughing at the other boys and making jokes but today he was right back to just wanting to kill them. And then there's the problem of the Hitler Youth.'

'What about it?' Frieda asked, very concerned.

'Well, you must have read that they're going to make it compulsory for every kid in the country to join. It's been all over the news.'

'We've rather given up on reading the German papers,' Frieda said gently. 'Not much fun in them for us. There's a Jewish sheet we see sometimes.'

'Well, they are,' Silke went on. 'Every German child belongs to Hitler and he wants to make it absolutely clear that he's their real parents and not their family.'

'How horrible,' Frieda said, shaking her head. 'Perhaps people will finally begin to realize what they've let themselves in for?'

'Too late now, I reckon,' Silke said. 'Anyway, the point is Otto's saying he won't join.'

'But why?' Frieda asked. 'He's already at a Napola school so what's the difference?'

'That's what I said, but for some reason he seems to have drawn a line. He says he just will not put on another Nazi uniform. I tell him I wear one and I'm a Communist but he says it's different for a Jew.'

'So he still says he's a Jew?' Frieda asked, almost smiling.

'Of course he does. You know Otto,' Silke replied. 'I thought *I* was stubborn. It's such a shame because things have been going really well for him at school despite him trying for them not to. He's a boxing champ, which they love, and of course they're thrilled about *me*.' Silke went the shade of red which occurred whenever she mentioned herself and Otto in the same breath. 'I go there in my BDM uniform and they think I'm his girlfriend.'

Frieda smiled. 'And *are* you, Silke?' she asked.

Silke went even redder.

'No!' she said, slightly too loudly. 'You know which girl Otto thinks about. Same as Pauly does. Dagmar of course.'

'But you *have* been seeing a lot of him,' Frieda pressed.

'Yes and I want to be able to keep seeing him and this business of the Hitler Youth becoming mandatory could make things go very wrong. If Otto refuses to obey the law, his teachers won't be able to help him even if they want to. He'll be arrested; it could actually mean a concentration camp.'

Wolfgang had been silent as he almost always was but now quite suddenly he slammed down his glass, spilling whatever foul-smelling spirit it was he'd been drinking on to the closed lid of his piano.

'He can't,' Wolfgang said in what was almost a croak. 'He *can't* go there. I *know* what they do.'

They all turned to him. Wolfgang never spoke of his experiences in the camp. He rarely spoke of anything much any more, particularly if he'd managed to find something to drink. Now, however, he was shaking with emotion. 'My little Ottsy can't go there,' he said, 'he just can't. The only way to survive in there is to beg and plead. With his character he'd be dead in a week.'

'I know. I *know*,' Silke said, 'but what can we do? You know Ottsy, he's so bloody-minded and he says nothing can persuade him to wear that uniform. He says he's been taking life too easy and it's time he let them all know he's still a Jew. I can't understand it. Everything was going so well and now he's just so *angry* again. I think something must have happened and he's not saying what.'

Paulus spoke up.

'I know what's made him so angry, Silks,' and then added quietly, 'and I know a way to make him see sense too.'

'Tell us then, Pauly!' Silke said eagerly.

'You're not going to like it,' Paulus went on. 'And for that matter nor am I.'

'If it stops Ottsy getting himself sent to a camp then I'll like it,' Silke said firmly.

'Why has Otto suddenly got so furious again, Pauly?' Frieda asked. 'Tell us what you know.'

'All right then. Ottsy tried to see Dagmar the other night.'

'Did you see him?' Frieda gasped. 'Did you talk to him?'

'No, Mrs Fischer would hardly let him in the house. Anyway Dagmar made me stay in her room. She thought it would be even harder to make him go if he saw me.'

'Dagmar spoke to him?'

'Not for long. She sent him away. She told him that he wasn't one of us any more. That she didn't want to see him because he had a life and she didn't.'

'What a bitch!' Silke exclaimed.

'Silke!' Frieda scolded. 'I hate that word.'

'Well, sorry. But I mean *really* it's not Ottsy's fault, is it?'

'Look,' Paulus said. 'Perhaps I'm not putting what she said very well. It made sense at the time and it was mainly Frau Fischer who spoke to him anyway. And of course by turning up he was putting them in a lot of danger. He really should have thought of that. Perhaps he did but he just couldn't stop himself . . . We all know how he feels about Dagmar.'

Silke looked away. Frieda reached over and squeezed her hand.

'So it's pretty obvious why he's started acting up again,' Paulus went on. 'Dagmar refusing to see him will have made him crazy. He wants to prove he's still a Jew. I know him. I *know* how he feels and he'd rather die and have her respect than live without it.'

Frieda's face contorted with alarm.

'You said you had an idea, Pauly. What is it?' she asked.

'Well,' Paulus said grimly, 'like I said, Dagmar's getting very depressed.'

'What's she got to do with it?' Silke exclaimed. 'We're talking about Ottsy.'

'I know that, Silks,' Paulus said patiently. 'But you know as well as I do that Dagmar is the key to him. Anyway she's kind of withdrawing within herself. Sort of giving up, a bit like . . .'

Paulus stopped himself but he couldn't help casting a glance in the direction of Wolfgang.

'Like me?' Wolfgang said with a bitter smile. 'Not quite as bad as that I hope. But if she is, you must make sure she avoids wood-based alcohol. It can blind you if you haven't built up a tolerance.'

'Please, Wolf,' Frieda said, trying to mask the distaste in her voice. 'We're talking about Otto. Go on, Pauly.'

'Frau Fischer's really worried about her,' Paulus said. 'Dagmar used to love to go out. She loves to *do* things. She's not like me. I can read a book, but she's a *physical* person and she's sort of *fading away*. She needs to be able to go swimming, she needs to go to cafés. Believe it or not, she needs tickets to the Olympics.'

Silke could hardly contain her frustration.

'Well, she *can't* go to the bloody Olympics, can she?' she snapped. 'What has all this got to do with—'

'But you see she can,' Paulus went on. 'All she needs is a good cover. All she needs . . . is a Nazi boyfriend.'

'You mean . . . Ottsy?' Frieda gasped.

Silke looked dumbstruck.

'Exactly,' Paulus said. 'If she was going about on the arm of a uniformed *Jungmann* from the elite Napola school, she could get in anywhere she wanted with no questions asked. He could even take her swimming, I'm sure of it.'

'Yes,' Silke conceded quietly, knowing instantly that her days as Otto's best and only friend were over. 'I suppose that's right.'

'And that's the way we'll keep Otto from causing trouble for himself. You have to go to him, Silks, and tell him that the better a Nazi he looks the more he'll be able to help Dagmar. That'll bring him round for sure.'

'Goodness, Pauly!' Frieda said. 'What a clever plan.'

'Isn't it?' Silke said glumly.

She and Paulus looked at each other. Both understanding the sacrifices they were each going to have to make.

Silke did her duty on the following Sunday, explaining to Otto Paulus's audacious plan.

'Dagmar needs you, Otts,' she told him. 'Pauly and Frau Fischer are really worried about her. She's going crazy all cooped up and losing hope. She has to get out. She has to have some fun. You're the only person who can do that for her so you really really have to start behaving yourself again and get them to trust you. Then they'll let you go out of school, like the other boys, and you can start getting Dagmar out of herself.'

Otto certainly did not need telling twice. In an instant his entire demeanour altered.

'Don't you worry, Silks,' he said with a broad smile, 'you can rely on me!'

'That's great,' Silke replied, her smile considerably less animated than Otto's.

That same Sunday Paulus put the plan to Dagmar.

'I don't know why I didn't think of it before,' he said. 'Ottsy gives you the perfect cover. You can be a German girl again and go where you please as long as you're with him!'

At first the idea of going out amongst Nazis turned Dagmar white with terror. But very soon the excitement of the adventure overcame her fears and her spirits began visibly to rise.

'Well, Otto *would* make rather a handsome beau,' she conceded.

'Try not to rub it in, Dags,' Paulus said ruefully.

'Silly!' Dagmar replied with a happy tone that Paulus hadn't heard her use in years. 'You know I love you both.'

It was decided that Silke would take Dagmar with her to the very next Sunday tea at the Napola. Otto easily got permission to have an extra guest as girls were always in very short supply at the boarding school social functions. Of course Dagmar had no BDM uniform but the fact that she would be arriving as Silke's friend would almost certainly be enough to ensure that no questions were asked.

The two girls travelled together across Berlin.

Having scarcely seen each other properly for a number of years they had very little to say to each other and conversation was very stilted. They tried to chat and joke a little about the old Saturday Club days, but apart from that shared history they had nothing else in common. They never had even before the Nazis, but now of course the gap between them was infinitely wider.

Spandau was at the very end of the line, after which they still had about a kilometre or so to complete the journey. Dagmar, who was wearing high heels, insisted on taking a taxi.

'Don't worry. I'll pay,' she said in answer to Silke's doubtful look. 'Mummy and I still have money, although they took a lot of it after . . . well . . . let's say they fined my father for the inconvenience of murdering him.'

As they sat together in the taxi, Silke took Dagmar's hand. Something she had not done since the days of children's games.

'I don't know if I ever said,' she whispered, 'but what has

happened to you is so terrible, Dagmar, and I'm so sorry. You know, about your dad and . . . well, about everything.'

Dagmar smiled.

'Thank you, Silke,' she said. 'You didn't say but I always knew you felt it. I may be mean sometimes but I'm not completely insensitive. Speaking of which, today for instance. I know how difficult this must be for—'

'It's fine,' Silke said briskly, 'absolutely fine. A really good plan. Pauly's plans always are.'

Within a very few minutes they arrived at the grand gates of the Napola school with the huge wrought-iron eagle and swastika mounted upon them.

'Oh God, I'm pretty nervous actually,' Dagmar admitted. 'I mean going in amongst all those Nazi boys.'

'You'll be fine,' Silke assured her. 'I'm absolutely sure of that.'

'How can you be, Silks?' Dagmar asked.

'Dagmar, they may be Nazis. But they're *boys*.'

Silke was right, of course. One glimpse of Dagmar at the school gates in her elegant, sophisticated, alluring grown-up clothes and she was the talk of the school. *Jungmann* Stengel, it seemed, had pulled off another coup, trading up from a nice-looking girl to a complete stunner. Certainly no one thought of asking such a beautiful creature for proof of her ancestry. Rather the excited boys would have queued up to lay down their lives for her.

Silke only accompanied Dagmar for one further Sunday before dropping out of the visits herself.

Her duty was done. Dagmar didn't need her any more. Otto's new companion was recognized and accepted by the school and had even been paid a toe-curlingly creepy compliment by the principal. Silke knew that no one would miss her and she couldn't wait to bow out. She didn't mind the other boys gawping at Dagmar but to see Otto doing it, panting and scampering about her like an eager puppy desperate to please, was hard for her to take.

Dagmar simply took over from Silke. More so in fact. Because whilst people merely *thought* that Silke had been Otto's girlfriend,

Dagmar immediately became it. And when she and Otto sat together beneath the oak tree looking over the soccer pitch they exchanged the kisses that Silke had longed would be hers.

Paulus's plan worked perfectly. With Otto beside her Dagmar was now able to enjoy the kind of fun that was denied to other Jewish adolescents. Otto was sixteen and could apply for evenings out and also Saturday afternoons. During these times he took Dagmar to parks and to the zoo. They sat together in cafés and occasionally even went to bars, most proprietors being pretty lax about youthful drinking, particularly with such an attractive young couple.

Otto had no money himself but he had his military-style uniform and he had grown quite tall and very strong. Dagmar did have money and she was happy to spend it on those precious times when she was able to be a normal young person once again.

And of course Otto took Dagmar swimming, which was her greatest joy of all. Soon Dagmar forgot even to feel nervous as they bought their tickets to the baths. No attendant ever once asked the beautiful girl with the Napola boyfriend for identification. She worried sometimes of course that she would be recognized, but she had been withdrawn from public life for so long that most people's memories of the heiress to Fischer's department store fortune were of a girl of twelve or thirteen.

Frieda now got her news of Otto from Paulus who in turn heard it from Dagmar. Silke still visited the Stengels on a Sunday evening to hear the news also. Smiling hard at every tale of the fun that Otto and Dagmar were having together. Just as Paulus tried hard to deliver the second-hand stories with the same joy and enthusiasm with which Dagmar had told them to him.

'They're both really having fun,' Paulus would say.

'Which is great,' Silke added.

And Frieda would look from one of them to the other and smile a sad little smile to herself.

On the Embankment

London, 1956

There was a decent moon and it cast a long streak of white across the cobalt black ripples of the Thames. A glittering, twinkling silver pathway stretching almost all the way from the Mother of Parliaments to the Royal Festival Hall.

'Peter Pan could'a danced along dat path,' Billie observed, 'on his way from Neverland to Kensington Gardens.'

'I don't think even Peter Pan could have survived a dunk in the Thames,' Stone replied.

They were standing together on Westminster Bridge. Neither of them had wanted to go home after their hurried exit from the pub, but Billie didn't want to drink any more so instead they had taken the taxi across Trafalgar Square and down Whitehall, and now found themselves standing in the moon shadow of Big Ben, staring down into the broad dark river as it hurried beneath them.

'I always like to t'ink of the Romans when I see the moon on the Thames,' Billie said.

'The Romans?' Stone enquired, somewhat surprised.

'It's jus' dis town's been here so *long*,' she explained. 'Amazin' to t'ink that people been lookin' at that same beautiful light on that same dirty ol' river for two thousand years.'

Together they made their way down from the bridge and on to the Victoria Embankment. Strolling past the various down-and-outs in search of an unoccupied bench.

'When I was a little girl in Trinidad,' Billie went on, 'me mudder used ta talk about how one day we be goin' to Englan' and then we'd have plenty money and anyt'ing we wanted to eat. An' then we'd take a pleasure trip on de Thames an' go see where ol' Henry de Eight be beddin' all his wives, one after another *after another*. An' then we'd go see where he killed a couple o' dem too. Cut off they heads in da Tower. An' we'd all be merry in merry ol' England. We did it too, you know. Me and me mudder. First Sunday we had money to spare for a day out, dat's what we did.'

'I wonder what old Henry would have made of that bloody awful Royal Festival Hall,' Stone said, glancing across the water at the controversial new building on the opposite bank.

'I like it,' Billie said. 'I t'ink it's very cool. Very satisfyin' spatially.'

'Too bloody Soviet if you ask me. Too much concrete.'

'Let me tell you, Paul. When you was born in a house wit' a mud floor, you don' mind a bit o' concrete. It be clean, it's cheap an' it don' blow down in a storm. That's a lot o' positive when you puttin' up a building.'

'Well, you're the design student,' Stone conceded.

'You can't study good taste, baby,' Billie replied. 'Nor common sense neither. I jus' be born wit' more than my fair share o' both, tha's all.'

They found an empty bench and staked their claim, Billie inspecting the seat carefully by the light of her Dunhill lighter before she would entrust her beautiful woollen coat to it. There was a cabbies' refreshment stall a little further along and Stone went and got them some tea and a bar of Cadbury's chocolate.

'You know those Romans who were staring at our moon from their wooden bridge got a nasty surprise,' Stone said when he returned with the two steaming china mugs. 'Boudicca and the Iceni turned up and they reckon as many as seventy thousand people died in the fighting and pillaging. Just about around where we're sitting now.'

'Well, d'ere's a gruesome t'ought for a romantic night!' Billie laughed. 'You always find a way, don't you?'

'But the good part of it is, that was the biggest slaughter that ever happened in the British Isles. No power-mad swine has topped it since in almost two millennia. That's actually an amazing statistic. How many other countries can say that the bloodiest catastrophe that ever occurred on its soil happened nineteen centuries ago? I'll tell you now. None. Lucky old Britain eh?'

Billie smiled and sipped her tea.

'Did you put three in?'

'Of course.'

'Don't t'ink you stirred it then.'

'Ah.'

Billie took a pencil from her purse and stirred her tea.

'You really love dis country, don't you, baby?' she said.

'I don't know,' Stone said thoughtfully. 'I'm not much good at love. But I do respect it, I can tell you that. I respect it deeply. And its people too.'

'Even after tonight. After you punched de landlord?'

'That was depressing. Very depressing. But I think in this country people like that are the rotten apples. When I was a boy they were the whole barrel.'

'Well, maybe.' Billie shrugged. 'Except I gots't tell ya I see a lot o' dose apples, you know. Teddy boy gangs comin' down Ladbroke Grove wit dere razors. You know when we first come here we couldn't even get no rooms because we was Negroes, oftentimes we still can't. No Dogs. No Blacks. No Irish.'

'I know, Bill. Of course I'm not saying it's paradise or anything. But all the same, it's still the most tolerant country I ever heard of . . . And the funny thing is they don't even know it. It makes me laugh sometimes to hear the Reds at work muttering that Britain's not much better than a Fascist state. I tell them, it may be elitist, snobbish, small-minded and class-obsessed, but in the middle of the nineteenth century they made a Jew Prime Minister. In the middle of the twentieth we murdered all ours.'

'We?' Billie said surprised. 'I never heard you talk about yo'self as German before.'

'Well, I am, Bill,' Stone replied. 'That's another funny thing. I'll always be German, or at least a part of me will be. The Germany of my parents and my grandparents. The one they loved. And I loved too. But the thing is, it got stolen. And that didn't happen here. The Fascists never got anywhere in Britain. We never let them.'

'We?' Billie laughed. 'So now you're British too?'

'Yes. I'm both. Or nothing at all, more like. But you know when we drove down Whitehall we passed Downing Street. We could have stopped the cab, got out and walked up to it. There's one copper outside. That's it, *one* cop. There's never been more than that, even when Britain ruled a quarter of the world. Isn't that something?'

'Yeah. I s'pos it is when you put it like that.'

She took his hand and he felt her thumb brush across his knuckles, discovering the scabs that had formed there.

'Ouch,' she said.

'Must have caught his teeth somehow. Didn't think I had. Thought I popped him clean.'

'Oh you popped him clean, all right, boy. Don' you worry 'bout dat.'

'I had to do it, you know, Billie,' Stone said.

'I don't t'ink you did have to do it. Not on my account anyways. I don't like violence.'

'Who does?'

'I don't think it helps.'

'Billie, I have a rule. When you meet that kind of attitude, you always have to fight it. It doesn't matter whether you're black, Jewish or White Anglo-Saxon Protestant, it's never good enough to walk away. You have to confront it every time you see it. I made that decision twenty-three years ago when I saw a young teenage girl running down the Kurfürstendamm in terror while they made her mum and dad lick the pavement.'

Billie smiled. 'It's still all about that girl, isn't it? Even now, when you're defending da honour of a Negro student in Soho in *1956*, you still be really doing it for dat little German girlie. You hit dat guy for her sake not mine.'

'No, Billie,' Stone protested. 'I did it for you. Really. And for my mum and my dad and Pauly and all the damned millions of others.'

'And Dagmar.'

'Yes. Of course. And Dagmar.'

'Dagmar most.'

Stone laughed. '*No*, not most. You most.'

'Well, gi' me some chocolate an' I'll believe you.'

Stone took the purple-wrapped bar from his pocket, tore

away the paper and ran a thumbnail along the groove in the foil.

'Wish I had some Lindt for you,' he said. 'Now *that's* chocolate.'

'I prefer Cadbury's,' Billie said, accepting a whole row of squares. 'I don' like posh choccie. Cadbury Dairy Milk an' a nice cup o' tea. *Dat* is livin', baby.'

Together they ate their chocolate and sipped their tea and watched as a coal barge slipped past in silence, cutting the silver ribbon the moon had draped across the water in two.

'So you an' Dagmar ended up goin' aroun' together then?' Billie said, resuming the conversation.

'Yes, that's right, we did. Her pretending to be non-Jewish and me pretending to be a good Nazi.'

'An' did you get to sleep wit' her?'

Stone coughed into his mug. 'Straight to the point, eh?' he said, wiping tea from his chin.

'Well, c'mon. It's the obvious question.' Billie laughed.

'Well, no, as it happens. We were only teenagers.'

'Haha! You was *sixteen*!' Billie snorted in amusement. 'Differen' times, baby! Differen' times.'

'Well, there wasn't really much opportunity for that sort of thing. Our time together was pretty restricted and we had no place to go to. It was still too dangerous for me to go to her house.'

'Bet you tried damn hard to find somewhere though.'

'I suppose in a way we did. We certainly messed around a lot, whenever we could. You know, alleys and park benches.'

'Oh I know. Been there meself. And she really was your girl? I mean for real? Not just because you could get her into the swimmin' pool?'

'Well I thought so. I thought she loved me. She said she did.'

'But she didn't?'

'No,' Stone replied, with a distant hint of bitterness. 'In the end it turned out I was just a convenient mate. She loved my brother after all.'

Reichssportfeld, Grunewald

Berlin, 1 August 1936

The roar was like nothing that either Otto or Dagmar had ever heard before.

Solid, like a blow. An assault on the senses. Thunderous. Volcanic. An eruption of noise. The air was dense and heavy with it. Noise as a palpable physical entity. Wave upon wave crashing against them. Assaulting them. *Punching them.*

Dagmar tried to speak, to shout, but her mouth seemed to move in silence. No single voice could prosper amongst those hundred and ten thousand joined as one.

Dagmar and Otto were drowning in a *sea* of sound.

It crashed into their faces like breaking surf. Filling their heads. Dizzying and disorientating them.

And just when they had imagined it could get no louder, the amorphous atmospheric cacophony took shape and form. Words as well as sound engulfed them.

'*Sieg heil! Sieg heil! Sieg heil!*'

Each '*heil*' an airborne battering ram. Shaking and vibrating their heads, their bodies and the concrete stand beneath their feet until it seemed as if it would crack under the pressure.

Dagmar pressed her hips against Otto's. He could feel her shaking and knew that he was shaking too.

Not with fear but with excitement.

It was simply magnificent. The greatest stadium ever built stretched out before them. A vast and elegant oval, surrounding the greenest of fields and the straightest of tracks, on which were assembled, in perfect rows, athletes from every corner of the globe. The finest human bodies on the planet, all gathered together behind their flags in celebration of excellence.

And beyond them, the great viewing platform. Far grander and more monumental than any Caesar had ever looked down on. And on it a tiny cluster of men, with one man standing completely apart. Forward from the rest and alone. His arm outstretched.

The Leader. Sternly acknowledging the familiar salute.

'*Hail victory! Hail victory! Hail victory!*'

The German team arrived last and stood closest to the podium. The largest team, it seemed to Otto, and clad entirely in white. Such a brilliant choice. Such a perfect piece of theatre. A deliberate and inspired contrast to the rest. Setting Germany apart completely from the various multi-coloured rigs worn by the nations that had preceded them into the stadium. The striped blazers, jolly boaters and bright ties, the garish turbans, and strangely incongruous bits and pieces of national dress. The flowing scarves, the rowing caps, the neckerchiefs in every hue. And the Italians, strangest of all in what looked like black battle tunics and military-style caps.

Only the Germans wore one single unifying visual theme. And that theme was purest white.

From the white caps on their heads to the white shoes and socks on their feet, they were the white team.

Like a regiment of angels.

The only splash of colour was the blood red banner behind which they marched.

One hundred and ten thousand people stood and raised their right arms in salute. Including Otto and Dagmar. They would have done as much for safety's sake in such a crowd, but in that moment and amidst that strange infectious madness, they actually almost *wanted* to salute.

Dagmar put her free arm around Otto and held him tight. He could feel her thigh against his.

Another roar rose up out of the ongoing noise as, far away across the hugeness of the stadium, Hitler approached the microphones. At such a distance he was but a tiny figure, and yet unmistakable. The most famous man in the world. Otto thought he would have been recognizable from across a continent.

The man just held himself in *that way*.

That particular *Hitler* way that cartoonists and comedians around the world had been ridiculing for a decade but which for all their efforts remained undeniably uniquely impressive.

Stern. Detached. Separate. *Alone.*

Few men who had come so far could have borne themselves with the same measured and quiet confidence at such a time. To stand before a hundred and ten thousand people greeting him as a deity and still remain somehow detached.

No triumphalism in his stance. No glee. Plenty around him of course, but not him. For him just the manner of a man who finds things in order and had expected no less.

The Leader's voice rang round the stadium.

'I proclaim open the eleventh games of the modern Olympic era,' he said, 'here in Berlin.'

Again a brilliant choice. Simple, like the white of his team. No ranting and raving. No spitting passion as the world had come to expect. Just the quiet authority of a man in absolute charge.

The Leader's brief address unleashed another verbal cannonade of siegs and heils which rang once more around the stadium. The Olympic flame was lit and the games themselves began.

Many spectators left at that point, preferring political theatre to athletics, but Dagmar and Otto intended to stay and watch every single moment that their tickets allowed.

'If only I could be one of them,' Dagmar said when finally it became possible to communicate at anything less than a scream. 'Imagine it! To be in the middle of all this. Ready to compete. Representing Germany. Dressed in pure white.'

'Ah,' Otto replied, 'but if you were competing, you wouldn't be able to stuff yourself with beer and sausages, which is what I'm going to get for us right now!'

They sat and watched the events all day. Finding themselves cheering on the German team despite themselves. Despite the fact that each athlete turned to the podium and gave the Nazi salute before and after they competed.

'Who else are we supposed to cheer for?' Dagmar asked, her mouth full of bratwurst and beer.

They drank all day without anybody seeming to mind their youth. Possibly the stall-holders didn't recognize Otto's black

Napola uniform was a school one, and Dagmar could easily have been twenty-one.

They were drunk of course by the time they drifted out of the stadium, and so instead of going home took the tram into the Tiergarten for coffee.

The whole of Berlin seemed to be celebrating the successful opening of the games and also the surprising number of early German victories, and Dagmar and Otto forgot their cares as they strolled together through the packed and happy throng.

'Don't you have to be back at school?' Dagmar asked.

'Fuck 'em,' Otto replied.

Dagmar's face fell. 'Otto, you can't say that.'

'Why not? They sent me to that school. I didn't ask to go.'

'Yes, but you have to stay there now, Otts. For my sake. The better a Nazi you are, the more you can take me out and we can have fun – that was Pauly's plan.'

'Oh yes of course,' Otto said quickly. 'I know that. Don't worry, I know lots of windows I can sneak back in through, and if they catch me I'll tell them the tram got stuck in the crowd or something. If I get a beating it'll be worth it. Just to spend a bit more time with you.'

'Oh, Ottsy. That is such a *romantic* thing to say. I remember the first beating you took for me. At Wannsee when poor Pauly got four extra for being too clever.'

Dagmar put her arms around Otto and kissed him. There were many couples doing likewise in the exciting twilight of the park and she kissed him long and hard.

'It's been so wonderful getting to go out again, Ottsy,' Dagmar whispered. 'I feel like I'm alive again.'

Otto felt alive also and hugged her closer and more desperately.

'Dagmar,' he half gasped, 'do you think maybe . . . maybe some time we could . . . '

'Yes!' Dagmar whispered. 'But not now. Some time . . . I want to. Really I do. But not tonight . . .'

'We could go to your mum's place,' Otto blurted. 'She never comes upstairs—'

'No, Ottsy!' Dagmar said, disengaging herself with reluctance. 'It's too dangerous. If you were seen there we'd be punished. Besides, you have to get back to school. You mustn't lose your privileges. You're amongst the elite.'

'Do you think I care about that?' Otto protested.

'You may not, darling. But I do. I like having an elite boyfriend.'

'Did . . . did you just call me "darling"?' Otto said, a huge half-idiot smile spreading across his face.

'Yes, I did . . . darling. Because that's what you are. My darling. All mine. Now you get back to school and *don't* get caught sneaking in. Because if they gated you then you wouldn't be able to take me out, would you? And that wouldn't do at all.'

A Holiday in Munich

1937

Frieda blamed herself. It had been she who had persuaded Wolfgang to leave the apartment for the first time in a month and go for a little walk. The result had been a nasty encounter with a Hitler Youth squad. He had limped back in agony and it was clear that whatever tiny improvements he had been making in his health and self-confidence had been set back tenfold.

'The little bastard just pushed me out of the way,' Wolfgang explained, his voice hovering between tears of anger and tears of despair. 'It was at the market. They were marching right through the middle, stamping and singing. What else do they ever do except stamp and bloody sing? I just couldn't get out of the way in time. I'd dropped some coins and I needed them. I was trying to pick them up. They could have gone round me but of course they didn't. The front kid just gave me a kick and I went rolling.'

Frieda was probing gently at his ribs. 'Well, it's either very bruised or you've cracked one again,' she said, trying to speak as if this was just a medical matter like any other, trying not to dwell on the fact that her husband had been sent sprawling in the gutter by a squad of adolescents.

The lift outside clanked. Paulus was home from school.

'Post!' he said. 'One from Australia, one from Britain.'

'Keep the stamps, don't forget,' Frieda said. 'The little Leibovitz boy absolutely loves them. He steams them off so beautifully – you should see his collection. He's so proud of it.'

'Yeah.' Wolfgang smiled. 'Little Jewish kids certainly have the best stamp collections. All the countries that don't want any Jews. Plenty of those.'

Paulus was already reading the letters.

'Interesting,' he said. 'It's from Government House in Darwin, Australia. The Northern Territory is definitely interested in doctors.'

'Well, they do need people down there. Why shouldn't it be us?' Frieda said as she unbuttoned Wolfgang's shirt and pulled the tails from his trousers. 'You've heard of Steinberg?'

'Yes, of course, Mum,' Paulus said. 'The Freeland League; he wants to buy a bit of the Kimberly and establish a colony of us. Believe me, there isn't a rat hole I'm not looking into.'

'Please don't call it that, Pauly.'

Frieda studied Wolfgang's chest and couldn't help making a little noise of concern. There were black bruises down one side of his white bony torso.

'Anyway,' Paulus went on, 'the point is they need working men as well as professionals. Maybe I'll end up shearing sheep and studying for the Australian Bar at night.'

'Ow!' Wolfgang gasped as Frieda applied a bandage.

His chest was so skinny and hollow and the flesh so sensitive that it was impossible to tie the bandage tightly enough for it to stay on.

'This one from England looks interesting too,' Paulus said. 'From the Central British Fund for German Jewry. They're happy to help us with visa applications but first we have to find people over there who'll put us up. I need a list, Mum. A list of every doctor you've ever been in contact with in the United Kingdom, in the States, France, Canada, everywhere. You've got to think back over all your years at the clinic. You went to international conferences back in the twenties. Forums on public health. Who did you meet? I don't care how briefly. I want their names, and especially any correspondence. We need somebody to focus on *us* specifically, that's the only way to do it now. Too many people are scrabbling for an exit. We have to find a champion, someone who'll take up our case. I need a list, Mum.'

'I know. I *know*,' Frieda said.

'You say that but you *have* to focus on it, Mum. We can't even *apply* for any foreign-entry visa unless we can prove that someone will take us in when we get there.'

'I have a lot to do, Pauly! I have patients.'

'There's plenty of sick kids in Britain and Australia that you can worry about.'

'Pauly. Those kids are not excluded from society. My patients have no one else. They *need* me.'

'We need you, Mum. We have to find someone who'll help us look for a place. We don't want much. Ottsy can stay here till we're established and Pops and Grandma won't leave so it's just three of us. You're a doctor, Mum! That's a huge plus. I'm young and fit and in a year I'll have graduated school, and I'm going to get top marks if it kills me. We have a lot to offer . . .'

Paulus's voice trailed away. As it so often did at this point in their desperate discussions. There was an elephant in the room. A poor half-crippled elephant. All three of them knew that Wolfgang's chances of convincing anyone that he could fulfil a 'useful occupation' had been slim enough when he was healthy but they were less than zero now.

'Don't worry,' Wolfgang said, laughing and trying to cover his son's embarrassment. 'I'm sure they have dishes that need washing. That's what most musicians do for a living anyway.'

'Yeah, Dad. That's right,' Paulus said. 'We'll be OK.'

'And in the meantime,' Wolfgang announced with exaggerated cheeriness, 'while you're trying to get us a bolt hole and Mum's attempting single-handedly to ensure the health of every Jewish child in Berlin, I'm going on holiday!'

Whatever Frieda might have been expecting her husband to say, it certainly hadn't been that.

'A holiday? Wolf, kindly explain.'

'Just a short one. A holiday for the *soul*.'

'Wolf,' Frieda said, smiling but with a touch of impatience, 'I don't really have time for games. What holiday? Where are you planning on going?'

'To the ends of the earth and to the edge of the conscious.'

'*Wolf!* I don't have time for this!'

'Into the minds of genius and to the furthest corners of my soul.'

He was almost laughing now.

'Right, that's it!' Frieda said. 'I'm not listening any more. Sorry, but I have to read up on rickets and juvenile malnutrition.'

'All right! All right!' Wolfgang said, producing a newspaper from his pocket and showing it to Frieda. 'I'm going to Munich to look at this. The *Entartete Kunst* – the Exhibition of Degenerate Art. They're actually mounting an *exhibition* of art they want people to hate. It's incredible. Every artist I ever loved – Kirchner, Beckmann, Grosz of course. Amazing names: Matisse, Picasso, look, Van Gogh! Can you believe it! All in one exhibition! And for free. All I need to find is the train fare to Munich.'

Frieda took the newspaper and looked over the article.

'I always, *always* think,' she said with a sigh, 'that they can't surprise me any more.'

'But they just keep on doing it, don't they?' Wolfgang replied almost cheerfully now. 'And for once, gawd bless 'em for it! I mean, this really is incredible. They've raided every museum and gallery in Germany. They're *that confident* in their Philistine vision that they're putting the best art on the planet on display on the presumption that people will laugh at it.'

'Incredible,' Frieda said, looking at the list and shaking her head. 'No rhyme nor reason, everybody in together. It says here it's all *Jewish Bolshevist* but most of these artists aren't even Jewish, or Communist for that matter.'

'Ah, but read on, it turns out the Leader has decided that it's possible to *paint* like a Jew even if you *aren't* one. Apparently it was *our* influence that created decadent art. I'd say we should be proud, only Pauly would leap down my throat. Anyway, Jew, Commie, Cubist or Expressionist, I want to see that bloody exhibition! So thank you, Herr Goebbels, for organizing that I may be suitably' – he quoted from the article – '*revolted by the perverse Jewish spirit which once penetrated German Culture.*'

'Wolf,' Frieda said with a look of concern. 'Do you really think it's wise? If they suspect you're not there to hate but to admire, and find out you're a Jew?'

'Frieda,' Wolfgang assured her with absolute confidence, 'I don't think I'm going to be the only one.'

Wolfgang was right.

He travelled from Berlin to Munich the following week on the night train, squeezed into a third-class carriage amongst a group of noisy soldiers who were being moved south to be deployed on the Austrian border.

During the night, bouncing along on the hard wooden bench, every jolt shooting agonizing pains through his chest, Wolfgang found his mind dwelling on memories of Katharina. She had made this very same train journey from Berlin to Munich in order to see Brecht's first play. Rattling through the darkness in search of spiritual balm, just as he was doing. That had been fifteen years ago and in a different country.

Arriving early in the morning, Wolfgang freshened up at the station lavatory, treated himself to one cup of coffee from the café and began making his way to the exhibition. This was being held in what had previously been the Institute of Archaeology, but the Nazis had closed that. They had no need of it. Clearly, having established their own thousand-year civilization, they saw no need to study any previous ones.

Wolfgang arrived very early at the venue, but it was fortunate for him that he did, for as he had predicted the exhibition was proving an enormous hit. Many thousands of people each day were struggling to have the chance to be properly revolted by decadent art, and even though it was scarcely seven a.m. the queue already snaked all round the building. Looking at the people waiting, Wolfgang could hardly believe that the Nazis could not see what was so self-evident to him. That almost without exception the people waiting patiently had come not to be outraged but to admire. There were no Brownshirts in the queue whatsoever, no party badges or police. Not a single one. The Exhibition of Degenerate Art was probably the only public event in all Germany that summer in which not a single uniform was to be seen amongst the clientele. Wolfgang thought that if the Gestapo wanted to make a good haul of the remaining free spirits hiding in Munich in 1937, they had only to attend their own propaganda exhibition and arrest everyone.

The exhibition was on the second floor of the building and it could only be reached via a small back staircase, up which it was really only possible to shuffle in single file. Wolfgang intimated from this that the organizers had not expected a big turnout. It was obvious that the exhibition had been mounted simply that it might be reported. So that the principle that there was such a thing as Jew-inspired 'degenerate art' would be established. That smug burghers might be able to sneer at an example or two offered up for ridicule each day in the newspapers.

The exhibits on display had been mounted in a deliberately alienating manner, crowded together, sometimes skewed, tucked into corners and placed in unsuitable settings for their scale. The place was also hot and the crowd thick, but Wolfgang determined to appreciate every item. To mentally isolate himself within the throng, focusing with all his might on each piece, allowing people to push past as he obstinately took his time.

Everywhere the organizers had posted little slogans in an effort to remind the patrons to make sure they continued to hate.

Madness becomes method!

The German Peasant through the eyes of the Jew!

Cretins and whores, the ideal of the Degenerate.
Nature through sick minds!

Wolfgang revelled in it all. *Wallowed* in it. Staying until the very last moment, leaving only as the doors were being locked behind him.

This was *his* holiday. A trip around the world and across the universe of the imagination in a single day.

Before he took his leave.

Because Wolfgang had a plan. A plan which he explained to Frieda in the last note he ever left her. On the kitchen table they had shared together all their adult lives.

He wrote it on the train back to Berlin. *My dearest, darlingest, beloved Freddy*, it began.

Please don't be angry with me. You must know that what I am doing is right.

You must also know that I have spent my last full day on earth in the company of some of the greatest spirits that ever lived. I would have preferred to have spent it with you, of course. But I couldn't. You would have guessed – you always do – and would have tried to stop me.

Fred. You know I have to leave you.

You DO know that.

There is no possibility in all the world of any country agreeing to take me as a refugee. I am broken and there's an end to it. If you insist on trying to take me, as I know you will, you will never leave this hell, and if you stay I do believe the end will be soon and it will be terrible.

You <u>must</u> get out and so must Paulus. Ottsy, too, I hope with all my heart. But you cannot if I am with you.

And so I must leave Germany by another route.

I pass without regret.

Believe that!

Believe it with all your heart or my soul will not rest.

How could I regret? I shared my life with you. No other man living or dead could ever have filled his time on earth more beautifully than that. To have lived life with you.

And with our boys.

But now that time is ended. Seventeen years of love.

And had those years been five or fifty, a minute, an hour or the half a century they should have been, it would have been just the same.

The same amount of time really. Do you see?

For in that time, no matter what length its earthly span, was contained all the love in the world.

Ha ha! There, you see! I <u>*can*</u> *say something without trying to be funny!*

And now it's goodbye.

Freddy.

Once again.

You know I'm right. You <u>*know*</u> *I have to do this.*

Here's hoping those heavenly choirs (in which I'm choosing at this last moment to believe) know some jazz!

Your own

Wolf

The night train arrived back in Berlin shortly before dawn. Wolfgang took a taxi back to Friedrichshain. It was an extravagance but a necessary one as he wanted to be sure to arrive home before Frieda awoke.

Asking the taxi to wait in the street outside their building, he crept slowly up the stairs to their apartment. He could not use the lift for fear of rousing Frieda. He tried hard not to wheeze as his infected lungs laboured with the climb, and almost held his breath as he approached his own front door. Creeping silently into the flat, Wolfgang left his note on the kitchen table and weighed it down with his house keys. Then, pausing only to pick up his trumpet, he made his way back out. He didn't linger. He didn't turn to look. He knew that had he done so the temptation to remain, to creep back into bed and kiss his beloved, would be too much.

And he had a taxi waiting.

Outside as the morning sun began slowly to find the first

colours of the morning, Wolfgang asked the driver to take him to the old Moltke bridge.

Once in the middle of the bridge, Wolfgang got out and watched the taxi drive away.

Then, taking his trumpet, he stood beside the sandstone parapet above the central arch and played. He played *Mack the Knife*, that mournful, hypnotic hook that Weill laid down to support Brecht's sinister lyric about the shark's teeth and the hidden blade. Back when Berlin was beautiful and crazy.

It took him a number of stops and starts to complete the short tune even once. Wolfgang's lungs were almost gone and even these few notes presented a challenge.

Then, rolling himself up on to the parapet, his trumpet still in his hand, Wolfgang Stengel threw himself off the Moltke bridge and into the river Spree below.

Later, when Wolfgang's body was dragged from the river and his death was duly recorded, it was said that he had committed suicide. But Frieda knew that he hadn't. Nor had any of the hundreds of other Jews who took their own lives that year when the whole world still recognized Hitler as a great and inspiring leader of the German nation.

'My husband was murdered,' Frieda said. 'They were all murdered.'

Frieda's Other Children

Berlin, 1938

In the spring of 1938, the German Government was flushed with victory after its popular absorption of Austria into the Reich.

This event had unleashed an orgy of anti-Semitic violence in the south, which was so far unparalleled in its spite and cruelty. Emboldened by what appeared to be a popular appetite for pitiless brutality, the Nazis began what they called the Aryanization of Reich assets.

'I think they're going to take our homes,' Frieda said to her mother and father on one of her Sunday visits.

'Nonsense,' Herr Tauber grunted over the empty pipe on which he still sucked despite the fact that it rarely contained tobacco. 'I won't believe it.'

'Dad. We have to *register* our assets. Property, possessions, the lot.'

'Well, it's like a census, isn't it?' the rapidly ageing man insisted, 'except instead of people they are taking an inventory of property.'

'Yes. Ours, Dad. No one else's. The Nazis want to know exactly what we own. I cannot think of any other reason for them doing that than that they intend at some point to steal it. Why else would they call a list of Jewish possessions "Reich assets"? They're certainly nothing if not shameless.'

The old couple tutted and protested into their little bit of coffee and bread and butter.

'But think about it, Frieda dear,' Frau Tauber said, 'if they took our homes, where would we live? There are thousands of us, they can't very well leave us on the streets. No. I won't believe it. It doesn't make sense.'

Frieda did not argue any further. In fact she regretted raising the point at all. Why should her parents face reality? It would do them no good if they did, for there was nothing they could do about their situation. They could not escape even if they had wanted to. No country would give them a visa. Better really that they should continue to live in denial, choosing to believe that somehow, in the end, the madness would stop. That it simply was not possible for the German State to be reinvented permanently as an entirely criminal organization.

Most Jews got through their days on just such brittle optimism. Refusing to accept that things were as bad as they were or that they would most certainly get worse. Frieda's parents, for instance, refused ever to talk about Wolfgang's suicide. For them, every person who gave up hope was another chink in the paper-thin armour of those whose chosen defence was blind faith.

'I'm sure that it's sensible for you to leave, dear,' Frau Tauber went on, 'but not for us. Everything we know and value is here in Germany and it's where we will stay.'

What Frieda said next surprised her parents greatly.

'I shan't be leaving either, Mother,' she said. 'I've decided. I will never emigrate.'

Her parents exchanged a worried glance. Frieda knew what they were thinking. It was clear that their faith in the eventual resumption of the rule of law held only in their own case. When it came to their daughter and grandchildren, they took a more realistic view of what the Jews might soon expect.

'Frieda, that is a foolish thing to say,' her father said sternly. 'Of course you must pursue your life abroad. There is nothing for you or for the children here. We are old. It is different for us. You must go. In fact, I forbid you to stay.'

Frieda, almost smiled at this effort on her father's part to assert an authority over her that he had not held for at least twenty years.

'Dad—' she began.

Her mother interrupted, cracks breaking into the measured delivery she was trying to produce.

'You cannot stay for our sake, darling! You are a doctor, you're well placed to run, and what's more to make a life elsewhere. Wolfgang's gone. We are old. There's only you and your children . . .'

'Exactly, Mum,' Frieda said quietly. 'My children. I have to stay for them.'

'But they'll go with you, of course! Ottsy, too, in the end,' her father said. 'If it's a matter of money, let us help, we'll sell everything we have. You say the government will steal it soon anyway—'

'Dad, I'm not talking about my *sons*,' Frieda said gently. 'They are both eighteen, they're men now. I'm talking about my *children*. The ones I care for. The ones I continue to deliver into the world, for whatever our Leader may hope for, nature takes its course and new Jews come. Tiny babies, who don't know they've been born in hell. Those babies, those children, need a doctor. *I'm* their doctor. I will stay with them and care for them for as long as I'm able.'

Her parents were astonished. It had never occurred to them that Frieda would take this view. She had spoken so often of emigration. She had written so many letters.

'When Wolfgang was alive it was different. I had to care for him and so I knew that if I could get him out I would have done so. But he's gone. He made a sacrifice for me and—'

'Exactly!' her mother exclaimed. 'He did that terrible thing *for you*. His note was clear, he was holding you back, making it so much more difficult for you to leave. But now that—'

'Now that he's gone I intend to honour him and our love for each other by staying.'

'It's not what he would have wanted, Frieda!' her father said, his voice rising.

'It doesn't bloody matter what he would have wanted, does it, Dad! He's dead! He doesn't get a vote!' Frieda's voice was rising too. 'He's released me. Given me back the time I would have spent caring for him, protecting him. I'm going to put that sacrifice to good use. The best use. Lots of people are never getting out, Dad. You two for a start, but a couple of hundred thousand others I'd have said at least. The very young, the very old, the ones with no money, no influence. They are all going to need a doctor. I'm a doctor. That's my job.'

'But what about the boys?' her mother asked, almost timidly now, taken aback by Frieda's passion.

'Paulus will leave once he's finished school,' Frieda said, her firm resolve in some danger of faltering. 'We have a place for him at Goldsmith's College in London to study Humanities, and the British Central Fund have a place for him in a hostel. And don't think it doesn't break my heart to let him go, but every child leaves the nest, and at least I'll still have Otto. Even if I can't see him I'll know he's near.'

Her father nodded. 'Of course, he's an Aryan. If you're to stay then there's no reason for him to leave.'

'He wouldn't have left anyway, Dad. He's in love.'

Her parents both smiled.

'The Fischer girl,' Frau Tauber said.

'Of course,' Frieda replied.

'Well,' Herr Tauber commented, 'you can't exactly blame him. She is a damned peach.'

'Yes. Poor Paulus,' Frau Tauber said.

The Taubers exchanged regretful smiles. Although they came from a generation that did not pry or discuss personal matters even within the family, they had been perfectly aware over the years of the feelings that both their grandsons harboured towards Dagmar Fischer.

'Yes,' Frieda agreed with a regretful smile. 'Pauly lost in love and he was heartbroken, of course. He still is. Young love can be terribly cruel. But of course the truth is it's worked out very nicely. Imagine if Dagmar had chosen Pauly, I know that boy and he'd be insisting on staying with her. He may be the clear logical one in most things but when it comes to Dagmar he's as crazy as Ottsy. Funny, you know, when they were kids, before all this began, Wolfgang and I used to watch them playing in their Saturday Club and we'd joke that one day Dagmar would love Pauly and Silke would love Otto. That's how it always seemed to us it would be. But love of course never turns out the way you'd expect.'

Herr Tauber frowned somewhat and tapped his pipe thoughtfully.

'And so Ottsy wants to stay on,' he said. 'That will mean being conscripted. He knows that, I presume.'

'Of course, he'll do his National Service after he leaves the Napola.'

'And after that? Those boys are all supposed to become *Gauleiters* and party leaders, aren't they?' Herr Tauber asked.

'As far as I can gather, his idea is to give the appearance of being as good a Nazi as possible so that he can do what he can for Dagmar.'

Frau Tauber frowned. 'Well, that's all very well at the moment while it's just a question of getting her into swimming pools and the like, but what happens next? They're growing up.'

The three of them exchanged glances.

'He can't *marry* her,' Herr Tauber said. 'It's illegal.'

'I know and I don't know exactly what they'll do,' Frieda said. 'All I know is that he's sworn to protect her. To be her knight in shining armour. I think eventually he thinks he'll smuggle her out, once he's in uniform, or later as a party official. It's not a bad plan – he's bold and he might pull it off. All I can say is that for the moment Otto isn't the worry. He's not a Jew, he's not in danger. Paulus is and it's him I'm going to get out.'

'And you really are determined that you will stay?' Frau Tauber asked.

'Yes, Mum. My boys are men. My husband is gone. I've told you. I have other children now.'

'Well,' her father said, pretending to blow his nose. 'You always did make us proud, my dear. Always.'

English Conversations

Berlin, 1938

Along with all her other frantic activities, Frieda decided to start an English language conversation group.

Even before the coming of Hitler, she had made a point of speaking English informally with the twins. Now she decided to spread her knowledge further. All Jews now being prospective migrants, it seemed like a sensible idea.

Frieda also knew she was looking for ways to help get herself through the lonely evenings. Paulus was still living at home but he was absorbed mainly in study and kept to his room a lot of the time. Frieda missed Wolfgang and Otto terribly and so tried to fill every waking minute in an effort to distract herself from the empty spaces they had left behind.

The group was an instant success. Quite apart from the practical consideration of gaining a language with a view to emigration, the problem of boredom was endemic across the whole Jewish community. Largely shut up and hidden away, people were simply going crazy with nothing to do.

Assembling the group was therefore easy, finding something for it to talk about proved harder. Or at least something that didn't concern the woes of their community. Frieda soon found herself developing rules and strategies to avoid falling endlessly into the same deeply depressing conversational ruts.

'We're playing that game again!' she'd say two or three times at every meeting. 'The game of who's suffered the most and who deserves it least.'

It was almost inevitable that most conversations degenerated into an exchange of misery. People fell over each other to describe the dreadful experiences they had suffered and which they were quite certain trumped anything that their fellow group members might have gone through that day.

Sometimes the exchanges became heated. Previously calm and temperate neighbours raised their voices at each other. Arguing passionately about whether being refused service in a shop by an old acquaintance was more outrageous than being spat at in the street by a small child.

'My daughter was ejected from the railway station lavatory.'

'They took my umbrella. Just took it from my hand.'

'An umbrella? So what! They took my bicycle.'

'Ha! They took my car!'

'I am a war veteran.'

'I've paid my taxes all my life.'

Then Frieda would ring the little 'no moaning' bell that she kept beside her and insist, 'We must stop this! And if we can't stop it we must at least be civil about it. We're all starting to bicker and snap at each other. It's hardly surprising, all cooped up together as we are, but that's all the more reason to try harder to show each other respect.'

Try as she might, though, it was not possible for Frieda to steer the conversation away from endless discussions about the rapidly deteriorating situation in general.

The truth was there was really little else to talk about.

The register of Jewish assets in April had been a huge psychological blow, and even Frieda herself could not help dwelling on the cruelty of the action.

'It's like a note through the door saying, *We're coming to get you*,' she said. 'Or a thug on the other side of the street just standing, watching you with a smile on his face, whacking his cosh into the palm of his hand. It's really quite brilliant. Making us *list* our things and then letting it hang over us. If they ever make bullying an Olympic sport, then Germany will win Gold in Tokyo in 1940.'

'*Ja, es ist absolut erschreckend . . .*' Morgenstern the ex-book dealer agreed in frustration.

'In English, please, Mr Morgenstern,' Frieda said. 'This is an *English* conversation group.'

'Yes. Of course,' the old man stammered, searching in his mind for the correct words. 'It is so very terrified, *nicht wahr*? I mean, is it not?'

'Terrify*ing*,' Frieda corrected, 'not terrified. *You* are terri*fied* because *it* is terrify*ing*.'

In June the conversation group lost a member when the government announced that any Jew previously convicted of an offence, even as minor as a traffic violation, could be *rearrested* for it at the discretion of the police and sent to a concentration camp.

Schmulewitz the ex-insurance broker fell immediate victim to this new decree.

'He was done for drunk driving in 1925,' his tearful wife explained, bravely struggling to deliver her dreadful news in

English as the rules of the group required. 'A local policeman Hans once challenged over insurance is now having his revenge, and Hans has been sent to Ravensbrück. For a glass of schnapps he was fined for in 1925!'

In July came news that was particularly demeaning for Frieda.

'I have to tell you all,' she told the group, in perfect English, 'that officially at least you must not call me "doctor". The medical certification for all Jewish doctors is to be cancelled. I am no longer qualified. They're only going to let us function as nurses and even then, of course, only to Jewish patients.'

'*So haben sie endlich einen Weg gefunden . . .*'

'In *English* please, Mrs Leibovitz,' Frieda interrupted. 'Always in English.'

'I was saying,' Frau Leibovitz corrected herself, 'that they've finally found a way to redress the so-called "imbalance" regarding Jewish doctors that used to worry them so much. We used to be told we had too many doctors, now we don't have any.'

In August came the shocking decree that all Jews were required to add the names 'Israel' or 'Sara' to their own names and that a large letter J was to be stamped on to every Jewish passport.

'They're marking us down,' Herr Katz said. 'Identifying every single one of us so we can't hide. Why? What are they planning? What more can they do to us?'

Frieda almost smiled. *What more can they do to us?* Each of them said it. To themselves and to each other, over and over again. Whoever could have imagined that such a phrase would be the most common English sentence used in her conversation group?

'Ah ah, Herr Katz,' she admonished gently. 'You know that I have banned that phrase as overused. Try to come up with an alternative construction.'

'Very well then, Mrs *Doctor*,' Katz said, his brow furrowed in concentration. 'How about – the end, where will all of it be coming?'

'Not bad,' Frieda said. 'The correct English sentence would be: *Where will it all end?*'

The Night of the Broken Glass

Berlin, November 1938

Otto was awoken by the familiar harsh rasping bark of a command delivered as unpleasantly and as aggressively as the speaker knew how.

'*Jungmannen!* Parade, you lazy swine!'

Otto looked at his wristwatch. It was nearly midnight.

Of course it was.

Midnight. The Nazis' favourite hour.

Everything felt more *special* at midnight, more sternly historic. Swearing-ins, oaths of allegiance, flag ceremonies. Brutal initiations and impossibly tough physical tasks. Why do them after breakfast when you can do them in the middle of the night? With bonfires, flickering torches and muffled drums?

Otto rolled out of his bunk. He had been asleep and lost in dreams of Dagmar from which he was most annoyed to have been torn.

'Turn out, you fucking swine,' the voice commanded. 'On parade! Civilian clothes.'

Otto's heart sank. It seemed to him that the dorm leaders had in mind their favourite torture. This was to force the boys on and off parade in all of their various kits in turn, summer, winter, sport, formal, swim, labouring etc., with ever decreasing periods of time in which to make the changes. Then when every single item of clothing and equipment in the school had been thrown on and thrown off in a frenzy of impossible deadlines, the leaders would call a dormitory inspection and punish the whole school for slovenly kept kit.

Otto's options on civilian dress were more limited than the other boys'. He was an orphan without personal means, supported by the state. The school board supplied him with everything he possessed, and while Otto's uniforms were splendid, they were not lavish with anything else. Otto had no long trousers to put on and so despite it being November he had to turn out on the frosty parade ground in shorts, which caused much sniggering amongst the younger boys.

Otto was just noting the identities of these juveniles for later payback, and also wondering why they had not already been sent running back to their dorms to change into another kit, when the headmaster himself emerged on to the parade ground in full party uniform.

'*Jungmannen!*' the principal began as every boy in the school stamped to attention in perfect unison. The man's face was aglow with excitement and it was clear to Otto that whatever was coming was to be no mundane dormitory punishment exercise. 'Tonight we are to be given the honour of acting alongside our party comrades in the SS!'

A shiver of excitement ran amongst the boys. The SS were heroes, Black Knights, the Death's Head Gang. At Napola schools they represented the ultimate glamour, far more so than the Wehrmacht. Otto, however, felt a grip of fear. Even though he had become somewhat immersed in school life now and in fact enjoyed its rigorous physical challenges, he never forgot who his enemy was. Or who his family was and, most of all, whom he loved. He always knew that by the very nature of being a Napola boy he would at some point be called upon to act against his own kind.

He also knew that he would never do that.

Even at the risk of discovery and punishment, even of death.

'We are also, by the way,' the principal continued with a beaming smile, 'to have a little fun. Because, my brave young German heroes, the time has come to settle one or two scores with those gentlemen and ladies who would do us harm. Tonight, lads, we have an appointment with the race enemy! With Germany's misfortune! With the Jew!'

While the other boys grinned and discreetly nudged each other, Otto swallowed hard and tried to concentrate. The atmosphere in the city had been tense for days. There had been a murder in Paris. A Jew had shot a German embassy man and there had been plenty of talk of revenge both in the papers and on the street. Could this be the moment?

Standing rigidly to attention, Otto listened intently, staring at the principal through the cloud of silver breath that hung in front of his face.

Then he noticed something else.

The sky towards the city was glowing red.

How could that be? The sun had set hours ago.

Otto felt his stomach turn. Nausea gripped at his gut and his bowel. Something very wrong was hanging in the cold night air.

'You will be aware, of course,' the principal continued, his voice harsh, like metal on stone, 'of the outrage that has occurred recently in Paris. A Jew has committed the vilest of murders. A crime against Germany, and tonight that Jew's cousins here in Germany will pay! All over the Reich spontaneous demonstrations of outrage and retribution are breaking out. You, my young men, are to have the honour of being a part of this great reckoning alongside the entire *Schutzstaffel* and *Sturmabteilung*. Think of it, boys! The SS and the SA – and you are to be their comrades in combat! Be it noted, however, that they have also been instructed to operate out of uniform. The reason for this is that no maggot from the foreign press may accuse these demonstrations of being anything other than popular and spontaneous. For they *are* spontaneous, you can be assured of that, lads! But spontaneity as we understand the word in National Socialist Germany! Spontaneity that is properly and correctly ordered in the service of the state!'

Otto was hardly listening. He was watching the sky. It was getting redder.

Berlin was burning.

Or at least parts of it were, and there could be no doubt which parts they were.

The urge to break ranks and run, to get to Dagmar as fast as possible, thundered in Otto's brain and pounded in his heart. He thought of his mother, too, but she at least had Paulus. Dagmar had no one to protect her at all. Otto struggled to remain at attention, he knew that to be of any use to her he must not panic, he must focus. He could see that trucks had been lined up at the end of the parade ground. Clearly he and the other boys were to be taken somewhere. It could only be into the heart of the 'action'. If he wanted to get to Dagmar, for the moment at least he was better off remaining with the school.

'These demonstrations of popular outrage are taking place across the entire Reich!' the principal went on. 'In every village, town and city. Wherever a Jew nest is found it is to be attacked. Our particular task is to pay a visit to the Kurfürstendamm! We are to make it clear to the whole world what Germany's youth feels about the fact that Jew Communist Capitalist Parasites still fester and breed in the heart of our city! The SS have asked only for our older boys to assist in this action but I have decided on my own authority to send the whole school. For Germany *is* its youth and none are too young to serve. And as the Führer has said many times, youth must lead!'

Otto looked across the parade ground to the youngest of the pupils. Eleven-year-olds all turned out in their scarves and mufflers and their plus-four trousers. All standing rigidly to attention on the glittering frosty parade ground. Clouds of breath hanging in the air in front of them, yellow in the lamplight. The billowing swastika banners fluttering in the breeze above them.

Some of the little boys looked nervous, scared almost. But most were grinning broadly. It wasn't every night that they were woken up and ordered by their teachers to go and smash windows.

Otto began almost to shake with frustration. When would they board the trucks? When would the old bastard shut up and let them go?

'These orders,' the principal went on, 'have come from SS-*Obergruppenführer* Heydrich himself, and they are to be followed with *absolute* discipline as befits Napola boys. All Jews, Jewish businesses, Jewish property and Jewish dwellings are to be attacked, and all synagogues, without exception, are to be destroyed. However, no foreigners are to be threatened and this is to include foreign Jews. Where fires are set, *extreme* care must be taken that no German property is damaged in the action. If in doubt, smash but don't burn. Am I clear? Gentlemen! The school maintenance department have supplied what hammers, sledge hammers, crowbars and spades are available. These are to be taken by the older boys. Signed for and returned!'

On command, the boys of Otto's class rushed to grab at the best weapons, but Otto held back. He did not wish to be encumbered by school property for which he would have to answer, and he had no intention of remaining on the Kurfürstendamm. Dagmar would certainly not be there in the middle of the night.

Dwellings, the principal had said. They were to attack dwellings and Otto could imagine that the richer the dwelling, the more gleeful would be the attack. The well-identified Fischer house was an obvious target.

The boys boarded their buses and there was much raucous singing as they drove through the darkness towards the city.

All the old schoolroom favourites.

The Jews' blood spurting from the knife makes us feel especially good.

Otto tried to join in, knowing that he must not arouse suspicion, but it was difficult for him to focus on the boisterous camaraderie. With each kilometre that passed, the scenes in the streets through which they were being driven grew uglier and more terrifying.

Every street contained at least one shop that had been smashed and set alight. Houses and apartment blocks were being wrecked, too, surrounded by wild mobs.

Pressing his face to the window, Otto saw many beatings. On every corner young men were being kicked on the ground. Girls thrown about by their hair and pushed into gutters. Mothers kicked and punched as they were dragged from their homes, babies screaming in their arms.

The air was very cold outside and with so many lusty voices singing inside the coach the windows were dripping with condensation. To see out, Otto had constantly to wipe a fresh gap in the wet film, and through this cloudy porthole a monstrous tableau of images was revealed.

He saw a man shot and another knifed.

Uniformed police were at the very heart of the disturbances. Over and over Otto watched as terrified young men were thrown into police vans, baton blows raining down on their defenceless heads.

Berlin's Jews did not live in a ghetto, they were an integrated part of city life, and so the whole town bore witness to the savage, hysterical attacks.

It was an apocalyptic scene.

A pogrom of unrestrained brutality.

Now the Napola coaches were crossing the river Spree, driving over the Moltke bridge, the very place from which Wolfgang had thrown himself the year before. Otto gave that tragedy only a moment's thought. A brief image of his father, putting his trumpet to his lips and then jumping from the parapet, passed across Otto's mind but then it was gone. The terror of the immediate blotting out all pity for the past.

Once over the river and through the Tiergarten, although still some way short of the Ku'damm, the school buses were forced to stop. The streets were now so littered with shards of broken glass that the drivers feared their tyres would be shredded. The boys were therefore assembled on the pavement and ordered to make their way on foot to the famous shopping street, and once there to attack anything Jewish at will.

At this point it was a simple thing for Otto to slip away.

They wouldn't miss him, it was chaos everywhere. The Napola group would never be able to stick together in such a frenzied crowd and he would not be the only straggler.

But Otto didn't care anyway; he was in a panic to get to Dagmar.

The glass crunched horribly beneath his feet as he ran, pushing his way through the baying, staggering, swaggering gangs of men and women, intoxicated on stolen booze and on power.

Absolute power.

It seemed to Otto as if the whole population was out on the streets, although of course he knew they weren't. No doubt the majority of Berliners were cowering, ostrich-like, behind their curtains. But there were enough people enjoying the party to make it look like the whole city, every thug, every thief, every bully, every disaffected inadequate with a grievance was on the rampage.

Many times Otto wanted to stop and try to help as pitifully defenceless people fell victim to the depraved savagery of the mob. A mob who had been whipped up into a storm of moral outrage against the 'crimes' of the race enemy.

These people *deserved* what they were getting.

Their attackers were actually the *victims*.

Forced to act having been goaded beyond endurance.

Torchlight flickered on faces that had become grotesque masks, distorted and bloated with righteous cruelty and untrammelled sadism.

Torch beams crisscrossed streets, searching for loot, for victims. For scurrying children to kick.

In every street Otto saw homes ransacked. He saw clothes torn from young women by mobs who chanted that they were whores. He saw five- and six-year-olds, their mouths so wide with screaming that their entire faces seemed nothing but great black wailing holes.

And other children silent, twitching, staring, dead-eyed and traumatized as their mothers and fathers were beaten in front of them. *Killed* in front of them.

Otto could not help them.

He scarcely registered them; they passed before his eyes like the disjointed imagery of a nightmare.

A dream.

Just two hours earlier he had been dreaming of Dagmar. Where was she? Was she already suffering at the hands of the mob? Were they pulling at her clothes? Were they beating her? *Murdering* her?

Desperate fear sent blood pumping through Otto's body and he ran as he had never run before. Past the old Kaiser's memorial church, along the Kantstrasse, where mobs of youths were starting bonfires of the Jewish property they did not wish to steal.

The contents of entire shops. Clothes, hardware, office supplies. Otto saw crazed women slashing at shop mannequins with knives. He saw men smashing typewriters and adding machines with sledge hammers. Entire telephone exchange boards torn from walls, hurled out of windows and reduced to splinters.

Snarling shouts and hoarse cries rang in Otto's ears as he ran.

Berlin's synagogues were burning, came the shout. The looted treasures of the temples lay scattered before Otto as he ran. Ground underfoot, hurled on to bonfires. Great and venerable leather-bound tomes fluttering like multi-winged moths on their way to incineration. Paintings, statues, carved lecterns, wall hangings and ornate furniture, all food for the flames.

Otto passed a gang of youths dancing about in stolen prayer shawls. They had made a patchwork on the pavement of some sacred embroideries and were forcing elderly Jews to urinate on them while their grey-haired wives stood by and wept.

'Make 'em wear the piss-soaked rags,' a teenage girl shouted at the boys, while her friends pushed a wailing old lady towards the scene.

Otto could do nothing.

He cared but he also didn't care. Because if all this was happening to every Jew he passed, what was happening to Dagmar?

The streets became a little quieter once he entered the expensive district of Charlottenburg-Wilmersdorf. There were not as many very rich Jews in Berlin as the Nazis claimed, and Otto ran through whole streets in which there were no disturbances at all.

Here and there a house was under siege, bottles thrown and windows smashed, but there were no random crowds of dazed thugs roaming about the prestigious streets. The police were seeing that better order was kept in so picturesque a suburb.

Briefly Otto dared to hope. Perhaps the madness had not quite arrived in Charlottenburg-Wilmersdorf, perhaps he was still in time.

Hope lasted only a moment. For on turning from one wide

tree-lined street into the one on which Dagmar lived, he saw flames ahead and in an agony that made him forget his bursting, aching lungs, he knew that he might already be too late.

The Fischer house was on fire.

A mob were gathered outside it, chanting, singing and dancing. Clearly they had already ransacked the place. Otto saw in one glance across the debris-strewn street many things he recognized from his visits over the years. Pictures, a gramophone player, beautiful cushions, shattered china and vases, small items of furniture, all smashed and scattered on the ground.

As he pushed his way through the crowd he trod on something soft.

Looking down he saw an old and frayed, knitted woollen monkey. Otto had seen that little stuffed toy many times before.

Lying on Dagmar's pillow. Or propped up on her dressing table, leaning against a tin of talcum powder. Or sitting on a box of tissues.

For all her grown-up sophistication, Dagmar still cuddled that monkey. And now it was in the gutter.

Which meant that they had been in her bedroom.

Her toy was on the street. Where was she?

Stooping as he ran, Otto gathered up the toy and shoved it into his pocket.

'Did you get them?' he called out at some idiotic prancing boys. 'The Fischers? Did the cops take them?'

'Cops? What cops?' the boys shouted happily.

'The Fischer women, where are they?' Otto said, and now dropping his pretence at a friendly enquiry, he grabbed one of the youths by the neck. 'The woman and the girl! Where are they?'

'Fuck off! I don't know,' the lad exclaimed. 'Probably still inside. That's where they were. Who fucking cares? Let 'em burn.'

Otto looked at the burning house. The ground floor was ablaze but the second floor wasn't burning yet. It would not, however, be long.

He tried to approach the house. The front door was already a furnace. There was no way that even driven by love he could enter there. The front windows too were impassable, fierce flames coming from every one. The great bay window that looked out from Frau Fischer's drawing room was a red-hot hole.

Then Otto heard the sound of sirens and clanking bells. There was a screeching of tyres and two large fire tenders thundered to a halt.

Otto dared to hope that all might still be well.

Firemen tumbled out as orders were shouted and with impressive efficiency the crew began preparing their hoses.

Otto ran over to the officer who was directing operations.

'Stengel, sir! Otto Stengel,' he said, snapping to attention and delivering the German salute. 'I'm a Napola boy.'

Otto knew that a panicked appeal would get him nowhere. He must be calm, authoritative.

That's how Paulus would have been.

'I'm busy, son,' the fire officer replied curtly.

'I think the Fischers are still in there, sir. I have been in the house. I know the layout. I can help you get to them.'

But the officer simply shrugged and turned to direct his men who now had their hoses unwound.

'Steady pressure!' the officer called out. 'One on either side.'

There was a roar and a gushing sound. The hoses which had been lying flat across the street squirmed and whipped into rigidity as the water engorged them and two great pressurized arcs shot from their spouts. There were three officers gathered around each nozzle struggling to contain and direct the water as the hoses twitched and slapped on the road, like tethered snakes desperate to break free.

For a second Otto felt relief, but only for a second. Relief was followed in short order by black horror.

The firemen were directing their hoses on to the houses on *either side* of the Fischer residence.

'What are you doing!' Otto screamed. 'There are people in the burning house.'

'Calm down, lad,' the fire officer replied sternly. 'If you're here from Napola you'll know the directive. We have been ordered to let Jewish property burn but to ensure that German property is not damaged. You may understand that the neighbours here are getting pretty concerned for their homes.'

For a moment longer Otto watched almost transfixed as the firemen, in accordance with a nationwide directive, dampened down the nearby houses while doing nothing to put out the actual fire.

Then he snapped out of it and ran. Crossing the front garden under the great arcs of water, skirting round the burning building and running up the dividing path that separated Dagmar's house from one of its neighbours.

As he ran he was drenched in water, fizzing and steaming as it cascaded off the roof of the next-door building, soaking him, which was a tremendous relief as the heat from the burning Fischer house was terrible.

At the back of the building the garden was empty. There was plenty of evidence that it had recently been filled with looters and vandals but now with the fire taking hold in earnest whoever had been there had clearly decided to join the main party going on around at the front.

Otto knew there was a ladder. He had been in this garden many times as a boy and had sometimes seen the Fischers' groundsman put a long ladder against the house to clear the gutters or carry out some minor repair to the roof.

He found the ladder just where it had always been, laid out on the ground behind the potting shed, and with a huge effort he was able to drag it out and get it up against the back of the house. Under the place he knew was Dagmar's bedroom window.

The fire had still not ignited the upper storey but it had certainly taken hold of the whole of the ground floor and Otto felt as if he must burst into flames himself as he stood on the lawn, wrestling with the ladder in the burning heat, trying to raise its upper section by means of the pull rope until he could get it high enough.

Somehow he managed the job and once the top end of the ladder was rested on Dagmar's windowsill, he scurried up, his skin burning at first but cooling as he got above the level of the flames.

Arriving at the window he peered into Dagmar's room. It was dark and he could see nothing through the glass. The power lines must already have been consumed by the flames because there were no lights on in the house at all. Otto banged on the window, getting ready to try and smash a pane.

Then, to Otto's relief and astonishment, the sash window began to open.

Sliding upwards in front of him.

Dagmar was standing behind it.

Her face a filthy, tear-stained mask of terror.

'Ottsy,' was all she could say.

'Your mother!' Otto demanded. 'Frau Fischer . . .'

'Downstairs,' came the croaked reply.

Otto climbed into the room and pulled down the window behind him.

'The draught,' he said in answer to the mute plea in Dagmar's eye. 'It'd fan the flames.'

As he said it he was hurrying across the room. He opened the door and stepped out on to the upper landing. It was already a furnace. The staircase was alight, the ground floor beneath a mass of flame. The heat and smoke were overwhelming.

Otto took one step forward, almost by instinct. But it was useless, he could not get another centimetre closer to the flames than he was already. No one could have done. Besides, if Frau Fischer had remained downstairs she was assuredly already dead.

Otto retreated into Dagmar's room and slammed the door behind him. Rushing to the window he opened it once more and looked out. He could see that below him the flames from the bottom floor of the house were already reaching out and licking at the lower part of his ladder.

If they were to get down that way they had only seconds left before their escape route was burned up beneath them.

'I'll go first in case you slip,' he said.

He climbed out and descended the ladder by a rung or two

then, looking back in, he noticed that Dagmar was in her stockinged feet. 'Grab some shoes, Dags,' he shouted. 'You must have shoes. We've got to get away from here and there's glass everywhere.'

The fact that Dagmar could scarcely speak did not mean that she was defeated entirely. Still mute, but active, she grabbed her strongest shoes from beneath the bed, and sitting on its pink coverlet for one final time managed to put them on without fumbling. Then she followed Otto out of the window.

'The last bit's going to be bloody hot,' Otto shouted. 'Let's get it over with.'

Together they descended, both in turn losing their grip on the red-hot lower section of the ladder and falling together in a heap on the back lawn, before picking themselves up and scurrying away from the flames.

Dagmar turned and looked back at the burning house.

'Mummy,' she whispered.

Shouts could be heard from around at the front. Shouts and laughter and singing. Clearly the crowd was enjoying the bonfire, watching a beautiful home burn.

Then a chant began.

Death to Jews. Death to Jews.

Dagmar began shouting.

'You got your wish!' she shouted back, suddenly hysterical and violent. 'My mum's in there! My mum's dead. My dad's dead too. You got them both. *The Jews died!* Isn't that enough!'

Otto grabbed her hand. He didn't think there was much chance of her being heard by the mob at the front of the house, but it would only take a few of them to decide to have a look in the back garden for him and Dagmar to be discovered.

Or she might run round to the front. With the wild way she was screaming and twitching there was no telling what she would do.

Otto could scarcely imagine what her mental state was after what she had been through. Only minutes before she had been resigning herself to being burnt alive.

He tried gently to pull her away but she wouldn't move. She simply stood, staring at her burning house.

'They kicked down the front door,' she said, quieter now but shaking terribly, her face and body flickering orange in the light of the fire. 'They went all through the house. They slapped and hit us. They tore pictures off the wall and pissed on the rugs. They took what money and jewellery they could find and smashed everything else . . .'

'Dagmar,' Otto whispered, gently tugging at her sleeve, 'we have to get out of here.'

'Mama was hysterical,' Dagmar went on. 'Beating her fists against her own head, that made them laugh. I locked myself in the lavatory and they left me alone in there. Thank God for the laws on racial purity, eh?'

Dagmar actually smiled at that thought, but it was a shocking, mad smile.

'Dagmar,' Otto urged again, 'we have to—'

'Then they went away and we thought it was over and we sat together amongst the chaos they'd made—'

'Dagmar—'

'Mummy was trying to gather up all the photos and albums that had been thrown around. By the time I realized they'd set the house on fire it was too late to get out. The hallway was burning and the only place to go was upstairs. I ran but she must have been trying to bring her photo albums. I only realized when I turned back at the top of the stairs that she wasn't following me. I could see her trying to pick up photographs and albums and bits of memories and then dropping it all as she reached out to try to gather more. I screamed at her to get out but it was too late, by the time she realized how close the danger was it was too late. All the papers and pictures around her were already burning. Then the ones she had gathered in her arms . . . her past life was her funeral pyre.'

'Dagmar,' Otto said, firmly now, 'we have to get moving. They're out for blood. You need somewhere to hide.'

But Dagmar wouldn't move. She was simply frozen with

horror. Having found the strength to get out of the burning house she now had none left to flee. The sight of the flames had transfixed her.

Then Otto remembered her toy. The stuffed monkey he had picked up in the street and which he knew had been with her all her life. Taking it from his pocket he pressed it into her hand.

'How . . . ?' she murmured, looking down at it.

'It was outside, on the road. I picked it up.'

Dagmar put the little woollen object to her face and breathed deeply, taking in its smell.

Somehow it seemed to help her. Otto's desperate effort at providing a distraction had worked.

'Where will you take me?' she asked in a steady voice.

Relieved, Otto led her by the hand to the back of the garden where there was a gate into an alleyway behind.

'I know how to get away from here,' he said.

Paulus and Otto had never told Dagmar but years before, when they had first fallen in love, they had sometimes made their way right across town together in order to creep into that same back alley and stare up at Dagmar's window. Hoping to catch a glimpse of her shadow on the blind.

'We'll go to my mum's place,' he said. 'There are no other Jews in our block so at least they won't have burnt it. There's a big order gone out about not damaging German property.'

'An order?' Dagmar said, almost to herself.

'Come on,' Otto instructed, 'we need to get a move on.'

The distance from the Fischer house to the Stengel apartment was a good eight kilometres clean across the centre of the city. A city they had known all their lives but one that had been transformed utterly into the most dangerous of jungles in which gangs of wild and merciless predators pack hunted Jews.

'We'll have to avoid the Ku'damm,' Otto said, as they hurried along. 'My school mates are all over it. I'm supposed to be a part of all this.'

'You mean . . . it's been planned?' Dagmar said in astonishment.

'Oh it's been planned. They read out an SS order, signed by Heydrich himself. The police have been told not to intervene.'

They were hurrying along through the crowded streets. Streets that appeared to be in the grip of some bizarre sort of carnival in which joyful revellers perambulated from one bloody entertainment to another.

'They're going to kill us all,' Dagmar said in a voice that sounded as if she was already dead. 'They're going to kill us all tonight.'

Otto kept firmly hold of Dagmar's hand and pulled her forward.

'Come on,' he said. 'We should be able to grab a tram at Zoo.'

With the town in the grip of a riot and the fire brigade at full stretch trying to contain the many and various blazes being set, it took them almost three hours to get to Friedrichshain. When they got there, however, the district was much quieter than the centre of the city had been. There were still screams and bangs and the smell of fire was everywhere, but the street on which the Stengels lived was free from hooligans.

Otto and Dagmar ran into the well of the apartment building and got into the lift which for once was at the right end of the shaft. They stood for a moment in silence as it began its noisy, ponderous way to the sixth floor.

'Dagmar,' Otto said falteringly, 'I'm so sorry – about Frau Fischer. About your mum.'

The words seemed so supremely inadequate that he wished he'd said nothing.

'I envy her,' Dagmar said, her voice hollow and empty like a freshly dug grave. 'Not the way she died, of course. But being dead.'

'No, Dags! Please,' Otto protested.

'It was what she wanted anyway. She talked about it so often that these last few months it's as if she's *been* dead.'

The lift crawled its way up the building. Otto struggled to think of something to say.

'You know I haven't been in this lift since I was fifteen,' he remarked.

'Should you risk it now?' Dagmar asked. 'You know you're banned from ever coming back here.'

'Fuck them. They don't know where I am.'

'Won't they miss you?'

'It was a free-for-all, I'll say I got separated. That I was chasing Jews,' he said, almost with a smile, 'which of course I was. I bet I'm not the only one of the older boys to have grabbed the opportunity to go off and please himself.'

Finally they arrived at the old familiar corridor.

There was no light on in the apartment and Otto of course no longer had a key.

'Oh shit,' he said, 'please don't tell me they're out.'

He knocked on the door and then whispered: 'Paulus . . . Paulus, are you there?'

After a moment they heard Paulus's voice from within.

'Who are you?' the voice demanded. 'What do you want?'

'It's *me*, Pauly! It's Ottsy,' Ottsy hissed. 'I've got Dagmar.'

The door swung open and within a moment all three were in each other's arms, hugging as if their lives depended on it.

'Fuck, Ottsy,' Paulus said eventually, 'look at you! You're huge.'

'Where's Mum?' Otto replied.

'She's everywhere,' Paulus said, 'the phone hasn't stopped ringing. There's so many people hurt. It's like they've actually declared war on us.'

'They have,' Dagmar whispered, cupping her hands around a mug of beef tea that Paulus had been preparing for himself and which he had now given to her.

'Everybody needs Mum,' Paulus went on, 'so of course Mum tries to get to everybody. You know her. She'll try and mend every broken head in Berlin.'

'Why aren't you out with her?' Otto demanded angrily. 'She's alone, you should be protecting her.'

'What sort of protection do you think I'd be? None. In fact, worse than none. Much worse,' Paulus replied. 'They're targeting young Jewish men, that's plain, they're literally pulling in any they find and throwing them into trucks. We've heard of twenty at least taken in this neighbourhood. They've come knocking here twice but I lay low and the neighbour said I was out.

'I still say you should have gone with Mum.'

'Ottsy. It would have put her in *more* danger.'

'All the same—'

'All the same nothing!' Paulus snapped. 'Ottsy! I thought maybe you'd grown up! You've obviously just grown muscles. There's no glory in being a dead hero. You have to *think*. We need to think now. We need to decide what to do about Dagmar. I'm presuming she can't go back to her house tonight?'

'Or ever,' Dagmar said without looking up.

In answer to his questioning glance, Otto explained what had happened that evening. Struggling in vain to find a way to mitigate the shocking and terrible news.

When he had finished Paulus did not know what to say. He opened his mouth but no sound came.

'Don't worry about my mum, Pauly,' Dagmar said, her voice still seeming to come from inside a grave. 'It's as bad for living Jews in this city as it is for the dead ones. Besides, it's just a matter of time for all of us anyway, isn't it?'

This was a subject on which Paulus could find words.

'No, Dagmar,' he said, 'that's not true. There'll be better times, I swear it, just you wait.'

It was Otto who replied to this.

'Wait? Wait?' he snarled. 'All we ever do is wait and what good has it done us? We need to *do* something.'

'Same old Otto eh?' Paulus said. 'What are you going to do? Mug another SA man? Somehow I think we're a bit beyond that.'

'Don't worry, Pauly,' Otto replied fiercely. 'I've got a better plan than beating one of them up.'

'Oh yeah? And what is it?'

Otto had been sitting on his father's old piano stool but now he stood up and stared for a moment at Paulus.

'I'm going to kill Himmler,' he said.

'*Kill* Himmler?'

'That's right.'

'Otto,' Paulus said aghast, 'it was killing one of them that started tonight's pogrom.'

'You think so?' Otto replied with a sneer. 'I don't. They were just waiting for an excuse, they'd have easily found another.'

'Yeah, OK but—'

'But nothing! It's time we started to fight back, Pauly. I can't see any other way of this ending. I've been thinking about it a lot. I'm going to finish school next month and guess what? They're going to have a passing-out ceremony and it's a big one too because we're the first graduation class. Himmler is going to be there.'

'Himmler himself?'

'That's right. Black Heinrich, head of the SS. The whole school's basically an SS project and he's going to give a speech. I reckon if I get hold of a gun from the armoury and sneak it into the passing-out parade I can nail the bastard. Do you hear me? I could kill Himmler!'

'Otto!' Paulus snapped. 'What are you talking about? You can't do that!'

'Give me one good reason why not.'

'I'll give you the best reason there is – Dagmar.'

'Dagmar?'

They both looked down at the girl they loved. She was sitting on the floor, leaning against the couch. Seemingly lost in her own thoughts.

'Of course Dagmar,' Paulus hissed. 'Even if you did manage to do what you want to do – which you wouldn't by the way – you'd get caught for sure and then what would happen to her?'

Otto nodded slowly and sank back down on to the piano stool.

'Oh,' he said. 'I suppose that's true.'

'Of course it is. You're her one chance, Otts. Her very best shot at making it. It's the same situation as it was two years ago when you started taking her out to the Olympics and stuff. You're a German. A Napola boy no less. You're going to go into the army. If things keep getting worse and she has to hide, you'll be better placed to hide her than any Jew ever could. You're a *German*, Otts, you have papers, you can *do* things. Buy things. Travel. Dag needs you. You can't save *all* the Jews, but you can maybe save the one that matters most to us.'

Otto looked once more at Dagmar. She was staring into her drink. He wasn't even sure if she was listening.

'Yes,' he said contritely. 'Of course. You're right. I didn't think of it like that.'

'Well think about it now,' Paulus urged. 'You might have to get her false papers, Otts, a new identity, God knows what. You'll need to keep a clean, a *very* clean slate while you're in the army and study hard—'

'Study?'

'Yes, so you can try and get an office desk, which will be safer for you and you'll have access to official stamps and passes and—'

'Wow, Pauly,' Otto said, taken aback. 'You've got it all planned out.'

'I have to, Ottsy. I *have* to have it planned,' Paulus replied, and it almost sounded as if he was pleading with his brother. 'I need to know that you're ready. That you're thinking straight. I was going to find a way of seeing you to discuss all this soon anyway. You see, I'm going, Otts. I'm leaving.'

It turned out that Dagmar had been listening after all because at this she looked up.

'You're leaving?' she said. 'Oh, Pauly.'

'Mum's managed to get me a place in England, to live and to study. I have the visas I need.'

'When?'

'Some time in the New Year. I want to graduate from school of course, but by the spring for sure.'

Otto and Dagmar were both deeply shocked.

'Is Mum going too?' Otto asked.

'You know she won't leave her patients. She says we're big boys now and don't need her any more but every day a new baby is born who does.'

Quite suddenly Dagmar began crying. She tried to stop herself but couldn't.

'You're so lucky, Pauly,' she sobbed. 'They won't give me or Mum a visa because of what Dad did. They've been watching us, warning us not to try to . . .'

Her words trailed away and she sobbed more deeply. Clearly only remembering as the sentence ended that her mother was now dead.

Paulus looked utterly wretched.

'Oh, Dags,' he said. 'You know that if there was one single way I could help you by staying, I would. But I'm a Jew too. I can't go anywhere. I can't *do* anything. Every Jew is a liability. To themselves and to those who care about them. With me out of the way Ottsy can focus absolutely on you and you alone. That's all that matters to me. You're all that matters to either of us.'

'He's right, Dags,' Otto said. 'It makes sense.'

Paulus turned once more to Otto. 'It's all down to you, Otts. And that's why before I go I have to *know*. I absolutely have to have your solemn *promise* that you'll look after Dagmar.'

Otto bridled at once. His fists clenched.

'Hey, Pauly!' he said angrily. 'I don't have to promise. You know damn well I'd die for Dagmar.'

And now Paulus too was angry.

'Oh for God's sake, Ottsy, are you really such a bloody moron?'

'What do you mean?' Otto asked, squaring up to his brother as he had done so many times before. 'Who's a moron? You asked me if I'd look after Dags and I told you I'd die for her and I would!'

'But I don't *want* you to *die* for her. *Anyone* can bloody *die* for someone. It's easy, just get yourself killed. I want you to *live* for her. Keep yourself *safe*. Keep your stupid head down. Make sure *everything* you do, you do with Dagmar in mind. Don't go trying to murder Himmler, and if there's a war, which obviously there's going to be, don't get yourself killed. Because if you did then Dagmar would be all alone. Alone! Do you understand, you idiot? The *last* thing she needs you to do is *die* for her.'

Otto was almost contrite.

'Oh. Well, put like that,' he said, 'I see what you're saying. You're right. Absolutely right, of course. You always are.'

'When I'm gone, Ottsy,' Paulus said solemnly, 'you have to pretend you're me. OK? Every move you make, every decision you take, you have to ask yourself, "What would Pauly have done?" Be calm. Be calculating. Be *careful.* Stay alive and keep Dagmar alive.'

'Right, absolutely. I get it . . . And once I'm in uniform,' he said, brightening, 'I can try and get her across the border and—'

'Otto, you're doing it again!' Paulus said, his face red with frustration. 'You have to *think things through.*'

'Well what's wrong with—'

'Quite apart from the fact that a lot more people have been shot trying to rush the border than have made it, there's no point. Dags doesn't have an *entry visa* any more. She had one five years ago for the States but not now. The Yanks are pulling up the drawbridge. Everywhere is. Even if you got her across she'd be sent back.'

'Oh,' was all Otto could say in reply.

'You have to protect her in Germany. And when the time comes, *hide* her in Germany, Otto. Do you understand?'

'Yes,' Otto said solemnly. 'I understand.'

Dagmar was looking at them both. A faraway expression in her eyes.

'You should go, Otts,' she said finally. 'It's nearly dawn. You have to get back to Spandau. They might accept you staying out all night but not all of the following day.'

'Yeah,' Otto said, 'that's right, I'll have to hitch a lift . . . I'd better go.'

Dagmar put down her mug and hugged him.

'Thank you, Ottsy,' she said quietly. 'You saved my life tonight.'

'That's what I'm here for.'

'It's what we're both here for,' Paulus added. 'We'll get you through, Dag. I promise. It looks like you'll be staying here for a while, too, until we can make a plan. You can have my room and I'll go on the couch.'

After Otto had gone, Dagmar and Paulus sat together in the darkened room for quite a long time without speaking.

Eventually Dagmar broke the silence.

'Pauly,' she said. 'Hold me.'

Rain on the Beach

Lake Wannsee, November 1938

A few days after the dreadful events of *Kristallnacht*, the Night of the Broken Glass, as the great November Pogrom had immediately come to be known, the Government announced that all Jewish children were to be expelled immediately from school. Paulus, who had been about to complete his final year, was dismissed that same day along with thousands of other bewildered pupils weeks before graduating. All denied the chance to take any examinations or gain any kind of certificate.

'Don't worry about the certificate,' Frieda assured him. 'They'll know about the new law in England and you have enough fine school reports stored up for any college.'

Dagmar came in from Otto and Paulus's old bedroom, which she had been occupying since *Kristallnacht*.

'Pauly,' she said quietly, 'since you'll have a bit more time now and won't need to be studying every minute, I should very much like you to take me swimming.'

Paulus and Frieda exchanged a worried glance.

During the previous week they had shared numerous whispered concerns about Dagmar's fragile mental health. She had scarcely spoken since she'd arrived and had not once mentioned her mother's death. The newspapers had reported that the fire had been electrical and that the widow of Herr Fischer had 'regretfully' been consumed in the flames. No mention was made of Dagmar, who had read the article without comment. She stayed mainly in bed or curled up on the couch clinging to the toy monkey Otto had saved for her, a deep fatalistic sadness enveloping her that Frieda and Paulus could find no way of penetrating.

Frieda was familiar with the signs of emotional withdrawal. She knew very well how many deeply damaged people were sitting mutely like Dagmar in cold bare rooms all over Berlin, dealing with their terrible reality by retreating from it.

'Dagmar, darling,' Frieda said gently, 'you and Pauly can't go swimming, I'm afraid. I'm sure you recall that the authorities have forbidden it.'

'Ottsy can take us,' Dagmar replied. 'It's never a problem.'

'Ottsy can take *you*, dear,' Frieda said. 'With Pauly it's more than double the risk. They're still targeting young men.'

'But we could go to Wannsee,' Dagmar insisted, her voice becoming firmer as she spoke. 'To the lido. We'll have the whole place to ourselves. They don't have staff there off-season.'

'Wouldn't it be a bit chilly, Dags?' Paulus asked with a smile.

'Exactly. Freezing. So nobody will be there. For once we'll be in the majority! We don't need an exit visa or an entrance visa. We just get on the *S-Bahn* like we used to do. Pauly, I want to swim. I *need* to swim. But I want *you* to come too, Pauly. I want both my boys, like it used to be.'

Frieda smiled. Dagmar had said more in five minutes than in the past five days.

'Do you know, I think Dagmar's right,' Frieda said. 'You both really do need to get out of this apartment. To get some exercise. And if Otto's with you I really don't think there's much risk.'

'OK!' Paulus said, grinning himself now, thrilled to see any sign of enthusiasm in Dagmar. 'Let's do it.'

'I'll write a note then,' Dagmar said, her eyes widening and her voice growing in confidence with each word. 'I'm sure Ottsy can get a pass out. They're all just waiting for graduation now. And he's such a school pet these days, and of course they still think I'm his Aryan girl. It'll be the three of us together again. A sort of farewell picnic. Farewell to you. Farewell to Mama. Farewell to everything really.'

For a moment Paulus's happy grin disappeared from his face. He looked closely at Dagmar, trying to gauge whether her plan was born of reviving spirits or was a symptom of a deepening despair.

'How about we take Silke?' he said. 'Make it a proper Saturday Club outing.'

'Ha, and share my boys with her?' Dagmar replied, and for a moment her eyes seemed to twinkle and her old smile appeared on her face. 'You know very well I'm *far* too mean to do *anything* so generous as *that*!'

Pauly smiled back. She sounded like her old self.

They met at Bahnhof Zoo.

The shattered glass that had littered the streets for days had been cleaned up but the burnt-out buildings and windowless shops remained as testimony to the violence of the attacks. The Jews themselves had been forced to clean up the wreckage that had been made of their lives and it had been a slow task, made harder because, as the newspapers were happy to crow, thirty thousand young Jewish men had been abducted from their homes and sent to concentration camps over the two nights of the pogrom.

What was not reported in the papers, but Frieda had ascertained through her medical contacts, was that ninety-one more had simply been beaten to death.

Now, however, everything seemed calm. The Jews were back behind closed doors and the majority of the population were going about their business as if nothing had happened.

Otto bought some nuts and apples for the journey and the three young people took the *S-Bahn* out to Wannsee. As they rode, the boys attempted to dispel the sadness that still radiated from their friend.

'Do you remember the swimming gala,' Otto said, 'when we took the blame for you breaking the trophy?'

'And I got four extra whacks because Otto was too bloody stupid to let me think up an excuse,' Paulus added. 'Come to think of it, I still owe you for those.'

'Any time, Pauly,' Otto replied, flexing his muscles. 'You're most welcome to try.'

The boys tried hard to be cheerful, and as the once-familiar stations passed by it seemed to have some effect. Dagmar almost smiled as they recalled the music lessons and the Saturday Club, and how angry Silke had been when Dagmar first turned up.

'Poor Silke,' Dagmar said. 'I don't blame her for being jealous. I know I'd have been if it had been her that you boys were chasing in the Märchenbrunnen. Do you remember how you used to trap me between Rapunzel and Little Red Riding Hood and try to steal kisses?'

And so they talked and even laughed a little together, revisiting the happy country of their youth, as the rain lashed on the windows of the train.

But then of course they ran out of happy memories.

Or, at least, while there were still some, any recollections of laughter and friendship that had occurred after 1933 were so entwined with darker experiences, of pain, loss and humiliation, that the three of them felt their smiles vanish from their lips.

'They took our youth, didn't they?' Dagmar said quietly. 'They stole our youth.'

There was thunder in the air and the rain came down in squalls as the venerable old train shuddered to a halt at Wannsee. As Dagmar had predicted, the three of them were the only passengers to disembark.

'You're braver than I am, kids,' the ticket collector remarked as they made their way through the barrier of that much loved little station, where Berliners had been disembarking with such excitement and departing with such regret for fifty years.

Paulus managed a smile in reply, his eyes flicking briefly to take in the first of numerous signs announcing that Jews were banned from the beach and its facilities.

The wet, windswept steps down from the ticket office boasted none of the festive garb that the three trippers remembered from happier visits. It being late November there were no flowers in the station windowboxes. No balloon-seller or ice-cream stand. The little wooden pretzel wagon was boarded up and padlocked and there was no accordion player in Bavarian costume with his feathered hat filled with coins.

But the sun peeped through the clouds momentarily, as it was supposed to do at Wannsee, and if they half closed their eyes and imagined that the limp and sodden swastika banners hanging from the lamp-posts were strawberry bunting, they could almost visualize the summer of 1930 when the great *Strandbad Wannsee* lido had been brand new. When Dagmar and her parents, stately in first class, and the Stengel twins with Wolfgang and Frieda in third, had joined the tens and tens of thousands of other holiday-makers thronging on to this very platform, all eager to see the gift to the people of Berlin from their municipal council. The new restaurant, the changing facilities, the easy access to the longest inland beach in Europe and, most important of all to the civilized citizens of Germany's capital, the splendid public lavatories.

The three of them made their way over the little railway bridge that crossed the platform and descended the worn-down old stone steps on the lake-side of the station to the promenade.

Of course every few metres they had to pass another sign forbidding Jews to visit, but in Otto's company Dagmar and Paulus felt relatively safe. They were young, fit and attractive, filled with life and vitality. It would have been a very great leap of the imagination for one of the ubiquitous police spies who hung about in the parks and pleasure palaces even in bad weather to mistake such a good-looking trio for any of those grotesque caricatures that featured in the pages of *Der Stürmer* or in the editorials in the *Völkischer Beobachter*.

The fat, top-hatted, hook-nosed gargoyle with its greedy, bulging eyes, grinning over money bags stuffed with Yankee dollars. Or the cadaverous figure with the hammer and sickle on its forehead, dragging a helpless maiden by the hair with one hand and holding a dripping knife in the other, a desecrated church left burning in its wake.

'Streicher and Goebbels might get mistaken for those people,' Dagmar said bitterly as they passed a poster depicting just such a wicked duo, 'but not us.'

'How do they *do* it?' Paulus said. 'How do they get away with these unbelievable pictures? I never saw *anybody* remotely like that in my life. Not even in a pantomime. Do people *really* believe they exist? I mean, it wouldn't be so bad but Adolf's entire gang are such a pathetic, weasel-faced bunch of cunts themselves.'

The next poster along was for the *Hitler Jugend* and the *Bund Deutscher Mädel*, which of course depicted the inevitable ideal of Nazi youth staring upwards with distant inspiration in their eyes. The funny thing was that, blonde hair aside, Paulus and Dagmar could quite easily have modelled for the poster. The two of them looked as fine and upstanding an example of German youth as any two eighteen-year-olds could be, and had Hitler been passing by in his open-top Mercedes, he would without doubt have nodded with approval and shaken them all sternly by the hand. Goebbels probably would have done more than shake Dagmar's hand. His reputation as a sexual predator was already well established and his particular taste was for sophisticated and glamorous young women with filmstar beauty. Dagmar would have caught his eye immediately.

Dagmar caught the eye of most men. Heads always turned to admire the tall, long-legged beauty when she walked about town, always elegantly turned out, with the handsome Napola *Jungmann* on her arm. None of those who grinned and nudged their friends and even wolf-whistled at her shapely behind as it swung past would ever dream that this lovely-looking Berlin girl was the same spoiled, cruel and wicked Jewess heiress of Goebbels' hysterical editorials, the pariah daughter of the Jew capitalist Isaac Fischer.

Dagmar had only been thirteen, still a girl, when she was forced to retreat from her life. The young woman who had emerged a few years later courtesy of Otto's Aryan ancestry was a very different creature.

But there were no passers-by to wolf-whistle Dagmar at Wannsee on that wet November day as they made their way down from the amenities blocks to the beach.

'Where shall we set ourselves up?' Dagmar asked.

The boys grinned at each other.

As if Princess Dagmar Fischer would have allowed them to choose. She had *always* decided where to sit, right back to the first days of the Saturday Club.

'Well, we've certainly got plenty of room,' Otto said.

The Wannsee beach was well over a kilometre long and they were the only people on it.

'But I think we should move along a bit,' he added, 'up towards the Glienicker bridge.'

Despite her current misery Dagmar found herself giving him a playful punch.

'I know where *you* mean,' she said, 'and we are *certainly* not going there.'

They all laughed. Otto was referring to the notorious nudist section of the beach, which had become even more popular under the Nazis, in their obsession with health and beauty.

'I'm not going nude in this temperature anyway,' Paulus said. 'My dick will disappear.'

'Not much *to* disappear if you ask me,' Otto remarked, chucking a handful of sand.

'Shut your face or I'll hit you over the head with it.'

A fight ensued between the boys, rolling together and tussling in the wet sand. Dagmar laughed. Something of the pent-up horror of the previous week and the terrible years that had preceded it was blown away for a moment at least in the fresh lakeside breeze.

'Stop it, you two!' she demanded. But she didn't mean it. She never minded at all when the twins showed off for her benefit.

'I think we'll sit here,' she said, putting her bag down on a secluded little dune where the lake wasn't too weedy. 'Look, there's even a *Strandkorb*. Somebody must have dragged it here and it's never been collected.'

Dagmar sat down in the middle of the padded, two-seater wicker seat.

'Don't think we'll need the shade,' she said, going to push the canopy back.

'Might keep the rain off a bit,' Otto suggested.

Dagmar squeezed at the cushion she was sitting on and it dripped water.

'Hmm,' she said, 'bit late, I think. Still, it doesn't matter, my bum can't get any wetter so I might as well relax.' She threw out her arms. 'Won't you two gentlemen join me on the *chaise longue*? Or is a girl to sit alone on the beach without an escort? How very *ungallant* of you.'

Neither Paulus nor Otto needed asking twice. They both rushed to squeeze themselves in on either side of Dagmar. For a little while all three giggled and flirted together, the boys exchanging insults while assuring Dagmar of their individual devotion to her, she laughing and scolding and giving them kisses on their cheeks.

'I'm going to swim!' she said suddenly, getting up and disappearing behind the beach basket to change.

'Don't laugh,' she called out. 'I'm wearing your mother's suit, which dates from the Stone Age, I think. It's also too small but since it's made of horrible baggy wool I don't think that matters. I had a *very* daring two-piece in pale pink satin from France but of course that got burnt when . . . '

Dagmar's voice trailed off. It was obvious to both boys that her *joie de vivre* was paper-thin, that beneath the surface the indescribable horror of the previous week was constantly with her. As of course they knew it must be.

'I always feel closer to Daddy when I swim,' Dagmar said as she emerged in the ill-fitting navy-blue suit. 'Mummy too, now, although she only sat and watched from the shore. She was always there though. Maybe she's here now, sitting on that bit of grass. Her and Daddy watching over me.'

Dagmar turned from them for a moment, sniffing deeply. Then she pulled herself together.

'It'll be pretty cold,' she said, 'but the only way to get in is to get in!' She ran splashing into the lake, leaving Paulus and Otto struggling out of their shoes and trousers so they could follow.

They couldn't catch her, of course, she was far too powerful and efficient a swimmer. What was more, that afternoon she swam as if somehow, if she went fast enough, she might wash away a little of her pain. She swam hundreds of metres out into the vast lake, breaststroke, crawl and backstroke. The boys, though good enough swimmers themselves, could not compete over those distances and were forced to wait impatiently in the shallows for her return.

It was pouring down now and so the boys eventually gave it up altogether, and filled in the time making a shelter for the picnic using an oilcloth groundsheet they had brought with them. They managed to knot it to the back of the *Strandkorb* for one half of the support and cut a couple of sticks from the scrappy woodland that fringed the lake for the other. In the end they were able to produce a decent enough lean-to under which they sat watching Dagmar powering her way back and forth across the storm-tossed lake.

The sky was even darker now and there was thunder rolling in from the direction of Potsdam.

'She'll have to come out soon,' Otto said. 'If there's lightning.'

'I'm not sure if she'd care.'

Otto nodded. He knew what Paulus meant. It was only a year since their own father had jumped from the Moltke bridge. There wasn't a Jew in Germany who had not at some point given thought to suicide. Dagmar had more reason than most.

'I think a girl like Dagmar wouldn't mind so much if she went like that,' Paulus continued, staring out across the wind-rippled lake to where Dagmar was churning up the water as if competing in one of those races from which she had been denied entry. Freestyle. Elbows up, fingers straight as they cut into the water, pulling her through it. 'In fact, I think she'd love it. To be taken in a storm, swimming at Wannsee, blasted to oblivion mid-stroke in a glorious instant. I don't think I'd mind much myself if I could go that way.'

They stared out at the distant figure. Crooked white arm followed by crooked white arm. Face emerging every third stroke.

'No. You're wrong,' Otto said finally. 'A girl like Dagmar will never want to go at all. She wants to live for ever. Something inside her will always make her want to live.'

'I certainly hope so. And it's our job to make sure she succeeds. It's your job, Ottsy. She's your girl.'

Finally Dagmar tired of her swim and began making her way back to shore.

'Well, let's drop it for now anyway,' Paulus said. 'After all, this is supposed to be a day out.'

Dagmar swam the last twenty metres breaststroke, heading straight for the boys, her head rising and falling, mouth opening and closing in a perfectly executed rhythm. She knew the shore well from childhood and found her depth at about five metres out, emerging from the water looking like the magnificent athlete she was, Frieda's sodden baggy costume clinging to the lines of her body. Paulus and Otto devoured the sight with hungry eyes.

'Now now, boys. I'll thank you not to ogle a lady in so obvious a manner,' Dagmar said, taking up a towel, which was of course as wet as she was. 'You look as if you're eyeing up your dinner.'

She stood before them, looking slowly from one to the other, patting at herself with the towel as the rain fell around her.

'Speaking of which,' she added, 'where *is* dinner? Why don't you lay it out, boys.' She threw the towel into the *Strandkorb* and plonked herself down on the ground beside the boys. 'I bags all the best bits.'

'You know you don't need to say that,' Otto replied, starting to lay out the food.

'I would if Silke was here!' Dagmar laughed.

Treats were no longer so easy to obtain in Berlin but nonetheless between them they had managed to assemble a decent spread, which they had kept dry in two biscuit tins. There was cheese, pickled gherkins, and even fresh white bread rolls. No butter of course, that had gone to make guns, but Dagmar had brought a little flask of olive oil and some salt. They had two bottles of beer, two packets of cigarettes and finally a whole bar of Suchard milk chocolate. The boys tried to insist that Dagmar should have all the chocolate but she had magnanimously suggested she take only half and they have a quarter each.

So they sat together in the pouring rain, half protected by their improvised shelter, and ate their meal.

And the emotions that crackled between them right from the start were as strong in their way as the lightning splitting the air above them.

Three passionate young souls, all huddled together on the wet sand beneath a dripping oilcloth. Breaking the bread. Sharing the cheese. Three histories, inextricably entwined. At first so very happy. Then so strange and so cruel.

Two boys desperately in love with one girl. Furtively stealing glances at her long bare wet legs, her feet folded beneath her bottom. The beads of rain on her slim arm as she reached between them for the chocolate. A chill wind blowing amongst them raising goose bumps on Dagmar's glistening white skin.

'Boys,' Dagmar said, offering round the cigarettes and lighting one for herself with some difficulty in the groaning wind, 'there's something I want to talk about. Something important.'

'Hang on!' Otto said through a mouthful of bread. 'Sorry! Got to take a slash. Been holding on but can't . . .'

Paulus grinned. 'Such a romantic, soulful spirit, eh?' he said as Otto scuttled off over the dune.

'Go properly away,' Dagmar shouted. 'I don't like hearing boys wee. You both used to leave the door open when we had our music lessons and I hated it.'

She laughed but the jollity did not ring true. There was a new tension in the air. She turned to Paulus.

'Pauly,' she said, 'was that your ticket I saw arrive in the post this morning?'

Paulus frowned and looked away without answering.

'So it was, then. I thought you looked a bit furtive.'

'Not furtive, Dags,' Paulus said, 'just . . . well, sad. And scared, I suppose . . . can we please not talk about it?'

'We have to talk about it, Pauly,' Dagmar said. 'When do you leave?'

'February. I keep telling myself maybe I could put it off. Try to change the ticket, wait a bit longer. But Mum gets angry about that and you know it's not like her to get angry about anything.'

'Angry?'

'Well, everybody's desperate to get out now. Since *Kristallnacht*. All the people who've been telling themselves for years it'll be all right. Like Pops and Grandma. They know now. But they're too late. It's insane the queues on the Wilhelmstrasse and at travel agents'. If I don't take my chance now . . .'

'I know, Pauly,' Dagmar said quietly, and now it was her turn to look away. 'I know.'

'I don't want to leave you, Dags!' Paulus pleaded, his face suddenly a picture of guilt and anguish. 'I can't bear it. To even think of leaving you when all I've ever wanted is to be near you.'

Dagmar leant over and squeezed Paulus's hand, looking into his eyes unblinkingly.

'And I can't bear the thought of you going, Pauly.'

'You know that if there was anything . . . anything I could do,' he began, but he could not continue because at that point Dagmar kissed him. She pushed her face forward across the remains of the picnic and locked her lips on to his.

Then her arms were around him and his around her.

It was utterly unexpected and Paulus was taken completely by surprise.

As was Otto.

Who emerged at that moment over the sand dune.

'Oi!' he shouted in surprise. 'What are you two up to?'

He scrambled down the dune looking red in the face and angry.

For more than three years, ever since the night he had mugged the SA man, there had been no doubt in Otto's mind as to who held the closer place in Dagmar's affections, and it was him.

She liked Paulus, sure. He was like her brother. But she was *his* girl.

There had never been any doubt about it. Never on all the many outings Dagmar and he had shared since the day when Paulus had first produced his plan for them to be together. All the kisses and cuddles, the hand-holding, the shared frustration of not taking it further when they both admitted they wanted to.

And now he found, on returning after an absence of just a couple of minutes, that she was locked in an embrace with his brother.

'Come and sit down, Ottsy,' Dagmar said. 'I have to tell you something. And Pauly.'

Otto did as he was told, a bewildered expression on his face.

Paulus too looked at a loss.

'Boys,' Dagmar said, taking a deep breath.

'This all sounds sort of ominous, Dags,' Paulus said, trying as ever to intellectualize the moment. To put his brain ahead of his fast beating heart.

'Ominous?' Otto blurted. 'Nice kind of ominous, if you ask me. Was that a "friends"-type kiss, by the way? Because it didn't look like a "friends"-type kiss.'

'Hey, Ottsy,' Paulus replied angrily. 'We were talking about me leaving. Amazingly, Dags is sad I'm going. Is that all right with you or does she need your permission?'

'Oh, so it was a *farewell*-type kiss then?' Otto asked.

'Look! I don't need to explain—' Paulus began.

'Boys!' Dagmar said sharply. 'Please. You have to listen to me.'

The Stengel twins fell silent.

'We've been best friends since we were seven,' Dagmar went on, 'and you know I love you both more than anything in the world. You *are* my world. Particularly now Mama has gone.'

The rain started to fall harder as she spoke, running down her cheeks and on to her bare shoulders, where it was gathering in numerous little glistening droplets. Paulus and Otto listened in silence.

'But we're growing up now. We're adults, not kids, and friendship's a different thing, isn't it? When you're grown up. Between boys and girls.'

Still neither boy replied, although the tension on their faces showed this was one observation that did not need making.

'You always said that one day I'd have to choose between you, didn't you?'

She looked from one boy to the other, her eyes big and sad.

Paulus found his voice first, although it was little more than a croak.

'I thought you had,' he said.

'Yeah,' Otto whispered, 'so did I.'

'I had,' Dagmar replied, looking at Otto, 'but it wasn't what you thought. Or what I made you think . . . I'm sorry.'

The rain was falling more heavily now, splashing on the remains of the food as the inadequate covering sagged under the weight.

'I'm in love with Paulus,' Dagmar said quite suddenly.

Both boys looked up astonished. Their mouths dropped open in silent surprise.

'I think I've known that for a year at least. Two. I don't know. Maybe more. I didn't want to say. I've never wanted to say. I shouldn't be saying it now.'

Her voice was shaking. Perhaps she was crying, it was hard to tell with the rain.

'Why did you kiss me,' Otto asked, and he too looked as if he might cry, 'that time when I brought you the buttons?'

'I was fourteen, Otts.'

'But since then. Lots of times.'

'I *wanted* to love you, Otto. I prayed that I could fall in love with you because I knew Pauly would one day have to go. That I *mustn't* love him because he would leave. That he would leave me and I'd be left alone and my damned life was going to be dreadful and hellish enough without a broken heart.'

Otto wiped angrily at his eyes.

Dagmar reached out to touch his hand but Otto pulled it away.

'I like you, Otts. I *love* you too,' she pleaded, 'I really do. You know that. But not how I love Pauly . . .'

Her voice trailed away. She turned to Paulus as if willing him to say something.

'But . . .' Paulus began, 'why have you never said?'

'Why do you think! Because you have a chance and I don't! And I never ever wanted to say anything to stop you. I knew you loved me and if I'd come to you a year or two years ago and told you I loved you, if I'd been your girl, would you have written all those visa letters? Would you have tried so hard? Would you ever have applied for that ticket that came this morning? Would you? If I'd been your girl?'

Paulus bit his lip.

'No, of course you wouldn't. I know you. You're both the same, you Stengel twins. You and Ottsy, the loyalest, bravest, best boys alive on this earth and I don't deserve either of you. And now I shan't *have* either of you because it's all set and that's fine and as it ought to be. You have your place and your ticket and you'll *live*, which is all I want. And Ottsy will be sent into the army, and whatever happens to me is my fate, that's all. And that's fine too because what will be will be. I kept my secret, Pauly, because I'd die before I'd stand in the way of your trying to get out. But now it's done and all our paths are set, I couldn't let you go without you knowing, Pauly. That's all. That wherever you go in the world, whoever you find in your life, there is . . . or there was . . . once a girl in Germany who loved you with all her heart.'

Otto scrambled to his feet.

'I'm getting out of here,' he said, trying to sound strong. In control of his emotions. But failing miserably. 'I'll see you two around, I guess.'

'Ottsy!' Dagmar called. 'Please, stay with us.'

'Can't,' Ottsy croaked, turning away. 'Gotta go.'

He ran back up the sand dune, clearly aware that were he to stay a moment longer he would bawl like a baby, and Otto was not the type of boy to want to be seen crying. Not by his brother, and not by the girl who had broken his heart.

After he had scurried away, a long silence ensued.

Paulus looked up and then looked down and then at the sky and the lake. Then he seemed about to say something, but could think of nothing to say.

Instead he kissed her. Just as she had kissed him. Long, passionately, putting his hand behind her head and pressing her face to his.

They kissed for a long time before either of them spoke again. Once more it was Dagmar who seemed to be clearer in her thoughts.

'I'm sorry I told you, Pauly,' she said. 'I had always planned not to. But then I changed my mind. I thought maybe it would help you . . . sort of sustain you. You've got a long road ahead.'

'Dagmar,' Paulus replied, finally breaking his silence. 'You loving me is the best thing that's ever happened in my life.'

Then they heard steps. For a moment they thought it was Otto returning.

But it wasn't Otto. Instead a different young man appeared. One who looked about sixteen.

In the uniform of the Hitler Youth.

'Hey, lads!' the boy shouted out, beckoning to beyond the dunes. 'Come here.'

Paulus swallowed hard. He should have been more careful, more aware. Everybody knew that out in the countryside the Hitler Youth and the League of German Maidens were everywhere, camping, marching, singing.

Spying.

Having Otto with them had allowed him to relax. But now Otto was gone.

With a rattle of boots and leather suddenly there were ten more of them, black shorts, brown shirts, swastika armbands. The two troop leaders had daggers at their belts.

'Heil Hitler, lads,' said Paulus with a cheerful grin, getting to his feet and delivering the German salute. 'Cold weather for a dip, eh?'

'Heil Hitler,' the lead boy replied. 'Please may I see your identification papers.'

Paulus had guessed it was coming. One of the principal duties of the Hitler Youth was to act as an observation auxiliary to the police. They were charged with the task of spying on the whole community, including their own families. Jews everywhere had learnt to beware these brown-shirted gangs of self-important young zealots, for if they found you where you shouldn't be, there was no possibility of getting away.

'Sorry, pals, can't do it,' Paulus said. 'Left them up with our stuff. Miles away. Didn't want them getting wet or lost in the sand.'

He knew it was a pathetic effort, but what effort would not have been? They were trapped. Ten eager little Nazis wanted to see their papers, desperate to catch an army deserter or a malingerer from state labour, or best of all a Jew where a Jew was banned. They would no doubt get an armful of extra badges for such a coup.

'You will take us to where you have left your papers, please,' the troop leader said. Paulus began to protest but the boy cut him short. 'Or you will come with us! And I warn you, if you waste our time it will be the worse for you.'

'Hey, lads,' Paulus said, trying hard to maintain his pretence at comradely familiarity, 'this skirt, she's not mine, she's another guy's. If we go back together he'll—'

'If you cannot produce identification papers, you will come with us this instant,' the leader barked.

'Yeah! And her, she can come with us too,' another lad, who held a dagger, said, smirking. 'If she'll go with this guy, she'll go with anyone.'

Paulus glanced at Dagmar. Her face white with fear.

The gang of youths now surrounded them. Dagmar got to her feet, taking up a wet towel to fold around herself, looking utterly vulnerable in her baggy bathing suit.

'Look, guys,' Paulus began, struggling to keep his voice steady.

'Silence!' the first lad shouted. 'I will give you one more chance and one alone to produce your papers.'

Paulus could only stand and stare, his brain working furiously. He could feel Dagmar shaking beside him.

The other troop leader spoke up. He was clearly the one to worry about. His face was nasty and sly. The first boy was trying to be correct but the other one just wanted to have some fun. If they were to be beaten where they stood, or worse, it would be him who would instigate it.

'Are you Jews?' the sixteen-year-old said cruelly, still smirking. 'Yes, I think perhaps you are.'

He took a step forward, then another, until he was standing quite close to Dagmar. He breathed in deeply.

'Yes,' he said, 'I think I smell Jews.'

He was looking hard at Dagmar.

All the boys were looking at Dagmar.

'We must take them to the police,' the first leader said. 'That is our duty as per our instructions.'

'You think I'm a Jew, you little bastard!' Paulus blurted. 'How about you take a look at my dick, huh?'

Would the old trick work again? It was a horrible prospect but preferable to capture.

'Don't be disgusting!' the first leader barked. 'You insult the badge I wear. The only thing I wish to see of yours is your papers.'

'*Her*, on the other hand,' the second leader leered, 'we could see more of.'

'No!' the first said angrily, 'none of that, Alex! We must take them to the police.'

Paulus weighed up the difference between the two senior figures in the gang, his mind searching desperately for a way to use it to his advantage.

'Yes,' Paulus said, 'let's go to the police at once and when I've made a call or two you'll see what a mistake you're making.'

'I said silence!' the first of the two shouted.

'You have no right to shout at me, kid!' Paulus shouted back. 'I am a grown man! Soon I'll be a soldier. I have my call-up papers already. Now, if you really insist on ruining my day, then let's get on with it. Come on. We'll go to the police now. But let me tell you, son, when we next meet there won't be ten of you, there'll be just you and me, and I'll make you wish you'd never met me.'

It had an effect. The first youth's face fell a little. Perhaps he was even considering dropping the whole thing.

But the other boy was clever. Clever and sly.

'What outfit are you joining? Come on! Come on! Which regiment are these papers you have for?'

Paulus tried not to look at a loss but he knew he'd blown it. He was one of the best educated young men in Berlin but he knew absolutely nothing about the Wehrmacht.

'I don't have to—'

'What outfit!' the boy shouted. 'Tell me now!'

'Rifles . . .' Paul blurted. 'The infantry.'

'There are more than a hundred infantry divisions in the Wehrmacht! Each containing a number of regiments! What is on your papers? Come on! Come on! No soldier who has had the honour to be summoned by the Führer would forget such a thing.'

Paulus was on the ropes and he knew it.

'I won't be shouted at by a boy!' he said. 'If you insist on keeping up with this bullshit then I demand that you take us to a police station.'

It was a horrifying indication of the level of danger they were now in that being taken to the police seemed to Paulus to be their best option. He did not like the way they were staring at Dagmar. If these boys decided to convince themselves that she and he were Jews, there was no telling what they would do, all alone on a deserted beach, hidden by sand dunes.

'So,' the meaner of the two leaders said triumphantly, 'are you Jews? I think you are Jews.'

'We should take them in,' the first lad insisted.

'What's the rush?' the meaner one replied, and it was clear to Paulus that the majority of the junior boys agreed with him.

'So, bitch,' the more popular leader said, putting his face close to Dagmar's, '*are* you a Jew?'

The game was up and Paulus knew it. His best shot was a long one but it was all that was left. The lead boy was much closer than the others, who were all still hanging back somewhat self-consciously. They were, after all, only boys, and Dagmar was a woman.

Paulus swung a fist into the vicious boy's face, knocking him to the ground with a single huge blow. Then, in a movement so swift that it was really a follow-through from the blow, he jumped down and tore the dagger from the boy's belt, pressing the blade to his throat.

'OK!' Paulus shouted. 'Fuck off or he gets it. I'll stick him, I swear! When you're gone I'll let him go, but not till then. Fuck off!'

The youngsters were not used to this kind of thing at all and were already stepping backwards in the face of Paulus's shocking fury. But then the other lead boy spoke. His character, which Paulus had at first thought might be useful, now proved to be their undoing.

'Stand ground!' the first boy shouted. 'Stand ground, I say! This swine has laid his hand on a *Hitler Jugend* dagger! Our weapon is our life! And like our life it belongs to the Führer! This man has stolen the Führer's dagger! Our honour is in his hand!'

The boy Paulus had by the collar was whimpering as he felt the knife on his throat, but there could be no doubt that resolve amongst his comrades was stiffening.

'Don't worry, Hitler Youth Man,' the first of the leaders assured his comrade, 'if this Jew swine dares to harm you, he knows what he'll get.'

It was a standoff that could go one of two ways, both the worse for Paulus and Dagmar.

Paulus dropped the knife.

Then another voice intruded on the scene.

'What the FUCK do you think you're doing, you little bunch of pricks!'

Paulus and Dagmar almost cried with relief. It was Otto.

He was standing on top of the sand dune. Two years older than either of the troop leaders. Muscular. Commanding.

Dressed in the same uniform.

'You want to mess around with a Spandau district unit, do you, you little arseholes?' Otto went on.

Paulus had told his brother to be sure to wear a uniform for the trip, and Otto had chosen his brown *Hitler Jugend* one because the school one was black and highly formal, and would have looked pretty grim after a day at the seaside.

It had been a fortunate choice. Not least because it carried on it the badges showing that Otto was of a considerably senior rank to that held by the two lead youths confronting Dagmar and his brother.

Paulus let the lad he was holding go. The boy snatched up his dagger from the ground, red-faced with fury but at a loss what to do.

The first of the troop leaders was in no such doubt. He leapt to attention.

'This man will not show us his papers, sir—'

'Well, of course he fucking won't, he's screwing the *Oberrottenführer's* bird! Would you want to be identified?'

At this some of the junior boys in the troop began to snigger.

'I just wanted to know if—' the leader protested.

'All you need to know, *sonny*,' Otto went on, 'is that *you* are a poxy little *Stammführer* while I am an *Oberkameradschaftsführer*.' Otto patted the badge of rank stitched to the arm of his shirt, above the swastika armband. 'And what's more, an *Oberkameradschaftsführer* from the Spandau district, who, as I think you know, are the meanest toughest bastards in the whole HJ. Even our BDM *girls* could kick your arses. What could our BDM girls do?'

The boys knew the authentic voice of brutal authority when they heard it and replied at once.

'They could kick our arses, Herr *Oberkameradschaftsführer* sir!'

'That's right,' Otto snarled. 'Now piss off all of you because there's a queue to get under that oilcloth with this bit of skirt and none of you are in it. So say *Heil Hitler* and fuck off!'

Otto clicked his heels and gave the German salute.

'*Heil Hitler!*' came ten instantaneous replies.

After which the two young leaders and their little troop of boys hurried away as quickly as they could.

Once more the three of them were alone.

'Shit.' Paulus whistled. 'Glad you came back, Otts.'

Dagmar sank to the ground.

'I thought . . .' she said. 'I thought they were going to . . .'

'But they didn't, Dags,' Paulus said quickly. 'They didn't, that's what matters.'

'I'm sorry I ran off,' Otto said. 'It was stupid and if I hadn't done you wouldn't have gone through any of that.'

'You couldn't have known, Otts,' Dagmar said.

'Of course I bloody could! There's danger absolutely everywhere. We all know that and I should have stayed with you. And that's what I came back to say, Dags. That I won't leave again, all right? Whatever you feel about Paulus doesn't make any difference. I still love you and I'll still look out for you, just like we planned. I promise.'

'No, Ottsy,' Paulus said. 'I think the plan should change.'

The Last Meeting of the Saturday Club

Berlin, February 1939

The four members of the Saturday Club met under the clock at the Lehrter Bahnhof.

Or rather under the great crimson slashes of red that hung beneath the clock.

The cavernous interior of the station was festooned with swastikas. More so even than usual. Hitler's fiftieth birthday was only weeks away and the station management had shown considerable ingenuity in finding places to hang banners where none already hung.

'Just when you think there's nowhere left to put a flag,' Otto murmured.

'Flags and parades. Parades and flags,' Dagmar said, without bothering to lower her voice. 'Don't they ever get *bored* with it?'

'Dagmar!' Silke hissed in exasperation. 'How many times? You don't have the luxury of being able to moan.'

'Nobody's damn well listening, Silke!'

'They are *always* listening.'

'Come on, let's not fight,' Paulus begged. 'Not on our last day together. You buy the tickets, Otts. I'll try and get us a table at the café. The train doesn't leave for another hour, we can have some coffee. Come on, Dagmar.'

Paulus led Dagmar away towards the station restaurant while Otto and Silke joined the queue at one of the numerous ticket office windows.

When they arrived at the window, the woman behind the glass gave the German greeting. It was a ridiculous sight. There was so very little room in her tiny cubicle that the woman was forced to make her gesture with a bent arm cramped close to her chest. More like the salutes Hitler gave himself at rallies, walking past a forest of outstretched arms, his own wrist merely flicked back at the shoulder in a self-conscious demonstration of absolute authority. Too busy, too weighed down with the cares of destiny to offer anything more than a limp parody of the straining adulation that surrounded him.

Otto returned the woman's salute. He had to.

The German greeting, as it was called, was not compulsory, and the ticket woman was being quite a zealot in greeting every single customer in such a manner. But having *been* saluted, it was certainly dangerous not to return it. Otto had seen people beaten up in bus queues for such an insult.

His own salute was no less comically inadequate than the one the ticket woman offered. With people pressing from behind he was also too close to the glass to do it properly, and so he was forced to stretch his arm out sideways, being careful not to knock the hat off the person in the next queue.

'*Heil Hitler*,' Otto said. 'Two tickets for Rotterdam please.'

It was just so absurd. Standing there with his arm stretched out sideways, invoking the name of the head of state while purchasing a train ticket. Otto doubted whether even the power-corrupted despots of Ancient Rome had expected imperial genuflections from their citizens in such mundane circumstances.

'Identification and travel visas,' the woman demanded.

Otto pushed two sets of papers under the window.

'First class,' he said loudly. 'Sleeper berths.'

It was extravagant but it was what Paulus had suggested when they had been planning the trip. The journey was a long one and slips of the tongue were a constant worry. As Silke had just pointed out to Dagmar, you never knew when the Gestapo or one of their millions of eager informers were listening. It was said that people had been given away by their own children after talking in their sleep.

The woman in the booth looked from Otto to Silke with suspicion. He was just nineteen, she was eighteen. A glance down at their papers showed that they did not share a surname.

'That's right,' Silke said from over Otto's shoulder, 'we're going to use the journey to see if we can't make a present for Heinrich to put in his Spring of Life orphanages! Wish us luck, won't you?'

The woman issued the tickets with ill grace and Otto and Silke retreated from the window, both trying not to laugh.

A brief moment of levity in a strange and horribly bleak day.

'Spring of Life!' Otto scolded. 'I thought you said not to draw attention!'

'I was just pretending to be a good Nazi girl.'

They made their way to the restaurant where Dagmar and Paulus had already bought coffee and sandwiches.

'Well, here we are,' Otto said, laying the sleeper tickets on the table. 'As Mum often says, "Everybody's looking for Moses", and here he is in the form of a ticket to Rotterdam.'

'First class, eh, Silke?' Dagmar said. 'All right for some.'

'It's what we agreed on,' Paulus reminded her, 'and it's worth it. We don't want Silke getting searched carrying my papers on her way back. Those Gestapo are all peasant snobs. They'll paw a girl in third class but bow and scrape to the ones in first. Besides, it's a present from Mum, we can afford it.'

'Yes, lucky your clever old mum thought to settle her money and property on Otto when she did,' Dagmar said. 'Every Jewish family should have an adoptive Aryan to look after the estate. Shame my parents never thought to adopt one. I might still be a millionaire.'

'Nobody should be a millionaire,' Silke said, 'and one day nobody will.'

'Bet you wouldn't say that if *your* father had been one,' Dagmar replied.

'Well,' said Otto, 'nice to know you girls are as good mates as ever.'

They were all uncomfortably aware that the moment had almost come.

'So this is it,' Dagmar remarked after a moment's silence. 'The final meeting of the Saturday Club, eh?'

'Not final, I hope,' said Paulus, 'but certainly the last one for a while.'

'Might as well be realistic,' Dagmar said. 'There's going to be a war. Do you really think all four of us will survive it?'

The other three did not answer.

'Your mother isn't coming then?' Silke asked eventually. 'To see her wandering lad off?'

'We didn't think it was a good idea,' Paulus said.

'The fewer Jews in the situation, the better, in this case,' Otto added.

'Well,' Silke said, trying to sound bright, 'at least this gets me out of a couple of days of slavery.'

Silke was a few months into her compulsory Year of Domestic Service, which all young unmarried women were required by the state to perform and which she never made any secret about hating.

'How did you get them to give you the two days off?' Otto enquired. 'I thought they were slave-drivers.'

'They are. But when you work as an unpaid skivvy in someone's house you get to hear things. And see things. Things I don't think Frau Neubauer wants me telling Herr Neubauer about.'

'You're a resourceful girl, Silke,' Dagmar said. 'You always get what you want.'

'No I don't,' Silke replied abruptly. 'I do *not* get what I want. You do.'

Silence returned for a little while longer as they ate their sandwiches.

'Well,' said Otto, raising his coffee cup. 'To the Saturday Club. Always loyal to the club and to each other.'

The other three raised their cups, repeating once more the childish oaths they had sworn on so many happy, carefree afternoons wandering the streets and public spaces of Friedrichshain looking for mischief.

'Except Dagmar,' Silke said with a giggle.

'Not including Silke,' Dagmar replied, smiling also.

Both girls showed each other their crossed fingers and laughed together.

'Just kidding!' Silke smiled. 'To each other!'

'Yes, to each other,' Dagmar replied.

Once more they raised their cups, demonstrating this time that their fingers were not crossed.

The station loudspeakers announced the number of the platform for the Dutch sleeper.

Silke drained her coffee. There was still half an hour until departure but there seemed little point in the four of them sitting staring at each other.

'Come along then, *Mister* Stengel,' she said. 'Let's be off.'

'Give our love to England,' Dagmar said.

The four of them got up.

Otto hugged Paulus.

'Until whenever, mate,' he said, forcing a smile.

'Yeah,' Paulus nodded, 'just till then.'

Then Otto turned to Dagmar.

'Goodbye, Dagmar,' he said.

Silke backed away discreetly, walking a few steps towards the platform. Paulus also turned away, retreating to a nearby newsstand.

Allowing Otto a moment.

Dagmar put her arms around him and hugged him tight.

'Goodbye, dear Ottsy,' she said. Her scent was in his nostrils. Wisps of her hair on his cheeks. 'And thank you, thank you with all my heart.'

'Well. I won't say it's a pleasure,' Otto replied, trying to make a joke. Then he whispered, 'I love you, Dagmar. I know I have no right to say that any more because you love Pauly, but I love you. And I always will. Paulus is there to protect you now and I'm glad because he's so much cleverer than me. But if ever you need me, I'll come. You know that, don't you? Because I love you. And I always will.'

Gently, she disengaged and smiled. 'Yes, I know, Ottsy,' she said. 'And don't you *dare* forget it!'

Then he left her, grabbing his bag and hurrying to catch up with Silke.

'You'll see her again,' Silke said as he fell in beside her.

'Maybe.'

As they made their way through the ticket barrier and then along the side of the train searching out their carriage, Silke put her hand into Otto's.

He was surprised and had she not closed her fingers tight around his he might have withdrawn it. They had often held hands as little children, and occasionally at Napola when Silke had been Otto's only friend, but this was the first time they had done it for years.

'Do you mind?' Silke asked quietly. 'Just for friendship. For comfort.'

'No,' Otto replied, 'I don't mind.'

He meant it. It was actually a comfort for him also. Good old Silke.

'It's so kind of you to come with me, Silke. To do this for us.'

'Hey, we're all in the same gang,' she replied.

As they walked along beside the hissing train, Otto felt a tiny increase of pressure from her hand.

Back in the main part of the station, Paulus and Dagmar were also hand in hand, walking purposefully towards the *S-Bahn*. Both of them knew that the best way to avoid detection, to avoid curt demands, searches and humiliation, banishment from the carriage and perhaps losing your watch and wallet, was to act with absolute confidence. Nazi officials had a sixth sense for fear so it was essential to show none.

To walk as Nazis did.

To strut. To barge. To bully.

'As Goebbels says,' Paulus remarked, throwing out his chest and fixing his face to an arrogant sneer, 'if you're going to tell a lie, make it a big one. Make it a bold one. If you're a Jew, act like a German. But don't worry, Dags. Once Silke gets back from Holland, I'll be a German and then you'll be safe.'

'I don't know why you can't be it already. You had an exit visa. Now that Otto's you and you're Otto, why didn't he leave on that?'

'This way we can be sure he'll get out,' Paulus said. 'A Jew's exit visa is worth less and less these days. War's coming and they're turning more and more of us back at the border. Some for no better reason than spite, but also because relations have deteriorated so badly with the British. As an Aryan he'll avoid any kind of trouble, and Silke will bring back his ID tomorrow.'

Dagmar put her arm around Paulus.

'You're so clever, Pauly,' she said, 'you think through every little detail. I certainly made the right choice.'

The Morning After

The German–Dutch Border, 1939

Otto was awoken by the jerking and shunting as the locomotive hauled its carriages into the customs siding for border inspection.

Otto had not expected to fall asleep. He recalled lying awake for hours. Staring at the second hand on his watch in the intermittent flashes of yellow light as the train roared through some town or other.

And now he was awake again.

Silke was up, rinsing her face in the little basin.

It was a lovely compartment. The stuff of happy daydreams. Cosy, comfy. Every little convenience tucked neatly away. Tooth cups in cavities secured by leather straps, concealed lamps and mirrors, an ashtray, water-glass holders, a fold-down table by each bunk, a little netted alcove for shoes. Everything in brass and wood and leather. Such a very nice place to wake up.

Unless of course that little compartment was carrying you away from everything you had ever known or ever loved.

Silke had her back to him as she bent over the sink. She had put on her skirt but not her blouse. The white straps of her bra stretched across a bronzed back and up over slim, muscular, slightly freckled shoulders, which her golden hair brushed as she flannelled her face.

How strange. How utterly surprising.

That he and Silke . . .

'You're not to be embarrassed or to hate me,' she said through the water and the cloth. Bright. Matter-of-fact. Jolly even. Yet every syllable strung tight with the shrill, brittle tension of having woken up remembering.

Otto hadn't realized that she knew he was awake. Her back was turned to him and he'd made no sound. But women seemed often to know things you didn't expect them to know, he'd noticed that.

Silke finished washing and reached out a hand, feeling for one of the starched linen face towels that were looped through the polished brass rings beside the basin.

'It happened, that's all,' she went on, towelling her face dry then taking up her sponge bag. 'I said you shouldn't have bought us all that brandy.'

She still hadn't turned around. Otto was in the top bunk so her mass of blonde curls were just a half metre or so from his face. A single bar of sunlight shining through a crack in the window blinds painted a blazing golden stripe across her shoulders.

She took a little tube of toothpaste from her sponge bag and squeezed some on to her brush.

'How many of those damned Hennessys do you think we had?' he heard her ask brightly.

Otto could not honestly recall. Four or five probably, plus the bottle of wine with dinner. They had certainly been the last to leave the dining car.

'Quite a few,' he said. 'And *guten Morgen*, by the way.'

How did you greet your oldest friend when quite unexpectedly you had made love to her the previous night?

'Don't worry, I know it didn't mean anything,' Silke said quickly, talking through the toothbrush foam in her mouth. She turned around to face him as she brushed. He could see her breasts jiggling very slightly in the cups of her bra as her arm moved back and forth and up and down. There was a wisp of rusty-coloured hair visible in the pit of her raised arm.

She turned back and spat the toothpaste foam into the basin and rinsed out her mouth.

'I know you don't love me. You love Dagmar,' Silke went on, using her ablutions to cover her embarrassment. 'Obviously I know that. God knows you've said it often enough and you talked about no one else last night at dinner, which was a bit boring, actually. And *slightly* rude. Of course, you didn't *get* her. That does have to be said. You lost that one but I know you still love her, so don't worry. Last night was about the brandy.'

As she leant forward over the basin he could see her ribs corrugated against her honey-coloured skin, the vertebrae standing out along her slim back. She was a very pretty girl.

'It was just for comfort. That's all, wasn't it?' she said, putting on her blouse.

'Yes,' Otto replied quietly, 'for comfort. Nice though.'

'Yes!' Silke replied, slightly too loudly. 'Very. Funny it should be the first time though,' she added, now a vivid crimson. 'I mean, for both of us.'

'Yeah. Weird. Kept it in the club, eh?'

'I always presumed you and Dagmar must have been at it like rabbits this last year or two.'

'No.'

'Sensible of her, really. Keeping that one in reserve.' As she said it her face fell and she added quickly, 'No, that was awful. I'm sorry, I shouldn't have said that, I didn't mean it. I don't know what I meant.'

Outside far along the corridors at the other end of the train, doors began to slam.

'*Raus! Raus! Ausweis!*'

As Paulus had predicted, the Gestapo were not being overly polite to the third-class passengers as they checked the credentials of those wishing to cross the border and depart the glorious Fatherland.

'You'd better get dressed,' Silke said, tucking in her blouse. 'They'll be in to see us in a minute.'

Otto was pulling on his pants beneath the sheets. 'Moment of truth, eh? Not that there's any risk. I get to be me for one last time.'

'There's always a risk with these people.'

All along the train could be heard protests and shouted commands.

Silke watched from the window as the Gestapo led away the ones who didn't have the required paperwork or whose faces they didn't like.

'Let us go!' a middle-aged woman was protesting. 'You don't want us. You hate us. For God's sake, why don't you let us go?'

There was much anguish at the border that day, as indeed there had been every day for years. Some of the older guards missed the days when theirs had been a happy job. Wishing people well as they went off on their holidays. Contented was the world when borders had been things that travellers crossed for fun.

There was a knocking at the door. More like blows, in fact, than knocks, as if the beautiful wooden panelling was being punched.

'Are these bloody people incapable of doing *anything* without turning it into some sort of violent assault?' Silke hissed *sotto voce*, running a brush through her hair. 'Tea time at Gestapo headquarters must be a *nightmare*. Breaking the crockery, spilling the milk. If they put on a ballet they'd do it in bloody jackboots.'

Otto laughed.

'Hey, I went to Napola! I've had three years of it. You stand to attention when you take a crap.'

'Actually I rather think that would be anatomically impossible.'

'Nothing is impossible to the German soldier!'

Another rattling bang on the door.

'*Einen moment, bitte*,' Silke called out.

Having slipped on her shoes, she opened the door of their compartment. There were three of them outside. A plainclothes officer and two Wehrmacht soldiers in steel helmets. Steel helmets in order to ask people on trains if they had visas. Even after six years of living under the Nazis, three at an elite school, Otto had still not got used to their deep psychological need to militarize *everything*.

'Papers,' the Gestapo man demanded. He was of course dressed in the usual gangster get-up, black leather trenchcoat and Homburg hat. All he needed was a Thompson sub-machine gun tucked under his arm in a violin case and he could have been in an American movie.

Silke handed over her passport and exit visa, while Otto sat up and reached for his in the jacket he had put at the other end of his bunk.

'What is your business abroad?' the officer snapped, having

gone through the documents, a task made difficult by the fact that he wore leather gloves.

'Just a little Dutch holiday before my Otto goes into the Wehrmacht,' Silke said. 'We will be back in a day or two.'

'We couldn't bear to be out of the Fatherland any longer,' Otto added. 'We might miss a parade.'

The Gestapo man clearly did not much like Otto's tone, nor did he think much of two such young people having the wherewithal to travel first class. However, their papers were in order and so, having thrust them back, he left them in peace. Or at least as much peace as could be had with the officer and his soldiers stamping and banging their way along the carriage to the compartments beyond.

'Well. Looks like that's it. You made it. You're out.'

'Yes,' Otto replied. 'I'm out.'

Through the window they could see those for whom departure had been denied being herded together on the platform under armed guard.

Together they began to put their compartment back into daytime order. Both self-consciously aware of their proximity as their hips touched while they folded up the top bunk into its wall cavity and turned the bottom one back into a seat.

'Seems funny to be coy now,' Otto said, 'after—'

'We were drunk,' Silke said quickly. 'We're not drunk now. And it was dark. Makes rather a big difference.'

'The attendant is supposed to do this while we go and eat a huge breakfast,' Otto said.

'I'd rather do it myself,' Silke said, reddening.

Hurriedly she gathered up her undersheet, screwed it into a ball and pushed it out of sight.

Afterwards they sat together on the seat and Otto gave Silke his passport and ID, the ones he had shown to the Gestapo man.

'So,' he said, 'you take these back then.'

'Yes.' Silke buried the documents deep in her handbag. 'I take them back and give them to Pauly. He's got someone who can change the photograph.'

Then Otto reached to the bottom of his own bag and produced a second set of papers.

'And here's Pauly's, with the photo already changed. He's bloody efficient, isn't he, my bro.'

Otto stared at the documents.

'Paulus *Israel* Stengel,' he said. 'Fuck. They know how to twist the knife, don't they?'

The train was pulling away, rolling slowly past the failed fugitives. All silent now, desperate figures, every protest stilled. Faces blank and cold with anguish as they watched their last hope of freedom leaving the station without them.

Otto looked down at the papers in his hand, at the large 'J' stamped across them, the letter that had condemned every yearning face they passed.

'Come on,' he said, 'let's go and have breakfast. We've paid a fortune for it, we should eat it.'

They got up and made their way down the very same corridor along which they had stumbled tipsily only a few hours earlier.

'First and last time I'll ever travel first class, I imagine,' Silke said.

Otto did not reply. That privacy which they'd paid for had taken such a very unexpected turn.

Why did he feel as if he'd betrayed Dagmar?

It was so stupid. After all, she'd rejected him for his brother, and it was very possible that he would never see her again anyway. He didn't intend to remain a monk for the rest of his life, so what did it matter who he made love to?

Even someone as unexpected as Silke. A friend. A dear old friend.

But still he felt deflated. Wretched almost. As if he'd despoiled something fine and noble.

Because he loved Dagmar. His first and only passion. He had told her so at the café at the Lehrter Bahnhof.

And then just a few hours later he had been in bed with another girl. What was that, if not a betrayal?

At the door to the restaurant car Silke stopped and turned to look at him.

'Don't feel bad about it,' she said.

Otto was completely taken aback. How had she known what he was thinking?

It was that woman thing again, they always seemed to know.

'I wasn't! Really, Silke,' he protested.

But she interrupted him.

'You were and you know it. You were feeling bad about last night. But please don't. For my sake. I'd hate it so much if you did. It was my idea . . . I wanted to, you see . . . Dagmar said I get what I want but I don't think I do at all . . . but last night, for just a moment, I did.' Now she reached out her arms to hold him. 'The thing is, I might never see you again and the whole world's about to go to hell and . . .'

'Silke.' Otto tried gently to pull himself away. 'Don't.'

'I *know*. I know you love Dagmar,' she said hurriedly. 'Of *course* I know. But it wasn't you last night anyway, was it? That's the point. It wasn't you.'

Otto was surprised. 'Who was it then?'

'Why that new fellow!' Silke said with a big broad smile that did nothing to disguise the tears standing in her eyes. 'Mister Stengel, of course. That very new, very handsome, freshly minted, soon-to-be Englishman. It was him.'

'Of course,' Otto said quietly, 'that's right, it was just Mister Stengel.'

'So that's all right then. No need to feel bad on his behalf, eh!'

For a moment they faced each other. There was a longing in Silke's pale blue eyes.

'Come on,' he said. 'Eggs. Eggs and fresh rolls.'

But she was holding him once again.

'We could skip breakfast,' she said quickly, urgently, 'me and Mr Stengel. We could go back to our compartment. Not you but that soon-to-be Englishman, the man from last night . . .'

For a moment Otto hesitated. Remembering those honey-freckled shoulders and golden curls, the strip of sunlight streaked across them. Her breasts moving as she brushed her teeth. The little wisp of hair at her arm.

And last night. That unexpected blur of drunken passion.

She was a very pretty girl.

But he loved Dagmar and he had promised that he would always love her. And Herr or Mister, Englishman or German, Paulus or Otto, whatever his name might be, yesterday, today or in the future, he would keep that promise.

Early Breakfast

London, 1956

'We parted at Rotterdam. Silke took the train back to Berlin and I took the ferry to Britain. I never saw her again.'

Stone was staring at the dark moonlit waters of the Thames. 'I never saw any of them again. I watched the continent disappear over the horizon and my whole life disappeared with it.'

Billie sipped at her tea. The fourth mug of the night. They'd been talking for hours. The taxi drivers had changed shifts. The rubbish barges had begun to remove London's daily tonnage of trash to wherever it was they took it. And there was a pale light beginning to glimmer in the sky.

'I entered England on Paulus's visa, took his name and the place that Mum had managed to get for him at Goldsmith's College. Humanities.'

'How'd dat go?'

'Not great.'

'What with you not bein' as clever as your brudder and all?'

'I lasted about three months. I tried. I really did but it was pretty grim. The charity had found a place for a clever kid. They wanted Paulus. A kid who could one day make a difference. Put something back in exchange for his good fortune. Help build the new world and all that. Instead they got me. I felt so guilty.'

Billie put her arm around Stone.

'So *that's* why all those law books be lyin' around your flat gathering dust,' she said. 'You're tryin' ta be your brudder. You're *still* tryin' ta replace him.'

Stone didn't reply. Instead, he snuggled a little closer. Embracing the tenderness. The companionship.

'So what shall I call you now, boy?' Billie asked. 'Are you Paul? Or are you Otto?'

Stone didn't reply for a whole minute or more.

'I think,' he began eventually, 'I think I'd like you to call me Otto.'

'There,' she said and kissed his cheek, 'was that so difficult?'

'As a matter of fact it was,' he said, 'it is.'

'So tell me this, Otto,' Billie said.

And still Stone flinched. 'Sorry,' he said. 'First time in seventeen years.'

'You tell me this, Otto,' Billie repeated, putting her head on his shoulder, 'why do you have to feel so guilty? It was all Paulus's idea, after all.'

'I know,' Stone replied. 'I know. But all the same, I've always felt unworthy of the life I took. Destiny had me dying in the Wehrmacht, but Pauly was too clever for destiny. He cheated fate and died instead. Mum, Dad, Paulus. All dead. The best of the Stengels. Only the adopted son survived.'

'Do you think they'd look at it that way?' Billie asked.

'No. Of course not.'

'Then I think you should show a bit more respec' to their memory,' Billie said. 'And you know what else I think?'

'What?'

'I think I need to find a loo.'

Arm in arm they returned to near the bridge, where there was a public toilet.

'Romantic eh?' Billie laughed. 'Too much damn tea.'

The dawn was really not far off now. There was more than a hint of it in the dark sky but neither of them wanted to go to bed.

'I can do college on no sleep,' Billie said. 'Damn, I'm the best they got even when I *am* asleep and they know it too.'

'I bet they do, Bill,' Stone said.

'So let's get us some breakfast.'

It wasn't difficult to find a café. London's early morning shift of workers was already mingling with the previous night's party-goers. Men in overalls and donkey jackets starting their day squeezed around Formica-covered tables next to men in dinner jackets and girls in pearls who were having a fry-up at the end of theirs.

Stone and Billie found a little corner in a greasy spoon near Waterloo Bridge and sat down to egg, beans, fried bread, toast and more tea.

'This is my kind of night,' Billie said, viewing the feast with satisfaction. 'Apart from you hitting that guy, of course.'

Stone shrugged.

'I'd do it again any time,' he said. 'It's my rule.'

'Yeah, you said. So come on then, you're in England, you're in school. What happened?'

'Nothing much more to tell, Bill.'

'Tell it anyway.'

'Well, like I said, I got away with it for a while at college. They made a lot of allowances for me being foreign and adjusting to a new country and all that. Then just as it was starting to get embarrassing, the war broke out and I got interned as an enemy alien.'

'They did that?' Billie asked in surprise. 'To Jews?'

'Well, they couldn't tell, could they? So they interned everybody. I didn't mind. I thought they had a point. After all, if you think about it, I *wasn't* a Jew, was I? I was a German travelling under a false identity. I didn't have any sympathy with the ones who complained about internment. The British had their backs to the wall after all.'

'And, of course, it got you out of college.'

Stone conceded that with a smile. 'That was a bonus. Anyway, they let us all out pretty soon and I went straight into the army.

That was how I got my British citizenship. It was after Dunkirk and they needed all the help they could get.'

Billie shook the brown sauce bottle over her second egg.

'You must have been pretty lonely.'

'I was very lonely. Very lonely indeed. The thing was, I didn't really want to make friends . . . I was sort of . . .'

'Wallowing in it?'

Stone laughed, spreading Golden Shred marmalade on his toast. 'I suppose you could say that.'

'I guess you had good cause, baby. More than most, that's for sure. Did you get news from home at all?'

'No. We could probably have corresponded via Switzerland in the early stages of the war but Paulus decided that with so many lies to cover the safest thing was to maintain separation. All mail from abroad was read by the Gestapo, of course.'

'An' from the day you left, Paulus became you? He was Otto Stengel, the ex-Napola boy?'

'That's right. Silke took my papers back to him. Paulus had found some old scrivener who changed our photos. There was a lot of forging going on around that time, as you can imagine. People trying to get that J off their papers. Apart from that, it was easy. All the addresses and family history were the same. I'd left the Napola but not yet joined the Wehrmacht. He just joined instead of me.'

'But what if he met someone who knew you?'

'He reckoned he was pretty safe. Don't forget, I'd been sent to boarding school. Most of my classmates were from other parts of the country. They went back to their own towns to join up, and most of them went in as officers. There were already more than a million soldiers in the Wehrmacht; soon there'd be millions more. Paulus reckoned he could keep below the radar.'

Billie whistled softly. 'Wow. Some guy, eh?'

'Oh yeah. My brother was some guy.'

'Joining the Wehrmacht out of the blue, when he was supposed to be a refugee studying in England. Giving up everything to join the *German* army. A Jew. You *both* gave up everything.

Jesus,' Billie exclaimed, 'this Dagmar must have been *some* chick.'

'She was, Bill. She was some chick.'

'Or you two were just crazy love-struck fools.'

They ate in silence for a little while. Billie using her fried bread to mop up her egg yolk with such dexterity that by the time she'd finished it looked as if the plate would not even need washing.

'And now you're going to find her. Right?' Billie said, having swallowed her last mouthful.

'What?' Stone asked.

'Dagmar. C'mon, P—, Otto. That's why you're going to Berlin, it's pretty obvious.'

Stone's eyes clouded a little. A beat of pain registered on his face before he turned it to a sad smile.

'Dagmar's dead, Bill,' he said. 'She died during the war. It isn't her I'll be seeing in Berlin.'

From Untermensch to Superman

Berlin, 1940

'Stengel! Step forward!'

Corporal Stengel rose from the wooden bench where he had been sitting alongside half a dozen other field-grey-clad soldiers, and stepped forward.

'*Ahnenpass*,' the SS-*Sturmscharführer* barked.

Paulus, now in the uniform of a Wehrmacht *Obergefreiter*, produced his 'pass of ancestors', that document essential to survival which proved that the previous three generations of his family had been of purely Aryan stock.

The SS sergeant-major studied it.

'Your name is Otto Stengel?'

'*Ja, Sturmscharführer* sir,' Paulus barked.

'Adopted?' the sergeant enquired.

'*Ja, Sturmscharführer* sir!'

'By Jews?'

'*Ja, Sturmscharführer* sir!'

He said this last with equal clarity, equal volume. Never show weakness. Paulus's year inside the German military had shown him that the only thing they respected was strength.

'And your blood family?'

'Parents dead. Grandparents abandoned me. The only family I knew were Jews, *Sturmscharführer* sir!'

He could almost feel the eyes of his fellow applicants opening wide behind him. Many men and women from Jewish families had passed through the dreaded Reich main security office on the Prinz-Albrecht-Strasse, but it was certain that prior to Paulus none of them had been applicants to join the Waffen SS.

The sergeant major was looking at him with narrow suspicion. 'An SS man brought up by Jews. That would be a first, I think,' he said curtly.

'I was less than an hour old, *Sturmscharführer* sir!' Paulus barked again. 'It wasn't my fault. As you can see from my record, I am a graduate of a Napola academy.'

The sergeant major smiled, clearly seeing some humour in the situation.

'Did they make you work for them? In the scullery, like Cinderella?'

'No. And they didn't drink my blood either,' Paulus replied. 'In fact, they were kind to me.'

'You defend them? You would stick up for the race enemy? For the people who stole you?'

'No, of course not, sir.'

'Why not? They're your family. You just said they were kind.'

'I do not defend them, sir, because they are stinking Jews and blood enemies of the Fatherland. I didn't know it when I was an hour old but I know it now because my leader has told me so.'

The SS man looked down at Paulus's papers. 'You served in Poland?'

'*Ja, Sturmscharführer.*'

'Must have been fun.'

'*Ja, Sturmscharführer.*'

Perhaps the sergeant major would have thought so. Brutality had without doubt become a sport for many of those brothers-in-arms with whom Paulus had stormed east the previous September. A lot of the guys had had 'fun'.

Once again in his mind's eye Paulus saw the eight corpses hanging from the hastily erected gallows. Their feet tied together and weighted with stones. Faces blue-green. Tongues distended like great crimson slugs exploring little dark caves.

Not dead yet, not for an hour if their tormentors had their way.

What village had it been? Rajgród? Witosław? Białowieża? They had been moving so fast it was hard to remember. *Blitzkrieg*, the papers were calling it. War conducted as fast as lightning.

Unless of course you took an hour to die.

An SS band had been playing in the mean, dusty patch of ground that served as a village square. Public torture and cold-blooded murder conducted to music. Military, marching music. As if it had been a flag the victorious army were raising over the village, and not the twitching bodies of husbands and fathers. With the noise of the music and of the truck on which he and his comrades were riding, Paulus could not hear the screams of desperate protest from the traumatized civilians.

But he *saw* them.

The mouths of the women and children open and wide, howling with an anguish that seemed to make no sound.

Like a silent movie shot in hell.

'Nothing like winning, eh?' the SS man added.

'*Ja, Sturmscharführer.*'

It was true. Winning had been unlike anything he could have imagined, certainly more terrible than if they had lost. He was sure of that.

'Strip,' he heard the *Sturmscharführer* demand.

Paulus removed his calf-length jackboots, his belt and webbing, his jacket, trousers, shirt and underwear, and stood naked and to attention as an SS doctor inspected him for any suspicious racial characteristics.

'So those Jews didn't circumcise you then?' the doctor remarked, taking Paulus's penis in the palm of his hand and staring at it as a farmer might inspect a bull.

'No. They were modern people and not religiously minded.'

'Well, it was decent of them anyway,' the doctor said, adding with a hearty laugh that it would have caused a few problems for Stengel in the showers if they had.

Then the doctor produced a set of measuring callipers, which for a moment Paulus presumed were to be applied to his penis but which instead the doctor applied to his head.

'Good cranium, I must say,' the doctor remarked with an approving nod. 'Teutonic shape, excellent Aryan lobes.'

'Thank you, *Herr Doktor*.'

On the wall was a chart depicting in what purported to be scientific detail the defining features of a Jewish skull. From what Paulus could see, the main characteristic appeared to be a forehead that sloped brutally backwards. Certainly the owner of such a skull would have a sneaky and ignoble look about him.

Paulus thought of his handsome father. His beautiful mother.

These people truly were insane. Could they really believe it?

Paulus knew that Otto had been subjected to the same inspection when he entered the Napola school. One Jew, one Gentile, no sense. This was supposedly the most technologically advanced army in the world and they thought they could define 'valuable' blood with a ruler.

Satisfied with the physical evidence of racial purity, the doctor turned his attention to the question of health.

'Mouth.'

Paulus opened his mouth. He had five filled cavities, one less than the maximum number allowed. Himmler had originally stipulated that an SS man must have no fillings at all, nor wear spectacles or indeed display any imperfection of any kind. How the stoop-shouldered, short-sighted, rat-toothed and chinless

Reichsführer SS could have written these instructions with a straight face was beyond most members of the public, even Nazis.

Unfortunately for the *Reichsführer*'s visions of a master race, the privations of the previous twenty years had ensured that almost no young German men whatsoever met the idealistic criteria of the *Herrenmensch*, and so the standards had been relaxed immediately. In fact, it was pretty plain that if you had all four limbs and weren't a Jew, they'd take you.

After Paulus had dressed, the interview continued.

'Why do you want to join the SS?' the *Sturmscharführer* enquired.

That was easy.

Because he was in love with a beautiful woman who was a Jew. And one day soon he knew he would have to hide her. And the closer he was identified with the murderer's gang, the less likely anybody would be to imagine that that was what he was doing.

Paulus had made his plan in Poland, when he saw for the first time what Hitler really had in store for what he called the *Untermensch*.

Until then, Paulus, like every half-civilized person in Germany, Jew or Gentile, had hoped that somehow, one day, a line would be drawn. That the steady erosion of all humanity towards the 'race enemies' would reach its nadir. Deprived of rights, property, dignity, security. Yes.

But murder? Mass murder? Surely not. That couldn't be.

Nobody. Nobody would do that.

Least of all the sons and daughters of Bach, Beethoven, Goethe, Schiller, Mozart, Bismarck, Gutenberg and Luther.

Murder all the Jews. *All* of them?

It couldn't happen.

And yet . . .

Maybe it wasn't planned. Maybe they scarcely even knew themselves that this was what they were about. But Paulus had seen in Poland with his own eyes which way the devilish wind was blowing. He had seen what sudden and absolute victory was doing to the men in black and, yes, also in field grey. They were supermen and they could do what they liked.

And what they liked, it seemed, was to kill defenceless people.

Poles, gypsies, the weak, the sick. And above all Jews.

Certainly it had seemed improvised and almost random; there appeared to Paulus to be no guiding system or specific orders. And yet everywhere he had been as the lightning war struck, he had seen dead Jews.

Or Jews for whom he could see no chance of survival.

Herded up. Shipped from here to there.

To where?

Three times the truck in which he was riding with his Wehrmacht comrades had been commandeered by the SS in charge of huddled masses of humanity being torn from their villages.

'Don't let them take us,' came the pitiful cries of children. 'They'll kill us.'

Paulus's comrades said they wouldn't.

Even they, who had passed village squares in which every father hung from a rope, still declined to believe it.

'They won't kill them. That's a Jewish lie. A slur on Germany. They're just shifting them out to make room for decent Germans.'

But Paulus could only ask himself the obvious question.

Shifting them to where?

If you tore every Jew from his home as clearly the *Einsatzkommando* of the SS were intent on doing, what would you do with them then? He had been told that they were being taken to the cities, massed in tiny ghettos from which they were not allowed to leave.

And what then?

Paulus thought that if he were Hitler he would kill them. After all, they were vermin and leaving them to starve would be messy and dangerous. A source of infection. A source of resistance. A source of witness.

Paulus had concluded that the path down which Germany was travelling could lead to only one dark and terrible place.

And his mother and his beloved Dagmar were trapped in Berlin.

Which is why, bumping along the dusty roads towards the charnel house that Germany was to make of the ancient city of Warsaw, he had made his plan.

'I want to join the SS in order to better serve my Führer and to cleanse myself once and for all of my shameful family history, *Sturmscharführer* sir!'

'Well done, lad,' the sergeant said. 'I think we'll take you.'

A Marriage is Discussed

Berlin, 1940

The newly appointed SS *Obergefreiter* Stengel turned left on to Prinz-Albrecht-Strasse and walked the length of the state security building. His jackboots rang on the paving stones as he passed the various queues of miserable people who had come with their papers in search of some stamp or other. Helpless suppliants begging for permission to survive.

He turned right on to Saarlandstrasse, a great blood-red double vein of fluttering flags, which led up to Potsdamer Platz. Two lanes plus a central island. So many flags. Red and black. Red and black. Red and black. All the way up to the *Haus Vaterland*.

He saw Dagmar before she saw him.

Which gave him a moment. A moment to drink her in. To savour. To treasure. To stand and stare across the thundering traffic at an oasis of poise and beauty.

She was standing beneath the famous Traffic-light Tower.

They loved the tower. Everyone in Berlin did. They had both been present at its unveiling in 1924. She a much-indulged little princess, separate and safe in a viewing area reserved for city dignitaries and leaders of commerce. He in the crowd, watching with his brother from atop their parents' shoulders, cheering and shouting as the policeman in his little box seven metres above the ground turned on the lights that would finally bring order to the traffic chaos of the Potsdamer Platz.

The tower had been a symbol of Germany's burgeoning economic revival. A miracle of modern technology, the first of its kind in Europe.

The tower was hung with swastikas now of course. The whole city was hung with swastikas and had been for six long years. Paulus no longer really thought of it as Berlin at all. Just Nazi Town, capital of Nazi Land, a hostile foreign country in which he was a prisoner.

Paulus looked once more at Dagmar.

How elegant she looked. From her fashionably broad-brimmed Homburg hat to her neat little lace-up brogues. No stockings, of course, they had disappeared from Berlin, but even ankle socks looked sophisticated on Dagmar.

It seemed to Paulus that of all the scurrying creatures hurrying this way and that across the great junction, Dagmar appeared the most naturally placed. Here in the heart of Berlin's shopping district, standing at the epicentre of its finest thoroughfares, she might have been posing for a fashion photograph to be placed in a stylish magazine. Or, more likely these days, to feature in one of those photo stories they published in *Signal*, to show the troops that life in the capital was still prosperous and normal and that the German girls were still beautiful.

Paulus's reverie was interrupted by a voice at his shoulder.

'Come on,' Silke said, 'I've only got an hour.'

In a rush as ever.

But there, just as she had promised. She never let him down.

Good old Silke.

Golden hair all wrapped up in a knotted scarf, someone else's baby's dribble on the shoulder of her housecoat. Shivering against the cold and damp for which she was ill-clad as ever. But smiling nonetheless. A big bright smile spread across a face so sun-browned it was still tanned even now as winter began to thaw.

She put her arm in his and at the automated bidding of the Traffic-light Tower (no friendly seven-metre-high policeman any more), they crossed the street together to join Dagmar.

The three of them were to have lunch in the magnificent *Haus Vaterland*. The internationally famous 'World in One House' where up to eight thousand people at a time could dine in the largest café in the world and at the various internationally themed restaurants. They could have chosen the Wild West American Bar, the Bodega Spanish winery or the Japanese tea room. There were Turkish, Hungarian and Viennese options too. With supreme irony there had never been a British or a French restaurant because the ultra-patriotic Herr Kempinski, the Jewish restaurateur who had founded Fatherland House, had never forgiven Germany's Great War enemies for the Treaty of Versailles.

When Paulus had come here with his parents and his brother back in the dream time they had, of course, always chosen the American Bar. Where they had steak and cornbread and a fancy coloured cocktail for Frieda. Now, however, being a good German soldier in uniform with not one but two girls on his arms, he steered the ladies towards the Lowenbräu Bavarian beer restaurant.

This was the loudest hall in the whole building, in which Nazi marching music blaring from loudspeakers competed with the beer-soaked din. It was a rowdy, triumphalist, unpleasant environment. Intimidating even. It therefore provided the best kind of cover for a planning meeting of race enemies and Communist-inclined traitors to the Reich.

Inevitably the *Horst Wessel Lied* was blaring from the loudspeakers as they entered the room and waited for a table.

'Don't grimace, Dagmar,' Silke said, smiling broadly.

'I can't help it. That damned tune. Don't they *ever* tire of it?'

'Well, at least there'll be no chance of us being overheard.'

This was the first time the three of them had been able to

arrange to get together since Paulus had returned from Poland and begun to set his plan in motion.

Dagmar was still living at the Stengel apartment, sharing the crowded flat with three other dispossessed Jewish households, including Frieda's parents, whose own apartment had recently been seized by a minor party functionary.

Silke was still in domestic service and so lived with the family that employed her, and Paulus of course had been first on active service and then tied up with his basic induction training with the Waffen SS.

Now, however, they could finally meet.

They ordered sausage and sauerkraut, which were still freely available in restaurants, plus beer for Paulus and apple juice for Silke and Dagmar. Dagmar fell on the food when it arrived. Rationing had been in place for the whole population for over a year, but Jews were only allowed the barest minimum and certainly no luxuries such as sausage and fruit juice.

'I'm going to speak quickly because we don't have much time,' Paulus said. 'The truth is things are going to get worse. A lot worse. What I've seen in the east defies description and I believe it's only a matter of time before it happens here.'

'What more can they do to us?' Dagmar asked angrily. 'We are forced to live like beggars, abused and exploited. My father's store has swastikas hanging from—'

'Your father's shop is gone, Dagmar!' Silke interjected, 'and so is your father. It's done, you can't look back.'

'It's easy for you to—'

'Please, Dagmar,' Paulus interrupted. 'Silke's right. What's done is done but I am here to tell you that what *has* been done is nothing, I mean *nothing*, compared to what's coming. He's said it. Over and over again. At the Reichstag, on the radio. This war will end either with the destruction of Germany or the destruction of the Jews.'

'Yes, but he—'

'He *does* mean it, Dagmar. The mass killing has begun, I've seen it, and I believe that once you begin on that path there's no turning back. I don't believe in five or perhaps ten years' time there will be a single Jew left alive in Berlin. We can't run any more, that option's closed to us. So you're going to have to hide.'

At that point they were interrupted, a Wehrmacht sergeant and two corporals appearing suddenly at their table.

'Hey, what's this,' one of them said, a big tough-looking customer. 'Keeping all the girls to yourself, comrade? That's not fair, is it? Two for one? I thought we were all supposed to be pulling together.'

The soldier put his beer down on the table and pulled up a chair between Silke and Dagmar.

'Excuse me, but we're busy,' Paulus replied quickly. 'There are free seats elsewhere.'

'Busy! I'll bet you're busy with two girls to yourself. Come on, mate, where's your army spirit? I can see you're bloody Waffen SS but we're all in this together you know.'

The soldiers' two companions were also pressing closer now. Breathing beer and tobacco over Dagmar and Silke's heads.

'These ladies are my sister and my cousin,' Paulus insisted. 'We have family business to—'

'We're in luck, lads!' the big sergeant shouted. 'This lad hasn't pulled either of them. Looks like we're three to two, not bad odds, I'd say. Hel-ooh, ladies!'

'Hey, lads, give us a break,' Silke said. 'We're talking here.'

'So talk,' the sergeant said, putting his arm around her.

For once Paulus was at a loss. Any kind of scene would spark an investigation, papers would be demanded which Dagmar didn't have. The sergeant outranked him by a stripe.

'You. Sergeant!' an imperious voice snapped.

Dagmar had risen to her feet, her eyes blazing. Her tone was loud and commanding.

'What is your name and what is your regiment?'

The sergeant was taken by surprise, recognizing a genuinely authoritative voice when he heard one.

'Now just hang on a minute, miss,' he replied. 'Why would you want to know that?'

'Because you and your friends are insulting German womanhood, that's why. The sister and the cousin of a serving man. And what is more you will be sorry for it because I am not some slut to be approached without an introduction. You will give me your names that I may report them to my fiancé.'

'Fiancé?' the sergeant asked, now clearly worried, his arm no longer around Silke.

'Yes, my fiancé. *Kriminal-Oberassistent* Heinz Frank of the *Geheime Staatspolizei* will be very interested to know how Wehrmacht non-commissioned officers conduct themselves on leave. You are a disgrace to the Führer.'

The three soldiers had had enough. Nobody in Berlin evoked the name of the all-powerful Gestapo without good cause. It was a name that was normally spoken of in hushed tones, not barked out with authority in crowded restaurants. The sergeant jumped up, mumbling an apology and claiming he'd been acting in fun. Muttering their names incomprehensibly, the three soldiers took themselves off as quickly as they could scurry.

'Wow, Dagmar,' Paulus said when they were gone. 'That was pretty crazy.'

'It got rid of them, didn't it?'

'It drew attention to you,' Silke said. 'You just can't afford to do that.'

'And what if I *hadn't* done it? While you sat there and simpered?'

'*Simpered!*'

'We'd be sitting here now trying to discuss our plans with three bloody Nazi soldiers groping at us, wouldn't we?'

'*Our* plans?' Silke snapped back. '*We've* been making all the plans as far as I can see. What plan do *you* have to save yourself, Dagmar?'

'I wouldn't *need* to save myself if people like your bloody mother hadn't decided I was subhuman.'

For a moment there was an angry silence. Then Paulus smiled.

'Nothing changes, eh?' He laughed. 'You two have been at each other's throats since 1926.'

The young women simply glared at each other.

'Now come on!' Paulus went on. 'We're going to have to learn to get along better than this if we're all going to live together.'

'Live together?' Dagmar gasped. 'All three of us?'

'Yes, that's my plan.'

'But . . . I thought . . . I thought *we* would live together,' Dagmar said, turning her huge brown eyes on Paulus. 'That you were going to look after me.'

'I am going to look after you. But I can't do it on my own. Silke has agreed to be a part of it.'

'A part of what?'

'You need to disappear, Dagmar. And to do it soon. There are thousands of Jews left in Berlin, and let me tell you when the whip comes down they're all going to be looking for a place to hide.'

'You think so?' Dagmar replied bitterly. 'I think they'll put their hands up and do what they're told like the bloody cowards they've all turned out to be. That's what we've all done so far, isn't it? Except my father.'

'And us, Dagmar, and us,' Paulus said gently. 'The point is we mustn't wait. We need to act now. Disappear now. Dagmar Fischer must die and you must become someone else. You need a new identity.'

'Who else? What identity?'

'Why, a respectable member of the Stengel household, of course. I'm a Waffen SS corporal, courtesy of my fine Aryan lobes, and I need a household befitting of my position. I need a wife . . .'

For the first time that morning Dagmar's face lit up.

'A wife! My God, what a funny way to propose!'

'Dagmar,' Paulus began.

'And what a wonderful idea. Of course, the wife of an SS man, what better cover could there possibly be? Well, it's not a very romantic setting to be saying it in, I'd always imagined Paris and the Eiffel Tower, but I accept.'

Silke stared at the table, drawing rings with her finger in the beer froth to cover her evident embarrassment.

Paulus took Dagmar's hand.

'Dagmar,' Paulus said, 'you know how much I would love it if that could be. You know how I feel about you.'

Now Silke turned away completely, staring at the barmaids rushing about in their Bavarian costumes with their trays full of brimming steins of beer.

'But you said,' Dagmar began.

'It's illegal for a German to marry a Jew, you know that.'

'But you said I was to have a new identity.'

'Yes, we hope, but not one that could possibly stand the scrutiny it would be under in a marriage contract. You know very well that any German, particularly an SS man's fiancée, must provide proof of racial lineage back to the eighteenth century before they can marry. Every church and civil record is checked.'

'Then what are you talking about?'

'Dagmar, a married German soldier is entitled to a home, and his wife is legally entitled to employ a maid.'

'A maid?'

'Yes. Tens of thousands of Czech and Polish girls are being stolen for domestic service in Berlin.'

Dagmar's mouth dropped open.

'I'm . . . to become a Polish maidservant?'

'To the world, yes!' Paulus said with a smile. 'It's a brilliant plan, though I say it myself. One set of forged papers plus a peasant's haircut and we're done. Nothing else, no records, no family, no past. No conversation even, since you don't speak German. You were snatched from your village three hundred miles away and forced into domestic service in Germany. These girls are getting off the train with nothing but a movement order. I've seen them; their lives begin at the station. Dagmar Fischer's life, on the other hand, is over. She left a suicide note like so many Jews are doing and threw herself in the river Spree, no body was ever found. Little Miss Czech or Pole, however, is working legally in Berlin for Corporal and Frau Stengel.'

'Frau Stengel,' Dagmar asked, 'and who's Frau . . .'

The penny dropped. She looked across the table at Silke.

'Who would have thought it?' Silke said. 'I'm marrying Paulus.'

'You –' Dagmar gasped – 'marrying Paulus.'

'Yes,' Silke said with a smile. 'Funny the way life goes, isn't it? When I was a little girl I can remember dreaming of marrying Otto Stengel and now I am. Of course, it's not the one I imagined, but we all have to make readjustments, don't we?' Silke raised her glass. 'Shall we do it properly and put an announcement in the *Völkischer Beobachter*, Pauly? Otto Stengel, betrothed to Silke, only daughter of Edeltraud Krause.'

Final Briefing

London, 1956

'You were right,' the man who looked like Peter Lorre said, 'Silke Stengel née Krause is an officer at the Ministry of State Security. Right at the heart of it, in fact. In Berlin-Lichtenburg on the Ruschestrasse.'

'Stasi headquarters.'

'Yes. Stasi headquarters. She has a service record dating back to shortly after the war. You say she used to be a friend?'

'Yes. A good friend.'

Stone closed his eyes.

Seeing once again the golden freckled shoulders. The thin strip of sunlight from the window moving across them over and over again as the train thundered towards Rotterdam.

Other memories flashed across his mind.

Silke at three or four years old in a flurry of tumbling wooden bricks, sitting first on Paulus's fort and then on his.

At the Saturday music lessons, singing and banging a tambourine.

Running, jumping. Dancing. Fighting.

Helping carry a body in a rolled-up rug into a lift.

Brown legs pumping at the pedals of her bicycle. Pretty legs, surprisingly pretty.

Lying beside him beneath the stars telling him for the first time about the *Rote Hilfe*.

Locking horns with Dagmar, the millionaire's daughter.

'She always was a Communist,' Stone said. 'I suppose she still is.'

'Well, then,' Bogart remarked with a gentle smile, 'here's your passport, all stamped and ready. Off you go.'

Mixed Marriage

Berlin, 1940

Neither the bride's nor the groom's parents attended Paulus and Silke's wedding.

Silke's father had of course last been seen disappearing from a boarding-house bedroom in 1920, and she and her mother had not spoken to each other since the mid-1930s.

Wolfgang was dead, which left only Frieda.

She stayed away as a matter of decorum. It would not have done for an SS corporal to have a race enemy attend his wedding.

Paulus had known that he must move quickly to get his domestic arrangements in order. Germany may have been victorious in the east but the nation was still at war with Britain and France and there was little doubt that a reckoning would not be long in coming in the west. As a soldier in the Waffen SS, Paulus would have to fight and might very well be killed, so there was no time to lose.

He and Silke had settled on a furnished apartment in his mother's childhood district of Moabit. Neither he nor Silke were known there, and it was also a goodish distance from the leafy suburb of Charlottenburg in which Dagmar had grown up.

As a single man and serving soldier it would have been out of the question for Paulus to have enjoyed the luxury of a foreign maid, so before Dagmar could be hidden away in her new home with her new identity, Paulus must first marry Silke according to their plan.

On the morning of the wedding, Silke and Paulus met at the apartment which from that day on they were to share.

'You look very nice, Silks,' Paulus said.

She was wearing a pale green two-piece suit and a cream-coloured hat with a feather in it. Her thick blonde hair had been set specially for the occasion, and, rarely for her, she was wearing lipstick.

She did indeed look nice.

'Thanks,' Silke replied. 'I'm trying to look stern and noble but also feminine and compliant. A credit to the Führer.'

'You got it bang on. Goebbels could put you on a poster.'

Silke smiled and looked Paulus up and down.

'I won't say you look *nice*,' she said. 'Not with that awful arm-band. But handsome. Very handsome. They do good uniforms, the Nazis, you have to give them that. I saw some photographs of British Tommies in a *Signal* magazine somebody left on the *U-Bahn* and they looked like plumbers in overalls.'

'Come on,' Paulus said, 'take a look at the apartment of the soon-to-be Frau Stengel.'

He took Silke's arm and guided her around the flat.

'I thought this could be your bedroom,' he said. 'I mean, if that's all right. Then Dagmar and I could take this one. It's up to you, of course. I mean, you can choose.'

'I'm fine, whatever you think,' Silke said briskly. 'I imagine I'll be out quite a lot anyway.'

They paused together outside the room Paulus had suggested for himself and Dagmar.

'Funny how things turn out, isn't it?' Paulus said.

'Do you think,' Silke began, and then stopped.

'Do I think what?'

'Nothing. It's not important.'

'I know what you were going to ask,' he said. 'Do I think Dagmar would have ended up wanting to marry me if there'd never been any Nazis? If she was still a Ku'damm princess and me the son of a trumpeter?'

'And a doctor.'

'All right, I have a bit more class on my mother's side, but I'm right, aren't I?'

Silke sat down in one of the easy chairs in the living room, giving a little bounce, testing it for comfort.

'Well, all right. If you like,' she said. 'I have wondered.'

Paulus sat down in the chair opposite, grimacing slightly as he detected a jutting spring in the upholstery.

'Well, she probably wouldn't, I imagine. I mean, it's impossible to know what might have happened in our lives if Germany had been a normal country, but I expect Dagmar would have gone to a Swiss finishing school and then married a multi-millionaire.'

'Yes, I think so too,' Silke admitted.

'But Germany's not a normal country. It's a nut house. Hitler won and so here we are. Making the best of it. As is Dagmar. I don't blame her for that. Come and look at the kitchen.'

They got up and went through into a decent-sized room with a modern gas stove. Silke opened the cupboards, running her finger along the shelves. A year of compulsory, unpaid domestic service had made her very aware of dust.

'And I do admit,' Paulus went on, 'that I like to think she *does* love me, however that love might have come about. She certainly *says* she does. Life happened, didn't it? She never did get to go to finishing school, and that's that.'

'And you've got the very thing you've wanted since you were twelve years old. So the really funny thing is, if it wasn't for Hitler, you wouldn't have got it. You owe Hitler for Dagmar.'

'I know,' Paulus conceded. 'I think that's what they call irony.'

Silke leant against the fitted drawer unit, her feet crossed on the shiny yellow linoleum.

'I was in love with Otto, you know,' she said.

Paulus had been checking a dud light bulb. He turned and looked at her.

'Were you?' he said rather weakly.

'Don't tell me you didn't suspect. Otto may have been pretty blind to a woman's emotions, but I always credited you with subtler instincts.'

Paulus looked a little embarrassed. 'I suppose I have wondered. Mum certainly thought you were.'

'And now he's gone,' Silke said. 'You persuaded him to switch identities with you.'

'Silks,' Paulus said very seriously, 'I didn't come up with my plan so I could steal Dagmar and cheat you of Otto. I came up with it to save her life.'

'The life of the person you happen to be in love with.'

'Are you blaming me, Silke? Are you angry? I really thought you understood.'

Silke looked away.

'I do, Pauly. Actually I do. I think you did have to do what you've done . . . I just wanted you to know, that's all. I was a bit fed up of suffering in silence.'

'Did you ever tell Ottsy?' Paulus asked.

'Sort of. In a way. On the train, but it was no good. He loves Dagmar. Just like you. So I was never in with any sort of chance really. *Bugger* that bitch!' But she said it with a laugh. 'Don't worry, I'll play my part, Pauly. I'm a Communist. I believe in helping my fellow man – and woman.'

Paulus smiled, and then Silke gave him a hug.

'It's a nice flat, isn't it?' Silke said. 'We're lucky.'

'I suppose so.'

'Do you think it was stolen from Jews? Like your grandparents' apartment was?'

'I don't know. I asked, but the agency said they didn't discuss those things.'

They were silent once more. Wondering if weeks before there had been children forced with clubs and rifle butts from the very room in which they were standing.

'I saw a lot of that in Poland, you know. Forced evictions,' Paulus said. 'It was just dreadful. Thousands of Polish families, not just Jews either, torn out of their homes in an instant. The radio left on, food still on the cooker, it was that brutal.'

'Come on,' Silke said. 'We don't want to be late for our wedding, do we?'

Paulus put Silke's bags in her room and took up his brand new SS forage cap from the little table in the hallway.

'Silke,' he said hesitantly, 'it's an amazing thing you're doing, you know. A wonderful generous thing you're doing for Dagmar.'

'I'm not doing it for Dagmar, you silly arse!' Silke laughed. 'I'm doing it for you. And for Otto. For the Stengel twins! Both of you. Because *you* want to do it for her. Because being men you both fell in love with the prettiest girl you knew, but she's a Jew so now we'll all have to spend the war looking after her.'

'And what about you?' Paulus asked. 'It means an empty sort of life for you. Married but not married. I mean, you can't build a life for yourself.'

'Bit late to try and talk me out of it now.'

'I'm not, it's just . . .'

'Look, SS *Sturmmann* Stengel,' Silke said, putting aside the little posy of primroses she was carrying and taking Paulus's hands, 'I *want* to do this. For a number of reasons. And it isn't *just* the Saturday Club or the fact that you and Otto have always meant everything to me. This is a good life, actually. It means I can leave compulsory domestic service, for a start, which believe me is no small thing. And marriage to a serving man, a serving SS man, brings lots of perks too. I'll eat well, I'll sleep comfortably. And most important of all, this isn't just good cover for Dagmar, you know. It's good cover for *me*.'

Paulus knew what she meant and he wasn't sure he liked it.

'You mean as a Communist?'

'Absolutely.'

'I thought your lot were Hitler's friends now,' Paulus said.

A spasm of sadness passed across Silke's features.

The Nazi-Soviet pact of 1939 had devastated what little remained of the underground German Communist movement.

'Stalin took a tactical decision,' Silke said defensively. 'He's buying time, I'm sure of it. One day there will be resistance again, and when there is, I want to be a part of it.'

Paulus didn't reply. There was nothing he could say. He was using her, he could scarcely object that she wanted to use him. They were all dependent on each other.

They left the apartment and took a taxi together to the Moabit town hall on the Tiergarten.

'We mustn't keep Herr Richter waiting.'

'Booking him must have taken some nerve,' Silke said, whistling through her teeth.

'Yeah. A bit,' Paulus conceded.

A week previously Paulus had put on his new Waffen SS uniform, marched into the local Gestapo station and asked to see the senior officer present.

Then, with great audacity, he had requested the Gestapo chief, whom he had never before met, to officiate at his wedding.

'I am the racially pure, adopted child of Jews, sir,' he said, 'hence I have no family and am all alone. My life and my marriage belong to the Führer. I wish to have the most authoritative witness to that fact. Therefore I am respectfully asking you to bear witness at my wedding.'

It was a brave and brilliant idea, which tied the local Gestapo into his name and his address, and indeed his life. Making the chief personally bonded to them.

As always, Paulus's tactical planning was faultless.

As Richter stood beneath the portrait of the Führer solemnly intoning the various oaths to State and Leader that a Nazi wedding required, he could not in his wildest dreams have imagined the truth. That the fine and upstanding young soldier standing before him and making those oaths would in a few short hours be grinding a glass beneath his boot in the presence of his mother and grandparents as he took part in a second marriage that day. This time to the woman he loved, who, like him, was a Jew.

Old Friends

Berlin, 1956

Looking out of the window of his Deutsche Lufthansa flight, Otto was struck by the fact that viewed from the air the layout of Heathrow formed an almost perfect Star of David.

He wondered if that was ironic. The British were supposed to be famous for their irony but he had never met a single one who could give him a clear definition of the word. Most of them seemed to think it just meant bad luck.

Otto decided that it was ironic. That shape, which had meant absolutely nothing to him until he was thirteen years old, and which thereafter had come to mean violence, abuse and death, was the last thing of Britain he saw as his plane disappeared into the clouds.

On his way back to Berlin. Where they had no doubt stitched that very same shape to the coats of his mother and his aged grandparents in order to mark them down for murder.

The stern-looking male attendant interrupted his reverie, handing out the complex and lengthy landing forms for the German Democratic Republic.

East Germany.

Otto folded down the little table on the back of the seat in front of him and took out his passport. Pausing for a moment to stare at it. He always paused for thought when holding his passport.

Such a precious document. So stately and imposing with its stiff, royal blue jacket. The copperplate text on the inside cover archaically stern and censorious. 'Her Britannic Majesty requests and requires . . .' It sounded good even with the Suez debacle only just concluded. Even with every editorial in the land screaming that Her Britannic Majesty was not in any position to request and require anything from anybody unless the Americans said she could.

Lots of people said Britain was sunk.

But those people were idiots, as far as Otto was concerned. Being British still meant an immeasurable amount. You just had to be born somewhere else to appreciate it.

Otto finished his forms. The first German document he had filled in for seventeen years, and the first he had ever seen which did not require him to state whether he was Jewish. He put away his passport and took a pull of scotch from his hip flask. He had not expected the airline to offer anything as bourgeois as an in-flight drink and so had come prepared.

He lit up a Lucky Strike, took another pull of whisky and tried to relax.

The pilot's voice came over the tannoy announcing that they had crossed the Channel and were flying over Holland.

Otto found himself smiling.

Holland. He had only been there once, passing through on a train. But he had lost his virginity there at a hundred kilometres an hour, so he always felt benevolent about the place.

He'd been with the girl whom he must shortly confront.

What would she look like now? he wondered.

Silke Krause.

Would her hair and skin still be golden? Or had a decade of service to the puppet masters in the Kremlin turned her pale and grey? She was only thirty-five of course, a year younger than him, but Otto had met Stasi officers before, masquerading as travel guides for East German delegations to Britain. Had Silke become like them, grim and unsmiling, dull hair pulled back into a starchy bun?

He would find out soon enough.

They landed at Berlin Schönefeld airport and were herded

together into the forbidding customs and immigration hall. Otto found himself thinking that Billie would approve of the building. Plenty of concrete. Funny to be in Germany, thinking of Billie, having spent seventeen years in Britain thinking of Dagmar.

Funny to be in Germany at all.

It was like a dream. To be surrounded by German voices again after so long. He was back. Back in Berlin. Yet feeling further from home than ever.

He wasn't in the hall long. If anything confirmed his assumption that he was the subject of a Ministry of Security sting, it was the speed with which he was ushered through the arrival formalities. His name was obviously recognized at the first barrier and he was fast-tracked from that point on. While his fellow passengers resigned themselves to hours of queues and questioning, Otto was nodded and stamped past desk after desk.

Of course, while the machinery of the state might be oiled by hidden forces, nothing could increase the speed of the physical machinery of the airport, nor the complexity of the bureaucracy under which it was run. Therefore having been spat out into the luggage hall in record time, Otto now found himself having to watch as most of the people who had been on the plane with him caught up while he waited for his bag.

It arrived at last, not on a moving belt as was now common in Western airports, but in a densely packed cage pulled by a tractor, which the passengers had to unload themselves, struggling to find their own under the weight of other people's.

Finally Otto spotted his old battered case being hurled to one side by a sweating traveller, and he was able to make his way into the arrivals hall. It was the same little case he had brought with him out of Germany seventeen years before. It was still in good condition; in the army he had used a kit bag, and he had not travelled since.

That case had stood on the floor of the first-class compartment when he and Silke had made love on her bunk. Otto wondered if she would recognize it.

He was in a hurry now, suddenly anxious to get the meeting

over with. The whisky buzz he had given himself on the plane was wearing off and he had decided it would not be sensible to give himself another.

Searching in his pocket for the little leather notebook in which he had written the address she had given in her letter, Otto scurried past the final line of customs officers unchallenged and began looking about for a sign to the taxi rank.

Perhaps that was why he didn't see her.

He was looking up. At the signs.

He hadn't expected her to meet him.

'Ottsy.'

He heard the voice and in those two syllables he knew.

Stopping dead, he stared about himself.

Shocked. Confused. Looking from one grey dowdy figure to another. Searching the monotone collage of depressed humanity. Cheap threadbare clothes. Sallow skin. A smile or two here and there but only brave ones. Weary ones.

'Ottsy, I'm here. I'm over here.'

That voice. That same old voice. Leaping across seventeen long years.

Turning around, he saw her.

And yet he didn't.

The woman he saw was a replica. The Soviet version of the one who owned the voice. As if they'd tried to make one like her but couldn't. Just like their awful gutless cars and leaking, lumpy refrigerators. Recognizable as of the same species as their glamorous, stylish, exciting American and European counterparts, but so obviously cheap, tawdry imitations.

The skin didn't glow. The hair didn't shine. The lips were still full but showed the pinched, pursed lines of a forty-a-day habit.

The eyes were the same, though. Big, deep and dark.

And sad. That hadn't changed either. Those eyes that had been sad since the morning of 1 April 1933.

'Dagmar?' Otto heard himself saying. 'Is that you?'

She flinched very slightly. Perhaps she knew what had flashed across his mind. Perhaps she thought the same thing every day herself, in her chicken coop Stalin-approved apartment, exchanging tired, worn-out glances with her mirror while she waited to see if the hot water would work or not.

'Yes, Ottsy,' she said. 'Of course it's me.'

She was standing perhaps three metres from him. People bustled between them. He stepped towards her, directly into somebody's path.

'*Entschuldigen Sie mich, bitte*,' he heard himself saying in that once familiar tongue, but the person merely grunted and was gone.

They were less than two metres apart now, but having been stopped once he did not seem to know how to cover the final distance.

'You didn't die?' he almost croaked. His mouth suddenly dry and his tongue sticky. Speaking in English again out of habit, in a daze, only half-conscious of speaking at all.

'No,' she replied in English, 'I didn't die.'

Then a beat. The tiniest of pauses. A flicker of what looked very like suspicion flashed across her face.

'But you knew that, Otto,' she said, 'you replied to my letter.'

'Yes . . . yes, of course,' he stammered.

So his first instinct had been right after all. She was alive! Once more she was breathing the very same air as him. Seventeen years of pain, longing and regret were suddenly and shockingly at an end.

He had been so sure she was dead. So sure it would be Silke.

Dagmar stepped towards him, deftly avoiding the scurrying people that divided them. With each step appearing more familiar to him. Her movements still graceful as of old, she even managed to wear her dull and threadbare suit with a flash of style.

'Won't you hug me, Ottsy?' she said, standing before him. 'Or don't you care to any more?' And then a smile, *her* smile. The lips more lined and the skin around them thinner but Dagmar's smile nonetheless and enchanting still. 'Have I grown too ugly for a kiss?'

'You Dagmar, ugly?' he whispered. 'Never.'

Stepping forward once again, he enfolded her in his arms.

And in the moment it took him to take hold of her, she was transformed. His Dagmar once more, the loveliest girl in Berlin, just as she had always been. He had only to blow away the dust of seventeen years and there she would be again. Dagmar Fischer. Princess. The woman who had owned his heart since he was a boy.

The stuff of dreams. Of fairy tales.

Tightly they held each other. As if fearful that hidden hands were threatening to tear them apart.

Otto wondered if he was going to faint, a sensation he had never experienced before. He felt levitated. Floating. Outside and above himself, watching the scene play out below. It was heady and intoxicating. He felt drunk.

She was *in his arms once more.*

Her hair again upon his face.

Her ear close to his lips.

Just *exactly* as it had been in the very moments when he had last seen her. At the station, when he went away. Then, as now, there were people all around, travellers hurrying back and forth, German voices on the tannoys announcing arrivals and departures. A coffee store and vending machines. It was as if the two of them had stood still while time had moved on. Frozen in each other's arms from 1939 to 1956 while the world hustled and bustled around them. The greatest war ever fought had come and gone. Empires had fallen and others had risen up. The single most terrible crime in all history had been perpetrated and now the places of those murders had become museums. Scientists were planning to place objects in orbit and swing bands were giving way to young men with greased hair and guitars.

And through all that and more, Otto Stengel had held Dagmar Fischer close in his heart. And now once more he held her in his arms. Time had indeed stood still.

And he had been so *certain* that she was dead.

Further English Conversation

Berlin, 1940

All day long Frieda had been seeing patients in the little 'surgery' she now conducted from a desk she had set up in her own bedroom. The tiny guest room she had previously used for this purpose was now occupied by Herr and Frau Katz the chemists and their grown-up daughter. The twins' old room had become home to her parents. There was a middle-aged spinster lady named Bissinger sleeping on the couch in the living room, and a widower called Minkovsky on cushions on the floor.

The problem of accommodation for Jews was becoming more acute each day, the government having introduced an ordinance as cruel as it was vague. It was to be left up to local residents themselves to decide how long they were prepared to 'tolerate' Jews in their midst. This meant that Jews could be turfed out of their homes on a whim, either through sheer cruelty or more often simply because a party official wanted to steal their home.

Frieda was even worried for her own apartment. The fact that it was now so full, coupled with the constant stream of patients coming to her door, had begun to cause tension with her neighbours. Up until now, relations had been good; the Stengels had, after all, lived there for twenty years and at some point Frieda had done almost everybody in the building a favour. Wolfgang used to play music at their children's birthday parties.

Now, however, tension was growing. There were whisperings that the Stengel place had turned into a Jewish ghetto. There were also complaints about the risk of infection caused by the flow of sick people making their way up the building. Most of all people resented the lift being used by so many outsiders. For months there had been angry mutterings about how the tiny lift always seemed to be on its way up to the sixth floor, and that when one did manage to summon it, it was unpleasant to share with sick, scared and pitiable Jews.

Eventually some people on a floor below Frieda's had put up a sign saying that the lift was for the use of residents only. This, however, was an unsatisfactory solution, since of course other tenants had guests whom they wished to be able to visit them without using the stairs. The next sign put up said simply 'No Jews', but again this did not work because Frieda was a legal tenant and continued to contribute her share of the communal running costs. Eventually it was decided that the sign should say that no Jews excepting *current* tenants were to use the lift.

Frieda found the use of the word 'current' ominous.

So far the situation had been left at that but nobody was satisfied with it. The sight of the elderly, the infirm and in particular of sick, undernourished children struggling up six flights of stairs was upsetting to the other tenants and Frieda knew that the next stage would be that she would be told her patients could no longer attend her surgery. She was currently trying to stave off this eventuality by making house calls wherever possible. This necessitated her running all over Friedrichshain, which was of course absolutely exhausting.

Frieda had arrived home after completing another gruelling day, hoping perhaps to have a moment when she could forget her troubles. A quiet bath even. Unfortunately she had forgotten that her English conversation group was meeting that evening and despite all the group rules to the contrary, trouble was all any of them seemed able to discuss.

The problem of food was becoming as serious as shelter. With the coming of war, rationing had begun in real earnest.

'And of course we get so many fewer coupons than anybody else,' Frau Leibovitz almost wailed. 'It's so *dastardly* to issue us with scarcely enough food to live and yet just enough not to die. We are all withering and wasting away.'

'Some people are saying that they intend to shoot us in the end,' Herr Tauber said. 'Ha! Shoot what? We're too thin to make a decent target.'

Frieda's father made his comment in German but Frieda let it go. Her parents were only a part of the group anyway because it took place in what was now their home, and besides which the incentive to improve people's English was now much diminished. With Germany having conquered most of Europe there was no longer any chance of emigrating anyway.

'Can you believe they won't let us in the air-raid shelters?' Frau Leibovitz complained. 'Hoping the English will do their dirty work for them, I suppose.'

'The English are finished,' her husband said. 'They'll get their necks wrung like a chicken, just like the French said.'

Frieda sipped at her acorn coffee, struck as ever by the strangeness of it all.

England. Otto was there! Calling himself Paulus.

And Paulus was in France, calling himself Otto.

In the Waffen SS.

'The Nazis will be across the Channel in a month,' Herr Leibovitz went on. 'The British will be swatted just like the Czechs, the Poles, the Norwegians, the Belgians and the French.'

'All right. All right!' Herr Tauber snapped. 'We know who he's damn well conquered, we don't need chapter and verse.'

'He's Satan,' Herr Katz said. 'He is, I tell you. He's the devil himself, or his henchman. How else can you credit it? Four years, Herr Tauber, that's how long you, me and the whole of the Kaiser's army were stuck in the middle of France. Stuck, I tell you! Couldn't move. Up to our backsides in mud. This man sweeps through in a fortnight. It's uncanny, that's what it is. He's supernatural.'

Herr Tauber didn't reply.

Perhaps Katz was right. The stunning success of Hitler's armies was without parallel in all history. Nobody had ever conquered Europe so quickly, or controlled so much of it. Not Hannibal, nor Caesar, nor Napoleon. The whole of the western continent was either occupied or allied to the Third Reich.

'That bastard Mussolini certainly made sure he was on the winning side,' Katz said. 'So now the Jews of Italy are going to get what we've been getting. And the newspapers have Hitler in the Pyrenees talking to Franco. Once he crushes the Brits his fortress will be complete.'

'Can we *please* all just *shut the hell up* about Hitler!' Frieda almost shouted.

She felt like screaming. After the day she had had and all the things on her mind. Hitler crushing the Brits? That would be Paulus. Silke kept her informed. Paulus was in France. He had been in the army that surrounded Dunkirk. He was part of the force being assembled in France for what the newspapers said would be the invasion of Britain. He had been issued with a cork life-jacket for the crossing. The papers were saying it remained only for the Luftwaffe to gain control of the skies over the Channel and that would be it for Churchill and his gang.

Paulus might be in Britain in a month.

Not as a refugee student as she had planned these last two years, but as a *German soldier*.

And Otto? Where was he? Was he in khaki? A British Tommy? Those same soldiers of whom her father had spoken with such grudging respect when she was in her teens. It seemed likely. Otto had been in the United Kingdom for nearly a year and a half now and there could be no doubt that the island nation was preparing to fight it out.

All these thoughts had been in her mind as she made her outburst. Now she looked around at the surprised faces. Frieda never lost her temper. She could see that they were shocked, upset, in fact. They relied on her strength.

'I'm sorry,' she said, 'that was rude. It's just that sometimes I get a little tired.'

She glanced across the room towards the piano.

To the piano stool.

It was involuntary. She still found herself doing it. Even now, three years on.

He wasn't there, of course. The Schmulewitzes were squeezed on to his little seat.

God, how she missed Wolfgang. The apartment was more crowded than it had ever been but she was so wretchedly alone. Most of the time she was too busy to think about it, but at home, surrounded by tired, terrified old Jews, it hit her hard. Her whole family was gone. Paulus. Otto.

And Wolfgang.

Her beloved partner and soulmate, lost beneath the cold dark waters of the Spree.

'We must try to be practical,' Frieda continued, as always taking refuge in her doctor's persona. Calm, efficient. Above all active. 'I've been thinking about this for some time. These restrictions are making life very hard but if we organize ourselves they can be tolerated. The evening curfew and the restricted shopping hours certainly present an organizational challenge—'

'Only between four and five p.m.' Herr Katz spluttered. 'Why? Why are we only to be allowed in shops for an hour each day? What possible purpose can it serve?'

'So that *decent Germans* may know when to avoid our infection, of course,' Herr Tauber growled.

'Well, with the few coupons they allow us and the little money they've left us,' Frau Katz chipped in, 'an hour is about fifty-nine minutes more than we need to shop anyway!'

'Please!' Frieda snapped once again, struggling to remain placid. 'We've moaned enough! I was trying to suggest that we start to organize ourselves better.'

'Organize, Frau Stengel?' Frau Katz enquired. 'What is there to organize?'

'What is there to organize, Frau Katz?' Frieda was angry. 'There is *everything* to organize. Most of our young people are gone now but we're all still able-bodied and can help those who aren't. The old, the sick, the little children and the mothers with young babies. How is a mother with small children and a husband stolen to the camps to get to the bread shop between four and five if the kids are sick? She can't but *we* can. *You* can. The curfew is causing some old people never to leave their homes; we need to find them and take them out. If only for a little walk – the streets are still free to us.'

'Not all of them,' Herr Leibovitz interjected.

'How many do you need for a stroll? You've only got two feet, haven't you! We need to make a list of every vulnerable person we know. And who *they* know. We need to set up some kind of telephone tree whereby everybody has a number they can call if they need help, even just for the shopping or a bit of company or . . .'

Then they heard the lift.

The creaking and the clanking as it settled to a halt on their floor.

All froze. It was probably only a late caller. A sick mother looking for Doctor Stengel, too tired to obey the sign in the lift. Or perhaps the gentleman friend of Fräulein Belzfreund.

But a knock at the door was always a cause for fear these days.

Later Frieda wondered at the coincidence that they came just then. Just as she had mentioned a telephone tree. It was almost as if they'd been listening.

Perhaps they really were the devil.

'It must be a late patient,' Frieda said. 'I've *told* them not to use the lift.'

But the sound of stamping boots quickly made it clear that this was no patient. It was a visit from *them*.

The whole room froze in fear. Even old Herr Tauber looked scared, until he realized this himself and settled his features in a mask of defiance.

There was a loud banging on the door. The usual thunderous clenched-fist assault.

Frieda took a deep breath and went to answer it. Before she had been able to reach the door the banging began again. When the Nazi authorities knocked on a Jew's door they expected instant access. Another moment and they would have kicked it down.

There were just two of them. A policeman and an SS trooper.

'Frau Stengel, formerly *Frau Doktor* Stengel?' the policeman demanded.

'Yes,' Frieda replied. 'How can we help you?'

'Your telephone,' he said.

'My telephone?' Frieda asked. 'What about it?'

'Hand it over,' the policeman said. 'As of this month, July

1940, by order of the Reich Government, Jews are no longer to be allowed to own telephones. All telephones owned by Jews are to be surrendered immediately!'

Frieda wondered if she had turned pale. It certainly felt as if she had. She thought of all the calls she made each day. Working old contacts, begging for drugs, bandages, needles from wherever she could scrounge them. The hours she spent trying to find accommodation for distressed families who had been arbitrarily thrown out on to the streets. Even that day she had put out a dozen feelers and was waiting on return calls that might mean life or death for patients in her care.

Now those calls would never come.

Frieda had only that very moment been explaining how survival could only lie in cooperation. In organization.

Clearly the Nazis understood that too.

Silently, she nodded to the little occasional table by the wall on which her precious telephone stood.

Without a word the SS man went and picked it up, tearing the lead from the wall.

The policeman scribbled his signature on a pad of printed forms, tore the top one off and handed it to Frieda.

'What's this?' she asked.

'Your receipt,' the policeman replied.

Frieda turned to the trooper, who was standing holding her stolen telephone. She looked at him intensely.

'It's Renke, isn't it? Thomas Renke.'

The trooper did not reply but it was clear from his eyes that Frieda was right.

'Your mother brought you to my surgery many times when you were young. Whooping cough, roseola, rubella, measles. Goodness, you had them all. You seem to have turned out well in the end though. Please remember me to Frau Renke.'

The black-clad figure remained silent.

'Come,' said the policeman, and the two of them left, SS Trooper Renke taking Frieda's telephone with them.

Frieda sunk into a chair.

'Drip drip drip,' she said.

'What's that, my dear?' her father asked, going over and putting a hand on her shoulder.

'It's how they've done it, Dad,' she said, wiping her eyes. 'Not all at once but one little torture at a time. Ban this, take that. For years even you were sure they would not go so far. But one drip at a time they've gone further and further. Further than we ever dreamt they would. Now we are not even to be allowed to communicate with each other. How far will they go? I wonder. Where will this end?'

Recognized

Calais, 1940

Paulus had been expecting it.

Every day since he had enlisted he had been on his guard. Certainly he was buried deep, the Nazi military machine was vast, there were millions of Germans now in uniform, and of course that uniform was the very last one anyone might expect the man they had known as Paulus Stengel to be wearing. Nonetheless, amongst those millions were some who would know him, whatever he wore. And who knew what he really was.

Paulus had been alert to such an encounter since the first day he had swapped identities with his brother, and now that moment had arrived.

He was sitting in a tiny country bistro about five kilometres from Calais, having ridden there on a motorcycle on an evening pass out. He had been in the process of writing a letter to Dagmar when he became aware that he was being observed.

No one called out his name or tried to speak to him but something told him there were eyes upon him. That he was being discussed. Perhaps it was a slight change in the tone of the murmuring that emanated from the only other occupied table in the room. Or else simply that inexplicable thing that people call the sixth sense.

Whatever it was, Paulus knew.

He had not particularly noticed the men coming in and taking their table. He had been too focused on trying to compose his letter. A letter in which he was struggling to give some hint to the woman he loved of the nightmare of being a soldier in Hitler's armies.

The nightmare of being a member of the Waffen SS. A soldier in the very regiment that bore the Führer's name: the division *Leibstandarte Adolf Hitler*.

The long-awaited military storm in the west had broken on 10 May when the German war machine smashed the Dutch border, swatting aside the feeble defences in an hour. So fast was their progress that at first it had seemed to Paulus as if he might even get away without personally shooting at the enemy.

The *Leibstandarte Adolf Hitler* reached Rotterdam in two days and The Hague in four, after which the Dutch surrendered and another country and its Jews fell into Nazi clutches. Without pausing for breath, Paulus's division had then swung on into France.

Paulus confessed in his letter that he had actually found the advance exciting. It was a heady experience to storm across sun-drenched countryside in pursuit of a retreating foe.

They had chased the British all the way to Dunkirk and would, in Paulus's opinion, have captured the whole of the expeditionary force had they been allowed to proceed. This was also the opinion of every soldier in his division, although it was one that had to be expressed carefully as the inevitable conclusion was that the greatest warlord in all history had made a stupid mistake.

It was in the approaches to Dunkirk that Paulus had witnessed an event about which he could not write but which had been on his mind ever since it occurred. The *Leibstandarte* had just taken the town of Wormhout, a mere ten miles from the beaches of

Dunkirk. A lot of prisoners had been captured and Paulus had been present when some men from the 1st Division had rounded up a group of about a hundred Tommies and herded them into a barn. Then instead of making them prisoners of war, as they were required to do under the Geneva Convention, they had thrown grenades into the flimsy structure. The few shattered British who managed to crawl out of the carnage were shot and bayoneted on the ground.

It was this incident that Paulus really wanted to put down in his letter to Dagmar, along with his terrible fears that one day he himself would be called upon to take part in such an outrage. He was prepared to fight for Germany, fate had put him in an impossible position on that score and he felt he had no choice. But he knew that he could not commit cold-blooded murder.

It was while he considered how he might hint at these tortured thoughts in his letter without alerting the censor that he had become aware he was being observed.

They were Wehrmacht. He could see their boots beneath the table opposite without raising his head from the page. Big hob-nailed jackboots, dusty and cracked. That made them army; no trooper in the Waffen SS *Leibstandarte* would have gone out on furlough without first shining his boots.

Paulus resisted the urge to look up. So far he judged they had not had clear sight of him. He knew his head had been partially bowed over the letter he was writing since they had entered the bar.

The exit to the bar, however, lay beyond the table on which the soldiers were sitting, so he could not get out without whoever it was getting a considerably better look at him than the one they were currently enjoying. Paulus therefore had two choices. He could either keep his head bowed and hope they would shrug their suspicions off and leave. Or he could brazen it out and leave at once, walking straight past them.

Paulus counted three sets of boots beneath the table. Not good odds.

The whispering continued.

The feet began to fidget.

It was clear to Paulus that if he waited for them to make a move he would be massively disadvantaged. He needed to take the initiative and time had almost run out. The chair behind one of the sets of boots was being pushed back. One of them had decided to act. To come across and challenge him. Paulus had seconds left to take control. If he waited a moment longer one of three would be in his face with the other two behind.

In a single and sudden movement, Paulus gathered up his letter, slammed some currency on the table and got to his feet. Heading straight for the door he flicked his eyes once to look at the men he feared.

One glance was enough.

The years fell away.

It was Emil Braas. The boy who had tried to turn the old soccer team against Paulus and Otto in the changing hut on their last day with the youth club.

'*Jude! Jude!*' they had chanted to the banging of a stick on a dustbin lid.

Emil Braas, who had been so jealous of them and had tried to take his revenge within a week of Hitler becoming Chancellor. Paulus had thwarted Emil then with a wave of his prick. Turned the crowd round and made the attacker look a fool. Such a trick wouldn't work again. Paulus had occasionally seen Emil Braas around Friedrichshain during the long years of 1930s, and foreskins or not, everybody knew the Stengel boys were Jews.

And just as in that instant Paulus recognized Emil Braas, he was quite certain that Emil Braas recognized him. Both of course had changed a great deal: no longer fresh-faced boys but battle-hardened men. The eyes, however, didn't lie.

The game was up.

Certainly Braas was confused. How could he not be? He knew that Paulus Stengel was a Jew. So the fact that his old enemy had turned up in a bistro in occupied France wearing a German military uniform with the dual lightning flash insignia of the SS on it was going to be a shock. But confused or not, Emil Braas knew him.

Although seriously outnumbered, Paulus calculated that for the next few seconds at least he still had the initiative. Braas was confused. He was not. That was a significant advantage if used decisively and Paulus, although never rash, was always decisive.

'Hello, Emil,' he said with a broad smile. 'What's the matter? Never seen a Jewish SS man before?'

And with that he was out of the door.

Paulus knew that he would have to kill Braas and also the men he was with. What was more he must do it at once before they had the chance to spread their suspicions further or think of calling the military police.

Outside he was relieved to see the dusty road was almost empty. He had chosen to visit that particular bar because of its solitude and isolation, and there were no other Wehrmacht personnel anywhere to be seen. Just an old peasant with a few goats a little further up the dusty track.

Paulus reached a hand into his knapsack.

Not being an officer, his usual weapon was a rifle, but he had left that back at barracks. The French countryside was completely subdued; their leader Marshal Pétain had called for cooperation with Hitler and so German military personnel did not carry their weapons when off duty. However, like many of his comrades, Paulus had picked up a souvenir during the recent fighting. A British officer's Enfield revolver. Paulus always kept it about him, well oiled and fully loaded for just such an emergency as this.

Pulling it from his bag he ran a few metres up the track and spun around just as the three men crowded through the front door of the tiny bistro in pursuit.

Had the pistol jammed even for an instant Paulus would have been overcome, but British engineering did not let him down. He opened fire immediately, taking the three soldiers absolutely by surprise. The gun was a double-action piece requiring re-cocking for each shot, but Paulus had been well trained in the use of small arms. His left hand flew over the trigger hammer after each shot, just like in a scene from an American western. The pistol blazed and his enemies were left with no time to do more than raise their hands in horror as one after another they took a bullet in the chest and fell. A further three bullets, one fired into each of their heads as they lay twitching in the dust, emptied the chamber and ensured that Paulus's secret was safe.

Paulus wiped the handle of the gun on his shirt tail, dropped it amongst the dead, mounted his motorcycle and rode off.

The People's Park

Berlin, 1956

Otto and Dagmar left the arrivals hall together and went to the car park where Dagmar showed him to an IFA F9 motorcar, a powerful, well-built machine which, although somewhat rusted and in need of attention, certainly indicated that whatever it was Dagmar did for a living, she enjoyed privileges that the vast majority of GDR citizens did not.

As they got in she raised her finger momentarily to her lips, clearly fearful that her car was bugged. The men at MI6 had warned Otto that he should presume all conversations in East Berlin would be overheard.

Otto was actually glad of the chance of a moment to think. It was all so very surprising.

And so very wonderful.

Dagmar was alive and surely that meant her letter was genuine. She had reached out to him to help her finally effect that escape which had been denied to her and her family on the boat train platform in 1933 and throughout the long years since.

Was he to be allowed the chance to be her Moses after all?

Dagmar made small talk as the city passed by the windows.

This was Berlin, Otto's home town. And yet he scarcely recognized it. Almost all of the buildings he had known had been reduced to rubble by Allied bombing, and in this eastern sector much of the damage remained unrepaired. Those buildings that had been erected were dull and featureless concrete apartment blocks. Although it occurred to Otto that they were not so very much uglier than those currently being thrown up all over London.

They drove quickly. There was not a great deal of other traffic apart from numerous bicycles, and soon they came upon a very familiar sight.

'I think you remember this park,' Dagmar remarked, and of course he did, having been there only recently in his dreams. It was the Volkspark, the very place in which he and his brother had chased Dagmar for a kiss amongst the fairy-tale characters of the Märchenbrunnen.

'It survived the war, you know,' Dagmar said.

'Yes, I heard that,' Otto replied. 'I was glad.'

Dagmar found a place to park her car. 'Come on,' she said. 'Let's go for a walk. I won't run away this time, I promise.'

They entered the park together.

'Can we talk now?' Otto asked after a few steps.

'Yes,' she replied, 'we can talk.'

Where to begin? What to say? There was so much to ask. A lifetime of questions.

But none so urgent as the present one.

'Why am I here?' he asked.

Perhaps she wasn't expecting it. It seemed to take her aback for a moment.

'I wanted to see you, Ottsy,' she replied.

Ottsy. How he loved to hear her use that name. It made him feel fifteen again.

'You wanted to see me,' he repeated eagerly, then, lowering his tone and looking away, 'Are you trying to defect?'

She seemed almost surprised.

'Defect? Goodness,' she said. 'You think that's why I wrote to you?'

Now it was Otto's turn to be surprised.

'Well, of course. You mentioned what my mum used to say,' Otto replied. '*Everybody's looking for Moses.*'

'I wrote that because I knew it would make you come. I knew it would make you know it was me.'

'But,' Otto said quietly, 'isn't that what you want? Aren't you looking for a way out of Egypt?'

A smile played on her lips. But it was a sad smile.

'Oh, always, Ottsy,' she said. 'Always that.'

Otto's mind was spinning. There were so *many* things he wanted to ask about. His mother, his brother . . . her. What had *happened* in all those years since he left Berlin? But again he knew that the present must be dealt with first.

'Dagmar,' he said, choosing his words carefully, 'I've been told you are a Stasi officer. Is that true?'

The smile remained for a moment, before fading slowly.

'Ah,' she said after a moment. 'I wondered if you would know about that. We try never to underestimate the British.'

'So it's true?'

'Yes, Ottsy. It's true.'

'Christ,' Otto said. 'The *Stasi*. Never in ten million years would I have predicted that.'

'Ten million years, Ottsy? Oh, I think it's been longer than that since I last saw you.'

They found a bench and sat down together. Otto produced his cigarettes. Dagmar accepted one eagerly.

'Our first shared cigarette since Wannsee,' she said, putting a hand on Otto's knee. 'Do you remember?'

Remember? Of course he remembered. He remembered nothing else so clearly in all his life as that day at Wannsee. He'd dreamt about it almost every night since.

Dreaming she'd chosen him.

But despite the temptation to dive at once into the past, the present remained more urgent.

'The Stasi, Dagmar?' he said.

'People change, Otto,' she said. 'I never picked you to end

up a civil servant in Her Majesty's Foreign Office either.'

Otto nodded, he could see her point.

'I ended up an army translator,' he said, 'towards the end of the war. I did a lot of German prisoner debriefings and a bit of work for the security boys. When I was demobbed they offered me a job translating at the FO and I took it. Nothing else to do really.'

He sparked up his Zippo lighter and lit her cigarette for her, which she drew on hungrily.

'Lucky Strikes. Your father's brand. I don't suppose I've smelt one since the early thirties. Funny, I quite often find myself thinking of Wolfgang.'

'Yeah,' Otto said, 'me too.'

'He was such a laugh. A character. He can still make me smile, even now, even after he's been dead for nearly twenty years.' Dagmar paused before adding sadly, 'I don't know anyone like that any more.'

They smoked for a moment in silence. Once more Otto found himself struggling to comprehend the enormity of the situation. After so very long, he was with her, sitting beside her. Smoking with her, just like they had used to do, in her pink bedroom in Charlottenburg-Wilmersdorf, in the house the Nazis burnt.

'So?' he found himself saying.

'So what?'

'So am I here to try and get you out? Because if that's what you want, I'll do anything to help. You know that. They'll help you too. The British. They want to bring you to the UK.'

'Ah yes. I imagine they do. If I'll talk to them. If I promise to tell them all about the Stasi.'

'Fuck them. You don't have to tell them anything if you don't want. Let them help me help you get out and then fuck them.'

'Ottsy,' Dagmar said with a sad smile, 'I'm not *trying* to get out. I work for the East German secret police. Believe me, they're as ruthless as the Gestapo and a lot more efficient. If I defected they'd find me and they'd kill me. I'll never get out.'

Otto was so confused now. 'Then why am I here?'

'Aren't you pleased?'

'You know I'm pleased.'

'Are you sure?'

'Of course I'm sure. How could you doubt it?'

Then suddenly he said it.

'I still love you, Dagmar. I kept my promise. I want you to know that. I've loved you every single day. On the ferry to England. In the hostel and the internment camp. Through the war years. Fighting in North Africa and Italy and behind a desk with the army of occupation. Then in London and for all those long, long boring years since I've loved you every minute of every day. I never stopped loving you and I never will.'

He hadn't meant to say it and yet somehow he had to tell her. He wanted so much for her to know that he had kept the promise he whispered into her ear at the Berlin station in 1939.

'And on the train?' Dagmar said, a wicked little smile playing on her lips.

'Train?'

'The train to Rotterdam, Otts. When you made love to Silke.'

He was absolutely stunned. It was the last thing he had expected her to say. He could feel himself reddening. Actually feeling *guilty*. It was so unfair; seventeen years of emotional self-denial and the first thing she brought up was him and Silke.

'Oh,' he heard himself saying. 'So she told you.'

'Of course, Otts,' she said, laughing now. 'We were cooped up together in an apartment for years. Girls talk. Oh, don't look so *bothered*, Ottsy. I was just teasing you. You were being so serious about how much you loved me. I couldn't resist! She *told* me it was nothing, she told me you were tongue-tied with guilt in the morning. That all you could think about was me.'

'Well . . .' Otto said, embarrassed, 'that's true, actually. We were drunk, you see. And it was an unusual situation.'

He could still scarcely believe that this was what they were discussing.

'And she *did* turn out quite pretty in the end, didn't she? Who would have thought it back in the twenties?' Dagmar laughed again. '*Please* don't look so upset, Otts. You promised to love me, not to remain celibate. I don't imagine you've been a monk since 1939.'

She stamped her cigarette out on the ground and accepted another. Otto thought of Billie doing the same thing on the Thames Embankment. Just a few days before and a universe away. For a mad moment he wondered if Dagmar knew about Billie too. She was in the Stasi after all.

'But you *do* still love me best of all, Ottsy. That's nice, I must say. Very nice.'

'I just wanted you to know. About my promise. I won't say it again.'

'Why not? I don't mind.'

'Well, it isn't relevant, is it?'

'Isn't it?'

'No more now than it was then. You chose Paulus, Dagmar,' Otto said. 'He was the one you loved.'

As Otto mentioned his brother's name he realized it was the first time he had done so. How could it have taken him so long?

'Paulus, Ottsy?' Dagmar said with a sad sad smile.

She tilted her head back and looked up at the sky. The clouds were grey but there were hints of sun rippling through them. There was no breeze and the smoke rose vertically from her mouth. After a little while she looked back at him and her eyes were glistening as if she was going to cry.

She seemed about to say something but then stopped, drawing instead once more on her cigarette. Finally her face seemed to harden a little with resolve and the words came.

'Oh, Otto,' she said as a tear trickled from her eye. 'I never loved Paulus.'

For a moment he wondered if he had heard her correctly, but there could be no doubt he had. The tears now flowing down her cheeks were proof of that.

'Dagmar,' Otto said, aghast, 'what do you mean? How can you say you never loved him? You told us . . . at Wannsee. On the beach. That you'd chosen Paulus.'

'Yes. That's right, Otts,' and she could not look at him now. 'I *chose* him.'

'Then what are you saying?'

'Oh, Otto. *Otto*,' Dagmar said, and it sounded almost as if she was scolding him. 'So *good*, so true. Just like his brother. Those terrible Stengel twins, eh? I didn't deserve them. I always knew that. But then I never forced them to fall in love with me either.'

'Dagmar, please tell me what you're—'

'Paulus was the *clever* one, Ottsy.' Dagmar ground out her butt, then took the lighter and another cigarette from the packet in Otto's hand, her fingers lingering for a moment on his. 'Don't you see? I chose the *clever* one. *Surely* you understand?'

'Not really, no,' Otto said, although he thought that perhaps he was beginning to.

'I wasn't interested in love, Otto. I didn't have that luxury. I was a Jewess trapped in Nazi Berlin. The mob had just *burned my mother to death*. I was interested in *survival*.' Dagmar lit her cigarette and collected her thoughts. 'I worked it out on the night you saved my life. On *Kristallnacht*. Do you remember what you said? When we got to your mum's apartment, me sitting there on the floor, hugging my little toy monkey. I still have it, you know. You said you were going to *kill* Himmler. That was your reaction to the Night of the Broken Glass. You were *always* saying that sort of thing. You were the boy who brought me the Brownshirt's buttons. Pauly *never* did anything like that. Pauly was too clever, too calculating. Pauly always had a plan. He had a plan that night too. He told you to forget stupid ideas like killing Nazis. Because you had to become a good German so that you could look after me. It was a *good* plan. But sitting there listening to it, not saying a word, I could see damn clearly that the wrong twin was going to have to carry it out. I needed the clever one. The calculating one. Not the wild one who wanted to kill Himmler. I didn't think I'd stand a chance with you.'

The cigarette packet fell from Otto's limp fingers. He stooped to retrieve it from the ground. Some children ran past the bench where they were sitting. He glanced up to see their legs flash past.

A boy chasing a girl.

Somewhere Otto could hear a band playing.

'You decided that night, then? On *Kristallnacht*?' Otto said, his words emerging as if from some strange other place. 'You decided to tell Paulus that you loved him?'

'Don't judge me, Ottsy.'

'Did you tell him then? That night after I went back to school?'

'No.' Her voice was tense but steady, almost as if it was a relief finally to be telling the truth. 'Pauly was dead set on his path; he was going to escape from Germany and be an English lawyer and build the future. I knew that if I was to keep him for myself I must handle him with care. I had so much to turn around and so little time in which to do it. After all, poor Pauly thought I loved you.'

The tune the distant band were playing finished. A smattering of applause drifted across the park. Then they struck up again. More marching music. Did they *never* tire of it?

'And did you?' Otto asked, and he was shocked to realize how eagerly he leapt upon the point. Had he won, after all? Had the pendulum to which he and his brother nailed their hearts as boys swung once again in his favour? '*Did* you love me?'

'Oh, Otto, Otto,' Dagmar replied wearily. 'You're a man now, not a boy. Surely you can see? Don't you understand? I never loved *either* of you.'

Otto flinched as if he had been struck. Dagmar too looked almost taken aback at herself, shocked at her own honesty. At the pain she was inflicting.

'I know how awful that must sound,' she went on quickly. 'I *adored* you. You must know that. Those crazy Stengel boys who loved me so. But even then we all knew that if it hadn't been for Hitler, me loving you would never even have been a question. Ours was a Saturday world, that was all. One day a week. And one fine Saturday I would have been gone. Away. Abroad. I was going to marry a millionaire just like my daddy was.'

Otto stared at the ground between his feet.

'Yes, that's what Silke always said.'

'Yes, I imagine she would have done,' Dagmar observed tartly, 'but Hitler *did* happen and I lost everything. Everything except my two darling protectors. That and a dedication to *survive*. A dedication that began on the pavement outside my father's store in 1933 and which I've carried with me every since.'

'You stole Paulus's life,' Otto said.

'He wanted me, Otto. He got me. All of me. I didn't ask him to love me.'

'But you told him *you* loved him.'

'So what?' Dagmar demanded, her voice brittle now, almost shrill. 'Not such a very big lie in the scheme of things. I'd have done a lot more than that to survive. I would have done *anything*. Pretending to love Paulus was easy – he was a wonderful boy, handsome and kind, and I didn't deserve him. But you might as well know I'd have killed him if I'd had to. The Nazis had already got my mum and my dad. I was the last Fischer and I was damned if they were going to get me!'

'You did kill him, Dagmar. He could have gone to England but instead he died at Moscow because of you.'

'Well, if you want to put it that way,' Dagmar snapped bitterly. 'If I killed him, I saved you. That's even, isn't it?'

'I didn't want to be saved.'

'That's your problem, Ottsy. And it's also why you were no use to me. Because you say things like that. And because you've spent the last seventeen years of your life forcing yourself to stay in love with a girl who rejected you. I needed . . . a pragmatist.'

Otto got up and walked around the bench, trying to order the confused, tumbling thoughts and emotions ricocheting around his head and his heart.

'So that day at Wannsee,' he said, 'when I ran off, before the Hitler Youth kids turned up – you asked him to stay? To swap identities with me?'

'Don't be silly, Ottsy. That's what *you* would have done but I'm clever like Paulus. All I did was what you know. I kissed him in the rain and told him that I loved him, not you. That I loved him but that I knew he had to go. That I *wanted* him to go. To live while I died. I knew that would be enough. That he'd do the rest. I knew Pauly's mind, you see. I didn't need to make the plan for him because given the right incentive he'd come up with it himself. And he did.'

The girl and boy ran past again. She was leading him a merry chase. He'd have earned his kiss if he got it. Otto found himself hoping she'd turn out to be worth it.

'Did you ever tell him?' he asked. 'After. When you were in Berlin living together.'

'Of course not. I didn't want to hurt him. Why would I? He was the best of men. I've told you, I adored him. Besides, I needed his dedication. I needed him to remain obsessed with protecting me. Silke suspected, though. I think she did from the very start and I believe she hated me for it. She loved you, you see, Otto, and when I stole Paulus for myself, I also stole you from her.'

The mention of Silke was like a light bulb turning on in Otto's brain.

Silke? Where was she?

Silke Krause. The woman whom MI6 knew to have worked for the Stasi since the war.

And why had Dagmar summoned him to Berlin? She didn't love him. She had never loved him. And it seemed she had no wish to defect.

'Why am I here, Dagmar?' Otto asked, his voice suddenly harder.

'Don't hate me, Ottsy,' Dagmar replied, surprised, it seemed, by the change in his tone. 'I couldn't bear it. Of course I know that now you'll finally have to stop loving me, which is a shame because not many girls get to be loved as long as I have by such a good man. But please don't hate me, Ottsy. Try to understand and to like me still. To love me still, at least a little.'

'Why, Dagmar? Why should I understand? And why should I love you?'

'Because you were never forced to lick a pavement while your mother dry-retched in the dirt beside you.' Dagmar almost pleaded. 'I was *thirteen*, Ottsy.'

'There's been a world of pain, Dagmar. Everybody's had a share.'

Dagmar's face, which had softened so entirely as she absorbed the fact that Otto's ancient promise to love her must finally be broken, hardened once more.

'Oh yes,' she said, 'you're right about that. There's been a world of pain.'

'Why am I in Berlin, Dagmar?'

'You know why, Otto,' she said coldly. 'You may not be as clever as Paulus but you're not stupid. You're being entrapped. We want you, just like your people want me. They're going to force you to work for us.'

'And how will they do that, Dags?'

'Dags?' Dagmar laughed. 'Long time since I heard that.'

'Blackmail, I suppose,' Otto went on. 'The usual dirty tricks.'

'Yes, I was supposed to get you into bed. An FO official photographed having sex with a known Stasi agent would not go down well with your employers.'

Otto almost laughed. The one ambition of his life had been to make love to Dagmar. And now it turned out he'd been so close.

'I told them I wouldn't do that to you, Ottsy.'

'Well, there's a comfort.'

'I told them I'd get you here but that I'd prefer it if they did their own dirty work. They never mind doing that.'

'So I'm to be drugged, am I? Put in bed with a couple of naked rent boys, Kremlin-style? Spy for us or we'll send the pictures to your bosses and the press?'

'That sort of thing. Yes.'

'Personally I preferred their first plan,' Otto said, 'the one where you did the dirty work.'

'Would that make things any better? Shall I sleep with you? I will if you like. I suppose it's the least I can do.'

A lifetime of faithful passion and pure devotion reduced to the offer of a compensation fuck, with the East German Secret Service recording the event for future blackmail. Otto actually laughed.

'Don't hate me, Ottsy,' Dagmar said once more.

'What happened, Dagmar? In the war. To my mother. To Pauly. Where's Silke?'

German Hero

Berlin and Russia, December 1941 and January 1942

A crippled soldier, his feet lost to frostbite, hobbled on his crutches up the steps of a townhouse in the district of Moabit and rang the bell of Paulus Stengel's apartment. Stitched into the lining of his cap was a letter, a letter from a dead comrade which the crippled man had promised on his life to either deliver or destroy.

'Paulus was the best of men,' the soldier said to Silke as he completed his task and turned away. 'A damn good soldier too.'

It was late January. The army telegram informing Silke of Paulus's death had arrived just after Christmas. His last letter was dated 6 December 1941.

My darling Mum, my darling Dagmar,

It is minus 40 degrees and we are halted before Moscow. Ivan has finally stopped us in our tracks and now the German Army struggles for its very existence.

We are told that if we can only hold our ground then Germany will survive to fight again next year. That may be so. But I must tell you both that I will not.

You know of course that my plan has been these last two years to be a good soldier of Hitler that I might best be in a position to help you both.

Now I find that I must change my plan. The evil that I have witnessed during these six months of campaigning on the Russian front leaves me no choice. The Devil and the Devil alone could have conceived of what is being done here in Germany's name.

It is in fact a comfort to be on the front line, dying by inches in a dug-out. For although this is a place of abject terror and quite bottomless misery, it is still preferable to being forced to witness the terrible truth of what is happening in the places we have conquered.

My darlings, this is a depravity beyond imagination. To say that we have laid waste to what we have occupied does not begin to describe the slaughter, the devastation and the endless cruelty.

And yet even now that is not enough to feed the beast that Germany has become. I do not exaggerate when I say that the principal concern of the SS Einsatzgruppen is that they cannot kill people fast enough. They are seeking to industrialize the process.

Language is inadequate. Goethe himself could not find words with which to communicate this unique and perverted slaughter.

Therefore, to come to the point, I have decided that I can no longer fight in this army. Even the love I bear for you cannot excuse me continuing to be a part of the most evil horde that ever made war.

On the pitiful and the defenceless. On the old and the weak. On babies and young children. On humanity itself.

My plan has changed. I will go to my commanding officer and volunteer to make a reconnaissance of the Soviet positions. Such a mission is often fatal.

I intend to make sure that in my case it is.

Thus in the eyes of Germany I will die an honourable, even heroic death, and as such Silke will be accorded the rights, respect and pension of a war widow. I hope in this way that the apartment in Moabit will continue to provide shelter for Dagmar, the only woman I have ever loved, and that also when the time comes Mum will hide there too.

I close by saying that despite this terrible darkness in which we all live, I die happy. Happy that I have been a good son to my mother and father, and that in some small way I have been worthy of Dagmar's love.

That love is the towering achievement of my life.

Goodbye, Mum. From your son.

Goodbye, Dagmar. From your devoted and loving husband.

Park Bench
Berlin, 1956

'Frieda never did come to live with us,' Dagmar explained. 'She told us that she intended never to go underground but to die with her patients.'

'Yes,' Otto replied, hollow-voiced, 'that sounds like Mum.'

He was trying to focus on the reality of finally *knowing* how his brother died. Otto had been a soldier himself; he too had crawled on the ground in the night seeking out a shadowy enemy. But not on *that* front, in minus forty degrees, creeping between the two most bitterly ferocious armies ever assembled on earth. Then standing up, the will to live crushed out of him, inviting the liberating bullet.

Had they shot him clean? Silhouetted against the frozen night sky?

Or had they taken him and butchered him for the devil's henchman they would have thought him to be?

Otto would never know. But he took some comfort from the knowledge that Paulus had *chosen* the moment of his departure from the world.

He had died as he lived, according to a plan.

They were still sitting together on the bench in the People's Park. Otto was vaguely surprised at that. He had been half expecting at every minute to be bundled into a police car by Stasi thugs.

But only children ran past them and in the distance the band played.

The cigarette ends were piling up.

He produced another packet from his case. He had bought a carton of two hundred at Heathrow.

He was beginning to wonder if that would be enough.

'When the final round-ups began and your mother refused to go underground,' Dagmar continued, 'Silke wanted to use the flat to hide others. She thought that she and I should at least share our rooms – there were so many people desperate to hide, you see. That caused plenty of trouble between us, I can tell you.'

'You didn't want to do it?' Otto asked.

'Do you find that shocking?' Dagmar replied. 'Why would I? Tell me? Why would I want to share? Every submarine Jew was a leper, a massive risk both to themselves and others. In constant danger of discovery and arrest. Of betrayal too. Oh yes, believe me, betrayal; dogs eat dogs when the table's bare. If I'd let Silke bring in even one more like me we'd have been doubling our chances of detection while halving our food and other supplies. We were entering the end game, you see, Otto. The condemned were getting desperate. On both sides, German and Jew alike. The fact that the Nazis couldn't beat Ivan sent them scurrying for easier victories elsewhere. That meant the Jews. The Final Solution was upon us. They introduced the yellow star and after that, unless you had a guardian angel like I had, there was nowhere to hide. The Gestapo began finally systematically clearing the Jews of Germany. They sent people letters and they just went, down to the station and on to the trains. Sometimes there was no letter, the police just turned up and pulled people out of their beds. Your grandparents went in November '42. Ordered to be at the station at such and such a time with one small suitcase each. They went, of course. Everybody went. They were told that there were homes waiting for them in the east, whole new towns even; people believed it, or tried to. Even after everything that had already been done to them they tried to deny the unthinkable. They simply could not comprehend that it wasn't homes but gas chambers that were waiting for them at the end of the line. Even after they'd been stuffed into cattle trucks. Pissing and shitting on each other, dying of suffocation and dehydration in railway sidings, pushing the corpses of babies out through the bars. They still could not quite believe that the Nazis actually meant to murder them *en masse*. That's why I have some sympathy for the Germans now when they say they never knew. After all, if the Jews themselves could scarcely believe what was happening to them, then why should the people who hurried by on the other side of the street looking the other way?'

Otto didn't want to talk about whether the Germans knew or not.

'And my mother? When did she go?'

'She lasted another few months. She lost the apartment, of course, just after Pauly died, in fact. No more silly conversation groups with old Jews moaning in English about not being allowed to buy soap or use telephone boxes.'

'She had a conversation group?' Otto said, half smiling.

'That and a hundred other things. She was everywhere, running all over town. On foot after they banned Jews from the trams and took their bicycles. I think she was personally trying to sustain the entire victim population of Berlin. I actually think it was what saved her for so long. The Nazis weren't stupid. They didn't want mass panic and they certainly didn't want resistance. They encouraged leadership amongst the Jews till the last. Your mother got taken to work in what was called the Jewish hospital, which the Gestapo still allowed to operate. They were doing everything they could to make the Jews get rid of themselves, you see. Lying to them, confusing them, sending mixed messages. The hospital Frieda ended up in was part of that. It gave people comfort when they got their movement orders. After all, if the Germans were still maintaining a Jewish hospital in Berlin, then perhaps they were also preparing homes for them in the east.'

Otto knew something of the psychology of Nazi tactics.

'Mum worked in the Jewish hospital?'

'I say hospital. It was more of a charnel house really. With no facilities or money whatsoever. And it was only for *Mischlinge* anyway, and the wives of mixed marriages. Jewesses with Aryan husbands in the army. When their husbands got killed at the front, the wives lost their special status and got shipped straight off to the death camps. Widowed and condemned to death in the same telegram. How's that for a grim joke?'

So much history all at once. Dagmar seemed to be finding some comfort in sharing it. Otto wished she'd stick to the point.

'What happened to my mother?'

The Jewish Hospital

Berlin, 1943

In January 1943 the Wehrmacht lost the battle of Stalingrad, thereby sealing the fate of the Third Reich. In response to this catastrophe, Josef Goebbels promised Hitler a Jew-free Berlin for his birthday.

Despite the massive strains on the city administration caused by the Allied bombing, the Berlin police authorities determined to make good Goebbels' promise.

In February 1943 the Gestapo began what was to be their final mass action against Berlin's Jews. Police supported by the Waffen SS spread out across the city. They smashed down every suspect door and invaded every cellar. They climbed through windows, sledgehammered walls and crowbarred locks. They burst into homes and factories. They opened drains, scoured bombsites and searched sewers. Working from meticulously prepared civil lists and with the aid of a small group of Jewish informers they sought out the last six or seven thousand Jews still living in the city. Scooping them up and taking them directly to a mass 'transfer site' on Levetzowstrasse into which they were crammed without toilets or water. This time there was no formal summons. People were simply snatched where they were found, children without their mothers, husbands without their wives. The comforting fiction of allowing people to prepare a bag containing 'work boots, two pairs of socks and two pairs of underpants etc.' was a thing of the past. The tactics learnt in Poland and the Ukraine had come home to Berlin.

For the time being, *Mischlinge* were to be spared, along with a tiny handful of privileged workers employed at the so-called Jewish Hospital. Frieda was one of these workers, but despite her special status she decided on that day in February when the last police action began that her time had come to join her beloved Wolfgang and Paulus.

It wasn't planned but it happened anyway. She had been

outside the hospital, walking in the frozen streets. Taking a few minutes' break from the nonstop work in which she was engaged.

With her yellow star on her breast she was accosted almost immediately. A van pulled up and she was ordered to get in by a policeman holding a wooden club on which Frieda could see there was encrusted blood along with skin and hair.

Frieda presented her special papers, which were all in order, and she was told that she could go. It was clear to her that some sort of arbitrary round-up was underway and so she began running back to the hospital.

However, on her way she saw another police van, an open lorry this time. It was pulled up outside a building that was clearly being used as a Jewish kindergarten. A terrible scene was unfolding as twenty or so children between the ages of three and eight were dragged by soldiers from the building and thrown physically on to the truck. An elderly woman who must have been the children's teacher was trying to protest, while all around her the children screamed and fell and soiled themselves.

A soldier began to push the teacher towards the truck, whereupon the old woman turned and slapped him in the face. For a moment the soldier and the old lady stared at each other, both equally shocked at what had occurred. Then the soldier simply drew his gun and shot her. After which he and a comrade hurled her dying body on to the lorry amongst the screaming children.

It was clear to Frieda, watching from the pavement, that the children were now completely alone. Whatever brief time they had left on earth they would spend in absolute terror and utter bewilderment without comfort or guidance.

'*Mummy! Mummy! Mum!*'

The small voices bleated for their mothers through terror-twisted mouths set in faces turned to grotesque masks of horror.

The engine of the truck revved up, almost drowning out their pitiful cries. Two soldiers got into the cab while two others mounted the running board.

As a soldier raised himself up, one of the smallest of the children reached out to him, no doubt in the childish belief that grown-ups could be trusted. The little boy's hand wiped at his wailing face as he stretched his little arms towards the man. There was so much snot, so many tears. The soldier recoiled, disgusted, punching the child away. The little boy fell back on to the dead body of his teacher.

And the children wailed. '*Mummy! Mummy! Mum!*'

The soldiers screamed back. 'Shut up! Shut your little mouths or we'll beat you, you Jew bastards! Shut up or we'll kill you!'

Brutality was their defence. Each young soldier had built a thick wall of cruelty around his corrupted conscience. A wall their leaders called 'strength'.

But the children didn't know how to shut up. They hadn't yet learnt to bow their heads and shuffle.

And so they cried, '*Mum! Mum! Mum!*'

Frieda heard those cries.

Mum? That was *her* name. It had been her name since 1920.

She was a mother.

And now she was their mother. Twenty more adoptions, all at once.

'Stop!' Frieda shouted at the last of the soldiers who was in the act of boarding the truck. 'Look! I wear the star! I'm a Jew! Take me! I will keep the children quiet.'

Continued Conversation in the Park

Berlin, 1956

'Frieda climbed on to the truck,' Dagmar said. 'Silke got the story from someone who saw it. Your mother couldn't bear for those children to spend the last hours of their brief lives without love or comfort, so she spent her own last hours giving them hers. She climbed aboard and she got amongst them and put out her arms and held as many of them as she could. Apparently the children clustered to her like bees around a flower. Then as the lorry pulled away she began to sing *Hoppe Hoppe Reiter. Hoppe Hoppe Reiter.*

Tears were streaming down Otto's face.

'She used to sing it to Paulus and me,' he said. 'I can hear her voice now.'

'We heard she was still singing when the truck arrived at the station, but by then somehow your mother had worked the magic that she always did and she had the children singing too. Even as they were pushed into the cattle trucks, crushed in with a hundred other condemned souls. "*Hip hop there, rider! Hip hop there, rider!*" Your mother went with those children to Dachau that very day. I imagine she led them singing into the gas chamber.'

Otto wept and wept. Thinking of his beloved mother and how brave her end had been.

She had died as she had lived, a beacon of goodness in a sick and dreadful world.

'And so there was only us left,' Dagmar went on. 'Me and Silke.'

Her voice was far away. Through his tears Otto understood that Dagmar needed to tell the whole story.

'We lived in Pauly's flat and of course we fought and fought. Two very different girls who never should have roomed together. Silke was trying to establish resistance connections. Can you believe it? Using her cover as a war widow to contact other Communists. She was a part of *Die Rote Kapelle*. The Red Orchestra – I suppose you've heard of it.'

'Yes,' Otto said, pulling himself together and blowing his nose on his handkerchief. 'The Communist-backed resistance. I've heard of it.'

'I warned her,' Dagmar went on. 'I told her if she was ever the cause of me getting caught I'd make damn sure she and her bloody idiot friends went down with me. That apartment was my castle. Paulus built it for me. Because he loved me. Me. Not some random bunch of self-righteous Reds.'

Her voice was starting to grate on Otto.

Incredible.

That same voice that had been nothing but music to him all his life. The voice he'd wrestled the telephone receiver from his brother's hand to hear, watching the clock, waiting his turn, jealous of every missed syllable.

Now it was actually starting to grate.

'Paulus may have loved you, Dagmar,' Otto said, a little more harshly perhaps than he had intended, 'but only because you lied to him.'

'*That* is a damned lie! He loved me because he loved me. Full stop. Just like you did. I didn't ask him to. I didn't ask either of you to, so don't start playing the victim now. If the bloody mad Stengel twins devoted their lives to me, it was because they *chose* to. What's more, I kept my half of the bargain with Pauly. We lived together in that flat as man and wife for the little time he had. That was what he wanted and that was what he got.'

'You fucked him. So what?'

'I *made love* to him, Otto, and never say I didn't! And he died believing in my love, which was just the way he wanted to die.'

'He didn't want to die at all!'

'Really? He always told me he'd rather die having won my love than live a life without it. How about you, Otto? How's the last seventeen years been for you? I never would have picked you to fossilize in a government office. You were always going to be a knight in armour. Wouldn't you *rather* have been a knight in armour? I think you would.'

Otto was stunned. She could always run rings round him. *Fossilize.*

She had his number all right.

'I'm sorry,' he said quietly. 'I don't suppose I have any right to judge you.'

'No one has any right to judge me for anything I did, Otto. Because of what Hitler did to me.'

She stood up, lighting her umpteenth cigarette with a hand shaking with emotion.

Something in what she said and the vehemence with which she said it brought Otto's thoughts back to the present.

'Dagmar,' he said, 'where's Silke?'

She turned and looked down at him. Her lip curling along with the smoke that drifted from it.

'God, Ottsy,' she said, 'didn't you work it out yet? Pauly would have got it at the airport. *I'm* bloody Silke.'

Jew Catcher

Berlin, 1945

The atmosphere was always heavy in the apartment on the days when Silke's shadowy Communist friends were due to visit.

Dagmar hated them with the passion of a true blue Conservative. And it was not merely because their presence in her home so dramatically increased her own chances of being detected, she hated them on ideological grounds too. She hated them for her father's sake. She thought they were nothing but self-righteous fools. A gang of egotists and fantasists who made themselves ridiculous with their solemn clenched-fist salutes, endless bickering over ideological details and expansive plans for future government conducted round a bare kitchen table by the light of a single candle.

Silke seemed genuinely to believe that she and her pathetic little group of unshaven conspirators were actually contributing to the defeat of the Nazis. She claimed that they passed information about police and Wehrmacht activities to the approaching Red Army.

But Dagmar did not believe for a moment that their tiny efforts would make even the slightest difference to the outcome of the war. In fact, she strongly suspected that they ran their little cell for entirely selfish motives.

'I know what you're doing,' Dagmar said when Silke informed her that another meeting of the *Kapelle* was to be held in the apartment that evening. 'You're feathering your nest for after the war. Establishing your credentials. When the Nazis are gone, you and your friends will claim the right to run the country, just like you tried to do the last time when the Kaiser left. When the Red Army arrives you'll run straight up to them waving your little secret code book and your party cards, shouting, "Comrades, we're the *good* Germans. We're the ones who've been sending you all those messages." And then you'll all get nice jobs with the party and all of the meat and white bread. I know you Commies. My father sacked enough of you.'

'Believe it or not, Dagmar, not everyone is motivated entirely by selfishness.'

'Ha! What could be more selfish than a Communist? You think you can tell everyone in the world how to run their lives and if they won't do it you shoot them.'

That evening, when the hour of the meeting approached, Dagmar would usually have retreated to her bedroom. But this time she simply could not face being confined once more in the space where she had spent the vast majority of the previous two years. After Paulus had died, Silke had been told that without a husband to look after she had lost the right to employ a maid. The authorities had demanded that the Ukrainian girl Bohuslava whom the Stengels had registered for rations be returned to the employment pool. Silke had therefore been forced to report the fictitious maid as a runaway, and since that moment Dagmar had been truly a 'submarine' with no papers or identity whatsoever, surviving in the half light, on food Silke still shared with her for Paulus's sake.

'You mustn't go out!' Silke said. 'You're crazy. You only need to be stopped once.'

'I'm sorry but I've got to, because if I don't I will go completely sodding mad. The war's nearly over anyway. Your precious heroic Red Army's in East Prussia and no doubt we'll all be Commies in a month.'

'With any luck we will,' Silke countered defiantly.

'Great. I can't wait to pull on my overalls and go work on a collective farm, but in the meantime I'm going to be a member of the *petit bourgeois* just one more time. I'm going to pin up my hair, put on some make-up, wear a nice pair of shoes and go for a walk!'

'For God's sake, Dagmar, you're safe inside. Why take the risk?'

'Because I want to be a fucking human being again!'

'Keep your voice down!' Silke hissed. 'You don't *live* here, remember.'

'You're all right!' Dagmar went on, only half heeding Silke's warning to speak more quietly. 'You've got your stupid politics. What have I got? Nothing. And I haven't *had* anything for twelve fucking years.'

'You had Paulus and Otto!' Silke snarled back, now raising her own voice.

'Oh for God's sake, enough with the Stengel boys,' Dagmar said, throwing up her arms in exasperation. 'They loved me, I *know*. What do you want me to do – whip myself with gratitude? They loved me. They didn't love you. I'm sorry. No doubt under Communism you could force them to love you, but your revolution's going to come a bit late for that, isn't it? Because Pauly's dead and Otto's gone!'

'You're a real bitch, Dagmar,' Silke said with tears starting in her eyes. 'A really mean bitch.'

'Oh grow up, Silke. I'm going for a walk. And what's more, if you've got any sense you'll come with me. Because this place is driving us both potty. I am going to go down to the Tiergarten, where I believe they still have cafés, and I'm going to buy a cup or a glass of whatever foul shit they'll sell me and pretend to be a human being for an hour or two, not a victim of the Nazis. Are you coming?'

'No, of course I'm not. I have a meeting.'

'Then goodbye.'

It was the hair and the make-up that were Dagmar's undoing. Perhaps as Bohuslava the maid in her headscarf, apron and dungarees, she might have passed unnoticed. But Dagmar Fischer always turned heads. Always attracted attention, even as pale and gaunt as she'd become. And she loved it. Basking in the appreciative glances thrown her way by weary soldiers as she swung along the path. And it was good cover too, just what Pauly had advised her to do at the station on the day Otto left. Walk with confidence and nobody will think to question you. It was those who skulked that got caught.

Besides Dagmar felt safe. No German would recognize her as the Jewish heiress who had supposedly killed herself in 1939.

But it wasn't a German who recognized the beautiful woman who was drawing all the admiring glances as she sat sipping her watery acorn coffee in the rubble of the Tiergarten.

It was a Jew.

'Hello, Dagmar,' a voice said. 'Surely you remember me?'

Dagmar didn't recognize the voice but when she turned around she knew the questioner immediately and her blood ran cold. The woman smiling at her was one just like herself. A beautiful young woman in her twenties. Another Jewish princess who had faded away in the 1930s. A blonde version of Dagmar, but one whose name was whispered in fear by every submarine in Berlin. Stella Kübler, the Jew-catcher.

The exquisite young woman with her Aryan looks and corn-coloured hair, who bought her life afresh each day by denouncement and betrayal.

The woman known to her Gestapo handlers as 'Blonde Poison'.

'I don't know you,' Dagmar stammered, attempting to disguise her German. 'I am Hungarian. A maid.'

'Come on, Dagmar,' the Jew-hunter said, 'the game's up. We went to half a dozen of the same parties together as girls. We were banned from the same pools. Goodness, my parents even went to your dad's leaving do at the Kempinski Hotel. I've often wondered if you'd ever turn up. Certainly never believed that suicide story, not Dagmar Fischer. You do look well, I must say. How have you managed it?'

There were two men standing behind the sinister beauty, two

men in coats and Homburg hats. They stepped forward and laid their hands on Dagmar.

The hiding was over. She was finally a prisoner of the Gestapo.

Between Rapunzel and Little Red Riding Hood

Berlin, 1956

'I've heard of Stella Kübler, of course,' Otto said. 'She got ten years, didn't she?'

'That's right,' Dagmar replied. 'They've just released her, in fact, and she's gone to the West. Perhaps someone will slit her throat. I hope so. Not that I can talk. I may not have betrayed two thousand like she did but . . .'

'You did betray Silke,' Otto said, finishing her sentence.

They had begun walking together through the park and had now found their way into the Märchenbrunnen, wandering amongst the hundred and six fantastical fairy-tale sculptures. It almost broke Otto's heart to remember the beautiful, carefree girl he had once known running amongst those figures. More enchanting than any fictitious magical creature could ever be. Laughing and shrieking and deliberately letting herself be caught between Rapunzel and Little Red Riding Hood.

She was a different person now. Only the physical flesh was the same.

'Yes. I betrayed her,' Dagmar said coldly, staring up at the stone figure that was letting down her long golden hair. 'It was me or her, that's all there is to it. No one was under any illusions by then about what the Nazis were doing at the end of their train tracks. The BBC had been telling the world for two years. If you were caught, you were killed, and I'd been caught.'

She sat down on the plinth of Rapunzel's statue.

'Do you remember, Ottsy?' she said with a smile. 'Kiss-chase in the park?'

'Of course I remember,' Otto replied. 'You, me and Pauly. And Silke. She was there too.'

'Yes. She was, wasn't she,' Dagmar said, trying to make her voice sound indifferent. 'Scowling as usual as I recall. Furious that you were both chasing me.'

'What happened, Dagmar?'

'The inevitable happened. The Gestapo took me in and I offered them a deal. Most people tried to do that. Trade their life for someone else's. There *were* heroes of course but a fucking sight fewer than they'd have you believe now.'

'Tell me what happened.'

'Well, unlike most of them, I really did have something to trade. I said if they'd let me go I'd lead them to a Red Orchestra cell. They couldn't believe their luck. I remember thinking, *why do they bother?* The war was so obviously over by then, the Russians were at the gates, but they seemed to care as much as they ever had about chasing Commies and Jews, like a chicken still running after its head's been cut off. Anyway, they took me to their headquarters and asked a lot of questions and filled in a lot of forms. Forms! Still forms, in triplicate and double-stamped while every building in Berlin was burning. I told them I was being hidden by Communists and where to find them. I said that after that I could recognize others if they'd let me out on a leash. They agreed and I took them back to the apartment and watched from the end of the street while they made their raid. Silke and three others were dragged out of the building. I remember her shouting, "All power to the Soviets." Can you believe it? She actually shouted it like she was in some Russian propaganda movie. Just ridiculous. They took them away and I was left with one policeman. I was just beginning to think about trying to seduce him when an air raid started. I say started, resumed would be more accurate. The Americans bombed by day, the British by night, it was pretty continuous. Anyway, the cop wanted to get to a shelter and he started running and I just sort of lost him. Just stopped running and let him go. It was such total mayhem in the city by then, bombs falling everywhere, and shells of course with the Russians so close. Anyway, when that particular raid was over I was alone. So I went back to the apartment, which miraculously was never hit. I had literally nowhere else to go and there was some food there and in those last weeks of the war you went pretty much anywhere for food, whatever the risk. I slept in the apartment that night with the whole place to myself for the very first time. I loved it. Just to have the space. The solitude. Just me and the little woolly monkey you saved for me on the night you also saved my life. Won't you sit beside me, Otts? It's hard to tell this story.'

Otto sat down beside her on the plinth of Rapunzel's statue while Snow White smiled at them from the other side of the path.

Two Women
Berlin, 1945

Dagmar awoke having slept for a long time. She stretched and yawned and wished she could have a wash but water had become too precious for that.

She got up and, collecting the rainwater tin from its ledge, began to prepare some herb tea. Astonishingly there was still gas for the stove. Bits and pieces of Berlin's civic infrastructure continued to function right to the end. One could just never be sure which bit. Dagmar had filled the pot with boiling water when she heard the front door.

She froze in terror. Sure that now it was all over. That it was the police come for her once again, and that they would either kill her or she'd be forced to become like Stella Kübler, a poison woman, living by betrayal and murder.

But it wasn't the police.

It was Silke.

For a moment Dagmar felt herself still in terrible danger. Silke must know of her betrayal. Were the three other Communists behind her with knives and clubs bent on vengeance? The Communists were nothing if not ruthless.

But then Silke ran forward and embraced her.

'They came for us,' Silke said. 'Thank God you were out! To think I tried to stop you.'

'What happened, Silke? I walked for hours and had to take cover from a raid. When I came home you were gone.'

'Somehow they found us. I've always known they would in the end. They've arrested so many of us over the years.'

'But you're here. You're free again.'

There was rubble in Silke's hair and her face and clothes were caked in dust. Dagmar guessed what must have happened but she let Silke tell it.

'The British saved me,' Silke said half smiling, the dust cracking at the corners of her mouth. 'The RAF.'

Dagmar could not help thinking how much Silke would have preferred it if it had been the Russians.

'The police station got hit in the night before they even had a chance to get to work on me,' Silke said. 'They'd put me in a separate cell to the men and that was what saved me. They died and I didn't. I don't know what happened to the Gestapo guys. Maybe they got hit too, maybe they took shelter, I don't know. All I know is that I was knocked unconscious and when I came to it was just me and a lot of bodies. There were no emergency services – perhaps they came later, but I doubt it. Anyway, I didn't wait around to find out. I just got up, walked out of the wreckage and came home. I came for my stuff. I'm going to need it soon.'

'They obviously ransacked the apartment when they took you,' Dagmar observed. 'Is there anything left?'

Silke crossed the little kitchen, turned off the gas tap and pulled the stove from the wall. Behind it was a bare brick wall from which she removed a loose brick, pulling out various papers and a little booklet from the cavity behind.

'My Orchestra stuff,' she said. 'I need to find another place to hide it now.'

'Stay a little while, Silks. I've made some herb tea.'

'The police might come.'

Dagmar looked at her watch. It was already mid morning.

'I don't think they're coming, Silke. Perhaps they're dead. Perhaps they've just finally given up.'

Silke sat down and drank her tea. Then they shared some food together and talked a little.

Still the police did not come.

Silke decided to sleep. She said she felt dizzy, and went to her room.

Dagmar sat in the kitchen and wondered.

Had Silke been taken to the same police station as her? It seemed likely. If she had, then the notes the police had made about Dagmar's arrest and confession, about her betrayal of the Red Orchestra cell, would probably have been destroyed in the air raid.

Probably. But not certainly.

Dagmar did not know what police station it had been. They had taken her to and from it in a sealed van. Somewhere in Berlin it was perfectly possible there remained a detailed police account of how, as the war drew to a close, the Jewess Dagmar Fischer had been caught and had subsequently betrayed a Communist cell.

And the Russians were coming.

Dagmar sat and wondered. What should she do?

The afternoon wore on.

Dagmar's shadow on the kitchen floor crept slowly towards the wall.

Finally Silke emerged. Looking a little bewildered.

Perhaps it was the strange noise that had woken her. A new sound in a city that had heard so many new sounds in recent years. A low crunching, jerking rumbling.

Looking out of the window into the street below, the two young women saw a new sight to fit the new noise. A Russian tank.

Silke actually shouted for joy.

'They're here!' she cried, grabbing Dagmar in a wild embrace and spinning her round. 'It's over. We're free!'

In the Garden of Innocence

Berlin, 1956

'Poor Silke,' Dagmar said, an empty deadness to her voice and to her eyes. 'When she saw that first tank in the street she actually cheered. She danced for happiness. She hung a Red eiderdown from our window for a flag and shouted down to the soldiers below. It was that damn flag that brought them to us first. While most sensible girls were hiding in cellars or being boarded up in attics by their mothers, that idiot Silke was shouting at those beasts. Calling out a welcome. Hey, boys! There's two young women here!'

There was a little drinking fountain nearby. Dagmar got up and went over to it and took a long draught. She had been talking for a long time. Her voice was dry.

Otto remembered his flask of whisky. He produced it and they shared a gulp or two together. The spirit made Dagmar shiver, or perhaps it was her story.

'Everything you've heard about what happened to the women of Berlin in 1945 is true,' she said in a voice of cold stone, 'and worse. The raping went on for weeks. Those Russian soldiers went hunting for women like the Nazis had hunted Jews, kicking down doors, shining lights in faces, seeking out girls in every rat hole, and if they could find no girls, then fucking their mothers instead. Silke and I were amongst the very first caught. We went through it all together. Sisters in misery. Those soldiers that she waved at in the street just couldn't believe their luck, two girls at once and in a nice apartment with beds and everything. A ready-made harem, one blonde, one brunette – we covered all the bases, as your American friends would say.'

Dagmar tried to smile but couldn't. She raised Otto's flask to her lips and took another gulp. It made her cough a little but also helped stiffen her resolve to resume her story.

'They kept us prisoners in that nice apartment Pauly bought. Using us as they pleased and renting us out to other soldiers for cigarettes and vodka when they got bored themselves. It was very strange really. They sort of set up home with us, going off for their army duties and then coming back to their sex slaves. Me and Silke together. Sometimes in the same room, sometimes separate. I suppose in a way it was even worse for Silke – she had to suffer the disillusionment. Those soldiers represented everything she'd hoped for. The future of the world. She flung open her door to them and they walked right in and started tearing off her clothes. Mine too, right there and then. Within a minute. Silke tried to show them her KPD card. But they didn't speak German and if they had they wouldn't have cared. Nor about the radio code books she kept behind the gas stove and her Resistance accreditation. They were hungry peasants and we were meat, that was all. Perhaps if she could have got out of the apartment, found an officer, someone to understand her, she might have been OK. There were decent ones amongst them I've heard. But we were trapped.'

'Did you tell them you were a Jew?' Otto asked.

'I tried once or twice but either they didn't care or they didn't believe me. All the German Jews they'd seen had been skeletons.'

Otto opened his suitcase and reached in for a third packet of Lucky Strikes. He could scarcely believe it, they'd smoked twenty each already.

'And how did it end?' he said.

'They started to get lazy and didn't bother to tie us up any more. I think they almost started to think of us as sort of wives. War wives, of course, but wives nonetheless. Sometimes they brought chocolate and one of them even made paper flowers to put in our vase. Of course that didn't stop him putting down his scissors and his coloured paper to rape us when his turn came around. They thought we were their right, you see. They didn't think we had any business complaining after what Germany had done to them. One night Silke had had enough. One of them had fallen into a drunken sleep right on top of her and was snoring in her face. Their breath was always indescribable. Onion and rotting gums. Silke squeezed herself out from under him, crept to where he'd left his belt on a chair and took his gun. I watched beside my own sleeping Russian as she started to put on her clothes. I can see her body now, white in the moonlight, black bruises on her breasts where one of them liked to squeeze her. I don't know what her plan was, she kept looking at me and putting her fingers to her lips. Anyway, she never got a chance to do anything. Two more came in, getting impatient to have their turn at us. Silke pointed the gun at them but the poor silly fool couldn't bring herself to fire. She always was a sweet girl and those boys were even younger than we were. So they shot her instead. Right there and then. I don't know what they did with the body – nothing much, I imagine. There were thousands of dead bodies lying around Berlin. And that was the end of Silke Krause, proud founding member of the famous Saturday Club.'

Otto wanted to say something but could think of nothing remotely adequate. More tobacco was the only comfort he could offer.

'If only she could have waited,' Dagmar went on. 'It only lasted another day or two, although it was a hard two days for me with twice as many soldiers coming at me as before. But after that they just went away. Simply walked out and never came back. Moscow had finally decided that enough was enough and had sent in the military police to restore discipline. Believe it or not, the soldiers left me some rations and a bottle of vodka. My pay, I suppose. What they thought a German girl was worth for more than a fortnight of pack rape. That and gonorrhoea. Thank God for penicillin, say I. I understood, of course. They were peasants, and after what the Nazis had done in the east I couldn't really blame them for wanting to rape a few German girls.'

'And you were left alone?' Otto said.

'Yes, all alone. And do you know what I asked myself?'

'No.'

'I sat there and I asked myself what Pauly would have done.'

Otto laughed. Dagmar laughed too, and their laughter sounded sadder to them than tears.

'Pauly would have made a plan,' Otto said.

'Exactly,' Dagmar replied. 'I needed a plan. The Russians were all over Berlin. This was way before the Allies arrived. Germany hadn't even surrendered. I was hungry and all alone. And I was scared too.'

'Of the soldiers?'

'Not so much, that period seemed to have passed. I was scared of what I'd done. Betraying Silke and her comrades. I couldn't know for sure who'd survived and who hadn't. Who might have seen me at that police station. And there was the report the Gestapo had written. Had it been destroyed? I hoped so but I didn't know. I was destitute and without protection. The Russians didn't like Jews and they didn't like millionaires' daughters either. I was alone and dazed from hunger and weeks of rape. I needed food and I needed to find a way to make my home secure. Dagmar Fischer couldn't get those things from the Soviets, but it occurred to me that Silke Stengel probably could. What was more, Silke Stengel had not been written up by the Gestapo as a traitor. On the contrary, Silke was a hero of the *Rote Kapelle*. Those two red soldiers had killed the wrong girl.'

'Wow, Dags,' Otto said, almost in awe. 'You really are something.'

'I'm still alive, aren't I?' Dagmar replied. 'I searched the apartment and found all the stuff that poor old Silke had tried to show to the soldiers. It was all there, scattered about, her whole Red Orchestra identity. Even her pre-war secret party card. Everything

I needed to be a Communist heroine. It was a risk, I knew, but not so great a one. I was pretty certain Silke's stepfather would be dead, and if her mother was alive she'd have gone back to the countryside, where she came from. Silke had always told me that the Orchestra acted in cells. Only her immediate comrades would have known what she looked like, and they'd all been killed by that lucky Allied bomb. So I made myself look as pretty as I could and I took my evidence to the Red Army authorities. I demanded that I be clothed, fed and given status befitting my lifetime's commitment to the German Communist Party. Pauly's rules, you see, walk with confidence. I guessed that they'd be looking for German Reds to help them run things, and I was right. They sent me straight to a German KPD man, who'd just arrived from Moscow as part of the team charged with re-establishing the party and making sure it got its people into the places that counted before the West could do anything about it. Astonishingly, this man knew of Silke. He'd been her Moscow control right back to the days when she'd been a young girl posting off *Rote Hilfe* reports wrapped up in women's magazines.'

Otto closed his eyes. Remembering the happy golden-haired girl who'd lain beside him near the stream on the night of their great bicycle adventure. She'd tried to tell him about the Red Help then. That had been twenty-one years ago.

Good old Silke.

Poor old Silke.

'Of course, he'd never seen her,' Dagmar went on, 'although being a man he'd fantasized that she would be a peach, and I could see how pleased he was when that's exactly what she turned out to be. I became his lover that night and he saw to it that I was given a new party card and a rank that reflected my long and heroic service.'

Otto stared up at the darkening clouds.

It was beginning to get late. They'd finished the whisky and his head was starting to ache. There had been so much to take in. And so many cigarettes. But of course the story wasn't over or he would not have been lured to Berlin.

'And you've been Silke all these years?' he said. 'It's . . . it's astonishing.'

'Not really. Can you even begin to imagine how many lives got reinvented or stolen in Year Zero? A whole continent had something to hide. I wasn't alone in keeping secrets, Ottsy. When the Allies arrived and the big four divided up Berlin, I could see I was better off where I was. My apartment, which, of course, as Silke Stengel I legally owned, was just inside the Russian zone and it was all I had. There was nothing for me in the West. Nobody was talking about compensating Jews then. There was nothing to compensate them with. This was the end, not the beginning. Germany was completely destroyed and utterly destitute. In the West I'd have been a homeless, penniless refugee alongside a million others, and of course there was still that Gestapo report to worry about. If it ever came to light I'd be put on trial for sure. So I bided my time in the East, which was when I was approached to join the newly formed, Soviet-run German police. I was the perfect candidate, of course. Silke Stengel, née Krause, Red spy since 1935. So I grabbed it. And for the first time in my adult life, I was in control. Overnight I had security, status and power. Imagine how that felt, Otto, to a Jew in Berlin in 1945. A Jew who'd been through what I'd been through.'

'But, Dags,' Otto found himself protesting, almost as if they were back in her pink bedroom arguing about their futures together instead of picking over their past, 'a police woman? It's just so unlike you. I mean, you must have absolutely hated it.'

'Hated it, Otto?' Dagmar replied, her eyes suddenly gleaming. 'I *loved* it. It was my fucking *dream* job. *I* was the hunter now. *I* was the bastard. All those little people of Berlin who'd sneered and laughed while my life was stolen were going to feel the toe of my boot every chance I got! I put on that uniform, pinned back my hair, went out on to the streets of Berlin and made life hell for *anybody* I could. I soon realized that in fact that was what the whole of the Stasi was *there* for, to make life hell for Germans. How perfect. How fucking ironic! I fucking loved it.'

'And that was it?' Otto asked, startled by the sudden venom.

'That's where you've been ever since? Making life miserable for the people of Berlin?'

'Exactly,' Dagmar replied. 'I couldn't have turned back even if I'd wanted to. By the time the West began to prosper I was in too deep and I knew too much. I'd made my bed, Otto. They don't let you leave the Stasi. If you try, they kill you.'

'So you're trapped.'

'I suppose so. But don't feel sorry for me, Otto. My life is good – better than yours in Britain, I think. As a Stasi girl I have the best food and the best wine. Caviar if I want it. We party people keep all the luxuries for ourselves, you know. I still live in Pauly's flat with my fashion magazines and any books I want and Western music too, all the stuff we deny to everybody else we keep for ourselves. I wonder what dear Silke would have made of that? Of the shitty corrupt little world her beloved Stalin made? And best of all, I still get to persecute the good citizens of East Berlin. The ones who let Hitler steal my life. The ones who looked away. The ones who stood in a circle around me and my parents and shouted that we should be made to lick the street.'

'Dagmar, you can't hate for ever.'

'Can't I? Try and stop me. I will hate for every second I'm on this earth. And when I'm gone and my body turns to dust, then each molecule of what was once me will still be hating.'

It was getting dark now. Young couples had replaced the children on the path through the gardens.

The story was almost over.

Otto had all of his answers now but one.

'And me, Dagmar, when did I re-enter the picture?'

'Oh, they've had their eye on you all along. Right from 1946.'

'Me?' Otto asked, very surprised.

'Don't be flattered. They watch all the Germans who work for the Allies. Big and small. They study their pasts, looking for ways to force them to work for us. They connected me to you via Silke's marriage to Pauly. I'm her, don't forget, and my married name is Stengel. It didn't take them long to spot the Jew Stone in the British Foreign Office who had once been a

Stengel and to work out that his sister-in-law worked for them.'

Otto actually laughed.

'Do you realize,' he said, 'you're talking about the Saturday Club? Paulus, Silke, you, me. Still connected, still a gang. Could anyone looking at us back at the beginning ever have imagined?'

'Every German story took a wrong turn in 1933, Otts. We're not so special.'

'I guess so. So they still don't know who you really are, then?'

'I don't *think* they do. You can never be sure. They love secrets and they bide their time. They certainly did with you. Once they'd made the connection between us they put me on notice that one day they'd require me to bring you to Germany. I think they were waiting for you to rise in your profession a bit.'

'No luck there, I'm afraid,' Otto said. 'I've not been much of a success at the FO at all. Or anywhere else for that matter. Same grade I started in.'

'We noticed,' Dagmar observed dryly. 'Anyway, a few months ago my bosses must have decided that now was as good a time as any to try and make use of you, and I was instructed to find a way to lure you over. I knew what that was all right.'

'Yes,' Otto murmured, 'you certainly did.'

'I told them the surest way to get to you was for me to assume the identity of a dead Jewess whom you had loved.'

'So that's you pretending to be Silke pretending to be you. Quite a labyrinth, Dags.'

'That's the way we like things in the Stasi. The more shadows and lies the better. So we re-established the Dagmar identity, made it official in case MI6 were watching.'

'Which by the way they were.'

'And here you are, Otto. It isn't all so very complicated really.'

'Maybe not for you, Dagmar. But it seems pretty bloody tortuous to me. I'm not the clever Stengel twin, remember.'

Dagmar looked at him and her eyes softened a little.

'You were clever enough to come to me and save my life in 1938, Ottsy. I'd have burned to death.'

She put her hand on his and squeezed it a little.

'But despite that, Dagmar,' Otto said, removing her hand, 'it seems you've been quite happy to entrap me.'

'Otto. I work for them. They don't give you a choice in these things. If I hadn't done it they'd have just pretended to be me.'

'Pretended to be you, pretending to be Silke, pretending to be you,' Otto corrected.

'Yes, that's right. Besides –' and she gave him a little smile, a smile he hadn't seen since the days of the pink bedroom – 'I wanted to see you. I thought you'd want to see me.'

'I did, Dags. You damn well know that. But the question is, what happens now?'

'They'll try to persuade you to spy for them inside the British Foreign Office. They're waiting for you over there.'

Dagmar nodded towards a bench situated beyond Snow White, which had been empty moments before but on which were now sitting two solid-looking men in the Homburg hats.

Otto stared across at them.

'The uniform doesn't change then? Different totalitarian ideology, same hats.'

'Yes, just the same.'

Otto sighed and lit a cigarette.

'One last fag, eh?' he said. 'The thing is, Dagmar, I can't help them.'

'They can be very persuasive.'

'No. I mean really. I really can't. You see, they want a spy in the Foreign Office, but in fact I won't be working for the Foreign Office when I get back.'

'Really? When was this decided?'

'Today. Here in the People's Park. I'm going to resign. And I won't be studying for any law degrees that I don't have the brains to get any more either.'

'You've been studying law, Ottsy?' Dagmar asked, very surprised.

'Trying to. Since 1947. You see, I've been trying to live the life Pauly lost. Isn't that silly? Ever since you caused him to give me his name and his prospects I've felt responsible. I've been trying to be him. For his sake and for Mum's – she did so love what she thought he'd become. But I'm going to stop now because it's obviously ridiculous. Suddenly I understand that. I can't be him and he wouldn't want me to. I've been Paul Stone for seventeen years but when I get back I'm going to start being Otto Stengel again. I don't know how I'll do it or what I'll do – sweep roads probably – but one thing's for sure. Whatever I do become, it'll be more fun than what I've been trying to be. And I'm afraid it won't be any use to the Stasi. Unless they want a spy in a woodwork class and an amateur jazz band, because I'll certainly be joining those.'

Dagmar smiled.

'Is there a girl?'

Otto thought about that for a moment. Then he remembered something and felt in the breast pocket of his jacket. He pulled out a paper tissue with a lipstick imprint on it. The one Billie had put there on the first morning he had been summoned to MI6. Something to remember her by, she'd said.

'Yes, actually,' he said quietly, 'I think there is a girl.'

'Ha!' Dagmar replied, looking at the red lips printed on the tissue. 'So you *did* love somebody besides me after all.'

'I didn't think I could allow myself to, Dagmar,' Otto replied. 'But now I know I can.'

Girl on a Pavement

London and Berlin, 1989 and 2003

In 1989 Otto Stengel heard the news of the collapse of the Berlin Wall while listening to BBC Radio 4 in the kitchen of the north London home he shared with his wife Billie.

The last of their four children had long since flown the nest and Billie was rushing off to her job as a fashion buyer at Marks and Spencer. Therefore Otto, who was a semi-retired cabinet maker, had the day to himself. He spent it in his garden workshop, listening to the unfolding saga of the people power revolution taking place in the city of his birth. Sometimes he paused over his saws and his wood planes to sip a little scotch, smoke a Lucky Strike and wonder what it might all mean for the East German official with whom he had last had contact in the Märchenbrunnen, thirty-three years before.

That same morning in Berlin, the retired Stasi officer known as Silke Stengel disappeared, leaving behind the flat she had lived in since the Second World War and no trace of where she'd gone.

Shortly thereafter Dagmar Fischer, a Jewish woman believed to have been dead for nearly half a century, reappeared in West Berlin. Her story of a life spent in the East was vague and confusing but her identity was clear. She had documentary proof taken from Stasi records filed in 1956, and subsequent DNA testing put the matter beyond legal doubt.

Thus established, Dagmar Fischer began a courtroom battle to gain compensation for assets lost under the Nazis and in particular to regain control of her father's department store on the Kurfürstendamm. This had been largely destroyed during the war and subsequently leased by the West German authorities to various retail chains.

Dagmar Fischer was successful in her efforts and the Fischer department store was restored to its former glory, reopening its doors in 1992. For the remaining eleven years of her life, Miss Fischer arrived in a limousine outside the store every morning shortly before eight thirty, in order personally to open the magnificent front doors of the shop on the exact stroke of the half-hour.

She was in the process of performing this self-appointed task on the morning she died, suffering a heart attack as she stepped out of her car. Falling to her knees on the pavement, she slumped slowly forward until her face was on the stones, her mouth open and her tongue lolling out. A concerned crowd quickly gathered round and a young man stooped down to ask if he could help her.

'You're too late,' Dagmar whispered to the paving stones as the breath of life left her body. 'Seventy years too late.'

Afterword
Biographical Reflections

This story is entirely a work of fiction, but it is inspired in part by a circumstance of my family history.

My father was a Hitler refugee. He was born Ludwig Ehrenberg in Germany into a secular family of Jewish descent. He came to Britain via Czechoslovakia in 1939 with his parents Eva and Victor and his older brother Gottfried. The great kindness of various individuals in Britain ensured the family's survival, as did the help of a small charity established in 1933 by British academics and scientists. The charity, now called the Council for Assisting Refugee Academics (CARA), still exists today.

Gottfried enlisted in the British Army in 1943, when, like the Stengel brother in my story, he was advised to anglicize his name in case of capture by the Germans. He became Geoffrey Elton and my father followed suit, changing his name to Lewis Elton. My grandparents remained Ehrenbergs until their deaths in London in the seventies.

Gottfried and Ludwig had a cousin, Heinz. Like the brother in my story, Heinz was adopted and, to use the Nazis' own term, of pure 'Aryan' blood. When his parents Paul and Clara Ehrenberg escaped Germany, Heinz elected to stay in order to farm the land his parents had acquired for him.

Heinz was soon drafted into the Wehrmacht and, like the Stengel brother in my story, was part of the army stationed on the Channel coast in 1940 in preparation for Hitler's planned invasion of Britain. Heinz also served in Italy; after the war, the family discovered that he and Geoffrey had come quite close to each other while fighting there on opposite sides.

Like the fictitious Paulus and Otto, my father and uncle experienced the segregation of school classrooms. They, too, were insulted by Nazi teachers and witnessed the confusion of the so-called *Mischling*. My father's best friend was half Jewish and, on being given a choice, bravely elected to sit with the Jews.

In the story, Paulus and Otto's grandfather had won an Iron Cross in the First World War. My grandfather Victor also served in the Kaiser's army and won the Iron cross in 1914. He fought in the trenches throughout the war, and my children have the piece of shrapnel that was dug from his leg in 1917. Like the fictitious Taubers, my grandparents loved the country of their birth very much and saw themselves as both Germans and Jews. When the family emigrated to England, my grandfather secretly brought his Iron Cross with him. On discovering this in 1940, my grandmother buried it in the back garden of the lodging house in which they were staying, where it has no doubt long since rusted away.

Like the Stengel boy in my story, my Uncle Geoffrey ended up with the Army Intelligence Corps as an interpreter. Geoffrey achieved the rank of Sergeant and throughout his life retained a deep affection for the British army. Indeed, it was said in the family that the army truly made him an Englishman. In 1989, when *Blackadder Goes Forth* was broadcast, Uncle Geoffrey was at first most unhappy at what he considered to be an insulting portrayal of the army; he later took the view that the satire was drawn with great respect.

Although my father's family were more fortunate than some in terms of the number of members who were able to escape the Holocaust, many of course did not. Lisbeth, my grandmother's beloved sister, for instance, died like the fictitious Frieda, having volunteered to accompany a group of Jewish children being transported east. Lisbeth was shot along with her young charges immediately on arrival in Lithuania in 1941.

An incident which I had hoped to include in my fictional narrative but could eventually find no place for concerned my Uncle Heinz and the death of my great-grandmother. In October 1941, she was still living in her home town of Kassel when the German authorities began a final round-up of Jews there.

Her grandson Heinz very bravely visited the Kassel Gestapo in his army uniform and asked that his adoptive grandmother, who was close to death, be allowed to die in her bed. '*Lassen Die mir die alte Judin in Ruhe*,' was his appeal. 'Let that old Jewess alone.' Perhaps his appeal was successful, because Emilie Ehrenberg did die in her bed soon after. She was spared the nightmare of transportation in a cattle truck to a death camp, but not that of having seen the country in which she was born in 1859 descend into insanity and barbarity without parallel.

Like Wolfgang Stengel, my family also had some experience of the pre-Holocaust SA concentration camps of the 1930s. My grandfather's other brother, Hans, was a Christian pastor, having been converted while he was a student. He was sent to Sachsenhausen Camp, where his good friend Reverend Martin Niemoller, the great anti-Nazi cleric and author of *First They Came . . .*, was also an inmate. Hans was eventually released, due largely to the efforts of the Bishop of Chichester.

He came to England, where, like the brother in my story, he was interned as an enemy alien, although, also like him, he did not resent it. Great-Uncle Hans returned to Germany after the war in an effort to continue his ministry, but my father and his family were happy in Britain, grateful for the safe haven and the opportunities this great country afforded. Having arrived as penniless refugees, they eventually prospered and made their mark. Both my father and my uncle married English girls and both became professors. My father held chairs in Physics and later in Higher Education, and in 2005 was awarded the Lifetime Achievement Award at the Times Higher Education Awards.

My uncle became a historian and Regius Professor of English Constitutional History at Cambridge. In 1986 he was knighted for his services to the study of history.

Geoffrey died in 1994, but at the time of writing my Uncle Heinz and my father are still alive; they still correspond and met quite recently. Heinz has even met my Australian wife, Sophie – at Geoffrey's funeral, in fact, making a connection that spans time, distance and history. I myself have been to Germany many times, where my plays are sometimes performed and also as director of the musical *We Will Rock You*. I have made true and lasting friendships there and have nothing but happy memories of the country of my father's birth.

Ben Elton, May 2012

Ben Elton is one of our most provocative and entertaining writers, author of thirteen internationally bestselling novels.

His multi-award-winning TV credits include *The Young Ones*, *Blackadder* and *The Thin Blue Line*. His stage hits include the Olivier Award-winner *Popcorn* and the global phenomenon *We Will Rock You*.

He met his wife Sophie in 1986 while touring Australia as a stand-up comedian. They have three children and call both Britain and Australia home.